LAST THINGS

LAST
THINGS

David
Searcy

VIKING

VIKING
Published by the Penguin Group
Penguin Putnam Inc., 375 Hudson Street, New York, New York 10014, U.S.A.
Penguin Books Ltd, 80 Strand, London WC2R 0RL, England
Penguin Books Australia Ltd, 250 Camberwell Road, Camberwell,
Victoria 3124, Australia
Penguin Books Canada Ltd, 10 Alcorn Avenue,
Toronto, Ontario, Canada M4V 3B2
Penguin Books India (P) Ltd, 11 Community Centre, Panchsheel Park,
New Delhi-110 017, India
Penguin Books (N.Z.) Ltd, Cnr Rosedale and Airborne Roads, Albany,
Auckland, New Zealand
Penguin Books (South Africa) (Pty) Ltd, 24 Sturdee Avenue,
Rosebank, Johannesburg 2196, South Africa

Penguin Books Ltd, Registered Offices: Harmondsworth, Middlesex, England

First published in 2002 by Viking Penguin, a member of Penguin Putnam Inc.

1   3   5   7   9   10   8   6   4   2

Copyright © David Searcy, 2002
All rights reserved

ISBN 0-670-03132-1
CIP data available

This book is printed on acid-free paper.

Printed in the United States of America
Set in Adobe Caslon
Designed by Nancy Resnick

For John, Elizabeth, and Anna

and wouldn't it be interesting if stars were ugly?
"Suppose someone were to say:
'Imagine this butterfly
exactly as it is, but ugly instead of beautiful'?!"
—Wittgenstein in *Zettel* 199
when seeing is a seeing as
the way out of the thicket
by definition the way into the thicket
and seeing through a puzzle is a puzzle. . . .
there is a gnomic economic
law involved here
that indicates an architect of thickets
for whom puzzles are a dank joy.

—GERALD BURNS,
from *Boccherini's Minuet*, "No. 22"

ACKNOWLEDGMENTS

Thanks to Steve Anderson, Tim and Melanie Coursey, Carol Drum, Mike and Anita Edgmon, Joe Henry, Randy Hill, Jeanne Larson, James Lynch, Doug MacWithey, Nancy Rebal, Steve Richardson, Ray Roeder, Bob Trammell, Adrienne Cox-Trammell, Dr. John Vorhies, and James and Charlotte Whitaker for reading, listening, and providing aid and comfort. I'm immensely grateful as well to my agent, Becky Kurson, my editor, Michael Millman, and to Deborah Treisman who let the first bit of this into print.

My friend David Wright, on whom the character of Luther is largely based, was my main informant. His help, and that of his family—wife Pat, sons Claud, Bobby, and Dr. Robby—was indispensable.

Thanks also to good old Yurang the first and, of course, to Gerald Burns.

1

The simplest sort of horror story (and the most gratifying some-how) starts with the damage—something ruined in ways too peculiar to explain, glimpsed, say, at high speed along a country highway at dusk just at that rosy half-lit moment before one flips on the headlights: Little jerks of their eyes now to the right—hers then his, but then it's gone and they fall silent watching the pink light leaving the tops of the pines: he looks back once in the mirror but everything's shadowy against the sky like one of those black and or-ange silhouette landscapes schoolchildren produce at Halloween—such an easy effect yet so dramatic with all the particulars of the world hopelessly lost in the radiance.

"Was that a scarecrow?" she says at last. And now the fact ac-quires a presence, seems to accompany them into the gathering dark, uphill and down along the blacktop with the pine trees closing in, losing all particularity. She watches his face now, how it brightens in the glow from the rearview mirror at the top of every hill but more and more faintly each time. She has to remind him about the head-lights. "Was that a scarecrow?" she asks again. He shakes his head the way he might at her concern for something dead in the road, some poor domestic animal, although in that case she wouldn't have said anything except "Oh dear" perhaps, bringing her hand to her face and glancing over to see his expression. Then, if he sensed her looking, he might shake his head and that would be that; but now it's unreasonable, she feels, inconsistent—she felt his foot come off the pedal, caught the deflection of his eyes. She looks behind for headlights, twists around and watches for a while the little lavender-gray slot of sky where the pine trees converge, hoping for someone else who might be observed to have passed the same spot and might be felt to intervene as it were, to interrupt the continuity and devel-opment of her thoughts, represent the succession of ordinary events across the moment, distributing it, delegating it in a sense. A couple of times she imagines a faint preliminary glow, a subtle brightening to the sky above the road but there's nothing further and presently she turns back around, sole custodian of what she now seeks to reevaluate in terms consistent with her husband's response: something dead, run over and tossed up onto a fence or a bush somehow, not a person but a deer, maybe a dog flattened by the impact like in a cartoon, unfolded, ears out sideways like a hat, all spread out and presented rose-colored in the sunlight in the corner of her eye, a scatter of teeth across its face.

He's shaking his head again very slightly.

"What?" she says.

He flicks on the brights which she dislikes along this stretch with the pines so close on either side because it seems so strongly to anticipate some sort of panicky event. Like shining a flashlight under one's bed when one was little, she imagines. He's flicking them off and on at the car that's been intermittently beaming over the rises, practically blinding now as it approaches zooming past hauling a boat at an alarming rate of speed. She turns to look, watching the taillights disappear and reappear, testing her sense of it and whether even traveling the wrong direction it might serve her purpose blowing past that spot in the dark, shaking the trees and ablating the fact to some extent.

"So what was it really?" She turns back around. The road's bending off to the right and the brights are shining into the pine trees faintly scanning across like a searchlight. She looks down. He's going to tease her, she suspects.

"If not a scarecrow?"

"Right." She closes her eyes.

"Well, just because you've got your category 'scarecrows'—let's call it a set—doesn't mean that under certain conditions, in the darkest recesses of the heart . . ." He pauses, turns and looks at her now; she senses it, opens her eyes and he's glancing over and smiling.

"What?" she says after a second, letting the question float away. He's doing something with his seatbelt, unfastening it finally and leaning back with his arms out straight, both hands on top of the wheel. The forest opens up now into meadow on either side, pale cattle here and there which, except for a couple right by the road, are hardly visible upon approach but as they are passed become luminous, their east sides lit by a nearly full moon just clearing the tree line. She brings her face against the window, cupping her hands around her eyes to watch the effect, the materialization cow by cow or sometimes several at once sort of rippling into visibility across the meadow into the distance, all standing, head down to the grass in that posture one associates with cows, represents them in their passiveness, their essential permanence and receptivity here presented out of the darkness one after another in such a spectral display, such a marvelous reiteration it takes away her breath for a moment, seems to absorb and neutralize her concerns altogether as if each glowing animal accompanied her like headlights past that critical point, as if all one's unpleasant thoughts in fact might be subordinate to a field of cattle in the moonlight. A rush of trees and everything's dark except for the moon itself peeking through like code—dots to dashes, now longer streaks as the woods start to thin, about to open up again she hopes on to pasture, a few more cattle perhaps just to establish the sense of them, or their luminosity at least, as an extended phenomenon like an aurora or a rainbow, something serene and transcendent like that, like a glimpse of the ocean to restore calm and lend perspective. The moon sweeps free of the trees, out over the meadow, which is black as felt—some sort of thick low cover like ryegrass or alfalfa—but no cows, not a glimmer. She wipes the window and looks again, holding her breath to keep from fogging the glass, extending her attention to every peripheral possibility the way one might hold oneself, jar in hand, toward the possibility of fireflies.

She turns away after a minute; the woods close in again; the high beams are shooting off between the trees in anticipation, she feels, of something darting across, lurching suddenly out of the woods into their path any second.

"It wasn't a deer," she says quietly. She looks over and he shrugs. A fall of yellow oak or sweet gum leaves swirls out of the dark across the headlights. The car rocks slightly with the wind. "It wasn't a deer," she says again just as quietly, looking down into her purse which she has lifted into her lap, fishing around now as if for evidence, withdrawing a probably empty Chiclets box which she squeezes and taps against her palm to dislodge any pieces that might be stuck. "You know?" She looks over at her husband again, tapping the box a few more times then stripping off the cellophane and starting to tear it from the top. "It looked like a person." She has it peeled apart now like a banana, laid out along its seams, nothing inside. "Didn't you think so?"

He glances over. "What have you got?"

She looks down at the box, holds it up by the corner, bringing her other hand to her face, unable to say anything for a moment, entirely surprised by her reaction to this: her operations upon the cardboard box, its inside-outness a sort of delicate indecency like a euphemism, like one of those naked female ivory dolls once provided to Chinese physicians to represent the unapproachable aristocratic sufferer—"Is there pain here?" He points and the answer comes from beyond the curtain, disembodied and, thus, inconceivably painful, unimaginably distant like something howling in the woods.

"No more Chiclets," she says.

"No indeed," he replies.

2

"Oh shit," says Luther Hazlitt and "Oh shit" again and again, looking down and shaking his head all the while as if to disperse some terrifically unpleasant realization burst upon him all of a sudden—some foul-up just remembered, irredeemable now: the gate left open, puppies gone and surely lost; cattle fled; insurance lapsed; house slowly filling with gas. And, notwithstanding mystical disciplines are outside his interest and experience, he's entered into it all by himself like a chant, a ritual syllable, soft and regular, an exhalation to clear the mind toward an eschatological point of view superior/posterior to the world whose very last and worst it subsumes and appropriates. "Oh shit," nearly a whisper, "Oh shit," like a sigh, like breathing, like an engine to evacuate belief. His big red chow is bewitched, deeply attracted and dismayed by the object of all this—what's hanging from the holly tree, its odd relation to the surroundings and how it moves slightly in the breeze side to side and up and down with the motion of the branches. He's circling around under the barbed-wire fence out to the shoulder of the highway and back, over and over swinging in each time a little closer, making a go for it now as Luther grabs him by the neck and hauls him backward all the way to the fence, having to get on his knees to jerk him down and make him sit with his blue tongue lolling out the side, eyes fastened across the fifty yards or so to where the holly tree dances in the wake of an eighteen-wheeler, dust lifting and settling, showing little rays of sunrise just coming through the thicket.

"Oh shit" at this distance loses urgency, fades and attenuates to a prolonged expulsion or breath, the dog panting little plumes of steam as Luther slips into a seated position with both arms around him, heads together as if to combine intellects in consideration of what sort of tragedy might be represented, what sort of accident would leave its residue hung out like laundry, like the discardable

parts of some insect metamorphosis—jeans, jacket, and shirt all together like in a department store display but with some essential
(one would think essential) fraction of their owner left behind, a
kind of mastic holding everything in place as if he had been jerked
out too quickly (like one of those impossible effects where high
winds are involved—straws driven through telephone poles and
such). The dog is whining a very thin sort of ventriloquial whine
with its mouth still open, tongue flopped out. A stronger gust of
wind whips through the thorn, across the dry grass blowing it flat.
Luther's looking up at the clouds. "Shut up, Yurang," he whispers.
He's imagining this object falling, watching it fall like a leaf,
trousers, shirt, and everything all of a piece floating down from a
great height to settle in the holly tree. Something from far away like
a loose kite, here by accident, unrelated to local events, more like
something meteorological. Who knows what can happen at high
altitudes, he thinks, what the soul leaves behind after a midair colli-
sion? Or even how often such things might drift down unnoticed
like cottonwood seed. Sun is streaming through now, catching the
holly tree in a golden light. There seems to be a sort of hat as well,
although it's unclear how it's attached, how it remains with the
ensemble—one of those woodsman's hats with earflaps it looks like
except the earflaps are stiff like horns, sticking out, the whole thing
like a vision, something religious the way the light strikes it now,
strikes the holly leaves around it making a halo that sort of flickers,
comes and goes with the breeze. He is reminded of those awful religious images he thinks of as Mexican—the iconography runs together: bleeding hearts, bleeding everything, the body of Christ
spattered red with little droplets all over like birdshot wounds (he's
imagining it again as it falls, folding and turning; plummeting like a
dove). Now Yurang goes for it with absolute conviction in spite of
everything—Luther yelling and trying to hold on to his tail, dust
and grass kicked in his face, having to go with the dog or lose his
grip altogether like hooking a fish too big for the line; he's being
taken right across (how the morning light shines on it, gleams from
glazed patches where the cloth has soaked through); he loses the
tail, kicks the hind legs sideways, spinning the rest halfway around,

makes a jump, falls and rolls with the dog whose aggression is instantly redirected into Luther's left forearm as they slide almost up to the holly tree, its burden lifting and falling slightly, sunlight peeking under the hat, making the interior, for a moment, glow red and yellow with the delicate and complex reduction of the structure like an eviscerated grapefruit which, he notices coincident with the pain in his arm, still supports a row of teeth.

"That is so stupid," says Agnes Peeler, splicing two big square Band-Aids into a bigger one under Luther's forearm, gathering up the wrappers and pausing to say it again right in his face: "That is so stupid, keeping a dog like that." She looks down at Yurang. "Chows are knowed for it—they'll turn on you; bite the hand, won't you sweetie?" Yurang wags his tail. "Bite the hand." She heads back into the kitchen talking louder: "'So what kind of dog is old Luther looking for?'" He can hear her making coffee. "'Well, sir, he kinda figured maybe he'd get him one of them dogs that'll bite him. Well fortune smiles 'cause I can let him have Old Arm-Biter here, Old Groin-Ripper, quite inexpensively today.'"

Luther walks out on the porch, holding the screen door for the dog, takes a seat in the ragged upholstered armchair, feeling the cushion first to make sure it's dry. Yurang plops down at his feet. After a minute Agnes comes out with the coffee, stands by the corner post looking into her yard—freshly raked, weedless, grassless sandy soil with white-painted boulders here and there looking arbitrary but very formal without flower beds or shrubbery, just the markings of the rake.

"I need some chickens," says Agnes.

"Come and get 'em," says Luther.

"White chickens," says Agnes reflectively. "I like to see 'em in the yard." Luther nods and shifts in his seat.

"So," says Agnes, taking a sip and looking over at Luther, "you gonna call Bobby? It's in the County, ain't it?"

"Over by Cook's." Luther nods.

"You want me to call him?"

Luther shakes his head, hoists himself out of the upholstered chair, feeling the back of his jeans. "You call who ever you want; it won't make no difference." He takes a seat on the steps.

"No difference how?"

"No difference at all." Luther's examining the Band-Aids, pressing them down around the edges. "No difference at all," he says again quietly but separating the words for emphasis, resting his chin now in his right hand, gazing across Agnes's yard whose rigorous vacancy has always seemed clinical although perhaps not so clearly and explicitly as now insofar as it encourages his sense of injury, its expansion or relocation from his arm to somewhere else, possibly more general, more interior.

Agnes is just looking at him now, holding her coffee, saying nothing.

"You didn't see it," says Luther.

There's a loose board at the edge of the porch; Agnes lifts it with her toe, nudges it back into place, and steps on it a few times.

"I don't think it's even from around here, anyway. You ever been dove hunting?" He looks at her. "You know how you can clean 'em just with your fingers?"

"Not with *my* fingers," says Agnes.

"But that's how you do it—you can just take your fingers and poke right through the feathers and everything and pull out the breast meat and that's it; that's all you do." Yurang's head is up, ears pricked, as colder air comes into the yard, the tops of the pines whip back and forth. "Nothin' to it"—Luther stands and steps back onto the porch with his hands in his pockets—"like it was a piece of fruit. Nothin' to it." He looks down at the dog, rubs his foot along his back; Yurang rolls over to present his belly. "Except this was pretty much all gone inside—whooshed out."

"Whooshed where?"

Luther shrugs.

"What do you mean 'whooshed'?"

"Just whooshed, like so quick everything else stayed put, like when they do that trick with the tablecloth and everything stays put and when you die and everything just stays put except you're dead and except for that you can't tell no difference. It looked religious."

"Shit," says Agnes.

"It did," says Luther. "It had a halo kind of; the way the light come through the bushes." Luther bends to get his coffee mug, slings the dregs out in the yard, making dark spots on the sand. "Sorry." He looks at Agnes. Agnes looks back for a moment, then goes inside. Across the road the pines are really starting to toss. Luther walks into the yard, scuffs sand over the coffee spots. Yurang follows him out to the fence. The wind is hitting the tops of the trees in gusts; a line of greenish-black clouds with swirly white underneath is coming over, little flickers of reflected lightning along the edge. Agnes emerges with a slap of the screen door, comes across the yard in a yellow plastic slicker like a child's.

"It's on his list already." She looks at Luther, making a face—gritting her teeth as her fingers work arthritically down every spring-loaded toggle fastener. "Somebody called Gilmer Police and they called Bobby and Bobby's got it on his list but it ain't very high up 'cause he's out checkin' his trotlines tryin' to beat the weather right now."

"Who called?"

"Don't know; just talked to Lisa. I think the whole department's gone fishin'. Somebody caught a three-hundred-pound blue cat last night."

"Ain't no such thing." Luther turns back to the storm. He can hear thunder now, a low, continuous vibration like heavy machinery in the distance.

"I'm going to run you on home," says Agnes. "Lisa said they're getting baseball hail in Sulphur Springs."

"Three-hundred-pound catfish," says Luther, shaking his head.

"You got your puppies inside?"

He turns back to Agnes. How old she looks in the yellow slicker, and how strange wearing the sort of garment that should contain a child—would, in a sense, be filled up by a child whereas Agnes seems almost to present a vacancy, an old woman like the ghost of a child, gray hair fanning out of the hood, shiny yellow becoming shinier as a spatter of rain strikes across it producing a tickety-tick sound further distinguishing the quality of the plastic from its contents—a clinical oppositeness like that between the glass jar and the pickled specimen, between the Band-Aid and the wound. His sense of injury seems to deepen. He closes his eyes for a second as more raindrops sweep across, icy-cold against the side of his face, the thought of the three-hundred-pound catfish suddenly coinciding with all this in an inexplicably unpleasant way, flopping itself like an extracted organ across all these inarticulate considerations. He pushes open the rickety little wired-picket gate, walks quickly across the oil road and throws up, leaning against a pine tree, kicking the dog away a couple of times, keeping his head down, breathing shallow breaths as the heavy rain starts to come through the forest in a wave.

It's that very eerie sort of luminous green thunderstorm that tends to come in spring but in fall seems especially threatening—that there's no call for it in a sense, no terrestrial necessity or balance, no seasonal polarity to direct all that uneasiness to a purpose. It's like an accident, a breaking down of equilibrium which, ungoverned, might release anything—cats and dogs, rains of fishes. Hail knocks intermittently against Luther's trailer house like thrown rocks; it carries that sense of intent, of thoughtful interval, makes it difficult, without power, for him to do anything except stand in the dark in the little kitchen area and listen to it, feel the house shake in the wind and watch the puppies, loose and wandering about, change positions stroboscopically, with every lightning flash reconfiguring themselves in sudden heaps and scatters like ball bearings in those little perforated puzzles you have to hold just right and tilt as Luther's trailer, in fact, is tilting now and then with the stronger gusts. It's not moored, not really a proper trailer house—more of a camper, retaining its wheels and, presumably, the capability of travel had he a vehicle to pull it; in which case he would have it under the pecan tree across the field facing east, parallel to the weather, build a little front

David Searcy

porch. As it is it's too exposed, where someone left it—dropped it off and drove away for some reason leaving it no place in particular, sort of adrift in a field of knee-high coastal Bermuda which looks like the surface of a lake, right now, the way the wind whips across it. He's leaning across his bed, looking out into the weirdly luminous darkness watching hail disappear into the grass.

The puppies have accumulated around his feet. It's time to gather them up and get them back into their box but he feels stabilized in this position with his arms out, elbows locked, against the back wall, pressing his knees against the bed frame, sensing the storm very distinctly this way which seems to provide a sort of relief, just for a minute, allowing his imprecise feeling of injury to spread out over a larger area, get confused with the buffeting and the racket, swept up with the weather in general, the agitation of the grass—how it ripples back and forth, light to dark, in streaks and whirls as the wind hits it from a number of directions simultaneously. There's a uniform wave from the left now; from the north a huge gust; all the trees on that side are bending in; the grass goes dark at the edge of the field and sweeps across all at once as he shifts to look out the other window. The impact knocks him off his feet, causes him to stumble backward over Yurang, come down hard on the floor with his head against the cabinets. Now the puppies are on him, overjoyed at the opportunity to get at his face, lick his ears, and tug his shirt as he comes to his knees with an armful, loses them again, has to find them after that one by one in the dark as they discern his intention.

The trailer lists a little, he thinks. It seems to shake more in the wind as if something underneath has given way. He sits on the floor leaning back against the bed with his eyes closed. After a while he slips all the way down to lie flat, arms out, letting the trailer be like a stethoscope to the weather, letting it extend his sense of the storm farther and farther out until he can imagine the object in the holly tree in the dark being shaken and battered to pieces as if it were brittle, not at all what he thought but made of something surprising like the sort of cheap papier-mâché they used to make jack-o'-lanterns out of. It seems implausible as that to him now as he dozes off, almost ridiculous, something cheap and imaginary falling apart in the storm bit by bit, crumbling away until it's entirely dispersed.

A flashing red light that seems to complement the throbbing in his arm brings him awake. Yurang's growling at the window, feet up on the back of the couch, making lunging motions every time the light comes across, bumping the glass with his nose as if he were about to jump through it. Luther's on the floor with his Army jacket over him and a pillow under his head, propped up now, rubbing his eyes—it's quite chilly; still no power, no light except the faintest predawn gray between the flashes. A short blurt from a siren sends Yurang into fits, barking and biting at the window like he might really break the glass. Now the puppies are getting into it. Luther pulls on his boots, stands with his legs wide apart shifting side to side to test the stability of the trailer, feeling the whole thing tilt a little as he moves to the door, shoves Yurang away with the side of his boot and steps outside.

Bobby's standing next to his squad car, grinning and reaching in to give another gratuitous burst on the siren (a furious commotion from the trailer).

"Shit, don't do that," says Luther.

Bobby does it twice again, looking at Luther and just grinning, the side of his beefy, red face flashing redder, grinning wider. "Agnes said you wouldn't believe it. This here's mine."

The trunk of the squad car is braced open. The sky is clear. The first pinkish glow has started to color a few high streaks of haze. Luther takes a couple of steps to the right. There's a sheet of half-inch plywood in the trunk with something tied to it. Lots of dirty cotton rope wrapped all the way around several times and just enough light to see, beyond the periodic red glare, the shiny mass of it bigger than the board, humped and bent around inside to keep the tail from flopping out.

"Caught him on chicken hearts," says Bobby.

Luther looks at him; then back at the fish. The rear suspension of the car is visibly compressed. Luther imagines it must tend to bottom-out driving around on these roads with all that weight. It's still alive, he suspects. Still wet with a smear of blood behind the gills, the head itself nearly lost to view up inside the trunk where the spare tire has been pushed aside to make room. Luther steps back, blinking at the beacon; it's the old-fashioned kind with the rotating mirror. He wonders why Bobby doesn't turn it off.

"Didn't have no decent bait." Bobby's grinning ear to ear, leaning back against the car, looking up as if to heaven, vastly gratified, reaching behind without looking and giving a shriek on the siren one more time.

"You been out there on 154 by Cook's yet?" asks Luther, rubbing his arm.

Bobby just shakes his head, still grinning, gazing heavenward, simply basking in the presence of what he's done as if he need never catch another fish, or a criminal for that matter, confront the problem of good and evil, this right here having summed it all up, lights flashing, dawn breaking pink and gold across the sky while Luther's dog, as a sort of background noise, has achieved a dreadful state of fury.

Only a single dead chicken but a white one. Luther turns it over, spreads its wings, lays it down by the stump where he sits. He can hear Bobby's squad car periodically, working its way around the lake—little celebratory yelps of the siren, now clearer, now fainter, depending on the distance and the direction of the wind. He picks up the chicken again, tries to locate the injury—a broken neck, he supposes; he can't imagine a chicken's head to contain a truly vital organ. He turns it this way and that, thinks briefly of plucking it but it's been dead too long; by now it's ruined. He holds it by the neck the way one holds a rubber chicken, stands, and lays it on the stump then goes to see about the trailer.

3

"Oh shit," in his sleep now, as if he were hovering at a slight elevation or standing in the back of a truck gazing over Cook's property by the highway on a very hot day taking note of all the cottonwood seed floating around. "Oh shit," in this case, is more reflective, more resigned and regretful than before, not obviously connected with the scene, yet, in the way dreams can permit one to separate from oneself, follow along beside like a dog, his mystification in no way disqualifies the fact that he's deeply affected, fully receptive to the emotional end of the situation without having to be informed.

So much fluff in the air seems self-evidently tragic, how it hangs and drifts about at every altitude and as far as he can see above the highway, over the thicket and across Cook's weedy, scrubby pasture down to the line of hardwoods along the creek like ashes, like chicken feathers—something residual, he might think if that were a word he ever used, and perhaps for that reason sorrowful. He's not used to taking naps, not comfortable on the couch in the afternoon with sun shining through his eyelids and, so, barely asleep—just adequate to maintain the dream as the bits of cottonwood fluff gradually disperse although not the sadness which seems, in fact, to concentrate, to sharpen to apprehension as he comes awake to the cool air moving gently through the trailer from the open window to his left across the bristles of his crew cut and through the door, carrying the sound of wet grass against the legs of someone walking slowly through it. He's up and looking out all the windows—mostly for Yurang who should be barking at the very least (those who know him know to honk and wait in the car if the dog's outside by itself). He can see the puppies in a heap at the front of their chicken-wire enclosure. He steps out the door and listens. One of those big crested woodpeckers is making a racket in the distance. He gets on

David Searcy

his knees and looks under the trailer, finds Yurang looking back. He scans the grass on the other side, stands up and backs away twenty yards or so, stops and listens again as Yurang trots on out to join him. It's in his head, he decides; something left over from the dream. He takes a walk around the trailer anyway, checking again for hail damage, getting the bottoms of his jeans wet, vaguely appalled at the spectacular inadequacy of it, how precarious it looks— not just structurally; he's tried to fix that by jamming a pair of railroad ties under—but, even beyond the sense of exposure, in some way that he finds difficult to articulate to himself. It's like being perched on a cliff. He walks on out into the field. Yurang's sniffing at something in the grass. Something dead, it appears by the way he wants to get right down in it, the way dogs do for some reason, crouching and rubbing in it starting with his face, both sides to ensure an even distribution.

"Get out of there," yells Luther. He's seen dogs go into a kind of ecstasy, roll around kicking their legs.

"Get out." He claps his hands. Yurang withdraws with great reluctance, shakes his head, gives a sneeze, and bounds over to Luther much invigorated.

"Jesus Christ," says Luther, keeping his distance. "Get on back." Yurang heads off through the grass and disappears under the trailer.

Luther waits; he can hear Agnes's truck coming up the road that cuts across the eastern edge of the clearing—crossing the little bridge at the tree line with a banging of the tailgate, lurching downshift and now rising slowly to grade as if surfacing in the field of Bermuda, mottled spray-can white over older and older touch-ups, very little of the original ivory color showing through. She comes right across the grass, revs the engine before cutting it off.

"So let's go have a look." She leans across, shoves open the door whose outside handle doesn't work.

Luther just stands there, shakes his head. "I don't think so," he says.

Agnes leans back leaving the door open.

"It don't make no sense"—he looks at her—"does it?"

Agnes shrugs, fiddles the column-shift back into first. The inside of her truck has that smell that cars made after the fifties can probably never have, the deterioration of early plastics in benign association, the synthetic analogue to mustiness. Luther climbs in, lights a cigarette. Agnes watches him for a minute. "Get to see Sheriff's fish?"

Luther turns to let his smoke go out the door, takes another puff, squeezes the fire off the end into the grass, placing the remnant back in the pack. "Fuckin' whale."

Agnes laughs. "Scared the bejeezus out of me—red flasher going, dragging me out there in the dark, give me his big old flashlight, and says go look at that jewlocker; go look in the trunk at that jewlocker, he says."

"Fuckin' whale," says Luther again.

They can hear the pileated woodpecker still going at it off in the woods somewhere—a very low and faintly disturbing frequency like a finger tapping on a window trying to get someone's attention.

"You better get on back to the path," says Luther; "this ground's real soft."

He shuts the door. Agnes flips the key and hits the floor starter, spins the tires, backs off and rocks it out quite expertly over the grass to the double-rutted track only marginally firmer than the surrounding meadow and which, in spring, tends to disappear altogether at times leaving the trailer completely isolated, more or less abandoned to all appearances except for the power line sagging out to it carrying the thinnest possible comfort, life hanging by a thread. He follows her to the chicken coop. "Got your onion sack?" he says. Agnes is kneeling, watching the chickens and making soft clucking noises.

"Six white leggerns," says Agnes.

"Seven," says Luther, indicating the one on the stump. "You can have that one for nothin'."

"Poor baby," says Agnes, standing and regarding it, looking back at the others, then at Luther. "Ain't got no onion sack. Going to make a proper crate when I'm ready." She continues to study him for a moment, makes a frown, looks past him, scans the area where they're standing. Yurang has come out to luxuriate in the taller grass nearby, thrashing about, twisting onto his back and kicking the air with his hind legs. "Where'd you bury the mother dog?" Agnes is backing up now, looking down.

"Out in the woods," says Luther. "He's been rollin' in something."

They turn to watch him contorting himself exactly like some wild animal that's been shot, dirt and grass flying everywhere, now and then pausing as if the agony were finally over then suddenly flinging himself back into it again, skidding around as if his forelegs were inoperable, plowing himself like that across the ground and disappearing into the grass on the far side of Agnes's truck, just a thrashing now, indistinct and emotionally indeterminate.

Repairing the henhouse is a matter of rearranging constituent materials—grafting bits of corrugated metal from less critical areas onto the roof of the north side, patching the holes thus created temporarily with whatever's available. It's already quite formless, having developed out of odds and ends—rusty corrugated, sheets of Masonite—found leaning against the trailer when he moved in a couple of years ago, took the caretaker's jobs, and decided the chicken coop, built impractically far from the house, might help to colonize the field, confirm his presence there in the middle of all that grass, discourage the investigations of local teenagers. For a while, before there were chickens, just the coop, he'd go out and look at it now and then, stand away in the grass and appraise it as if expecting something to happen automatically, as if chickens might flock to it like purple martins.

The whole thing has shifted in the storm. A triangular sweep of bare ground at the back shows how the wind brought it around a couple of feet on one side leaving a gap where the chicken wire buckled up next to the structure. He puts in a stake to keep the wire down, counts the chickens again as Yurang—never interested in chickens except when Luther is—stalks them, in his pungency, like death around the perimeter, following them this way and that wherever they wander, wherever the center of the group is sensed to drift (individuals are disregarded within limits), always keeping himself at that point outside the fence closest to them which can sometimes involve a dramatic 180-degree repositioning in response to a very slight general excursion.

The sun is already below the tree tops from Luther's viewpoint; although to the east the pines are still bright and half the meadow beyond the road. He stands and watches for the two or three minutes it takes the first shadows to bleed across into the woods and start to climb. It makes him feel especially cut off, left behind, this moment on sunny days when the field falls into shadow a little before the rest of the world, as he imagines or merely senses without really thinking about it, a sense of falling out of phase, not to rejoin the normal progress of events until morning when the sun, shining down equally, brings his situation back into line, pulls him abreast of everyplace else—still isolated but, at least, simultaneous in some way.

The puppies are whining, bunched up at the front of their pen, ready to come out for their customary frolic at this hour before being taken inside. He lifts off the wire loop, bends open the corner section, and waits to receive them as they come tumbling out—two gray and four red—making straight for Yurang, a cloud of puppies enveloping him, inescapable as flies, going everywhere he goes stiff-legged across the yard, under the trailer, out into the tall grass at which point Luther calls them back and gathers all except Yurang into the house for the night.

There's no cool left in the refrigerator. He takes all the luncheon meat out—the kind with olives and pimientos—makes a big sandwich with most of it (white bread, American cheese, a smear of bright yellow mustard), breaks the rest up for the puppies and tosses one whole piece out the door. He lets down like an ironing board his stowable kitchen table surfaced with the same gold-flecked white Formica as the countertop and the interior of the shower that doesn't work. In the gloom at this time of day the gold bits catch the last light from the window above the couch, look like fairy dust from a certain angle if he keeps his head very still, eats his sandwich without bending.

Sometime after midnight Luther's power comes back on. The

David Searcy

sound of his radio, off station, volume low, reaches him gradually, brings him awake, just the static coming and going with an irregular beat, a sort of swishing sound like walking through grass. He lifts his head and listens in the dark to how it changes: faster and slower, gaining and losing just the edge of a signal, just enough to make a noise, slowly diminishing, swishing away, drifting finally into silence like someone passing on by across the field into the woods.

4

I t's Agnes again. He can hear her coming across the bridge too fast, making an awful clatter and grazing reverse on the downshift. He has to hurry getting dressed as she charges the house, getting Yurang too excited, yanking the door without even knocking, bringing her face to the little window so he has to open it very carefully, boot and sock in one hand, to keep from pushing her off the step. Even so she jumps back, more of a skip and then another, holding her hands, palms together, in front of her face in a girlish attitude of constrained delight, doubles over, starts to laugh, hardly able to speak at all as he pulls on his boot and begins to bring out the puppies, waiting for Agnes to settle down, letting her help in the manner of a bucket brigade, handing them to her at the door one after another which sets up a sort of escapement for her mirth, permitting her to tell him, a few words at a time, at each exchange, about the catfish and how Bobby's placed it on display at Joe's Big Juicy right in town and is taking money just to see it (here the escapement breaks down briefly, she has to pause to wipe her eyes), how, Lisa says, he's had to put it in Joe's freezer, which meant Joe had to do something with all that hamburger (she loses control utterly at this point, hands the puppy back to Luther and goes to lean against the truck with a handkerchief to her face) and so tonight (this is the hard part; Luther's afraid she's going to collapse) he's having a special (she shakes her head); he's having a special, she explains in a squeak before reaching inside the passenger's window to open the door, hoisting herself onto the seat with a great sigh, looking away across the field still with the handkerchief to her face, giving a little shudder now and then.

Luther finishes with the puppies, goes to check on the chickens, Agnes behind him now, more composed, firmly insisting he's to accompany her into town this very evening after she gets back from a

David Searcy

trip to the Canton flea market and brings him the roll of tar paper he wants (except she won't unless he agrees) and besides she'll pay for it and, oh my God, it's been a hundred years since she had a date.

There's no haze in the air; the sky is blue-black all the way down to the horizon when he can see it turning and looking back up the road out the rear window of Agnes' truck. The air feels thin somehow as well—whistling in through the little triangular window vent, makes him nervous, the sense it delivers of breathlessness, augmented by the respiratory constraints placed upon him by his fancy bright-red cowboy shirt, for the last couple of years his only good one, about to pop its pearly buttons. He watches the side of the road, the particulars going shadowy, indistinct, patchy forest turning to thicket and just at this moment, as the light seems to leave, perfectly receptive to whatever notions he might have, whatever objects his imagination cares to locate among the trees and undergrowth beyond the fence where certain areas, clotting to darkness a little sooner than others, suggest debris of various kinds.

At Joe's Big Juicy it's like a funeral, a sort of wake: the slow procession down the long, narrow aisle between confronted ranks of school-desk-style seats, a certain confusion and commingling of purposes between those there for the half-price hamburgers and those come to see the fish. Outside there's a banner across the window covering up the "Joe's Big Juicy" ("Hamburgers" long ago having been erased from the bottom by the backs of seated loiterers taking advantage of the sill, the obvious solution to which problem—painting the sign on the interior surface—Joe rejected because he was certain that would cause it to appear backward from the street). The banner itself is not as legible as an advertisement ought to be, seeking to explain too much—the hamburger discount, the cost of admission, the variability of each upon the other all disappear in the red-marker urgency of it, the bursts of extra information, the rush to completeness not unlike the exegetical signage one gets with certain street-corner apocalyptics. The essential fact—the size of the fish—is embedded deep within the text, already encrusted, as it were, with consequences and derivatives although, getting past all this and passing beyond the nave-like dining room (special vouchers to be redeemed upon returning through the kitchen), a sudden clarity is encountered, almost brutal, almost scientific. The top of the big horizontal freezer has been replaced by a sheet of plywood (reddish stains suggest the same one Luther saw before) into which has been inserted—taped around with silver duct tape—a plastic window. An orange extension cord, secured at intervals with the same silver tape, leads across the floor, up and into the freezer standing next to which is Bobby himself in full regalia (stag-handled .45 in customary full cock on his hip) and casting hardly a glance toward the pale, unearthly glow that issues out through the view plate, as if at this point he were beyond mere subject matter, nothing more were necessary, no fish required, simply having established these conditions were sufficient to invoke any miracle one wanted to insert (if there were nothing in the freezer but the light, who could complain? Who would go away unhappy into the dark across the square and get in his car and drive away without a feeling that something extraordinary had at least been approached in some sense? Whose life would not be changed?).

The woman just ahead of Luther has lifted up her little boy so he can bend over the window and bring his face right down on it as if he were making an ice cream selection or Xeroxing himself, occulting half the area so the little back room, otherwise unlit, becomes much darker, Bobby receding for a moment into the shadows, then, as the child is withdrawn, reappearing very dramatically.

"Hey, Sheriff," says Luther.

"Hey, Luther," says Bobby; "it ain't got no littler."

Luther leans across the plywood, gazes into the cold white glare just long enough to make out the huge frost-whitened shape of the fish and read the hand-lettered weight of it on the card also starting to gather frost as if even this massless statistic were already passing into legend, lifts his head to look at Bobby who has come forward to lean over him, white straw cowboy hat reflecting down into Luther's eyes like an interrogating lamp.

"Makes it look like marble, don't it."

Luther squints at the hat.

Bobby squints back, glances away for a second, nods and smiles at a couple of people then brings his face down even closer, big white hat even brighter.

"Ain't even no eggs in that jewlocker." Then he smiles again, stands up and returns to his station where the woman with the little boy waits to have a few words, taking Bobby's hand in a gesture that seems, in the oddly military/funeral context, to contain both praise and consolation.

Agnes is out front sitting on the sill under the banner looking serene, gazing off into the emptiness of the square beyond the immediate goings-on.

"Ain't you even going to go look?" He sits beside her, untucks his shirt a little.

"Don't need to look. You get your cheeseburger?"

"I ain't real hungry." He looks at Agnes. She's wearing makeup. The light from behind shows the places she missed—pale gill-shaped streaks where the skin appears to have folded as she applied it. He looks away across the square, leans back and sits there for a while next to Agnes, saying nothing.

A few more cars are starting to leave, some circling back for another pass as if not quite ready to depart some deeply celebratory moment like a prom or a tent revival; people emerging onto the sidewalk are hanging around, strolling about. Luther turns and peeks under the banner. Bobby's up front with Joe by the cash register now, holding his hands apart for someone—farther and farther apart in dramatic increments, getting that beatific look on his face again as he extends his arms straight out all the way to indicate a fish immeasurably vast, palms open like a crucifixion, head back, eyes to heaven, white hat like a halo.

Luther starts to feel sick again, stands and walks out to the curb, looks back at Agnes.

"Hey," says Luther. Agnes opens her eyes. "'Bout ready to go?"

She smoothes back her frizzy gray hair, follows him out of the light down the walk to the corner where Luther waits for her by the pickup.

"Don't need to look?"

"Don't need to look." Agnes swings up into the driver's seat. Luther stands there by the window, untucks his shirt the rest of the way.

"Why the hell not?"

"You walkin' home?"

He goes around and gets in the truck, has to shove the door open again and slam it. "Just sort of figured you might want to take a look after carryin' on the way you did."

She pulls out and heads up the street, slowing down as she passes Joe's. "Already seen the damn thing didn't I. Look at that."

Luther looks. "Jesus Christ." People are praying. It appears the woman with the little boy has decided to conduct some sort of service. She's got Bobby by the hand again—head bowed along with Joe and a couple of others, all right out front on the sidewalk under the fluorescent light which is going bad and starting to flicker: now you see them, now you don't; now brightly lit, now silhouetted against the garishness of the banner, its urgent and complex invitation flashing red through the butcher paper, Luther leaning out and looking back until they pass around the courthouse.

5

How depleted the morning feels as it enters Luther's trailer. How like the smell that seems to have seeped in from under the house where Luther's dog has had to sleep the past two nights and of whose quality the light partakes, draws upon to carry the same faint sense of loss one sometimes awakens to on the couch in the afternoon. He thinks of the drifting cottonwood seed again, sustains the image as he dawdles about unfocused, watching the puppies, starting his coffee, standing in his Jockey shorts by the bed and looking out across the grass. He touches the window—how warm it is. He pulls on his jeans and steps outside, walks a ways into the tall grass the better to present himself to the possibility of briskness, any disturbance of the room-temperature stillness. He swings his arms for the sensation, as if to agitate the air. Yurang watches from under the trailer, wags his tail at Luther's whistle but stays put, has to be coaxed, Luther approaching, squatting down and clapping his hands to bring him out in a pitiful crawl that looks like contrition.

"What'd you do?" Luther lifts Yurang's head, the eyes half closed and slightly fluttering as if anticipating punishment. "What the shit you do?" He sniffs the dog, gets up and goes to inventory the chickens. Yurang creeps back under the house.

The chicken count has not declined. The dead white Leggern is still on the stump. It's got flies now—just like that. A little warm weather is all it takes. He looks around. Yurang has withdrawn all the way back under the trailer. The faintest breeze moves over the grass. Luther just stands there for a minute, barefoot and shirtless, feeling exposed in senses concentric and increasingly emphatic like a target, the rings of water around a splash, with the pines outermost and himself at the center perfectly still trying to listen beyond the little scratchy sounds of the chickens, extend his attention across the field, across the surface of the grass which catches the raking light in such a way that it seems to ripple here and there with subtle currents, little movements of the air too slight to feel. He crouches down, which changes the angle. The grass no longer appears to move. Yurang's a shadow. A shadowy tail wag and here he comes— out from under and over to Luther, licking his face, as if an all clear had been sounded.

Luther pulls Yurang around, makes him sit, grabs his ears and looks him directly in the face. There's nothing there, nothing whatever on his mind—tongue out, eyes vague with that faintly Down's syndrome expression chows get. Luther gives him a little shake. Yurang growls and Luther smacks him on the head. "What's the matter with you?" he says, shakes him again and repeats the question.

"Hoo baby," in that sudden wild falsetto country people can produce and which can startle, even demoralize, those not used to it. "Hoo baby," shrieks Luther again in a voice intended to engage the attentions of dim-witted cattle over considerable distances and which has paralyzed the woman standing near him in the pasture, caused her to stiffen, not move forward, not accompany him as he walks along with a slit-open feed sack under his arm, letting the pellets trail out behind. The cattle converge; she reaches to pat one on the flank, a huge Black Angus, withdraws her hand without quite touching—it's much too large and the effects of contact too uncertain, like trying to touch a passing truck. "Do you know about cattle?" she wants to ask (she and her husband know practically nothing) but Luther's still running out the bag. She moves to catch up but Luther raises his head to call; she stops and turns. She can see her husband across the pasture examining the stock tank, walking thoughtfully around its craterlike perimeter. "Hoo baby." It shoots right through her. Inexplicably hateful, especially the ease of it, the effortlessness, as if these people might always be about to produce that sound, release a blast of something animal, possibly sexual, as if the most ordinary pastoral activity might always degenerate into a shriek. She reaches into her purse for the box of Chiclets, takes one. He's coming back now, folding the sack, surveying the cattle, counting them probably. She's deeply hopeful they've all arrived.

"Gettin' after it now." He's got the sack folded up under his arm, standing a little too far away for easy conversation. "Ain't been out here for a couple of days."

She walks over to him. "Is that all they eat?" He looks at her briefly then back at the cattle.

"No ma'am, they graze. Them's just field cubes."

"Field cubes," she repeats softly, bending down, picking up a handful. "They're cylindrical."

"Yes ma'am." He kicks a few scattered pellets toward a very pale sandy-colored cow feeding near them.

"What kind is that?"

"Charolais."

"Charley?"

He tries again.

"Is that French?"

"Lord I guess."

He's ill at ease and looking around. For a moment she fears he's found one missing, about to call. She turns to the pale Charolais, braces herself but nothing happens. Her husband's here.

"Is that all they eat?"

"No sir, them's field cubes."

Her husband rolls one back and forth under his sneaker. "They're round." Luther just looks at him. Her husband looks at her and grins. "They're round," he says again. "Pie are square; cubes is round."

She gives him an admonitory glance but their guide's not paying any attention: he's just looking over the pasture, standing in that asymmetrical way that reminds her of Praxiteles and younger men—hip cocked, weight thrown to one leg—although his paunch disrupts the line. She contemplates the configurations: her portly husband, belt high where his actual waist must once have been—the Tweedledum shape as she secretly thinks of it—versus the kouros encumbered. In the first case the weight is accepted, belted in, a part of the self. In the second it is refused but has to be carried around like baggage; the belt tilts down in front assuming almost the function of a truss, the weight pendant and distinct like a goiter obscuring but not really quite belonging to the self which is left to retain its youthful stance. She tries to imagine her husband standing like that, poised off-balance slightly, the implied athleticism. But he would look ridiculous. It's as if, at some point upon the approach of middle age, men decide which sort of creature they wish to become and so adjust their belts accordingly the way certain hive insects, she seems to recall, select the type or caste of individuals by adjusting their diets in some way. She tries to imagine her husband making that yodeling scream to call the cows and it's worse than ridiculous; it's appalling. She imagines it could only sound like anguish. She pops another Chiclet into her mouth, walks past the Charolais, touching it carefully, feeling the seismic thump thump of its hindquarters shifting very slightly in response. They're talking cattle now; she can hear her husband slipping into his information-gathering mode, a bit too earnest, more rigorously attentive than the data would actually seem to require. She's walking toward the stock tank, stops and turns, points to the Charolais and calls to her husband.

"That's the kind." He looks over, cups his hand behind his ear. "That kind right there." She points emphatically, making little jabbing motions. He turns to Luther; back to her.

"Charolais," he calls out.

"I know."

"Charolais."

She nods vigorously, thinks of the name as she makes her way to the tank, walks up the side to the edge of the water—how gentle and permanent it sounds. "Charolais,"—"ais" at the end she hopes, for the way it would look written on postcards, say, or maybe letterhead. It would be too pretentious to have a sign since there'd be only ten or twenty at the most and just to have them; not for beef, not for slaughter. The water is muddy and opaque. Her eyes defocus toward the reflection of a buzzard. She looks up. It's circling gradually to the west. She goes that way, decides to leave the men alone for a while, descends and follows a path across the pasture, through a gate, over the cattleguard into a field of taller grass dotted here and there with even taller clumps of tiny yellow wildflowers. She stops and takes off the sweater she had put on out of habit, ties the sleeves around her waist. How still things are in the sudden warmth as if life were in shock—the kind of silence that might follow some disaster. She snaps off a cluster of the little daisy-shaped yellow blossoms, takes it along twirling it by the stem, bringing it to her nose. They have a resinous, medicinal smell—or it might be the foliage, which is slightly sticky. It's like the smell of freshly sawed lumber and seems to carry, by implications both medicinal and mechanical, a faint residual sense of violence. She seeks the curative associations, lets it remind her of something rubbed onto her chest when she was little, hot towels placed over as if to drive the vapors deeper down through her muscles into her lungs, or into her heart as she imagined, as if people could really be so permeable. There's a sort of steaminess to the air. She thinks of the flowers in the heat releasing some penetrating essence, closes her eyes for just a second as she walks, pretending to present herself to it as she might to a vaporizer.

There are little stands of hardwoods now, without leaves, very thin and vertical—young sweet gums possibly. She threads her way in and out among them, pausing at one point to locate the sun, trying to keep it on her left. She can see the buzzard gaining altitude, wheeling away higher and higher, out of sight finally in the haze. The trees close around; she's in the forest, luminous shade, bright yellow elms and cedars mostly underneath, pines and oaks and a few big sweet gums forming a canopy, an arcade above the overgrown road or footpath she seems to be following. It's very dramatic, like entering a tunnel; she can see the end of it straight through, not far away—a golden glow as if it led to a better world. It reminds her of a photograph, presumably famous, much reproduced: a pair of toddlers, brother and sister, seen from behind as if the camera, and hence the viewer, might not follow for what she sensed were allegorical reasons insofar as it appeared to her (notwithstanding simpler, happier interpretations) these were dead children entering paradise.

There was even something about paradise in the title and it disturbed her whenever she saw it—the terribly sad and, as she felt, erroneous sweetness. Up ahead it's quite glorious, fairly dazzling yellow light. She glances back the way she came and it's nothing like that, light breaking through now from the sides as she approaches, as the forest opens, sheets of yellow left and right then all around as she wades out into a broad corridor of wildflowers so dense and uniform it looks like something intended to be seen from the air like one of those bizarre landscaping projects conceptual artists sometimes come up with—a great yellow slash right through the forest, straight as a highway, cutting over a slow rise to the south and to the north falling away in a long sweep, crossing a road maybe a half-mile away before rising through plowed fields, the solid yellow breaking up, starting to fray as the flowers give way to grass. It's a pipeline easement of some kind—probably gas; the countryside is dotted with little wells. She closes her eyes again. The medicinal scent is in the air; a comforting glow from underneath comes through her eyelids. She keeps them shut, breathes in deeply as she walks very slowly, the sticky foliage grabbing her jeans. A distant call. She thinks at first it's calling her, that it's time to go. But it's calling cows. "Hoo baby," very thin and far away. "Hoo baby." She shuts her eyes more tightly, endeavors to walk a little more noisily through the flowers. It's her husband trying to make that awful shriek but sounding like a drunk or a crazy person—somewhat worse for being distant, disembodied in a way. She's trying not to lose the moment. Surely he's quit. She stops to listen, eyes still shut. It's perfectly quiet. She looks around, feeling suddenly rather exposed. She's been walking downhill, drifting out to the middle in the general direction of a cross-shaped structure which at first looked like a deer feeder or some sort of valve stem for the pipeline. Now it resolves into a scarecrow. She quickly looks down at the flowers. They're waist-high and so thick she can't see her feet. The medicinal smell is overpowering, no longer therapeutic, merely suggestive of illness or injury. She looks up. It's facing away, hanging from a horizontal cross beam on a post like a regular scarecrow—big puffy-looking head, forearms dangling, what look like garden gloves for hands. Maybe the flowers are actually cultivated. She sees no birds to be discouraged except a buzzard which, if it's the same one, has returned with two companions, wheeling high above the clearing. She gets the Chiclets box from her purse, taps it once into her palm, starts to tear it, puts it back, looks up again. An ordinary scarecrow, she decides, might be beneficial, might help to normalize her thoughts. She walks a few steps farther toward it, pauses to consider how its edges and the pattern of its coat (it wears a rather handsome herringbone jacket) seem slightly variable, somewhat blurred. She's maybe twenty feet away. The air is still. The smell of the flowers has become explicitly unpleasant. She leans forward as if at a barrier, as if seeking to advance just far enough for information to occur in whatever provisional way might not preclude a swift emotional withdrawal. But it's too late; other facts converge—a whispery buzzing, the worsening smell—and it's perfectly clear that the blurring effect, the soft penumbra, is a swarm of flies.

"Goddamn it, Luther, why don't you get a phone?"

" 'Cause you wouldn't never come see me."

Willis Beagle (Deputy Dawg as he is known) backs off the step to let the door open a little more. "Shit, pull that to," backing off a little further. Yurang's trying to insert himself into the gap, barking crazily, truly desperate. "I'll blow his head off."

"No you won't." Luther grabs the dog by the collar, pulls him back, and shuts him up in the tiny bathroom, then returns to crack the door again just a couple of inches, "Aw, go ahead," before flinging it open slap against the side of the house in order to watch Willis Beagle go for his gun and throw a fit.

"Goddamn it I'll do it"—his face bright red—"that dog get loose around me I'll blow his head off"—stepping to the right to look past Luther into the house—"blow his motherfuckin' head off," calming gradually, dropping his hand, just standing there now regarding Luther with faint malice that slowly slides back over his buck teeth into a grin that rediscovers his official advantage in this situation.

"You want to talk out here?"

"What are we gonna talk about?"

"We're gonna talk about that woman."

"What woman?" says Luther.

"What woman," repeats the deputy, shaking his head, looking around. "I don't see no others to confuse her with—you keepin' a woman out here, Luther?" He's immensely pleased with this approach. "Thought you favored dogs"—a delighted display of dental pathology—"what the hell woman you think?"

Luther looks out across the field beyond the squad car—a hazy whiteness to the air, the morning sky completely colorless—looks back at the deputy; it's already warm enough to make him sweat a little under his arms, hands on hips, stupid grin just starting to fade as Luther turns to get the puppies, bringing them out now two at a time.

"You know what I'm talkin' about." He's lost his grin and, somehow, the initiative. "You know what woman."

Luther plops the last pair into the pen. "Let's do it like this"—he gets the hose to freshen their water—"you tell me what I'm supposed to know and then I'll tell you if I know it."

Willis is grinning again. "Got you on the arm didn't he," he says.

"What?" says Luther.

"One of them dogs."

Luther glances at the bruise, the scabbed-over punctures, smiles at Willis. Willis grins back, which seems to establish a kind of equilibrium.

"That rich one you had here yesterday."

"Yeah," says Luther.

"You want to tell me what happened?"

Luther slips the wire loop over the gatepost, whips the hose back up against the trailer.

"Well, Willis"—he turns to face him—"I guess I clean just forgot to file a report; I mean them coming all the way out here to look at Mr. Tuel's cattle and wantin' to know about field cubes and how to call cows and what not; I guess they must be spies, don't you figure?"

"Shit," says Willis, walking away a couple of steps, taking off his cowboy hat, looking at the sky, his sweaty black hair pasted down like a wig. "You must be a goddamn degenerate"—he looks at Luther—"I want to see this fuckin' scarecrow."

They can hear Yurang inside scratching furiously at the insubstantial plastic door to the bathroom—a little slapping sound every now and then as it bends out and springs back. Willis puts on his hat, glances toward the open door to the trailer, back at Luther, buck teeth starting again to emerge very slowly as if whatever thought delights contains complexities, requires assembly. Suddenly he goes into a half crouch, draws a monstrous automatic pistol and points it at the trailer. "Bet I get him before he clears the step." Yurang's making an awful racket; now an ominous silence; Luther imagines him getting his nose through, bending back the plastic.

"What scarecrow?"

He cocks the hammer. "You tell me."

"What fuckin' scarecrow?"

From inside there's a snap like something breaking. "Here he comes."

"Goddammit, Willis"—another snap, more furious scratching—"what is that thing?" It's the biggest handgun he's ever seen.

"Desert Eagle three five seven mag."

"What's that thing on it?" Momentary silence again from the bathroom; Luther glances at the door, back at the pistol.

"Laser sight."

"You're shittin' me."

"Look yonder at that dot." He indicates with the pistol as if the red spot should stay put, holds it steady again, maintains his stance—a faintly luminous red spot jiggling against the side of the trailer next to the door.

"I don't see nothin'."

"The hell you don't, look at that." He waves it in a circle.

"Nope."

"Shit, you're blind. Look here." He brings it toward them across the trailer. (A soft scrabbling sound—claws tearing at shag carpet; something cracking.)

"I don't believe it." Luther whoops to keep his attention, glances at the door again. "Put it on my hand. Does it hurt?"

"No it don't hurt, you idiot. It's just a light." He uncocks the pistol, shines a brilliant tiny spot on Luther's palm.

"Hey, do it over here." Luther trots over to the door, swings it shut. "Do it again." Holds out his hand. The little spot glows in his palm, seems to tingle. "Don't that beat all." A soft low growl from just inside. "How much that set you back?"

"More'n that whole trailer's worth I reckon." Willis Beagle looks vaguely dejected.

"Bet it did," says Luther. "Bet it did."

"One-fifty grain Eldorado Starfire bullets. Know what those are?"

"Sure don't," says Luther.

"You can't get 'em."

"Well goddamn," says Luther quietly. They're standing on the rim of the stock tank looking west.

"Just Police. They open up like little buzz saws when they hit you"—demonstrating with his finger—"spin right through."

Luther glances at the finger, out across the pasture. "Let me see one." He's scanning around. "What'd she say about the flowers?"

"A bunch of flowers is all." He produces a cartridge. "Stuck way out in a bunch of flowers."

"Yellow ones?"

"Shit I don't know. Here, look at that, look at them little things, them little ridges." He holds up a jacketed hollow-point bullet with tiny ribs radiating from the tip, pulls it away as Luther reaches for it, brings it back slowly toward Luther's stomach, turning it like a screwdriver. "Them little things open up like a flower"—twisting it now into Luther's paunch—"spinnin' round, cuts you all up." Luther steps away. Willis grins, makes a feint, goes for his paunch again with the bullet, pulls up and looks at Luther sideways. "Bobby says she's real good lookin'."

"Bobby talk to her?"

"Yeah, not me—well not her neither, not really. Talked mostly to Roly-Poly."

"Her husband?"

"Yeah."

Luther looks away toward the woods; Willis is studying his bullet, turning it this way and that. "She wouldn't get out of that car," he says after a minute. "You see that car? Shit. Bobby went and poked his head in but she wouldn't get out. Said she was real good lookin' though"—puts his bullet back in his belt—"good enough to eat." He grins at Luther. Luther smiles, walks down the embankment and across the pasture—"Know what I mean?" yells Willis—out the gate and into the meadow. He thinks for a moment he can detect a trail, a faint disruption of the grass the way she went but he really can't. He can hear Willis fiddling with the gate, negotiating the cattle guard in his high-heeled pointy boots, walking up behind him and just standing there, doing something with his equipment, adjusting his holster. Luther imagines he can feel a slight tingling on the back of his neck.

"You really got somethin' might be scarin' purty ladies you ought to let me see it." Luther turns. Willis grins. "You got a big old nasty scary thing?"—vastly amused—"I know I sure do"—grins hugely now, "but I don't know about you; don't see nothin' here"—regarding Luther with what should probably be mock dismay but which his physiognomy, overtaxed, renders merely as a sort of feral ardor whose effect on Luther is unsatisfactory. His teeth withdraw, he takes off his hat again, runs his hand back over his hair, wipes the sweat off on his shirt, scans the meadow. "Shit," he says, "I don't need this," and turns to go, turns back at the gate, completely official. "How many acres Tuel got out here?"

" 'Bout eight hundred," says Luther. Willis thinks about that for a minute.

"How come she didn't say nothin' to you?"

"She was locked up in that big old Mercedes when we come back. He had to bang on the window to get in."

Willis reaches for the latch, remembers something, walks over to Luther, hands him a moist twice-folded sheet of paper. "Bobby told me to give you this," then turns and passes through the gate and across the pasture with the receding sound of his equipment slapping softly against his leg.

Luther walks a little farther into the meadow and stops, looks around. A flight of crows swoops out of the woods and disappears back over the trees. It's as still as yesterday. He unfolds the paper, some sort of flyer—little schematic Christian fish at top and bottom, a Xeroxed photo of Bobby's catfish still lashed to the plywood, and an announcement: "These are the Last Days of the world when wickedness shall be shed like the skin of the serpent." And below in smaller letters: "Last Days Covenant Church—First meeting Monday, November 20, 8pm at Joe's Big Juicy Hamburger Restaurant." He studies the photo of the catfish propped up on its plywood sheet, somebody's hand coming over the top, grabbing its mouth to keep it from slumping. It seems unclear whether it's intended to represent something ominous and prophetic or just a special added attraction. He folds the paper and puts it in his pocket. Off to the west the crows are complaining, making a commotion, cawing to one another more and more frantically, louder and louder till the woods are filled with their distress.

6

Into Luther's thoughts sometimes at night comes an image of his trailer out in the dark by itself in the middle of the field. It becomes obscure to him in ways themselves obscure but quite disturbing, as if explanation were required beyond the obvious for such a thing, for someone living in this situation. He sees it as if from a distance, from the edge of the clearing perhaps, across the moonlit grass, indistinct, just a pale shape out there in the open and, as in the vision of the drifting cottonwood seed above Cook's pasture, with a sense of tragedy or profound apprehension at least the way it sits there so provisionally (which is not his term but his impression) as if at that moment of greatest potential, greatest peril, just at the cast as the top-water lure lays on the water before the line whips up and back. He jerks his head around to the window. The high waning moonlight fills the field, glints along the power line at the curve where it dips away out to the road. He thinks of the lake and the giant catfish, frosty white, white as marble, imagining it in the water like that, pale and rising, mouth agape. He kicks off the covers. Yurang's alert. He's up on the couch looking out the window. Luther can see his face in the moonlight, ears forward, mouth shut, perfectly still. A red flashing in the corner of Luther's eye; he sits up quickly. It's just the little digital clock needing to be reset. An interruption during the night; a twitch in the line. He wonders what time it is, leans over against the screen, craning his neck to locate the moon but he can't quite see it; looks over at Yurang, muzzle presented to the window, to the cold white glow like a refrigerator light. It must be just about overhead, the way the light barely slips in across the dog's face and the back of the couch. He turns the clock away. It bothers him flashing "12:00" like some sort of alarm—like flashing "empty." He swings his legs over and sits there for a while on the edge of the bed watching Yurang and how the moonlight diffuses into the trailer, appears to accumulate like dust. It seems important to know the time. Yurang's not moving, not even a reflexive wiggle of the tail as Luther gets up, goes to fiddle around in the drawers to find his watch—a complicated plastic one with a broken strap. He holds it up to the little window above the sink, gives it a tap, presses the buttons. The battery's depleted but there's something there almost, he thinks: a flicker of numerals under the surface, black numerals rising to the screen like one of those fortune-telling balls. For all he knows it could have enough juice to keep the time without quite displaying it. He holds it higher, angling it down to catch the moonlight from outside. He tries all the buttons down at once. Even the wrong time, visibly passing, would confirm its progress, correct the feeling of its having run out somehow all of a sudden. He taps it again, holds it nearer the window then puts it down, turns and leans back against the sink, looking at Yurang and out at the tall grass—too bright it seems, pale as frost although it must be eighty degrees outside at least. He goes over to the couch, slumps next to Yurang. "You see a rabbit?" A twitch of the ear. "You see a rabbit?" Luther turns and rests his chin on the back of the couch, touches the window. It's hard to tell; contradictory signals—the wintry aspect of the field, the warmth of the glass—make it difficult to estimate as if things canceled out, yielded no particular temperature, no clear determination. Yurang has raised himself a little, front legs stiff. Luther lifts his head to see where he's looking. "Wanna get it?" The glass fogs slightly. "Big old rabbit." A circle of breath. "Big old swamp rabbit." He scans the field beyond the tire tracks, looking for a ripple, the sort of undulatory darkening of the surface that you see when something's moving through the grass. The light's ambiguous, almost grainy like old photographs, faded-looking. His eyes lose focus after a minute; there's nothing to see; he shifts around a little more and brings his head down onto his hands.

No eggs this morning. Luther ducks out of the henhouse, flings a little more scratch around, checks the water and the laying mash,

David Searcy

stands and watches them for a while, six Leggerns and eight Reds, their peculiar, jerky agitation. Yurang's just waiting by the gate. The chickens are too scattered about the yard, too disorganized to be stalked.

Luther takes a brick and knocks some plywood back into place then straightens the gatepost, leaning and pounding on it till it's more or less upright, jams the brick back under the corner of the coop where it's lifted up. He walks out to the path, Yurang following, rubs his arm and looks out over the field, up to the road and back along the car tracks to where they fade in the taller grass. A mournful mooing from beyond the trees. He looks at Yurang, squats and scratches him behind the ears. "Cubes is round," he whispers; Yurang closes his mouth and then his eyes, maneuvering around to submit his hindquarters.

Nothing much in the refrigerator either. One brown egg, a half package of American cheese slices individually wrapped. He swings it open all the way, stands with the cool air coming around him and out the open door of the trailer right behind. He turns, letting the sweat chill through his tee shirt under his arms and down his back. A cloud of gnats hangs over the field, perfectly stationary, somewhat ghostly in the ripply heat above the grass. He shuts the door, shuts the refrigerator, sets the oscillating fan going on the counter, lets down the little gold-flecked Formica table and sits, hands folded, leaning back. The plastic fan makes a squeal at the end of each half-cycle—unusable at night, the whir of air across his face and then the screech like some sort of bird diving past him in the dark.

After a moment he gets up, takes the cheese and the egg from the refrigerator, heats a pan, swirls a pat of butter around in it, breaks the egg into a bowl. He stands there looking at it for a minute, butter sizzling, turning dark brown in the pan. The bright yellow yolk is shot with blood. It's very unpleasant entirely aside from ruining the omelet—faintly traumatic, the brilliant yellow stained with red. He has no rooster and there's no reason for it, a fertilized egg, immaculate conception, somehow pathological there in the bowl like some alarming physical symptom. The butter's scorching, going black. He turns it off. The little fan hasn't had much effect.

He steps outside into the hazy glare, sits in the doorway, and lights a cigarette. The gnats have receded across the field, spread horizontally into an attenuating smoky layer that shifts very slowly this way and that. It extends itself gradually, thinning out, losing coherence after a while, breaking up into fainter wisps that glint in and out of visibility, then seem to evaporate all at once.

"Dammit, y'all get out." The puppies are on him, going for his face, restricting his movements as he tries to crawl up under the trailer. His attempts to sweep them out of the way with either arm in a sort of breaststroke make it worse, heighten their fury, broaden the attack to the point it's impossible to withdraw the nail-studded scraps of lumber without risk of puncturing one of the dogs. He decides to go limp, give them the victory, endure their celebrations for a minute or two then make his move as they lose interest, but it's all too exciting, too good a game; he has to back out, turn around, and kick what boards he can out the other side.

It's lousy lumber in any event—most of it split, half the nails too bent to straighten. All the good parts went to the henhouse and the little step he made for the trailer. He corrals the puppies, gathers tools, lays everything out in the trampled grass. He can hear the oscillating fan inside making its noise every couple of seconds. He feels incapable. It's hard to imagine making anything. He takes a split plank, stands it up, yanks it apart the rest of the way, tosses the pieces off to the side. He kicks the two best boards together, sits down and looks at them for a while.

The saw doesn't work right. It's not rusty; it must be the weather. Too much humidity or too much heat getting in the wood, which is what an old black gardener told him once, how heat can soak into the trees and make them difficult to prune. More like heat getting into the gardener, he thought at the time. Or more than heat, an overwhelming vagueness. He looks up. The sun's just a brightening in the haze, hard to locate with precision. It must be three or four o'clock. He jerks the saw out. It's drifted too far off the mark; he marks it again a little farther in, gets his knee down on it right at the edge of the step, goes very slowly, then quite brutally forcing the saw to seek the line, hacking it through at a shallow angle to keep from jamming into the dirt.

He's turned off the fan. The faintest breeze comes through the little louvered windows, the sound of a redbird peeping its monotonous evening song. The trigger's the hard part—all the clumsiness brought to a point, a dependable consequence. It makes him think of a TV show Agnes made him watch about some place in England where prehistoric people did astronomy with a bunch of boulders. He has it on the table, a long cobbled-together wooden box, one end closed with fine screen mesh, the other open with a guillotine-like sliding door suspended above. He's on his knees peering into it, lining it up with the fading glow from the larger window over the couch. He can see the trigger now, the whittled stick in silhouette, gives it a nudge with the handle of his hammer. It slips a little, then releases up through the hole. The sliding door binds halfway down. He adjusts the rocking-arm mechanism on top and tries again, then pries the guide rails out a little; same result. He gets some soap, a desiccated remnant, pauses to wrestle with the door to the bathroom, kicking at the bottom where Yurang popped it, bent it out so it refuses to latch.

The haze has thinned. Real shadows now behind the red-tinged yellow light move almost visibly across the grass. He soaps the track and then the edges of the wooden trapdoor, works it manually up and down a number of times, recovers a Coke bottle from the trash, places it inside and gives it a roll. The door slaps shut. He stands up and steps back, walks around to the other side, regarding the trap from every angle, stops and listens. The bottle is slowly rolling back. It hits the door with a gentle thump. He's gratified vastly beyond the facts of the achievement, beyond the prospects for the stewpot. It's as if some greater principle were at issue—the bottle defined as well as captured, knowledge snatched from out of the fog. No mystery here—he looks at Yurang, opens the trap, and lets the bottle roll onto the floor, turns to the refrigerator, finds his very last can of beer and pops it open, chugs about half then quickly assembles a thick cheese sandwich with all the slices left in the pack. He cuts it in two, considers a moment, cuts it into quarters, stuffing one in his mouth and taking another over to the trap, having to reach in as far as he can to place it just between the wire screen and the trigger.

"Get on back in"—Yurang wants to follow him outside—"don't need you smellin' everything up." He shoves the door shut with his boot, turns to the meadow whose possibilities seem to disperse, become obscure with the light's withdrawal across the grass. He carries the trap against his hip, walks very slowly into the tall Bermuda, looking down into the warm gold streaks and patches between the shadows streaming almost to the road. It's like casting a line—not something to think about very closely, requiring focus as down along the creek, say, you can spot where things have been, their tracks in the sand, the little trails they use. Any place will do. He puts the trap down, squats next to it, working the door a few more times before setting the trigger, catching the notch right at the edge of the hole, right at the point where something's instincts will give way just an inch or so toward the sandwich and that will be that, down comes the door. Maybe he'll hear it if he's awake. He stands and backs away a couple of steps. The rosy light has thinned to gray. How nice, he decides, were he able to hear it way out in the field in the middle of the night, uncertainty collapsing with a little slap. He heads back to the trailer, turning now and then to mark the spot. The pines to the east are going dark, losing the glow from the bottom up until there's just a brilliant red-gold fringe set off by shadow, briefly radiant, as he pauses to watch, and then suddenly gone.

It was about sunrise, he thinks in the gloom, finishing his sandwich—what the boulders were for, the prehistoric boulders—catching the sunrise one day a year, some special occasion, a dazzling flash through a crack in the rock blinding the camera, very dramatic. "Imagine that," Agnes had said. And he supposed he could. He could imagine setting up a couple of sticks to do the same thing with a lot less trouble. But maybe there was more to it, something he missed. The redbird has stopped. He drains his beer and closes his eyes—the slightest hint of exhilaration, the faintest alcoholic glimmer. What if right now he heard the trap—he holds the thought and tries to remember how to skin a rabbit, if it's an *R* month, and something else, something elusive as the intoxicating effects of half a beer, yet which fastens his concern to the extent that this night, when, after a while, he goes to bed and lies awake, what enters his thoughts, what yields a vision, is not his trailer but the trap. And in the imaginary moonlit darkness it presents a similar aspect, the same proportions—a shadowy box across the grass yet more concise, a sort of refinement.

7

Joe looks at the voucher, looks at Luther. "That ain't no good." His little Nehru-style paper hat has begun to split along the crease, slipping to his ears, making him look moronic and immune to argument.

"You turned your grill off?"

"No I ain't turned it off"—he glances behind as if to make sure—"I ain't turned nothin' off." He shoves the ticket back at Luther. "That's just a onetime deal."

"Don't plan to use it more'n one time."

"It's out of date." He turns back to the kitchen, makes a show of being busy. Luther walks over to the drink box, gets a root beer, takes a seat, looks at the Dr Pepper clock above the empty benches across the aisle—two thirty-five. He squints into the glare out front where Yurang is moored, flat on his stomach, head on his paws, completely inert. "Ain't no date on it." No response. Luther gets up, goes back over to the tiny service window, nudges the ticket across the counter toward the kitchen. "How 'bout some water for my dog?" Joe scoops some ice. "Don't need no ice." Joe dumps the ice, fills the cup.

"When you gonna get a truck?" Joe slides it across.

"Just soon as Tuel dies and leaves me all his money."

"He oughta get you a truck."

Luther looks back and grins, steps out the door. Yurang drains it, getting his nose right down in the paper cup then lapping the dribbles as Luther pours. There's hardly a soul out on the square. Luther untangles Yurang's leash, reties him nearer the post, and sits there at the edge of the walk for a while drinking his root beer, wadding the cup into a tighter and tighter waxy ball. Across the way at Hudgins' clothing store there's some activity but that's about it. Housecleaning it looks like. No one actually visible, just odds and ends periodically flying out the front door onto the sidewalk, unidentifiable bits and pieces. Now a leg. A human leg. The bottle slips and root beer fizzes down his shirt. The delayed sound of plastic hitting the concrete. Next an arm, a shapely torso, a bunch of stuff that looks like wigs.

Joe's at the griddle flipping a patty. "Servin' burgers at the Wal-Mart now," says Joe over his shoulder.

"Yeah?" says Luther, grabbing some napkins and dabbing at his shirt.

"Takin' over everything. Oughta go ahead and call the whole town Wal-Mart. Just change the name and be done with it. 'Welcome to Wal-Mart.'" He comes over to the window. "What you want on this?"

"Whatever you got."

"Welcome to Wal-Mart," mutters Joe, piling on the extras in a demonstration of home-owned generosity. "Wal-Mart, Texas." Wraps it up in translucent paper fastened with a toothpick.

"Things pretty slow?" Luther takes it over to the seat next to the Coke box. Joe just stands leaning on the counter, shaking his head, gazing out from the little window down the empty shotgun-style interior into the bleary light beyond. Luther removes the toothpick, spreads the paper which nearly covers the little half-desk, holds the cheeseburger just above to keep the spillage—a fairly steady precipitation of chopped lettuce and onions—off the floor.

"You ever trap rabbits?" he says around a mouthful.

"Huh?" says Joe.

Luther swallows, takes a swig. "You ever trap rabbits?" Joe comes around to the other side.

"My daddy did. He used a box—not much on snares; he'd cook 'em ever which way. Squirrels too."

"Ever had any get away?"

"Get away?"

"Get out of the trap. Take the bait."

"You mean just sittin' out, nobody messin' with it?"

"Yeah," says Luther, gathering the salad bits to the center of the paper and reinserting what he can.

"Not rabbits. You leave one out there long enough he'll start chewin' around that hole where the stick goes up. He ain't gettin' out though unless maybe you forget about him." He takes a school desk on the other side, props his head up in his hand, watching the street, after a couple of minutes turning back to Luther, studying him awhile. "I believe you're done." Luther's folded the now-transparent greasy paper into a trough, tilting it to his mouth, giving it a tap. Joe takes his ticket book over to the register. "Coon'll do it though. You catch a coon, he'll take the bait and back right out; use his hind feet to grab the door and slide it up. Seen that happen." Luther banks the wad of paper into the trash, picks up his backpack, drops his empty in the rack. "Half price on the cheeseburger, not the drink." Joe hands him the slip.

"Y'all don't plan to go worshipin' that thing do you?" Luther counts it out in change, looks up at Joe, who looks back blankly. "Sheriff's fish." He indicates the stack of flyers by the register. They look like Xeroxes of Xeroxes of the one Luther received, the picture of the catfish so far removed from the original, so indistinct, it's hard to tell what's being grasped, being presented by the now strangely disembodied hand. Joe turns one of the flyers around as if it were necessary to consult before responding. "Not near as I can tell." He shuts the register, looks out the window. Somebody's backed a truck up to Hudgins' door, loading all the manikin parts and whatnot. "Shuttin' down," says Joe. "No kidding," says Luther. "Sure are," says Joe. "Seventy-somethin' years. Welcome to Wal-Mart."

The gently rising oiled sand road that goes to Mount Pisgah crosses the highway outside town. It runs past scattered, perhaps once actively agricultural, little properties whose sustained dilapidation Luther likes somehow, finds vaguely reassuring—all the cars and stuff in the yards, the sense of a sort of neutral buoyancy. He lets Yurang off the leash to range ahead a little ways, one side to the other, sniffing at a spot, lifting his leg, now back across, trotting slowly along the fence where a number of fish heads have been hung up, one per post, salted, dried, black catfish heads of various sizes,

46   David Searcy

mostly big ones nailed through the lower lip, one after another, like trophies of war rather than sport; like a display of scalps.

It's enough of a hill to be able to look off to the right and see the highway now and then where the fields run together: a yellow bus from Harmony School gears down the grade, flashing to turn, and passing it now, heading out of town at a high rate of speed, a county patrol car flashing its own lights and blipping its siren for no particular reason Luther can determine, with no other traffic, blurting and blinking over the rise, all that excitement somehow inappropriate, fading away, lost in the quiet. The air seems too heavy, hangs in hazy layers which, from this perspective, look sort of like milk left standing out, starting to separate with the translucent part at the bottom, gradually thickening, going whiter the higher you look without quite defining, actually coagulating, into clouds. The sun is there but imprecisely, a brilliant blur.

Yurang's flushed something by the fence—a rabbit or a rat, just a skittering through the weeds, shooting out across the field and disappearing, leaving Yurang by the barbed wire in a crouch. He sits up, panting, waiting for Luther, jumps up on him, bounds away across the road. The school bus is coming up the hill behind. Luther whistles. Yurang races back across, trots next to Luther as it passes—pale, haphazard little faces turn to look; one, with his lips pressed to the glass, makes kissing gestures then, much congratulated and encouraged, renews these demonstrations from the rear window as the bus moves down the road for a hundred feet or so, coming to a stop where a long straight path leads past a partially dismembered Camaro to a house quite badly in need of paint except for the trim which is turquoise green. The face at the window is suddenly gone and after a moment a boy emerges, stands in the dust and the blue exhaust, watching Luther and Yurang approach, leash reattached. He drops his binder, gathers it up, walks down the path to stand by the Camaro as they come by, watching them steadily without expression, clutching his schoolbooks, lips still red from his exertions.

• • •

"Ever which kind of trap you could desire," says the owner of the Mount Pisgah Feed and Grocery, "over yonder by them pellets." Actually there aren't very many kinds: two sizes of live trap—one for rabbits, one for coons, both double entrance, heavy wire mesh with a bait-tray trigger in the middle—and various kill traps of the usual sort for mice and rats. They look obscure and somehow ineffective—even the mousetraps—although, no doubt, they all work fine. He takes down the coon trap, studying its subtlety, the complex linkage between the bait tray and the doors, the indirection of it all.

"Got to have a college degree." The owner's behind him, laughing and reaching around to cock the trap, tripping it now with a ballpoint pen. Whack, go the wire doors simultaneously. "This little deal here"—he indicates a small, hinged metal flap—"locks everything down so he can't push out. What you trappin'?" Luther looks at him—a large red-haired man whose name he forgets, who requires good humor and straightforwardness, would not be receptive to Luther's thoughts, his strained uncertainty on this matter.

"Somethin' after my chickens," he decides to say, lifts the little metal flap and lets it fall.

"Big somethin' or little somethin'?"

Luther works the doors up and down to feel the tension. "I ain't quite determined yet."

The owner comes around to look at him. "Is he goin' over or comin' through?"

Luther smiles. "Not neither one."

The owner appears to consider then reject this information, "Coons and bobcats'll go right over, take 'em and run, chicken to go"—he shoots one palm across the other with a slap—"same thing with a possum except sometimes he'll just gut 'em and make a mess"—glancing up front now—"be right there"; he holds up his hand with three fingers curled, two extended to count the remaining possibilities. "Weasels'll slither through like a snake—if you get a chicken up against the fence with his head chewed off, that's gonna be a weasel"—jabs with his thumb—"bull snake leaves a little pile of eggshells where he's spit 'em out." He keeps his fist up for a second to signify completion and simplicity, nods, and goes off to other business.

Luther picks up a plastic basket, gets six apples, a small jar of peanut butter, a loaf of white bread, two packs of cold cuts, and one of those little half-cartons of eggs. Also he needs a very large nail—a twenty-penny nail or possibly one of the even bigger kind referred to as spikes. The selection is limited but he rummages around among the bins and comes up with a pretty good one which he takes with his groceries up to the front.

"He bite?" asks the owner, looking outside.

"Naw," says Luther.

The owner shakes his head. "I always heard chows are liable to bite." Yurang's acting the part, straining at his leash, periodically growling at something not apparent from inside. "Tend to be unpredictable," says the owner, examining the nail, elaborately folding it up in a little sack and tossing it in for free as Luther stuffs everything into his backpack. They stand for a minute watching the dog, his peculiar aggressions toward nothing in particular across the road, the conspicuously empty mown field falling away in the hazy distance to clumps of trees and spotted cattle.

"You know chickens don't never sleep."

Luther looks at him.

The owner laughs. "You ever hear that?"

Luther smiles and shakes his head. Yurang's just sitting there now, tongue lolling, gazing off into the heat.

"Don't never sleep," says the owner, "scared all the time. Just the way they are. Never close their eyes, even at night."

The owner follows Luther outside. "That's what I heard"— watches as Luther unties the dog. "What's he weigh?"

"'Bout seventy pounds. Use your hydrant?"

"Go ahead."

Luther lets it run for Yurang, then cups his hands, takes a drink himself splashing his face and the back of his neck. The owner's still there. Luther wipes his face on the front of his tee shirt which smells like root beer.

"I guess they're good watchdogs," says the owner, kneeling—not extending his hand but as if considering it. Luther shortens the leash.

"He'll do more'n watch."

The owner looks up at him.

"He's okay just tied up out here."

The owner stands, puts his hands in his pockets, looks off across the field. The little semicircular drive has a recent layer of asphalt—black and crumbly, uncomfortably absorbent to the heat of the day. Luther turns to go.

"Where do you get them dogs?"

Luther stops. "I got six pups."

"You raise 'em to sell?"

"Yeah, pretty much. I might keep one."

"Tell me somethin'"—but now he's distracted by someone leaving, having to go over and exchange a few words while Luther waits. It's getting late. He can imagine the mess in the puppies' box when he gets home. The owner returns with the other man who stands slightly away, both regarding the dog.

"He's seventy pounds," says the owner, looking over at the man, making no introductions, everyone on the asphalt sweating a little. Yurang's indifferent, sitting and panting, occasionally shutting his mouth and pricking his ears at the smaller, darker man, a receding presence who keeps his distance as if automatically, as if it were some habitual form of resentment rather than caution that required the interval.

"How bad'll he do?" A voice so reluctant Luther can't hear it. He looks at the owner standing between them like an interpreter.

"Against a trespasser," says the owner, "somebody comin' in. How bad'll he do."

"If I don't do nothin'?"

The owner nods. Yurang lies down, puts his head on his paws.

"Likely to kill him."

The small man rubs his stomach under his tee shirt which is olive drab with a much-laundered emblem involving a parachute, some kind of skeletal-looking device, and over it the slogan, "Death from Above." He has one of those anomalously dark complexions which unsupported by the other evidence—dirty-blond hair, pinched thin-lipped face—has the quality of stain.

"What you take for him," he says.

"He ain't for sale."

"He's sellin' the pups," provides the owner of the Mount Pisgah Feed and Grocery.

"Don't need no pups." He rubs his stomach. "Don't need no pups." He turns and spits a wad of something complexion-colored toward the road.

"Don't need no growed one, that's for sure." Yurang rises as Luther takes a step in the man's direction. "You got to raise 'em yourself." The man looks away as if Luther weren't there. "That way they're family. You get one growed, you can't be sure of him." Luther glances at the owner. "He might be unpredictable." The small man walks over to the road, spits again, and returns to stand at his former distance.

"How long 'for he gets mean?"

"They ain't mean. Just protective."

"How long for he gets protective?"

"Eighteen months."

The olive-drab tee shirt has begun to soak through, darkening him further, making him recede further, look more uncomfortable and more resentful. For a few seconds they all stand there on the asphalt saying nothing, then the blue-green pickup across the drive lurches slightly as something inside very large and pale makes a sudden movement. A couple of short honks followed by a long, declining bleat as she leans on the horn, draining the battery for the entire time it takes him to walk across, open the door, and push her away. They just sit there in the truck for a minute or so, apparently giving the battery a chance to recover; then there's a click, a discouraging tug as the engine turns once, surprisingly catches, revs up past the redline three or four times and they head off throwing a little asphalt, trailing a thin white pall of smoke.

"Leonard's troubled," explains the owner.

"So's his wife," says Luther, unwinding the leash from around his wrist, hitching up his pack. "What'd you need to ask?"

The owner looks puzzled, shakes his head. "Musta got covered," smiles and walks back into the store.

8

Past Agnes's house with its TV-lit interior flickering in the dusk, they follow the road to where the fence breaks in for the power lines, cutting through there taking the easement between the planted pines on the right and on the other side mostly thicket which gradually thins then opens abruptly onto the broader corridor for the gas line angling straight back to the southeast. Luther lifts the barbed wire for the dog then holds the top strand down with his backpack, straddling over, losing his balance, doing a little dance on one leg and falling backward to the ground where he lies for a moment considering the clarified blue-violet sky and how unpleasantly it strikes him for some reason, the way the stars just now appearing seem to descend into visibility like bits of something floating down. He sits up and pushes Yurang away, retrieves his pack and checks the eggs.

The pipeline passes out of the trees downhill through open fields to the road that runs along the north edge of Tuel's property. Luther guides Yurang under the wire again—his fur is sticky from all the wildflowers whose resinous scent seems to reactivate his former pungency to a degree. Luther slips through right behind, laying his pack across the bottom strand, jumps the ditch, stands in the road looking at the Milky Way sweeping clear across the sky east to west, listening to a faint, very distant whispery sort of noise like that of wind coming through the trees, or maybe a gas well somewhere wheezing through its cycle. He follows the sound of Yurang's tags; it's too dark to see him, too dark now to see very much at all, even the road. He tries to keep to the very center, sensing the slight crown of it, not wanting to drift over into the ditch, keeping the jingle straight ahead. Yurang's receding, trotting away as he usually does when they reach this point, out of earshot after a while. He'll wait at the place where they always cross, sit by the fence, let Luther know if he should miss it in the dark. The other noise seems to come from nowhere in particular—more of a hissing, not really the boiling teakettle kind of sigh the gas wells make although like that it carries a sense of something depleting, leaking away.

Periodically the gas wells multiply. Production falls below some critical level, well-density restrictions are suddenly revised under rules which, governing property deeper than ordinary property, are more profound, subtend all others; and overnight the number doubles, up they pop wherever they will—the three big tanks along with the separator and all the pipes and various gizmos—sometimes right in somebody's backyard. It occurs to Luther to wonder if there might not be a consequence—some sort of deflation or subsidence—to the evacuation of so much material, so much content, leaving a shell like something gutted, all the insides finally whooshed out, turned into water, gas, and kerosene. He stops to listen. It is in fact an empty kind of sound, like something hollow held to the ear. It gives him a hollow, uneasy feeling in his stomach. He takes a deep breath, cups a hand behind each ear and turns in place like a radar dish. There is a difference—a little more audible from the south, from the direction of the property. He tries to think what kind of insect might make a sound like that, something hatched out prematurely in the heat. He turns to listen down the road—the faintest jinglejangle of dog tags, Yurang scratching himself and waiting.

In the woods Yurang goes crazy, back and forth, this way and that as if there were rabbits running everywhere. After a minute he settles down but intermittently stops in his tracks, growling softly, causing Luther to stumble over him. Luther puts him on the leash, wrapping it several times around his hand, shortening it right up to the collar as they emerge into the clearing, squatting down now, making Yurang sit beside him. "Shit," says Luther. The clearing whispers. "Shit," whispers Luther again to himself a couple of times. The smell of Yurang seems to associate itself with the noise, makes Luther imagine a vast swarm of flies. He stands up, lets out the leash. He can see the trailer, the back of it way out there in the field, so small and indistinct, removed somehow as if by some sort of tragedy, as if in his absence some catastrophe, always threatened, had finally occurred, played itself out and left behind this empty whispery sound like smoke. Yurang wants to make straight for it, tries to bark as Luther pulls him back, tells him to shut up, jerks him along, circling away to come in obliquely, backpack slapping against him awkwardly, making it hard to keep up the trot. He arcs in gradually from the west side trying to distinguish more clearly the henhouse and the trailer, get a shadowy sense at least of the situation, where things are and what looks different. Something's different. He kneels in the grass. A big pale something next to the trailer seems to be where the noise comes from. He loops the leash around his belt and ties a knot, holds Yurang's dog tags in his fist and moves in closer, staying low, tapping Yurang on the nose to keep him quiet. It's a car. He kneels again, removes his pack, takes out his little two-bladed pocketknife, puts it back. The stars are brighter than he can remember, sweeping across in streaks and clouds, hardly twinkling, the way he imagines they might look from outer space—the way they might sound he imagines as well, a steady, soft celestial hiss. It's hard to concentrate. He digs into his pack, pulls out the eggs, the peanut butter, and everything else to find the nail. Yurang's gone to stalking mode, taking up the slack to Luther's belt and causing him to pivot slowly clockwise. Luther yanks him down next to him, wads the little paper sack around the nail head to make a handle, a sort of cushion for his palm, undoes the leash from around his belt and now unclips the other end, keeping the tags against the collar in his fist. "Okay," he says. Okay to the dog and to the fact that he has nothing really to lose no matter what; and off they go straight for it now, Luther loping in a crouch as if he knew what he were doing, as if he had seen this in a movie. There's the henhouse. Just the dark shape on his left, nothing added, nothing moving. There should be movement any second, he expects, sudden voices, flashlight shining in his face—in that event he'll let the dog go—anything but flat-out panic on their part, any challenge whatsoever, let the dog go, move away and listen first to all the noise they're bound to make as Yurang hits, let all the yelling tell him what he's got to deal with. Here's the

David Searcy

trailer. Nothing looms, nothing lurches, just the noise. Yurang's making for it, going right for the car. Luther stops him, hauls him down and taps him lightly with the nail across the muzzle. It's a patrol car. In the starlight he can see the County emblem, the lights on top. He drags Yurang back across to the trailer. The door's still locked—an excited chorus of yipping and whining as he fiddles with the key, holding the nail between his teeth, shoves Yurang in and shuts the door.

He stands for a minute catching his breath, regarding the patrol car. He walks over to it, touches the hood. It's been here awhile, apparently just parked with the radio turned way up, tuned to nothing, hissing away. He can see stars reflected in the windshield. He leans closer—and among the reflected stars now, faint and tentative like a nebula, delicately lit by some very soft interior source, the face of Willis Beagle, mouth wide open, hat tipped forward over the eyes. Luther goes around to the window, looks inside. The radio dial gives a greenish glow. There's a lot of trash. All over the seat there are wads of foil, paper sacks, empty cups—Dairy Queen debris. No sign of trauma. Luther steps back, slips the nail into his pocket. Willis stirs. He seems to gather himself out of the noise, out of some deeply disordered state that takes a moment or two to consolidate, to organize, as if individually unpleasant behaviors had to be individually started up. "Motherfuck," he says, shifts himself around slightly to permit a prolonged and evidently gratifying flatulent release. "Jesus Christ. Jesus fuckin' Christ," he murmurs, turning down the radio, pushing his hat back, fully emergent now with a belch as the light clicks off and everything's silent except for a mournful sort of sigh that trails off gradually. Luther becomes aware of the periodic squeal of the little fan inside the trailer, the sound of traffic off to the east.

"Where's that dog?"

It sounds like a semi gearing up the steep grade south of town, winding out endlessly gear after gear. It must have fifty gears. It goes on forever.

"Goddammit, Luther."

"He's inside."

"Let me see your hands." He turns on the dome light.

Luther squints and puts them up.

"Not that. Come on around here, get in the car. I want to see your hands." He rakes the trash off onto the floor as Luther gets in. It smells like the men's room at the Dairy Queen. "Hold 'em out here." Luther complies. "Turn 'em over." He takes his time, looking very closely, turning his head this way and that. "What's on your shirt?"

"Root beer," says Luther.

"Root beer," says Willis, shaking his head. "Root beer," he says again, flipping off the dome light, leaning back. "Where you been?"

"Town," says Luther.

"Town," repeats Willis as if to suggest how thoroughly dubious all this was, this going to town and spilling root beer on his shirt. Luther lets his eyes close for a minute. He can still hear the semi, just barely, a very thin receding whine.

"What's all the lumber?"

"For traps," says Luther.

"Traps," says Willis. "You gonna trap yourself a woman?" Now he's into it. "That's it ain't it?" Sits up and turns so his teeth shine softly in the starlight, then withdraw as inspiration seems to depart; "Bet that's it," slumps back in his seat. Luther wonders how long he's been sitting out here. He kicks the trash out from under his feet, leans forward and rests his arms on the dash, looks up at the stars as if he were hanging out here voluntarily, waiting for friends or something just parked out here in the dark looking at the stars. He's too depleted really to care what it's all about; the adrenaline drains away like a solvent. The stars don't twinkle. Somehow they're flat, very bright but lifeless like smeared fireflies.

"Found your scarecrow."

The stale cheeseburger smell is starting to get to him. He leans back.

"'Bout the nastiest thing I ever seen." Willis coughs something up, spits out the window. "Anybody could of seen it." He seems to turn to look at Luther. "You know that? Anybody could of seen it right off that dirt road over yonder. Right up there on the pipeline out in the middle of them little flowers. Shit," says Willis, after a minute says it again and then falls silent as if, having drifted too far from sarcasm, he were at risk, too much exposed. Luther can just discern the outline of his cowboy hat and his prominent ears against the window but nothing within it, no features at all—Willis erased, Willis empty. Luther gets out of the car. Something about the smell is just too much. He runs his hand back over his crew cut, leans on the fender gazing south across the field. Somewhere way off in that direction he can hear wild dogs or possibly coyotes—anymore they're so interbred there's not much difference—making that gibbery high-pitched racket. Regular dogs, it seems to him, never make that sound unless they're injured. In any case it sounds like injury, received or inflicted, one way or another. Willis climbs out. Luther can hear him adjusting himself, arranging his equipment. He comes around and walks past Luther toward the field a couple of steps, stands for a moment. "I hate them things." The howling and squealing seem to be drifting away farther south. "You gonna let me look in your trailer?"

Luther turns to walk back toward it. "Look all you want."

"Ain't got no warrant." Willis follows.

"Ain't nothin' to see."

Willis disappears behind the trailer while Luther struggles to transfer Yurang, furiously reluctant, and then the puppies into the pen. He throws a layer of newspaper over the mess in the puppies' box, sits on the bed, and closes his eyes against the seventy-five watt overhead light and the sound of Willis, who seems to be standing right outside pissing on the trailer. It sounds like rain, very slowly tapering off then gently dripping pitter-pat. The trailer tips as he steps in, fully restored, all squinty buck-toothed application to the problem of evil latent in the ordinary, the glaringly drab. It's as if that were the point, the irreducible bleakness of Luther's trailer out here in the dark, in the middle of the field, as if that were the mystery. He gets right down as close as he can above the counter and especially the sink, making that face as if the real truth might be startled, flushed like rabbits, carries his scrutiny up the ripply plastic paneling, across the wall, in and out of the bathroom, over to the couch, beneath the dog-stained once-green cushions, into flimsy butt-jointed plywood drawers and cabinets incapable of holding, it seems to Luther, any secret at all much less whatever Willis has in mind, although he almost wishes there might be something like that, something for Willis to pull out slowly, mouth agape, hold up in the terrible bare-bulb glare.

He's paused at last, run out of places except for the smelly cardboard box. He stands above it, gives it a kick. "So what's this shit?"

"That's what it is."

He kicks it again, seems inclined to accept this declaration, brushes his hair back under his hat and kind of slumps, walks over to sit in the open door looking out into the dark.

The little fan has gotten worse. Now it's making a distinctly predatory-sounding shriek. Luther gets up and turns it off, looks for his cigarettes which he remembers are in his backpack where he left it out in the field. Willis has his gun out, playing with it. "Hey," says Willis, "you know that dummy somebody put out there on the highway on Halloween?"

Luther walks over to where he can see what Willis is doing. "Yeah," he says.

"That somethin' like what Agnes said you saw? Somethin' like that?" He's playing with that sight thing, making bright red squiggles on the side of the squad car and in the grass the way a child plays with a sparkler.

"Nope," says Luther, "not like that."

"Maybe worse?"

"Yeah worse," says Luther. The dancing dot is getting Yurang all worked up. Luther moves in a little closer. "You want to get ready to shut that door when he comes tearin' over that fence." Willis angles the dancing dot over toward the dog.

"And you ain't been makin' no scarecrows, huh?"

"Nope," says Luther, stationing himself right behind Willis. "Didn't y'all go out there to Cook's and have a look?"

"Yeah we did but not real quick, figured it was just another one of them jokes. Looked like animals got most of it." He must be flashing it in Yurang's eyes, driving him crazy. The chicken-wire fence is not going to hold.

"Willis," says Luther softly, bending close to Willis's ear, "you need to put that thing away or I'm going to stick it up your ass."

Willis pauses, seems to consider, twists around, grins up at Luther, and puts it away without complaint. "You know what they said over there in Tyler?"

"Who?"

"The coroner." He gets up. "The goddamn coroner," steps back inside. "We had to get that thing hauled out there like a body." He goes over to the table and starts to fiddle with Luther's trap. "'Ain't no zoologist.' Shit I know he ain't no fuckin' zoologist." He's lifting the little sliding door and letting it fall. "'Take it to a vet'"—the coroner's absurdly petulant, whiney tone of voice is a sort of refinement of Willis' own—"'can't think of no reason to be bringin' this shit out here to me.'" Now he's playing with the trigger, trying to catch it as lightly as possible so all it takes is the slightest tap to make it fall. "'Take it to a vet.'" He mouths the words, trips the release, looks over at Luther, fixing him now with the squintiest possible sort of stare, holds it awhile, seems to arrive at some sort of decision. "Remember that head-on out by Kelsey? Remember that?" Luther nods. Willis nods back. "Shit, I seen all kindsa shit"—now he turns back to the trap—"all kindsa shit, bodies and shit. This here was worse." He's bending way down over the trap now using both hands to set the trigger. "Animal parts. All different kindsa animal guts and shit stuck up inside this coat and pants and everything all stuck together, tied up some way with string or something. That anything like what you saw?"

"Maybe," says Luther.

"Not filled up though. Kinda hollow."

"Yeah," says Luther.

He's trying to set it much too lightly and it keeps slipping up through the hole.

"Yours have a head?"

Luther would prefer Willis not assign it to him that way. "Not much of one. Had some teeth."

"Teeth," says Willis, tapping the trap to no effect, resetting the trigger. "This one we got had a big ole puffy head—some kind of sack stuffed full of grass." He stands up now, looks over at Luther. "Had great big Donald Duck eyes drawed on it like they was lookin' up at the sky. No mouth or nothin', just Donald Duck eyes lookin' up." He lifts his gaze to illustrate, turns back to the trap, regards it awhile. "Shit," he says, unbuttons his shirt pocket, takes out a folded sheet of paper, hands it to Luther. "Need you to sign this," gives him a pen.

"What for?" says Luther.

"It's a consent."

"Consent to what?"

"Look in your trailer."

"You already done that."

"Yeah I know. Just go ahead and sign it."

Luther signs it and hands it back. Willis kicks the table leg and the trap slaps shut; he walks to the door. "So what you plan to trap with that thing anyway?"

"Rabbits," says Luther.

"Rabbits," says Willis—a trace of a smile as if he sensed an important derisive opportunity just beyond his grasp. He turns and heads out to the car, taking a moment to assume his crouch, draw down on Yurang, and send him into a frothing rage, before getting in and driving away.

Luther's lying awake in the dark listening to the puppies settling down, seeking to make themselves a heap, scrabbling of claws against the cardboard, tearing of newspaper—this goes on until they reach an equilibrium, every puppy nuzzled up to every other, fitted back into that wad from whence they came. Yurang sighs, shifts on the couch. Luther can see a star through the open louvered window above the table. He can see it reflected in the narrow strips of glass as it descends which makes an interesting illusion, false stars appearing and ascending toward the real one over the half hour or so it takes the star to cross. After a while there's another one, later a pair. At some point the eastern sky starts to glow with the rising moon and Luther sits up on the edge of the bed, looking at the floor, rubbing his arm where Yurang bit him. He gets up and goes over to the cabinet under the sink to find his flashlight, holds his palm across the lens, flicks it on and off to make sure it works, pulls on his jeans, and steps outside. Yurang's got his face up to the window making sniffing noises. "Shut up," whispers Luther. He walks very quietly out to the henhouse, through the gate and up to the door, squatting down there right outside, breathing silently through his mouth. Not a sound. No movement of chickens. He stays there like that as long as he can—till his leg starts to cramp and the diminished yellow moon peeks over the trees—then he turns and points the flashlight, flicks it on and sure enough they're wide awake, not even startled.

9

"That religious woman's sayin' it's the Rapture." Agnes is sitting on the tailgate of her truck watching Luther in the grass going through a shoe box full of drill bits, screws, and whatnot. Now and then he'll take a bit and hold it up next to his twenty-penny nail to compare diameters, put it back and hunt for another. He looks over at Agnes, returns to the shoe box. Some of the bits are shaped like blades, flat and pointed, some are spirals. All are rusty. He's got one of each type now, holding them up against the sky.

"Like on them bumper stickers," says Agnes. "You seen them bumper stickers about the Rapture." Luther's fitted the spear-shaped wood bit into his drill, now tightening it down, gazing off at a flight of vultures wheeling slowly above the pine trees to the south. "Guess not," he says.

She's leaning forward, swinging her legs. "'Warnin',' " she says, "'this here vehicle bein drove by a self-righteous idiot who's liable to let go the wheel any old time he gets a twinge the Good Lord's fixin' to reel him in and maybe sometimes just for practice.' Things like that."

Luther smiles, unhooks the trapdoor from the mechanism, withdraws the door, and turns the trap over on its side. "You want to come lean on this a minute?"

Agnes hops down off the tailgate, comes over to kneel next to the trap, holding it steady as Luther drills through the side of the door track at a shallow angle, going slowly to keep from drifting. She watches the procedure for a moment, then studies Luther. "Ain't you never been to church or nothin'?"

"Nope," says Luther. "You're lettin' it slip."

Agnes turns around and sits on the end of the trap. "She calls them things 'the blessed.' "

"Who?" says Luther.

"That religious woman. Them scarecrow things. Says things like that are bound to happen. Says they're blessed."

Luther pokes the drill through carefully, runs it back and forth a couple of times. "Blessed what?"

"Blessed nothin'; blessed leftovers I guess. She says that's what's left behind when somebody gets raptured, says it ain't like what you think and don't have to happen all at the same time to everybody at once, everywhere at once. Says it's like the Renaissance."

"Renysance," says Luther. "You can get up." Agnes rises. Luther puts the trap right side up, inserts the door then slips the nail into the hole. He pulls on the door to test the lock. "What's like the renysance?"

Agnes has hopped back on the tailgate. "The end of the world near as I can tell." Her legs are swinging like a schoolgirl's. She's watching the vultures circling away in the morning air which is already hazy, already warm enough to sustain them. She shakes her head. "My heart goes out to that little boy."

Luther's got everything reconnected, tripping the trigger, letting the door fall with a ratchety sound like running a stick across a washboard. Now he tries it with his hand placed in the entrance. The door thumps down. He stands with the trap clamped on his hand, holds it up like that, smiles at Agnes.

"So what's that for?"

Luther brings it over to the pickup, lays it on the tailgate, withdraws the nail to release the door, and resets the mechanism. This time he reaches all the way in. It shuts on his arm. He lifts it up to show it's locked. "This way don't matter if his tail or whatever's stickin' out"—he swings his arm with the trap still on it—"locks right down." He puts it back up on the tailgate, removes the door along one edge of which there's a series of steplike notches. He runs his finger up the notches. "Slides down easy"—then tries to go the other way jabbing his finger into a notch—"but won't go up unless you jerk the nail out; see?" He removes his finger, moves the door up and down in space.

She cocks her head slightly, regards him with exaggerated sympathy. "Sweetheart, them bunnies ain't got no tails to speak of."

"Yeah, well this here one's kinda different; likes cheese sandwiches. You got a hacksaw?" He's scratching a mark a couple of inches below the nail head with his knife.

"Back at the house."

"Let's get your Leggerns." He puts the trap down, lifts Agnes's chicken crate out of the truck and helps her carry it. "Put you a roof on this thing you won't need no henhouse."

"Two-by-fours is what I had."

He leaves her alone, lets her get silly as she wants about the chickens, squatting down there in the chicken yard next to the absurdly over-built crate, clucking and talking as if there were qualities here to discover, personalities to discern. He sits on the step and lights a cigarette, Yurang plopping down beside him. From the gas well just beyond the cow pasture to the west comes the faint periodic wheeze, the pneumonic sighing away of fluids; clearing the pipes. Sometimes at night it keeps him awake although not the sound so much as the interval—the waiting for it, the soft iron lung–like exhalation. He squeezes the fire off and puts the cigarette back in the pack. The vultures are specks now, riding the thermals higher and higher. He wonders what business they have at such altitude, what sense their low and narrow concerns could possibly make of that perspective.

"Can you tell me what this is?" She's still in her robe, sitting outside at the round teak table under the big white canvas umbrella, holding a scotch and looking at the flyer, turning it sideways. "I'd like you to tell me what this is."

He comes out with a paper plate filled with little triangular constructions of toast, cream cheese, and salmon. "Want one?"

"No."

"Better eat."

"What is this?"

He sets the plate down on the railing, stands, and watches a startled heron sweep out of the bayberries, circle the pond, and disappear around the point. "An invitation"—he turns and leans against the rail—"to the wonderful world of local cults. Took it off my windshield."

"What's this picture?"

"Some sort of fish?"

She turns it right side up again, shaking her head.

"It's a fish-handling cult"—he pops one of his delicacies into his mouth—"the absence of danger induces a kind of religious ecstasy."

She looks at him, frowns, takes a drink, and twists around to present the flyer to a better light. "That's not a fish." She gives a little shiver.

Her husband shrugs, turns back to the pond. "Maybe it's a deer." He takes another triangle. After a minute she gets up quietly and goes back inside.

"Just kidding," he calls.

She freshens her drink, takes a seat on the sofa drawing her legs up under her robe, resting her scotch in the little hammock between her knees. She closes her eyes for a couple of minutes, opens them again. Her husband has taken her chair under the luminous white umbrella. How pale he looks in his pale blue shirt. How pale the sunlight is through the haze, how whited-out things seem in general—overexposed the way movies look when they want to suggest memory or a dream. She swirls the ice with her finger. A steady drizzle of little leaves the size of snowflakes yellows the lawn, carries a sense of snow somehow in spite of the heat, in a black-and-white movie would look like snow. She drains half the scotch, gets up to replenish it, returns with the flyer placing it upright at one end of the couch, curling up at the other, taking a sip. Her husband's just sitting out there beyond the French doors watching the pond, perfectly still, paused with his elbow on the table, a salmon-and-cream-cheese thing halfway to his mouth as if suddenly arrested by something observed, something surprising out in the water or up on the far bank among the pines where deer sometimes cross. She waits for his arm to complete the intention, wants him to continue, follow through as if there were some risk of getting caught, losing oneself to such little moments, small apprehensions like having to sneeze, requiring a blessing to bring the soul back to the body. A yellow leaf falls to his shoulder. It makes her wince. She looks away.

There is a fish. She tilts her head sideways. But it's superficial—a vague sort of fish shape there in the middle, running top to bottom, a vertical fish. She straightens her head and it goes away, recedes to vacancy, a gap between somethings or where something's torn, twisted apart—a car wreck suggests itself; some awful thing, some fundamentalist premonition so frightfully admonishing, so eagerly rushed into distribution it's unrecognizable like one of those anti-abortionist placards—what was that? you think as you pass it, knowing it has to be really hideous to be worth all that trouble, blown up that large, held out to the traffic all day long. She looks at her husband. Now he's composed. Slumped in the chair, arms folded, head back, eyes probably closed. She takes a long drink, twists around on the couch. How odd one can tell when a picture's a photograph and not make out anything of what it actually is—that sense, regardless how poor the copy, how many iterations removed from the original, that photographic data, uniformly degraded, remain somehow definite, hold one's attention, one's will to believe, to the same degree even prior to comprehension, which leaves one uneasy, somewhat exposed. I have something to tell you, someone says urgently with such perfect authority you know it will be true whatever it is. But for a moment there's a blank, you can put any urgent thing there at all and you'll have to believe it, wonderful or terrible, believe it already, just need to be told. How scary that is. She's right at the edge of having too much, needs to decide which way to go, which way the day is likely to go. Her husband's immobile. She gets up and goes to the south windows, stands there for a while gazing out across the lawn, across the drive, the new white five-rail fence and the pasture beyond where the cattle will be when they come. It's such a gentle and uniform drifting of little leaves. She squints at the distance— everywhere the same, like migrating butterflies. She drains her scotch. You think oh a butterfly, what could be more simple and accidental, then three or four more butterflies and more after that until you lift your eyes entirely away from the particular, into strata of butterflies, thousands and thousands, rank upon rank of what you had imagined were, by all impressions, the least rankable, least steerable, most fluttery, frivolous, insubstantial, and contingent of creatures here arranged upon some Hindenberg-like principle of the world. She goes to the kitchen, refills her drink, then to the bathroom, selects an unopened bottle of some clear antidiarrheal medication, pours a little in the dosage cup, dumps that in the sink, carries it all back to the front. Her husband's asleep. The pond is yellow around its margins with swirls of leaves. The day's declining already it seems but she places the medicine out on the table where it can confirm her indisposition, where he can see it should something come up.

Luther's gone stupid, incapable again. He can't decide where to place the trap. Can't bring himself simply to put it down. Whatever directed his decision the first time no longer operates. Something has changed. Maybe the trap itself, more specialized, more accurately adjusted to special circumstances, requiring greater accuracy in its deployment. Like trading a shotgun for a rifle. It's charged with a whole cheese sandwich now. Loaded for bear. He keeps walking farther out into the field, holding the trap in both arms before him like he was dowsing or something, like it was some sort of instrument. It's as if the notion to put it anywhere, no place in particular, had acquired a certain rigor. He's looking around and gauging the distances to the trailer, to the trees and the road until these all seem about the same—the middle of nowhere or as near as it's possible to come given the situation, his trailer actually marking the cosmological center of the field as a whole, the middle of nowhere proper; the trap, then, belonging at the center of this half where the trailer faces, where he can regard it, think of it (in ways inarticulate, experimental) in sympathy with his trailer and so, in some sense, his own predicament. He puts it down and sets the trigger. He's added a small sophistication—a strip of tin now bears on the hacksawed end of the nail, acts as a spring to keep the door locked even should some creature in its struggles knock the trap over on its side.

. . .

She's moved to the bedroom, the little built-in desk in the corner with the windows that look out on the drive and the parking area which is paved with coarse volcanic rock of some sort—loose chunks that, as dusk approaches, make a complex network of shadows. She rests her chin on her hand and lets the pattern go out of focus, become detached, a screen of random lights and darks that tend to consolidate into fanciful shapes—faces mostly, then exclusively, cartoonish faces, some grotesque—coming and going, changing aspect, shifting generally toward the malevolent if she concentrates on one too long. She tries to reverse this, make a bad face become a good one, but it doesn't work that way apparently. She finishes her scotch, the last of it; she'll have to drive all the way to Gladewater to get more tomorrow unless it's a Sunday. What is today? She can't remember. She can't make it look like the driveway now, can't seem to reclaim the reality—as when looking through a chain-link fence at something beyond, the fence will suddenly detach from proper space and seem to float both near and far at once, undeterminable until you reach out and actually touch it. Her husband's entered. He closes the curtains across the windows facing the pond, saying something in that elliptical, apologetic way he has of transmitting an accusation. She receives the tone before the sense, deflects the sense, attends the faces as they darken—more and more shadow, less and less light, more and more difficult, sad and ambiguous until it's all gray and there's nothing to do but let the covers be turned down, her slippers removed, her head placed on the pillow, kissed, forgiven like last rites and put to bed.

Luther's stopped for no particular reason, come to a halt among the chickens, caught in the evening's rosy light. He's feeling removed, illuminated, apprehensive, struck by the oddness, the arbitrariness of things in general—all that walking, he imagines, all that stuff with Willis Beagle catching up; and evenings worst in any case: how like a military flare the way the sun breaks through the haze picking things out, showing them up for just a moment, stark and vulnerable right at the last. Yurang's sitting out in the field with only his head, lit coppery-orange, above the grass, slit-eyed, looking into the west. It's not a comforting, resigned, and restful evening light. It compromises, seems to call things into question—all the scattered odds and ends, the ripply foil-like corrugations of his trailer, silver-rusty propane tanks, aglow, discovered, caught for exactly what they are, lit from the side as if surprised. There's something final about it, nothing picturesque. Yurang's gone, submerged again. Luther watches to see if he pops up somewhere else, detects some turbulence to the southeast toward the road but nothing more. The tree-shaped shadows creep across, the chickens peck their way back over toward the coop—he watches the three remaining Leggerns (the ones without charm, the ones deficient in personality) follow the Reds, preparing to roost. Across the road the meadow dims and then the pines from the bottom up, light seeming to concentrate toward the top, intensifying the way burning cigarette ash will do as you squeeze it off. For a while he stands and listens to nothing, the ebb of events—no birds, no traffic, silence as if the air had been sucked away with the light as if it were really the end of the world in some sense at least, locally at least, right here in the field.

She has a dream. Or not a dream, an intuition like a dream and like a dream hard to retain. She's sitting up. The curtains are luminous. There must be a moon. She's frightened, shivering, terribly thirsty, but afraid to get up. The sound of her husband breathing beside her carries no comfort. It's like the sound of an appliance—cool air blowing, dishes washing. What she'd like is a drink of milk, right from the carton—whiteness, coldness, qualities of cleansing and neutralizing. A drink of milk would be like water in the face. One's thoughts must settle, visions vanish drinking milk straight from the carton, that much closer to the source, calming as cows, a glimpse of ocean. Now she fastens on the curtains, glowing softly, pale as milk. That will do, she thinks—a blank screen to diffuse whatever thought she thought she had like in that movie where the hero had to make himself think "brick wall" long enough to blow up himself along with the evil blond-haired telepathic children with glowing eyes. She brings her hands up to her face. The screen's not blank enough. There are shadows, variations. She closes her eyes, attempts a wall, then flings her hand out to the light switch, hits it. Pain and light at once. Her reading light, the little recessed focused spot, shines on her hand, the back of which is injured, gouged right in the center, starting to bleed. How strange it looks, so very dramatic. She gets up slowly, keeping it raised, goes to the desk, turns on its light with her other hand and opens the drawer, takes out the flyer, looks at her hand, looks at the flyer, looks out the window at the dark. Her eyes are tearing. She takes a deep breath, looks back down. The primary image, the fish, the car wreck or whatever, the original photographic image is still there in its original ambiguity—a drop of blood falls to the desk, she looks away, retrieves a Kleenex from the dresser, dabs her eyes and then her hand—but now—she can't stop shivering—now there's something else just as she feared. Why is it fearful? Is it always fearful? Even to those others you hear about from time to time, the ones you imagine must be so childlike and unquestioning? Does the condition of the mind make any difference? Maybe it's worse for her—now she's crying—the way a fever or chicken pox is worse beyond a certain age. How much easier, more graceful, it must be to find the miraculous without effort in the scorch marks on a tortilla; have one's neighbors, sympathetic, reverent, gather to watch the revelation cast in accidental shadows on the garage door after dark. But here alone, sophisticated, it's so terrible. She can't bear it and now can't bear to look away. It's like those "magic eye" illusions that her husband, unable to see them, finds so frustrating especially now that they're everywhere—calendars, cereal boxes—the more you look the more you see, the easier it gets, more and more random bits of data are enlisted to the image, the crown of thorns is now so clear—how could she ever not have seen it—eyes uplifted, pained, a squareness, roughness to it like a painting by Rouault and the mouth so strange, wide open just like on that figure on the bridge in the famous picture by Edvard Munch.

David Searcy

The scream jerks Luther awake and makes him bang his head against the wall, sends Yurang scrambling back and forth from one end of the trailer to the other, hopping up on Luther's bed then back to the couch and so on. Luther's stunned, not sure what woke him up, what kind of sound it was; he thinks maybe a weasel or god-knows-what has gotten inside, skittering around with Yurang after it. If it's a raccoon it could be dangerous; a big one cornered can kill a person—he's heard of that. He's up on his knees. He can't detect any other movement in the moonlight, just the dog, back and forth, acting crazy. Luther grabs him, feels him twitch around, the teeth against his arm just holding back, not quite enough to break the skin. He hooks the collar, pulls him down, applies a headlock, starts to rap him on the nose. From way out in the field it comes again—a scream which, interpreted as having its source nearby and suggesting one sort of thing, suggests something altogether different relocated, understood now to be coming from way out there across all that open grassy expanse. It expands accordingly. Weasel anxieties, magnified, become unthinkable; hardly permit interpretation, make the short hairs on the back of Luther's neck stand up, his arm tightens around the dog until he chokes and wriggles free, withdraws to the couch where, nose to the window, he stations himself the rest of the night.

10

Certain things are easier to see just before sunrise—just when you can barely see anything at all, in fact. The gray light seems residual, to have settled over the tall grass like clear water, perfectly smooth and uniform and you can see into it, see the general structure of the grass and across its surface like a pond so any disturbance, any departure from the pattern, is apparent. If you wait for better light you've got all the contrasts, all the shadows confusing as ripples which is all right if what you're looking for is large enough and simply an object of some sort; but the subtler record of the night's activities will be obscured. The silence seems to help as well; the tree frogs have stopped their high-pitched twitter and the birds won't start for maybe half an hour—no distractions except for the faint mosquito-like whine of a siren somewhere off to the south.

A little mashed-down spot in the grass shows where the trap was. And a few feet away is the rocking-arm part that went on top with the trigger at one end still attached and at the other just a broken string. More puzzling is the thrashing about that seems to have occurred over quite a broad area and of course what's become of the rest of the trap. Luther backs away a little, looking behind to stay on the barely detectable trail he's already made, not wanting to confuse things. He turns around, looks again at how the grass has been disturbed. Sometimes in the woods you'll come upon a little clearing where the grass looks rumpled like an unmade bed. where the deer have spent the night. This looks like that a little—although deer would never choose any place so exposed, and whatever churned the grass up here did so more violently, whipping it around more than compressing it, the overall effect much less distinct. He thinks of Yurang's violent contortions out here that time. He moves closer again and sniffs the air, squats on his heels—there's something, he thinks; but hard to say if it's in the air or just the association, the memory of Yurang's pungent rollings about. He stands and turns, studies the irregular trace of his passage across the field, how it tends to get lost among the natural variations and interruptions, but how if he slightly averts his gaze, as it were pretends to look away, he can make it out pretty well for fifty yards or so. He suspects were the trail even an hour older he wouldn't see much. Still, he turns and addresses the problem, backs off again, tries the averted gaze technique to gain a better sense of the disturbance, its extent, its shape, and whether at any point it leads away to show which direction his trap has gone. It's hard to imagine what sort of creature would be large enough to leave this sort of evidence yet small enough to get its head caught in the trap. He thinks of the scream. He can still hear the siren—very thin and very faint now wailing away off more toward the east. After a couple of minutes he heads back to the trailer, stands for a moment watching the sky, his hand on the doorknob. It's stiff for some reason. He turns. It gives very slowly. He jiggles the door—there's no slack. He twists the knob hard as he can and the door flies open, throwing him back as Yurang bolts.

There's no stopping him this time. Luther watches him tearing across the field. And no reason to, really. He gathers a couple of things—an apple, his pocketknife—checks on the puppies, picks up his cigarettes on the way out, locks the door behind him. He squints at the field. For a minute there's nothing then way out in the middle a sort of eruption. It's fairly implausible; not your ordinary recreational thrashing about; it's almost ridiculous, like one of those dust devils that spring up in summer, bits of grass actually flying up, bits of sod as well it looks like—even from here he can see dirt in the air. He heads out toward it. Now a grassy ripple shoots off to the west, seems to curl back and dart away in another direction, stop and reverse itself again. Another pause, then what looks like that zigzaggy thing dogs do when they're about to get the bearing, jerking this way and that as if caught on a line that goes slack at each tug. Luther breaks into a trot. There he goes, no slack now—a flash of red, an actual glimpse of the actual dog heading straight to the south, straight as an arrow. Luther tries to pick up the pace but fails pretty quickly. He's not going to catch him, not even thinking of calling him back. He slows to a walk as he passes the twice-devastated patch of grass, the second wave having obliterated all evidence of the first. Even the stick, the rocking arm, is gone. He looks to the south where Yurang went. He can just detect Yurang's wake in the grass. The sun will be up in a couple of minutes and already the light's become superficial, the field brighter and more opaque. He tries to listen for Yurang's tags but he's probably out of earshot, and now there seems to be another siren.

Luther's got himself caught in the thorn. The vines are everywhere, covering the scrub and forming deep mats that require much back-tracking, constant attention to where he steps. It's one of those intentionally blighted areas—all the hardwoods poisoned back, sprayed from the air, to make room for pines that, for whatever reason, were never planted. The thorn took over. And now he's got so far up in it he's not quite sure how to get back out. He's not even sure Yurang came this way. It looks less and less likely. He reaches down to untangle his foot—he's still got his apple, puts it in his mouth while he detaches the vines and slowly high-steps his way over to where a fallen tree makes a place to sit and catch his breath. His tee shirt is soaked. The air is dead here a little below the highest weedy humps of thorn. There's nothing to see except the sky, already dead white. He must be a couple of miles south of the property. Yurang's probably gone back home. He regards the apple, takes a bite. A fly alights on the bitten portion. He waves it away. The fly returns. He gestures more vigorously, swinging around to straddle the trunk, then scooting back so he can lean against a branch. He runs his hand across his hair. It's gone to seed, hardly a crew cut anymore. He rubs his eyes, his bristly face. He repositions himself a little to take better advantage of the branch, letting the fork at its upper end support his head. He waves at the fly. There's an almost-subliminal sound of insects. His sweaty stomach, round as an apple, shines through the tee shirt. He lifts the bottom of his shirt, flips it up and down a couple of times to get some air, some evaporation. More flies are buzzing around the apple. He lets it drop. There are quite a few—not exactly a swarm, just a lot of flies now that he looks. He pulls his shirt down over his stomach. Not like there's any particular reason, anything dead, more like just part of the general blight. It's suffocating. He waves the flies away from his stomach. They must like the sweat. He sits up slowly. A barely perceptible breeze causes movement that catches his eye. Something's hanging in the tree. A little something draped over a twig on one of the few remaining branches. He stands on the trunk and gets his balance, takes a step toward it, takes another, and stops for a minute. He still can't tell quite what it is. This part of the trunk has lost its bark; he takes little sideways steps to keep from slipping. It's dangling just above his head. It looks like a little pair of legs. He waves at the flies and steps in closer, starts to touch it, then recoils, then goes ahead. He pulls it down. It's just the crust from a piece of bread—just one long piece with all the white part nibbled away the way a child might do. The way a child might leave it, one side broken in the middle and hung on a twig so each right-angle end looks like a foot.

No sign of the dog. Nothing all day. Luther stopped calling after a while, stopped scanning the field, had supper alone, watched the little gold flecks in his Formica table twinkle and fade, gathered the puppies into their box, stood around doing nothing, and now in the last gray light he's back. It catches Luther by surprise—a glance out the window and there he is, a shadow just standing out front, no celebration upon arrival, hardly a wag as Luther comes out to see if he's injured. Luther stops a few feet away. Yurang sits. "Jesus Christ," says Luther. It's worse than before, beyond mere dabbling, the occasional frolic, intoxicating romp, or whatever it is at death's fragrant outskirts. This is more serious. Backslider's wine. Yurang lies down, puts his head on his paws. Luther gets a squeeze bottle of hopelessly delicate floral-scented dishwashing liquid, goes to uncoil the hose, returns with it running, wets Yurang down in the twilight, feeling for maggots and holding his breath.

11

"I hate to see that," says Agnes.

"What?" says Luther standing in her yard, hands in his pockets, looking at the chickens.

"Them little marks."

"What little marks?"

"Them's teeth marks; tell me they ain't teeth marks."

"Shit," says Luther.

"Tell me they ain't."

"Shit," he says again more softly, walking away, rubbing his arm.

"Shit yourself." She's raking her yard, pulling the sand into regular furrows that pass around her decorative white-painted rocks like running water. It looks very formal and somehow restful and she's going at it furiously, bending over now and again to remove some unwanted bit of stuff and fling it away, not appearing to mind, however, the chicken tracks.

"Just bruised," says Luther.

"What?" She stops and leans on the rake, glaring at Luther, who feels like a schoolboy caught muttering some impertinent self-defense. He's never seen her quite like this.

"Goddamn, Agnes. Didn't even break the skin. Don't amount to nothin'." She just stands there, rake in the sand, pulling a little, back and forth like it was on idle.

"Break the skin?" She's clawing a trench. "Oh let's wait"—she turns back to it now smoothing over where she paused—"let's wait and see if it breaks the skin somewhere it hurts." She's at a big rock, white paint worn where people sit; she sets the rake against it edgewise, walks in circles all around it making rings that look like ripples, shaking her head. "Hurtful things," she says, "let's get them hurtful things; let's seek 'em out and bring 'em home"—she stops again—"where is he?"

"Home," says Luther, still standing away, "he's got all stinky."

"What, again?"

"Yeah, worse though."

"Dogs get maggots sometimes."

"Yeah I know."

"Like rabbits get."

"I washed him down."

"You ever seen them big ones rabbits get? Big as your thumb?"

"There weren't none on him."

"Wolves. You ever wonder why they call 'em that? Them great big horsefly maggots wolves?" Luther says nothing. "Gives me shivers; always did, hearin' my daddy call 'em wolves. We'd hear howlin' sometimes at night when I was little and I'd think it was them things makin' that noise. Scared me silly—can you imagine that? Thinkin' them maggots was out there howlin' in the dark?" She lifts the rake, comes toward him now. "Can you imagine that?" He backs up. "Anything worse—and to a child—than thinkin' somethin' like that?" He's against the fence. "What would the world be with somethin' like that in it?" She's put the rake down, taken a tissue from her pocket, dabbing at her face, not even looking at Luther now, gazing away down the black oil road. "I just can't believe somebody done that to that baby."

"What?" says Luther after a minute.

She turns to face him. Her eyes are wet. "Leavin' all that hair behind like that"—she closes her eyes and seems to shiver, turns and looks back down the road—"little bits of hair like in a barbershop, like he just took the parts he wanted, spit out the rest—little bits of hair all over that poor little baby's room." She faces him again. "You know if it was mine I think I'd sooner it be blood, just let it be blood all over; least you'd know; trace the life and see where it went. But just hair. Can you imagine?" She peers at Luther. "Shit," she says and leans her rake against the fence, goes in the house, comes right back out, takes up the rake, hands Luther a copy of the *Gilmer Mirror* and returns to raking, moving quickly across one way with narrow sweeps of short brisk passes then back the other way much more slowly, smoothing it out, keeping the pattern, placing the tines in the previous marks.

"Toddler Vanishes." He unfolds the paper; a picture of a trailer—not like Luther's, bigger than that but still not much, lots of junk around it, rickety swing set, somebody standing off to the side, maybe a deputy. It's not a good picture—overexposed, not quite in focus. Farther down is one of those photographs that, soon as you see it there—no need for headlines, no need for anything—lets you know that person is dead or good as dead, that someone had to reach back into the residue, rummage around in boxes and drawers to retrieve a likeness: a blank-faced, moonfaced little girl so pale and accidental, so faint in a pale dress in the dirt next to a little dog she seems, even more than such photographs usually do, inserted at random, unspecific like those people in pictures ready-made picture frames come with; she could stand for any lost child, seems already about to vanish. Luther looks up at Agnes. She's nearly done. She's raked rings around all the white rocks above a certain size. The parallel furrows cover the yard. She's at the fence now across from Luther, finally just standing, holding the rake, looking at the yard. Luther's not sure where he's supposed to step, never having been present at a proper raking, the full-scale operation. She seems to be observing a moment of silence as if that were part of it, or maybe she's still thinking about the little girl. After a minute she glances over at Luther, chin lifted slightly as if looking down, as if he had just crept in beneath her notice; then without hesitation or any particular care she walks right across, takes back the paper, and heads for the house stopping to look back at Luther still standing against the fence. He follows, finding himself trying to stay more or less in her footprints. He stops on the porch.

"You got a loaf of bread?"

She sets the rake down, drops the paper in the upholstered chair. "You come out here just for that?"

"Sort of. You got one?"

"Expect I do."

"A new one?"

"Ain't we picky."

"Don't want it to eat. Just want it to look at. How it looks on top—the way them creases run." She just looks at him. "You know. Them wrinkles on top."

She opens the screen door. "I do for a fact know them wrinkles on top." Luther follows her in. "Got a bag of prunes here too you're welcome to gaze upon." She's got one whole unopened loaf of Mrs. Baird's white bread and half another. She puts the whole one on the kitchen table. Luther stands and looks down at it, pats the sides to line up the slices. He looks at Agnes. "Can I see that other one?" She presents it. "See," he says, "they ain't the same." She's frowning. "Here." He steps away, looks all around.

"It's on the porch."

He goes to get his pack, returns with it open, withdraws a shoe box which he places on the table, taking a seat and placing his hand on top of the shoe box. "Didn't want nothin to get squashed." Her frown has deepened. He opens the box, takes out the end of a loaf of bread, three or four slices, folded up in the wrapper. "Other night somethin' got my trap"—now he produces a little flat foil package, spreading it open—"made this god-awful scream." He stops, looks up at her and lifts his arm. "That's why he done that. Fit to be tied. Don't never want to go grabbin' one when he's like that." He looks at her a moment longer, goes back to the package—"weren't his fault." He's got it spread out now into a square in the middle of which is the crust of bread with the ends rejoined so it forms the original outline. He unwraps the other package, takes the topmost slice of bread—"look here now"—places it very carefully on top of the ghost slice on the foil, gets down on his knees to line it up. "Look here." He motions for Agnes to look, to get down also but she just stands not looking at the bread, looking at Luther. "Come on." She glances at his demonstration. "Ain't that a match?" He picks it up and brings it over holding it so she can see. "Lookee here, right here that side part where it kinda bulges—that part, too; ain't that a match?" He takes the whole slice off the top, replaces it with one from the end of her half loaf, brings it back to show the disagreement.

Agnes goes over to the refrigerator, gets a pitcher of something, and pours two glasses, hands him one.

He puts down the exhibit. "That's my bait." She sits at the table; Luther stands in the middle of the kitchen holding his lemonade. "Whatever made off with my trap did that, hung it up in a dead tree off to the south, just hung it up there like some kid'll eat all the soft part, leave the rest, and play with it like that. Hang it up there like a kid." He takes a sip and makes a face. "You use any sugar? Shit." He shakes his head with some violence. "Goddamnedest scream I ever heard." He walks to the window. "I tell you what—you hear somethin' like that you be fuckin' glad that dog'll bite. You better believe I'll take old Leg-ripper." He looks at Agnes. "Whatever you said."

She shakes her head and takes a drink, smacks her lips, looks out the window by her chair. "Hell of a rabbit."

"Shit, I guess."

"Cheese sandwich?"

"Yeah, a whole one. Didn't see the other half."

"That trap with the lock?"

"Yeah, went nuts with it. Broke part off and tore the grass up thrashin' around."

"You got a monkey."

"What?"

She takes a drink and nods. "That's how you catch 'em—take a coconut, hollow it out, and make a hole just big enough he can get his hand in, put somethin' in there he really likes, and tie the coconut to a tree."

"So how's that catch him?"

"He won't let go."

"Oh shit."

"I seen it on TV."

He takes a sour drink of lemonade, then drains it looking at the little bit of yard outside the window raked exactly like the front. It's like that all the way around—scraped down to nothing by some necessity almost medical it seems to Luther, in its severity, its protocol. He finds it comforting. His throat burns slightly from the astringent lemonade. Here come the chickens around the corner of the house.

"Or maybe a wolf." She watches them peck their way out to the fence and down along it toward the back. "We got them little red wolves; you know that?"

Luther looks at her—the evidence plain as day right by her arm. He can't imagine what she's thinking.

"Could be they sound weird as they look. You ever seen one?" Luther shakes his head. "Strange-lookin' critters; you never know, one get his nose caught up in there might make a sound you never heard before in your life"—she's moved her chair closer to the window to watch the chickens, sounding detached, a little dreamy— "could be more'n one thing's involved—first one thing, then another and maybe another, birds or somethin' that don't like the crust. Insects maybe. Maggots are picky—you know they still use maggots to clean out wounds sometimes in this country; seen that too on a TV show; right here in America; hospitals do it somebody gets gangrene bad enough; regular old maggots; take what they want, take all the rotten, leave the rest." She's leaning over, gazing down along the side of the house, eyes half closed, resting her head against the window. "What you don't want," she says after a minute, "is somethin' mixin' them two things—makin' that howl then goin' and nibblin' that bread like that. Both them qualities mixed together. That wouldn't do."

12

The sound of an airplane wakes him, one of those little planes. It seems to draw him out of a dream, fluttering by up there so slowly. A dream about snow. He sniffs the air. No trace of Yurang. It's very late. The puppies are stirring, starting to fidget around in the box. The sky's bright white. He hardly ever sleeps this late. He sniffs again. It smells like snow. He brings his face up to the screen of the open window by his bed. Not really snow but something different. A change in the weather. Yurang's way out there by the road, sitting in the short grass perfectly still except for his nose which periodically he elevates to test the air. It's a wonder he can smell anything at all. Luther leans back, plumps his pillow, kicks the covers all the way off, and tries to make himself receptive, let it come to him through the screened and louvred windows of his trailer what portends like a sudden chill. After a minute he sits up. It's hard to hear because of the puppies, hard to tell if there's something different in that sense too—a different sound, a sort of ringing. He stands and stretches, goes to the door and steps outside in his Jockey shorts, looks at the sky—a flicker of something way up in the glare, a flash of something, maybe several somethings going whiter, disappearing; now just "floaters" in his eyes, the specks and swirls you get when looking too hard at nothing. He looks at Yurang standing right out in the road now, turning one way then the other, undecided, lifting his nose. A bit of something white descends beyond the field into the pines, too big for a snowflake, maybe a leaf the way it seems to dip and swoop; a piece of paper. Now another right over the field. It comes down slowly and somewhat erratically, floating, dipping, and veering a little this way and that as it descends. It is in fact a piece of paper. Luther can see it's a piece of paper as it settles in the grass. Two more come down behind the trailer. He looks up, squints at the haze. He can make out several now drifting across like cottonwood seed, like butterflies. And even more much higher, way up there like birds he's seen in flocks that in the distance sort of shimmer in and out of visibility as they swerve one way or another—just like that, as here and there the paper's whiteness for an instant catches the light to match the glare, then shifting darker—reappearing slight displaced—it's like there's something meteorological going on, the sky itself mixed up in the process, generating all this stuff, these little leaflets. A few more drift into the field. Most seem to hang, sustained somehow, dispersing, floating gradually off beyond the trees.

He looks around. He listens for cars then trots across into the tall grass, gets the nearest one, trots right back, stands in the doorway for a minute looking at it, bouncing a little on his heels and feeling the trailer's instability with his weight there at the door, how it rocks and starts to tilt but doesn't quite. The puppies think it's time to play, scrabbling around trying to climb out of the box. He sits on the bed. There's a movement of air through the little windows, hardly a breeze, and what he thought he heard resolves. They're drilling again. Somewhere to the north, going through rock, making that screech you can hear for miles as the bit wears out. It comes and goes, rising and falling. Luther scoots back on the bed. "Behold," it says. He rests his head against the wall. "'He is coming with the clouds . . .'—Revelation 1.7." This handwritten in a very ornamental script above a picture, a photograph apparently, so poorly reproduced it's indecipherable and below which in the same elaborate cursive: "'. . . waterless clouds, carried along by winds; fruitless trees in late autumn, twice dead, uprooted . . .'—Jude v. 12." He looks at the photograph for a moment, lays the leaflet on the bed, goes over to the trash and rummages around, getting the puppies all excited. He comes back with the flyer Willis gave him, spreading it out and placing it next to the smaller leaflet. He kneels and looks at them awhile. Without the reference there'd be no way to make it out; it's worse than the ones he saw at Joe's—the giant catfish on the plank has completely degraded, lost its outline to the contrasts, the bleeding of darks into each other, the violent erosion of the image like something blasted, hit with birdshot. He turns it over. The back is covered in little print:

Find the Savior. Can you find Him? Many did at the Last Days Covenant Church on Monday. Look at the picture on the front. It is unretouched but has been copied many times, each copy made from a previous copy of an ordinary snapshot of the wonderful catfish on display at our meeting place. Look again. You should turn the paper over quickly. Be in a calm and well-lit place. He may startle you. Does He look like Jesus? What does Jesus really look like? Can you see the crown of thorns? The anguish? Some can see him right away. Still, others need more time. Yet time is short. That He is expressed within the commonplace this way suggests He is both imminent and immanent, both arriving and arrived. His presence implicates itself at his approach the way a tingling may precede a lightning strike . . .

Luther flips the leaflet over—not a thing; a messed-up picture of a catfish—flips it back.

. . . the way the wind precedes the storm. Come join us Sunday Dec. 10 at 8 P.M. See the largest catfish in the world. Learn how the world can end a little at a time.

Down at the bottom flanked by schematic Christian fish is the address at Joe's Big Juicy. Luther gets up off his knees, looks out the window. Yurang's off somewhere. The drill is really singing, hitting a clear and urgent note as if the bit were finally worn away completely, trying to polish through the rock unable to stop, making a sound like squealing tires.

13

The heat gets worse, gets into things, expands to take the place of events. It gets too hot to walk to town, to go see Agnes on Thanksgiving. Mr. Tuel drops off a gallon of gasoline, a heavy weedeater, and instructions to clear the fence line to the west and at various points where he's determined it's too weedy, too untidy from the road. It's hard to start. As if the heat's got into it too. Luther pulls and pulls, adjusts whatever's to be adjusted, pulls some more then lays it down. White smoke has settled in the grass and takes a long time to disperse. The smell of gasoline hangs around as well and doesn't go away. Whenever Luther steps outside to try again or opens the door at all it smells like gasoline which makes the heat seem even hotter, the air combustible. It's an uneasy sort of heat in any case, inappropriate as that autumn hailstorm, not like regular summer heat which in some sense has work to do. It's like a mistake, a malfunction, heat from an electric motor or something jammed, the insulation starting to go. He tries all day to start the weedeater, each time waiting a little longer. He pulls the plug and cleans it, checks the gap and tries again. After a while he settles into a kind of routine. Maybe a couple of times a day he'll pick it up and try to start it, maybe more if he thinks about it, alternating left and right hands tugging to make the sputtery little sound the engine makes when it can't quite start, can't quite get going enough to run but just enough to make a thin white smoky haze. His efforts slacken after a while, his sense of duty attenuates and modifies to require just this periodic, nearly pointless obligation toward the weedeater like massaging the limbs of the comatose. He'll take it out every couple of days into the field, away from the trailer, stand and tug as the white smoke drifts across the grass like some sort of fumigant, practical or religious, sense the almost but not quite absent will to life of the little motor, nearly catching, fluttering awake almost at times, pouring smoke then losing compression, sucking air.

He finds more leaflets—all the same. He acquires a pretty good collection, makes a stack and adds to it regularly, keeps an eye out for them, finds them in the pasture among the cows, in the trees, the chicken yard; and in the tall grass now and then he'll spot another. He takes an obscure sort of pleasure in it, thumbing through them like baseball cards, content to have them in their revelatory potency albeit entirely denied to him.

He takes the gas can out in the field it stinks of gasoline so badly. No one can see it in the grass. It's not likely to be stolen. Sometimes looking at the tall grass out the window by the little Formica table in the evening he imagines he can see a breeze across it, ripples, faint ones; and he'll pause, put down his sandwich, wait to feel it, but there's nothing.

Yurang takes to spending more and more time out in the open, sometimes ranging back and forth, sometimes just sitting, lifting his nose above the grass. Whatever excited him so much before is absent now. He seems determined to regain it. Luther, too, pays more attention to the field, his sense of floating on its surface, the instability; he thinks about it, has that vision every night where he's standing somewhere far away and seeing his trailer in the dark way out in the middle of the grass all by itself. The drilling finds another pitch. They must have changed the bit or something, hit different rock, a deeper stratum which returns a shriller note. He can't imagine what's involved, whether they actually know where the drill is going or just keep drilling till there's gas; whether it's really possible to know. No one can see down there of course. How can they know anything beyond it's where the gas comes from. He thinks of what Agnes said about the trap and imagines the drilling, blindly reaching into the earth, sounds like a monkey with its hand caught in the coconut. It's that sort of notion which once conceived is hard to shake, takes all his attention to ignore and not be startled when after a period of relative quiet the screeching starts up in the night.

. . .

The trailer needs some extra bracing after all. The railroad ties aren't quite enough. Just walking one end to the other now he can feel it wobble slightly and what makes it worse is that the fulcrum, the point of maximum instability, is along a line that intersects the little table where he likes to take his meals. It's not really a matter of practical concern—it's far too slight to cause any trouble—just disconcerting to take a bite, lean back, and gaze outside and feel this vague uneasiness as the weight shifts, this gentle hint at the precariousness of one's established frame of reference. He was once surprised and appalled to learn from a TV show he watched with Agnes how many people on the *Titanic*—quite a number in fact, and not just those asleep—had no idea there had been an accident; appalled to think that such a catastrophe—and after all a simple mechanical one—might transcend a person's ability to detect it. In effect a person simply sitting at that moment in the silence drinking coffee— tea, whatever—had for all practical purposes already sunk beneath the waves without even knowing it, so complete from the very first was the disaster, it seemed to him, as if "that's that" were what the silence had to say.

There's not much lumber left. He stacks up what he's got next to the step. It seems the ground has dried so much it's slumped a little here and there beneath the frame so the railroad ties now, in fact, support too much of the weight at a point very near the center of gravity, causing the whole thing to teeter a bit. The leveling jack at the front is rusted so he jams a couple of boards up under it. This helps some although there remains, he thinks, a barely perceptible shiftiness, a certain sense of insecurity. He tends to move over to the couch now with his coffee or his sandwich. He can turn sideways, lean his back against the wall to see outside. Not that there's anything to see except the grass—like so much water. People like to stare at water, stare at ocean, he supposes; stand on the beach and gaze at nothing, look out portholes he imagines much like this. After a while the trees don't count; or if they do it's in an insubstantial way like distant clouds.

The puppies have lost all their exuberance in the heat. They decline to follow him into the grass, decline to romp. He stands there calling. They prick their ears and look uncertain, scratch themselves, and sprawl about. Yurang maintains a sort of desultory patrol; he lifts his head at Luther's whistle, then continues through the tall grass on his way.

The grass is hot. It seems to hold heat. Standing in it he can feel it on his legs, how warm it is. He's heard of hay baled up before it's properly dried out simply bursting into flame, barns burning down. Spontaneous combustion. This whole field—a hundred acres, he would guess—might yield 10,000 bales of hay. Not very good hay—mostly stalk, too long unmown, a sort of matting from the leafy part, the good part bending over and finally breaking. But good enough at least for cattle. Tuel should mow it, make some money; make a lot more if he didn't let it go so long next time. It's irritating and so, he decides, is the grass itself, the dust it throws, the sound it makes when you walk through it. He tries to avoid walking through it now unless required to by his duties toward the cattle or the weedeater or to check the well behind the trailer. The water has begun to taste like sulfur.

Sometimes he thinks of the little girl, her pale and empty-looking face; how empty it feels to think of her lost so thoroughly—diffuse, the very idea of her spread out so thin it almost vanishes like the thought of someone lost far out at sea. He sits with his coffee gazing out, his thoughts diffusing across the grass. He wonders if under the right conditions a field of grass could just ignite all by itself; become so thick and hot and matted, start to smoke like one of those bales and just go up. How nice it would be if it were gone; to be able to see the ground out there clear out to the edge, know where things are.

14

"Look," says Luther's barber, Royce, "watch now, see if she does it now." A squad car's passing down the street. The huge woman in white sitting with her dog on the sidewalk bench in front of the barbershop doesn't move.

"That's City," says Avery, who runs the chair right next to Royce's, sitting in it at the moment, reading the paper. "She don't get up unless it's County." Royce looks at Avery. Avery goes back to his paper. "She was here at nine when I come in," he says. "She'll do it if it's County."

You can see the County Courthouse across the street with a big perfunctory framework Santa hung with limp red tinsel propped up on the lawn—not one of your picturesque county courthouses, more severe, a ziggurat, beige brick, mean-spirited with reluctant Art Deco touches. Royce has turned the chair a little toward the window. A couple of white deputy sheriffs' cars are having a conference side by side across the way in front of Joe's. After a minute one turns into the courthouse parking lot; the other comes around the corner up the street. She rises now and places the little dog on the bench, steps off the walk which here presents a pretty good drop. She lurches heavily against the front of Agnes's truck, recovers, walks out into the street so far the squad car slows, unsure of her intentions as she stands and leans toward it slightly, watching it pass. She continues to stand there in the street for a moment longer, then she turns and comes back slowly, using Agnes's fender to help herself up. She must outweigh Luther by a hundred pounds. Her white nurse's, waitress's, or whatever uniform is wet in places, bra straps visible, supporting structures showing through which adds to the overall sense of strain, imminent collapse. The bench sags a little. She takes the dog—some sort of terrier, white with pricked ears—into her lap, leans over it, hugs it, gives it a kiss, and lets it down.

"That's five or six," says Avery, reorganizing his newspaper, flapping it open and folding it back. It's almost noon. The little window unit's laboring, hardly cooling. "Five or six times since I been here."

"So what's she doin'?" Luther asks. Avery shakes his head.

"Got me," says Royce. "Hold still." He's giving Luther a final pass. "Can't get no shorter with a flattop less you wanna risk gettin' scalped." He brushes him off, shakes out the cloth, looks over at Avery. "She does that thing with the dog too, don't she?"

"Every time," says Avery, "gives that thing a smooch."

"I seen a dog just like that somewhere," mumbles Luther into the towel he's using to wipe his slightly sweaty face and neck. Avery rises folding the paper carefully, placing it on the stack in a corner chair. He stands and stretches gazing out onto the square which is mostly empty—a couple of sheriff's officers in big white hats and khakis coming across for lunch next door at the Waffle House. The glare off the bleak, flat-fronted courthouse makes him squint. He looks at his watch.

"Ain't no sense in this"—he turns to Royce—"let's shut her down." Royce deposits Luther's five ones in the register, locks it up, puts the two quarters in his pocket. Luther's sitting in the corner with the papers on his lap going through them one by one. Royce starts rinsing out the sink.

"Here," says Luther. "Right here's a dog just like that there." He jabs a finger at the picture of the vanished little girl, the little prick-eared squatty terrier there beside her in the dirt.

"Sure enough," says Avery. Royce comes over drying his hands, looks at the picture, looks at Avery. "Oh, hell," says Avery. A sudden catastrophic-sounding whine comes from the front like a gas line blowing, or an a/c compressor letting go. They all look. The woman's standing with both hands up to her face, her body heaving, making that noise which seems to have brought the cowboy-hatted, lunch-bound officers to a halt out in the street. It's Bobby with his head turned oddly, looking sideways at the woman; one of his deputies looking confused. She teeters forward, screaming now, hands plucking at herself, her hair and clothes, as if some tiny automatic bit of mind had disengaged itself to worry about her appearance. No one's

moving; there's no traffic, no activity on the square, just the shriek-
ing woman huge and white, her sweaty uniform going translucent
down her back and under her arms as she steps into the sunlight, bra
straps and underwear elastic standing out like veins and tendons. It's
hard to tell if she's screaming something, if there's anything in it.
Some words suggest themselves then break apart, get blown to
pieces in the rush like bits of mechanism flying off some sort of engine out of control. Little bursts of spray coming from her mouth
glint in the sunlight. Avery, Royce, and Luther move up to the window. Now she leans against a concrete trash receptacle. Now she's
throwing stuff at Bobby and his deputy—paper cups, big wads of
paper, Coke cans, bottles—all the trash comes out, gets flung into
the street as Bobby backs up with his hands held up. She tries to
push the trash receptacle over, fails, and lunges off the walk, falls to
her knees, screams even louder picking up some odds and ends already flung to fling again then all of a sudden utterly collapsing,
curling up there by the curb reduced to faint asthmatic sobs.

By now some people have come outside. The Hispanic lady who
runs the Waffle Shop makes a move to render aid but Bobby stops
her with a gesture, keeps his hand out as he negotiates a very cau-
tious circumambulatory approach suggesting he's seen this sort of
thing before, she's only wounded, doubly dangerous, very likely at
this critical moment to rise and charge. He comes up to her from
behind, leans over to look, and finally prods her with his boot.
Luther can't believe it but he does. Not roughly, not a kick at all but
still it seems profoundly thoughtless. Then he motions to his deputy
and together they get her up, she neither helping nor objecting only
moaning a little louder. Bobby waves at Royce and Avery in the
window. "Shit," says Avery. Royce goes over to hold the door and in
she comes, all blubbery, sweaty, weirdly fragrant in her misery, white
hose bloody at the knees. She starts that plucking at herself, urged
into Royce's chair and seeing herself in the mirror across the room,
gets really frantic with her hair, eyes wild and looking now at Royce,
who's got a cloth soaked in witch hazel for her cuts. She starts to
heave her body, gasping, jerking her foot which is caught somehow
beneath the footrest. With a groan and a mighty effort she twists

around and pulls it free. They all step back. She rises, stands there for a moment looking down, her wheezy breathing coming slower. "Mrs. Pitt," says Bobby. She ignores him, bending over, getting down now on her knees. "Mrs. Pitt"—he steps toward her—"you wanna let me run you home?" She's carefully, quietly gathering all the clippings into a pile. "I'll get Troy here to bring your truck." She's reaching all around, back behind the chair, under the footrest, getting all she can, sweeping together all the faintly reddish, blondish bits of hair. Luther rubs the back of his neck, runs his hand across his flattop. Bobby takes another step. "Mrs. Pitt." She's having trouble getting up not using her hands, holding the hair. She staggers a little, gets her balance, stands and looks at Bobby now. "Mrs. Pitt, the Good Lord. . . ." he begins. She throws the hair right in his face. He spits and backs up, wiping his eyes. She's out the door. Royce gets his whisk broom, tries to administer to the sheriff, gets pushed away. She's out there standing and looking around, speaking now—pleading or something—with the Hispanic lady, looking up and down the street, under the bench. "Oh God," she says clear as a bell even through the glass. "Oh God. Oh God."

"That dog run off," says Avery. Everyone looks at him. "Hell, he took off soon's you brung her in." They look outside. She's gone. The Hispanic lady's gone. The glare off the courthouse brick is terrible—if it were glass they'd all be fried.

"Shut up," says Agnes. "I know what I'm doin'. I been out here before. You just hang on." Luther's haircut makes him irritable, uncomfortable as it always does like some sort of creature newly emerged—a soft-shelled crab or a snake—from its cast-off shell or skin, a little bit sensitive, somehow, to things, to all this bouncing around in Agnes's truck in the heat through these fields of whatever it is.

"What is this shit?" A dried-up chunk of something like a miniature ear of corn whips through the window against his chest scattering dusty seeds or kernels and little crawly insects everywhere. "Shit," says Luther.

"Capper corn," says Agnes.

"What?" says Luther. "Shit." He bangs his head. "Slow down."

"Got sandy patches. Gets this dry you're liable to sink." More shriveled, brittle ears of whatever thump off the windshield, graze his arm. He pulls it in. It's not a road, hardly even a path through half-dead yellow-brownish stalks. Dust fills the cab. "It's feed corn. Capper corn. Same stuff goes in scratch."

"Don't look like much." He picks a fragment off the seat and throws it out.

"She lets it go."

"Your cousin?"

"Yeah, gets mad at somebody or somethin', lets it go—to hell with it. Always been like that." The wheel twists out of her hands; the truck goes sideways; now they're plowing right across the rows, bouncing wildly, trying to duck all the stuff that's flying in the windows. In a second she's back on track though, right back in the seam which is all it is, just a narrow parting in the stalks.

"How far we goin'?"

"I don't know. She don't remember. Might not be nothin'."

For a while they're quiet. Agnes slows a little, has the technique now apparently, the stalks and leaves just slapping gently against the truck.

"So what he say about all that?"

"Nothin'. Washed his face off."

"Nothin'?"

"Nothin' really. Talked about her like she's a fish, joked about it, said 'Them old big ones get away sometimes and just as well 'cause he didn't want to have to get a bigger freezer.' Stuff like that."

"She find her dog?"

"Hell I don't know. I seen her drivin' around in that truck. I think I seen that truck before and her husband too."

Agnes shakes her head. "Poor baby girl." A flock of quail breaks right in front, whirring all around like little rockets as the truck veers off, bursts through a row of corn into the open. Agnes stops, turns off the engine. The dust they sucked along behind them catches up, surrounds the truck, floats in the windows.

"It looks real small," says Luther.

"Does it?" The engine's ticking, cooling off. He opens the door, gets out and stands there by the truck. He can hear the insects, all the insects in the corn. It's a little clearing where a hogpen used to be, way out here in the cornfield, not much left, some two-by-sixes along the ground, a couple of cedar posts with hog wire stretched between. It's on the hog wire. Hung out like somebody might do a catfish head or a coyote although it looks something like an angel. A little angel. He wipes his eyes. The dust's still settling. Agnes just sits there in the truck. He crunches across the cobs and stubble, squats down near it, sniffs. It looks like it ought to smell pretty bad and it probably used to. One wing has come loose from the wire, looks stiff but droops a little; the other's spread out all the way, still tied with string it looks like—chicken wings, some sort of chicken. The rest is made from something else. It's hard to say. He stands. His haircut makes him feel exposed, prickly all over. The prickly whisper of the insects makes it worse. He tilts his head. A squirrel perhaps. A cat, its features rearranged and shriveled now, the whole head smaller than it should be, like one of those rubber shrunken heads yet from a distance—now he stands back—from this distance, so you can't see how the jaw has been separated, the mouth propped open with a stick, so you can't see the details, it's like an angel, in proportion to one's notion of an angel, just the shape, the general shape. He turns and walks back to the truck, climbs in, and lights a cigarette, looks at Agnes. "You sort of like to get up right next to it then don't look." He opens the door to let out the smoke.

"It looks like an angel."

"It ain't though," says Luther. "Not how you think of 'em any-way." He takes a long draw, squeezes the fire off onto the ground. "When she find that thing?"

"Last summer. Seen it and left it alone. Didn't say nothin'. That's how she does. I guess it could be older than that."

"I guess it could. Don't look like no animals messed with it though. Maybe it was dried out first."

"God it's hot."

David Searcy

"Maybe it's the first one."

"God." She's fiddling with her hair as if suddenly now after all these years, out here in the cornfield she's decided it might be possible to do something with it.

"You seen them paper things?" says Luther.

"What paper things?" She's trying to brush it behind her ears.

"Them pieces of paper somebody dropped."

"I seen 'em."

"What you think?"

"'Bout what?"

"'Bout that picture. What you think?"

She sighs and leans back, puts her hands up on the wheel.

"You read it?"

"Yeah."

"You look at the picture?"

"Didn't make no study."

He looks at her a minute. "See."

"See what?"

"See how you do?"

She starts the engine; he shuts the door. She sits there gazing across the clearing for a moment, letting it idle, shakes her head. "Poor little baby," he thinks she whispers; he says, "What?" and she says, "Nothin'."

One by one the chickens gather into the shadows under the cedars at the back of Agnes's house, flutter up into the branches for the night.

"They always do that?"

"Every night."

"What's that?" He points at her chicken crate set on its end against the house with perfunctory tar-paper sides and roof.

"Made a coop out of it like you said."

"Don't like it huh?"

"Not one little bit. They like them trees."

"You figure they're scared?" He takes a sip of lemonade.

"Of course they're scared. Chickens are scared. Don't never sleep. You ever hear that?"

"Yeah I heard that."

"Well it's true. Don't close their eyes. Don't never sleep."

Luther's got a brand-new spark plug, got it gapped. Now he's waiting to let the chamber air out a little. Yurang's sleeping under the trailer. The puppies are scattered, lying about. He's poured the old gas out of the weedeater, put in fresh, and now the smell of gasoline hangs in the air, an aggravation to the stillness and the heat. He puts the plug down, takes the gas can back into the field, stands there a minute, then walks on out to look again at how the chicken wire's been kicked in on one side of Agnes's crate, the solid trapdoor he rigged up still locked down tight, the sandwich gone. No scream this time. No sound at all or none, at least, he couldn't sleep through. There might be a smell but he's not really sure and nothing to track (Yurang just circling, whining a little). He didn't think to check first thing. He squats beside it. It's like something couldn't see the wire and tried to go right through it.

Now he's got the plug in, torqued down with his channel-locks, now he pulls, the engine sputters, makes some smoke. He stands there tugging, absentminded, watching the thin white smoke drift slowly across the field.

"You got a camera?" he asks Agnes.

"Used to. Oh God lookee here." The room's lit only by the TV. Agnes is cross-legged on the couch, now twisting around to pay attention. Luther sits back down to watch. It's Bobby himself right there on the news, big as life.

". . . to talk you've found the little Pitt girl," says the tiny news reporter struggling for gravity under an absurdly buoyant hairdo.

"No ma'am, no." He looks so strangely, monumentally benign, his hat pushed back, his paunch secured, presented, shirt tucked in

around it, hands on hips to represent the massive, round avuncular-
ity of the law. "I wish I could say somethin' 'bout that baby's where-
abouts. No ma'am, what we got's folks talkin', that's 'bout all." He
beams.

"No body?"

"No ma'am."

"No articles of clothing?"

"Well now"—he smiles, rears back a little—"we ain't quite sure
on that one yet."

"You did find something, isn't that right?" She looks at the camera. "Near the Pitts' house in a tree?"

"You know I can't get into that." He turns to someone to his right
just out of view; there seems to be a commotion behind the camera,
some sort of banging; Bobby's looking back that way; the camera
jerks around, flares white into what seem to be glass doors, bright
sunlight, violent-looking movement—they're in the courthouse;
something's going on outside—the camera's back on Bobby pointing. "She needs an escort." Whoever's holding the lights gets jostled;
all you can hear—it's all just shadows for a moment—is Bobby's
voice: "She's going to need an escort now please; right this minute."
The light's back on, the news reporter looks uncertain, waits too
long to regain the interview; Bobby's talking to someone else, and
now he's leaving. "What about . . ." She turns and reaches with the
microphone. "Sheriff?" Yelling: "All this talk, these accusations?"
The camera whirls around again into the light, much confusion on
the steps, the reporter's voice, "Please don't do that," then it goes blank
and back to the newsroom anchor couple each earnestly turning to
regard the other's earnestness in turn the way they do: it was, in fact,
the baby's mother outside the courthouse this afternoon; there was
no body in the tree as first reported although there may have been
some sort of hoax which, "Scott, I'm sure you will agree." Scott's
head nods grimly. "Will not amuse the people here in Upshur
County." She hits the remote. The room goes dark. A sigh from Yurang on the floor. "Up in a tree?" says Agnes. Luther gets up, goes
over to the screen door, looks outside into the gloom. A drill rig's
squealing somewhere way off to the east.

"You got a camera?"

"What for?"

"Thought I'd take a picture."

He can hear her rise and walk into the kitchen, turn on the water, splash some water on her face it sounds like, come back, just a shadow, take a seat in the rocking chair over by the window.

"Don't seem to cool off none at all," she says.

"Sure don't," says Luther. He can hear her rocking. He can see stars through the screen. Between the porch roof and the tree line across the road a band of stars that flicker oddly, seem to sift right through the screen when he moves his head.

"Picture of what?"

He's leaning over, looking sideways, holding his hand up to the screen to see its outline against the stars. "Oh well, just somethin'. I don't know."

"How come you live out there like that?"

"Like what?" A finger by itself tends to disappear, tends to get lost—too small, too simple—within the interstellar distances, the gaps; but as a part of the whole hand he can make it out. How strange.

"Out there in the middle of nothin' like that."

"Like what?" A fist, though—simple as that is—is big enough to see. "In the middle of nothin' like what?" He drops his hand and stands up straight, looks over toward Agnes. After a minute she says, "Shit; ain't none of my business." He says nothing. The squeal of the gas drill comes and goes and for a while that's all there is—the intermittent, distant screech and the sound of rocking, opposite sounds in some sense not entirely clear but perfectly opposed it seems to Luther nonetheless at just that moment in the dark.

David Searcy

15

He's got the weedeater with its pole against his shoulder, its motor braced between his boots, the spark plug with the wire attached—holding that in one hand, the starter cord in the other. He gives it a tug. He can see the spark. He pulls again. A hot blue spark. There's nothing at all wrong with the magneto. He lays it down and opens the gas can, sniffs it, pours some on the ground, tosses a match. It makes a whump and burns with a bright orange-yellow flame. He sits on the step and watches a while as it flickers away; then he screws the plug in, removes the carburetor, checks for clogs, shuts both needle valves, and backs each one off two-and-a-quarter turns—the all-else-fails resuscitation mode for small two-cycle engines. He stands and pulls. The white smoke drifts into the grass. He takes a few deep breaths himself. There's a sense of airlessness. He looks around at everything, the stillness and the grass, and pulls again. It's like emphysema, what that must feel like, all the machinery wheezing away to no effect. He's moved to the edge of the tall grass, tugging, making it sputter, watching the nylon line spin around each time he pulls. He stops and stands a minute or two to catch his breath, then takes the weedeater by the grip as if it were running, sweeps it slowly back and forth across the grass in an easy motion letting it swing from the shoulder harness the way it's supposed to back and forth, back and forth in easy arcs as easy as Agnes raking sand.

He can't sleep in the quiet. Nothing stirs, not even the puppies. The drill's gone silent. The wheezy gas well's holding its breath. He gets up and puts his clothes on, steps outside, hears Yurang lift his head—a tiny jingle—then lie back down. He shuts the door. No moon, just stars, the Milky Way sweeping above the trees over to the west and down to the north behind the trailer. He steps across the ruts into the grass, looks all around at the vague horizon, the blank unmoonlit curtain of trees. He stands for a moment, looks at the stars, looks down, and leans over to touch the grass, its surface just above his knees, moves his hand across it back and forth. He walks a little farther out into the field. He stops again. He can hardly stand it. The feel of grass against his jeans, the swishing sound. He rubs his hand across his flattop, back and forth and down his neck. He turns and looks back at his trailer. It's not like the dream. In the dream there's moonlight. He reaches down and grabs some grass with one hand, tries to pull it up, then tries with both hands, squats and tugs without success. His hands slip off. He's cut his palm. It stings like a paper cut. He holds his hand up to his mouth, looks at the Milky Way awhile, looks down, and kicks the grass, just kicks at it in a general sort of way. It seems to help in a general way. The way some injuries—to a knee or an elbow, say, with so many nerves involved—can seem to benefit from being struck again, slapped on purpose to confuse the signal, spread the damage out or whatever. He kicks again with a little more force, a little more swing so the grass tends to catch on the toe of his boot, whip around, and tear. There's something faintly rewarding in that. He tries his left foot, nearly falls. It requires a certain amount of force but not too much— you kick too hard, you swing right through and lose your balance. He tries again; moves farther out into the field. A running kick seems best, the way you kick a ball—a step and hop to get the weight of the body into it, bring his whole self, all his concerns, right to the point as if, beyond the question of pain, to test the injury in the most direct and brutal way, just go ahead and force the matter, see what's what, get down to basics, get that swishing sound, that grassy-dry sensation aggravated, get that dust up in his face, make bad things worse, think to himself right here it's getting out of hand, right at this moment his volition falls away and all is lost, all left behind, it's sink or swim, a sort of lunging twisting lope now seems to do it, takes him with it, lets him dig his boots into it left and right in easy swings, the dead and matted bits come flying like something thrown off by a baler, bits of nothing, a sort of cloud, a sort of halo

David Searcy

which he imagines must accompany such exalted states of fury like in a cartoon, which must surround him now and probably in the daylight would be visible from a distance ("Look," he imagines someone saying, "what is that?"), he's got the stroke, the perfect rhythm, self-sustaining, as it seems, in such a rarified environment, way out here in the middle of nothing, under the stars, the accumulation of empty gestures yielding an actual sense of emptiness, discovering a sort of richness to it, what it really is to get down in it, right down into the substance of that vacancy, all that failure and dissolution just like Yurang rolling around in all that shit, disporting himself in all that dead and rotten shit. His legs give out. He's on his face. It's all just breathing for a while. Eventually he rolls over onto his back.

How still it is. Just like it was. No background noises. Not a ripple. Not a sound. Absorbently quiet. Respiration, the ache in his chest, the prickly, dusty sense of himself all seem to subside, be drawn away into the grass. His arms are flung out to the side. He's lying awkwardly, twisted a little, but he's not inclined to move. A hint of breeze too faint to reach him makes a whispering in the grass, brings a sweet wet-blanket sort of smell—the final stages of some small departed creature. He allows a certain fellowship, a certain warmth of feeling toward it. They diffuse toward one another in the grass. He's gone too far now, he supposes. This is in fact what dogs do isn't it—give themselves up to it somehow after all that thrashing around, take leave of themselves, become inert as if having rolled around in death to the point of overdose or something. What if he's slipped at last so far he's into sympathy with that? Able to share in that experience? The air is quiet again. Perhaps a little cooler. He feels the heat still in the grass along his shoulders and down his back. It's not so bad. He can see the Milky Way through the grass, the part that arcs down to the north. In his mind he traces it all the way back to his trailer, now very distant he feels sure. Barely a speck as he imagines. He thinks of Yurang, thinks of him standing on the couch, nose to the window, tensed and stiff-legged, looking out. He thinks of the chickens wide awake and the little girl again, her simple, vacant face. He closes his eyes. The smell comes over him. His other senses more or less deprived, it seems to expand, involve the whole field as a kind of expression of it, the animal tragedy incidental. It smells like emptiness itself; the sweet and pungent scent of absence in whose presence the heart grows fonder. Or at least alert to the possibility. Alarmed perhaps at the possibility. He tries to hold himself as quietly as he can toward such a delicate apprehension. He recoils a little from the thought—not quite developed, not yet arrived yet still enough to give a start. (What is it dogs do right at the last? They catch themselves—all stiff and twisted, legs in the air, they give a twitch, the head cocks funny as if at the very last possible moment they stop and think what am I doing, then they're up and shaking themselves all back to normal, trotting away as if there was never anything peculiar going on.) There must be limits, being dogs. It can't be simple after all—one's relation to this sort of thing. It's not like milk, say, going sour—just unpleasant and nothing else. The breeze again. He still can't feel it but it brings a sort of chill. It can't be a simple thing like that—were that the case then you could think well that's all right, whatever it is out there it's sad but just misfortune pure and simple, things like that are bound to happen, dogs would tend to walk around it, it wouldn't require elaborate observance, so much attention, so much fragrant dishwashing liquid. But in fact—and it seems quite clear to him reduced, as he feels himself to be right now, to these essentials, to these lowest common terms—it presents a dilemma: here you're out for a little romp, a sniff and a roll, and all of a sudden it goes too far and you find yourself confronting this deep and paralyzing uncertainty—life or death, let's get it straight now which is which and which am I? It throws you into a kind of shock. His arms feel numb, the way they're spread. The grass has started to lose its heat. His back is hurting. It's like that moment playing tag or hide-and-seek when your pursuer comes so close you think you musn't move even slightly from whatever cramped or strained position you've managed to get yourself into. Or when you think he's close but really can't be sure and after a while you really start to get uncomfortable, thinking maybe it's all over and everyone's playing something else but now you've got so much invested. You feel cut off; sort of ghostly. What if the numb-

David Searcy

ness in his arms spread through his body? What if he stayed out here like this. Let everything go. Just faded away. Can such things happen? Sometimes people just burn up like bales of hay. He's heard of that. He saw a TV show about it—people just go up in smoke; don't feel a thing. They find a trail of ashes, maybe, where they got up from a chair, walked into the kitchen or over to a window and that's that. They never know it. What a thing. He sighs. The ashes he imagines blowing softly across the floor like those of the vampire at the end of some old movie he remembers.

It's an odd sort of breeze it seems to him. Very intermittent. It comes in gusts but very soft ones. It has the quality of someone blowing in your ear to wake you up but softly, teasingly so you don't really consciously feel it; you twitch a little, brush it away; you think it's something like a fly, some ordinary thing, a bit of feather. He wonders what it was that died. The particular animal, not that it matters. Something small. A rabbit maybe. Much larger creatures, say a cow—you can smell a rotting cow for half a mile and even that far off it's different, like a disaster, the massive, overwhelming fact obscuring finer considerations—larger creatures leave too much of themselves behind. But little animals—barely here at all somehow—leave behind a whiff of something else. He saw a rabbit once—a cottontail—get run over; a truck just ran right over the top of it, the rabbit rolled a little ways and Luther walked over to where it was—pretty much undamaged except it was dead and lying near it in the road was the rabbit's heart, itself undamaged, beating away as if the rabbit and its life were separate things that might get along without each other; and for a moment you could see that. How the heart didn't even know about the rabbit. It might be beating for a possum or a squirrel for all it knew or, as in this case, for nothing at all. You had this rabbit, then over here you had its heart and in between there was this distance, absolutely nothing. The breeze has stopped. There's nothing now except the smell. He thinks perhaps it's not a rabbit after all. He doesn't know why he should even form an opinion. He's being as still as he possibly can. Breathing softly. He thinks of the owner of the Mount Pisgah Feed and Grocery, his simple red-haired matter-of-factness, how there was something he wanted to ask but never did. What would he think if he were out here, constrained somehow to lie here obviously and heavily in the grass and give his opinion: well like you say it's sort of sweet—a little too sweet seems to me; inappropriate I would say and yet (his orange-red eyebrows knitting with the thought) you got this powerful sense of loss (he shakes his head and folds his big red-freckled arms) like love is lost, like everything is lost, ain't no hope left; no sir (he'd whisper) that ain't no rabbit (then he'd lie here like that listening for a while); and furthermore it ain't dead neither cause it's moving.

Luther opens his eyes. The stars have a scattered, grassy quality. The breeze has gathered for a while beneath his notice, rising gently, very gradually, very softly into his awareness that it's not a breeze at all but some sort of subtle, local movement in the grass so indirect, somehow, so delicate he'd generalized it. He does, in fact, feel numb all over, afraid to try to move in case he really can't. He breathes through his mouth to make less noise. He lifts his arm and brings it over, wets his finger and slowly raises it like a periscope. There's no breeze. He holds it there. The whispery sound is rather faint but almost continuous now, a soft and wavelike rustling in the grass. He brings his hand down, makes a fist. He uncurls a finger. He thinks of the way an armadillo, practically blind, will snuffle along, make sudden, tentative little probings. Not like this. He uncurls another. A snake won't make any noise at all. A raccoon—three fingers now— a raccoon is much too smart (too clean as well—is there a taste? a cloying taste that he's inhaling?), much too wary to get this close. (It is, he thinks, a little closer. Or it's louder. Or he's simply paying attention.) Same with a bobcat—almost out of fingers now; why shouldn't he just get up and see? Why should he lie here like he's paralyzed or something? There's no change in its position. There's no movement in terms of angle but he hears it so it must be moving toward him or away. It's like in a submarine, he thinks—the way you imagine it, past the point of useful action, everyone braced, unfocused, listening in the half-light to that little metallic ping (a skunk, perhaps); or watching storm clouds, trying to tell which way they're going, how that requires an uninterrupted yet undirected, incremental kind of attention as information stacks up somewhere behind the eyes (the Mother of skunks) and suddenly you know what you need to know. His fingers spread across his chest, across his heart. The smell, the sweetness, overwhelms him altogether and just for a second or even less than that, before he jerks away from a sort of stinging in his arm that feels like a paper cut again but worse, before he flings himself across the grass, goes scrambling through it on all fours, he thinks well this is surely it, what keeps the chickens awake at night. And then he's up, the gentle whisper now replaced by a terrible scream that spins him around and makes him completely lose his bearings, keeps him twisting this way and that with his fists up, waiting, although by now it's perfectly clear it's only the gas drill screeching away and there's nothing at all to be seen in the grass; it makes no difference. After a moment he settles down and stands there for a while just listening to it; a little later lowers his hands, holding his arm which has begun to hurt, watching the grass, watching the east begin to glow. It takes forever for the glow to look like sunrise, for the light to reach the ground.

16

S he wants the tiny pearl-like interval of silence to expand, be like a gas, combine with heat and fill the room. She wants to close her eyes again. The sheriff sits down, yawns, "You take ole Deputy Dawg there" (indicating Willis who is not happy to be indicated in this fashion, turns his doglike face to the service window to watch the hamburger patties cook), "he don't get no sleep, don't close his eyes lest he's got some eelectronic racket in his ears, got that radio or that TV turned way up and tuned to nothin'. Makes it easy to catch him sleepin' on the job though. Ain't that right?" he yells at Willis— a sudden, feral sort of bark.

"That's not uncommon." She tries to deflect him.

"Hey, ain't that right?" It hurts her ears. She hates that instinct, whatever it is, the way it pops up automatically, the sound it makes in such a long and narrow, hot, high-ceilinged room.

"Hey, Deputy Dawg."

"You can buy white-noise generators now," she tries again, her voice too faint.

"Hey."

"Yep," says Willis to the hamburgers softly, "yessiree."

The sheriff turns to her and nods, leans way across the single school-desk seat between them. She can smell him. There's no air. The oscillating fan up front is useless. "Just like a blanket. Meaner they are the more they need some kinda blanket."

She looks at Willis, head down waiting for his burger, fiddling with something on the counter, making it spin, stopping it and spinning it over and over. She shakes her head.

"You think I'm jokin'? Willis, get over here."

"Oh no. Please." She sits up straight. "Really . . . no, that's all right . . ." Willis has turned, leans against the counter holding the object he was spinning. It looks like a bullet. ". . . I was thinking in general—these days, that's all, how it seems so hard to sleep, for me at least, you know, with everything." The sheriff gazes at her a moment, smiles, leans back. For a while there's just the sound of burgers cooking, sizzling quietly, white noise filling the empty space. Willis has turned around again to spin his bullet. The sheriff's looking at his hat.

A certain quality of having had too much to drink the night before—not quite a hangover, short of that—affects the sense of space and distance. Until the sheriff and his deputy came in, the empty room seemed much too large and now it's small, its width at least, its narrowness much too long and narrow, unadorned, white-painted, like some sort of corridor to somewhere else, not very comfortable, like being punished—that sort of uneasiness—like being sent out into the hall, placed in between things, not allowed a place to be. A penitential hamburger restaurant. And she a sort of *penitente* or *penitenta*, whichever it is. She looks at her hand with the little round Band-Aid on the back. She looks toward the front, into the glare. She wonders where her friends could be.

Joe's scraping the griddle, finishing up. "Here you go." He spears each paper wrapper with a toothpick, comes around from behind the counter with a little red plastic basket for the sheriff. Willis takes his standing up, gets a soda from the box. "Bring me a K-Orange," says the sheriff. "Gettin' all fancy, baskets and everything."

"Sure you don't want nothin'? Ain't no charge." Joe's paper hat is just about gone, ripped up the front, the advertisement for some bread company smudged, illegible.

"Oh no thanks." She can smell the sheriff. And now his lunch. How strange, she thinks, maybe even disturbing, the overlap of human smells with those of cooking. The similarity. Such incompatible categories—emotionally anyway—running together. She glances at him. It's hard to tell now which is which. She smiles and squeezes out of her seat. Joe's at the front, standing by the fan, looking out the door which he's got propped open with a big white chalky ammonite that must have come from somewhere else—down here it's all just clay and sandstone.

"Think they're lost?" asks Joe.

She looks at her watch. "No, I don't think so. They're bohemians, not very strong on punctuality"—Joe's looking at her—"Hippies sort of. Arty types." He seems uncertain, takes his hat off, folds it, places it by the register.

"Neon, right?"

"That's what they do. That's all they do. They have a book out—did you know that?" He shakes his head. "*Historical Neon.*"

"Historical neon," he mouths the words, whispers them softly to himself, steps toward the doorway lifting his apron, wiping his hands.

She stays by the fan which seems to help—the periodic breeze across her face. She lets her eyes close and for a while that's all there is.

"You gonna be here for the next one?" calls the sheriff. "That was somethin'." She can hear him getting up. She turns. He's brushing off his shirt, hitching up his belt into that trusslike configuration, low in front, high in back—it's hard to imagine how it stays that way with everything, his pistol and whatnot, hanging from it. Now he's fixed up, all arranged, just standing, looking. She's aware of how her hair, at intervals, blows across her face; her rather thin white cotton blouse, and that she's backlit. Willis is looking at her too. She moves away to the other side, stands by the gum and candy rack, adjusts the flyers stacked next to it.

"I guess your husband," says the sheriff, "he don't get involved too much in all this."

She's using one finger to nudge the stack until it's even with the front edge of the countertop. "He tolerates me."

"Tolerates you?" He glances at Willis. "Hell, I guess." Willis grins through a bite of cheeseburger. "Hell, I guess," he says more quietly. She looks at the floor, looks out the window. Joe's out front now by the curb, just standing and waiting, smoking a cigarette. The sheriff nods in his direction. "Expecting somethin'?"

"Well I suppose you could say we are waiting for a sign." She smiles, perhaps too nicely, now he's coming over, taking a flyer from the stack and looking at it, looking up and getting the joke. "Waitin' for a sign?" He grins. "What Joe's been talkin' about?" She nods. He studies the flyer again, after a moment shakes his head, looks over his shoulder, "Goddammit, Willis." Willis puts his bullet back in his belt and goes outside. The sheriff shakes his head again. "I just can't see it. I don't doubt it—hell, I seen that old woman faint—but I can't see it." He holds it out and starts to come around beside her. He wants her to show him. He's going to have her point it out: this is his mouth and here are his eyes and this is the blood from the crown of thorns. And she can't do it or even look at it right now; the odor—the sheriff, the hamburger or whatever—the confusion of categories is much too disconcerting, her grasp of ordinary spatial reality none too secure just now in any case and there's the sense she has that the whole thing, if she's not careful, could very easily get out of hand somehow, start happening anywhere at all without permission or compelling cause like Jekyll and Hyde, or that's not right but that's how it feels—appalling to think it more horrific than benign. She's backed away. The sheriff has stopped. He's smiling now, tilting his head at a funny angle, holding the flyer, extending it toward her, shaking it slightly. "Tell you what, though—I believe I do see somethin' in that catfish now and then." He laughs. "The way it kinda changes. You like fishin'?" He nods encouragingly.

"I don't know."

"You ever seen one big as that?"

"I really don't know."

"Don't know?" He approaches.

"No."

"Don't know?"

She shakes her head.

"Why not?" He looms.

"I haven't seen it." He just stands there. He seems to expand, become even larger, his hand on her shoulder guiding her now, back toward the kitchen and the little room beyond.

One Halloween when she was ten or eleven she was taken with a friend by the friend's older sister to a "haunted house" that had been set up out in the country and which, unlike the usual kind, was notoriously unsponsored by school or charity or any other civic organization. It was a rogue haunted house someone had constructed inside a bleak and isolated and very ordinary old gas station with no attempt whatever to modify the exterior so that it presented in the glow of its old fluorescents and the lights of parking cars such utter seriousness, such contempt for introductions, such perfect confidence in whatever horror it contained, she absolutely refused to enter. She had to stand outside and listen to all those sounds coming from inside the gas station where she knew, even at that age, there was typically no room for anything extraordinary among the tires, the lift, the counter with its revolving rack of sunglasses, some with silver-mirrored lenses. That such banal, confining, unexotic space could contain such terror filled her with dread and for quite some time would cast, periodically, a sort of doubt upon the commonplace facts of life, would cause her to shrink from certain places and situations that seemed—arbitrarily to everyone else—to provide special purchase for these doubts. And in fact a certain residual sensitivity in this regard is what disinclines her toward the exhibit of the giant catfish stuck back here behind the kitchen like in a closet, like something stuffed up under the bed. She's seen those catfish heads on fence posts, after all, and that's enough. She's absolutely certain she's seen enough on all accounts. He finds the switch and the light fans up across the wall, across the confusing, densely red-lettered paper banner carefully taped now above the freezer. She's in the kitchen, hanging back. He's moved to the freezer, leaning over it, lit from beneath as by a flashlight under his face to frighten children.

"Come here." He beckons with his hand. How heavy his hand, how thick his fingers. How could those fingers point to anything she'd care to see; how could they indicate, discriminate, with any accuracy, blunt as clubs. No wonder he's blind to the sacred image. It must be like trying to pick up a pin compared with fishing: grappling with things in their rudest state before they're Xeroxed, disseminated and transformed. It really does look like a sort of Neanderthal photocopying machine. She steps up to it, bends over the view plate. "What is it?" she says. "What am I seeing?"

"Hoooey," a yelp from out front like calling cows but more jubilant. "Hooooey!" it comes again. It must be Joe. She turns and steps into

David Searcy

the kitchen, looks out through the service window. He's jumping around and waving his arms. "It's the universe!" he seems to be yelling. A truck with a huge A-frame-type structure on the back is turning around and backing up next to the curb. "Hoooooey," he yells. The Emerald City Neon Sign Company of Dallas, Texas, has arrived.

"Wayne, Joel, this is Sheriff Size." The sheriff nods.

"Size large, I'd guess." Joel grins, the tall one with the scraggly reddish beard. "I bet you get that all the time." The sheriff nods.

"And this is Joe." She looks behind her. Joe's dancing around to the other side.

"Hoooey!" says Joe.

"We need to tell him that's not it," says Wayne, the beardless not so tall one with the earring, looking concerned. "This is it right here—but not bad, huh." He takes a step back to admire the somewhat weathered arc of blue-enameled sheet steel with the radiant neon cross. "Look at that pattern"—he indicates the radiating neon elements—"it's like a meander—the way it's squared off at the ends, makes all those rays. They call that 'sunlight.' Could be thirties."

"Very nice," she says.

"Oh Jesus, look at this. Whole goddamn universe!"

Joel looks at Wayne and shakes his head. Wayne looks at her. "We better tell him."

"Tell him what?" She smiles. "What is it?"

"Well that's the thing." Joel rolls his eyes, looks down and shakes his head again.

"That's why we're late," says Wayne, touching her on the arm. "This moe-foe here is one in a million."

"One in a million," echoes Joel. "It is the thing, the thing of things, the sign of signs." They guide her around.

"Good Lord," she says. It's hard at first to see what's what, it's so elaborately padded and strapped to the tilted frame.

"Transportation nightmare." Wayne backs out into the street for a better look. "Forty miles an hour all the way." Joe's sitting across on a concrete bench on the courthouse lawn now, head in hands gazing at the sign in a sort of trance.

"From where?" she asks. She can't imagine what sort of East Texas enterprise might adorn itself like that; it's more like Las Vegas, the explosive sunburst shape of the painted metal background with smaller neon-outlined planets and stars and galaxy-looking things all flying away. Across the bottom, maybe ten feet long, is the word "universal" in red and yellow neon letters. She looks at Wayne.

"Podunk," says Wayne.

"Dry Gulch, Nowhere," says Joel.

"Universal what?" she wants to know.

"Curb feelers. Gromets. Universal Gromet; hell we don't know." Joel's bobbing slightly up and down in his delight. "A dream deferred, man. That thing was still inside its crate in like this abandoned warehouse or whatever in this little bitty town outside of Quitman—not even a town, man; can you believe it? Crate was trashed but the sign"—he steps back next to Wayne—"look at that. That sucker's never been plugged in." He's started bouncing on his toes. "This here"—now pointing—"this here's the cover of a brand-new book." He looks at Wayne.

"*Universal Neon.*"

"Man, that's it."

"Got the vertical taken care of, the historical coordinate—now the horizontal, geographical."

"Cosmological."

"Theological."

"Oh man, that's it."

"Hoooooooey," says Joe. They turn. He's standing on the bench. The sheriff and Willis are leaning on a squad car across the street. A few other people have gathered around.

"Don't tell him yet," she says.

"Why not?"

"We need to talk."

17

Agnes steps down out of her truck into a piranha-like mass of puppies who think her flat, black package might be something edible.

"Found that camera," she calls and shows it to the puppies who, undiscouraged, interpret this as a playful gesture. "Ain't got no film." One has her pant leg. "It's pretty old." She looks down, tries to shake it off, takes a couple of steps, looks down again. After a moment it loses interest. Luther's taping something up on the side of his trailer, standing back and looking at it. She comes up and stands beside him.

"You make that out?" asks Luther.

"Make what out?"

"That there. What that is."

She walks over to it. "Tar paper." He goes inside, comes out with another sheet which, like the first, is lightly spattered with white paint. He tapes it up.

"How 'bout now?"

She looks at him. "This somethin' like them wrinkly pieces of bread?"

"No, look. It's different. That one's different."

"More white paint."

"That's right."

"That it?"

"No that ain't it." He goes over and places his hand against the second sheet then takes it away. "See there?"

"I guess."

"It's a hand."

"I suppose it is. What happened to your arm?"

He glances at the bandage. "Nothin'. Look here." He puts his hand against the first sheet then removes it. "See. Same thing. Same thing both times but one's got thirty drops of paint and one's got forty. Just that much'll make you see it"—he stands away and folds his arms—"makes a picture." He cocks his head. "Like a shadow."

"A stencil."

"Yeah but it's a real thing, not just flat. A real thing." She studies him for a moment. The corrugated siding is hot, uncomfortable standing this close. The Scotch tape is peeling away from the tar paper; first one sheet falls, then the other. They move away, walk toward the chickens. Yurang crawls out from under the trailer to trot behind.

"Here's how you do it." She flips a lever on the front and tilts open a door in the top of the box until it clicks, then reaches in and withdraws the lens and bellows assembly until it too clicks into place. "And there you go." They stop; he takes it.

"Never used one."

She points to a prism-shaped attachment perched on top. "You look in there"—indicates a lever on the side—"push that little thing to take a picture. No, you hold it down like this." She demonstrates. "Look in the top." He gives it a try, looks in the viewer, scans around.

"I can't see shit."

"You gonna tell me about the tar paper?"

"Can't see shit."

"It's pretty dirty."

He's walking away. "Goddamn, it's backwards"—walking out into the tall grass, peering down into the camera clicking the shutter— "How come it's backwards? Does the picture come out backwards?"

"I don't know. I can't remember—don't make no difference I don't think; you get a negative; you can turn it, make the picture any which way you want."

He's on his knees now in the grass, pointing the camera at the dog who's coming out to join him—clickety-click, taking empty photographs, watching the image, reversed, approaching. He lifts his head and looks at Agnes. "It don't make pictures?"

"Not right off, not like one of them Polaroids." She walks out to him. "What are you doin'?" He's on his stomach inching forward with the camera toward the dog, peering down into the viewer. "What happened to your arm?"

"What if it's dark?" He gets to his feet.

"My goodness, Luther; you use a flash. What happened to your arm?" He's fiddling with an adjustment on the lens. "You know," she says, "I knowed this feller had a brother got his privates all ripped out by one of them. . . ."

"Dammit"—he hands the camera back—"goddammit, ain't got nothin' to do with him."

She looks at him a second, carefully folds the bellows back into the box, shuts the door with a little snap. He's turned away now holding his arm, touching the bandage very lightly, looking out across the grass. "Ain't like I live out here on purpose." A single crow sweeps over the trees, dips low and glides across the field. He turns to watch as it lifts and flaps down onto the road. "You hear any more about that baby?"

"That little girl?"

"Yeah."

"No."

"They ever say what was in that tree?" The crow's found something it really likes now on the far side in the grass, tugging at it. No response. "So where do you go to get a flash?" He turns. She's heading back to the truck. "Goddammit, Agnes."

"Goddamn yourself."

He catches up. "You gonna let me use your camera?"

"You don't want it. You don't want nobody neither."

"Goddammit, Agnes. It wasn't the dog." He watches her go, the puppies after her again, all agitated by her pace, all underfoot and growling, grabbing at her jeans.

It's bleeding again. He pulls the tape off, lifts the red-soaked, folded toilet-paper pad. The cut runs right across the red mark from the first time Yurang bit him. The little bruises, just above, from the second time are almost gone. It makes him think of a piece of bait, a minnow dangled unsuccessfully too many times, too much nibbled, hardly worth another try. He should get stitches. He pours some mineral spirits on it, grits his teeth and waits a moment, rinses it off, and holds it closed while taping straight across it, then a new pad and more tape on top of that. He sits on the bed and shuts his eyes for a couple of minutes, then gets up to stand at the table, looking at the white-spattered gardening glove and the sheet of tar paper under it. It's not like a photograph—he picks up the glove; it's still sticky with paint—but closer, somehow, to the thing or to touching the thing; not, he decides, like a picture at all, more like a trophy, getting it, lifting it free of the ground and the grass, separating it from everything, holding it up in the starlight like a rabbit held up by its ears or a fish on a line. He looks over at his leaflet collection—the stack of them next to the stove. That's what happens, he thinks. You don't capture a thing with a photograph. You capture a story about it. It stays tangled up with the stuff that's around it—that board and that rope and that place. And that makes a story and stories get changed. He nods to himself. Stories get changed.

He pours some white paint in a cup, adds a capful of mineral spirits, mixes it up. He wants it thin enough to flow, to run off the end of the mixing stick, but not so thin it makes a splatter. He holds the stick above the target. Outside the sun's so bright through the haze, so bright on the grass, it hurts his eyes to look out the window. He can hear a truck coming slowly up the road—it sounds like a truck, sounds like it's stopping and turning in. It's not Agnes, though. A drop of paint falls, makes a perfect little asterisk. Yurang's growling—a subtle vibration through the floor. He covers the paint and steps outside. A blue-green pickup has pulled in and stopped just off the road. Yurang eases out from under, slow and threatening, growling softly. Luther reaches for his collar. The truck pulls forward a dozen yards and stops again. It's not the woman's—someone smaller, it looks like, darker. The sky's reflecting off the glass. A tug from Yurang. Luther puts him in the pen and herds the puppies in as well. The truck creeps up a few more feet. The engine stops. Smoke drifts away. The door swings open. For a while that's it, that's all. Then he gets out. So small and dark against the brightness; even darker, more receding than before, as if compressed or desiccated, shrunken into himself. He spits. The spit seems darker too. Like blood. Like something concentrated. He approaches looking left or right but not at Luther, stops almost too far away to talk. A few more crows have joined the first one in the field across the road. They're making noise. The man looks like he's saying something. Luther steps a little closer.

"What?" says Luther. The man steps slightly to the side and spits again. He shouldn't do that, Luther thinks as if there really were too little left to waste. Now Yurang's barking. "What?" says Luther.

"Shot herself," he seems to say as if to no one in particular. His name is Leonard, he remembers. Leonard Pitt. The puppies join in—too much racket, crows and dogs. Luther comes around to where he can see his mouth, read his lips a little, just enough. His lips are dark brown at the corners. "Got up this mornin'"—they hardly move—"got up in that tree some way or other"—he looks past Luther across the field—"and shot herself." The crows and dogs have fallen into a sort of rhythm, call and response, as if their base concerns had joined, found common cause. He moves to spit and Luther backs out of the way. He wipes his mouth with the side of his hand. "Said if that woman"—he wipes again—"that woman was right then she was goin' too, gonna be blessed too; cut all her hair off, went and got up in that tree and shot herself right in the face." He turns and looks over at the dogs, just stands and studies them for a while. "How much you askin' for them pups?" and starts to walk in that direction. Yurang's snapping at the wire as he approaches, lunging at it. It won't hold him very long which should be obvious— Leonard's rubbing his stomach and standing right there watching like it's chain-link fence or something. Luther's feeling somewhat dazed—the noise is confusing, seems to carry away the sense of the situation. He hurries over; yells shut up. The dogs shut up. A rush of wings and the crows depart. They stand there looking saying nothing for a minute.

"How much for that'n?" He points to a male, one of the gray ones, still excited, trying to grab on to Yurang's ear.

"Hundred and fifty."

"Hundred and fifty dollars?"

"They got papers."

"Papers?"

"Registered; they all been registered."

He shakes his head and walks away. "Don't need no papers."

"They come with 'em." He just keeps walking. Luther follows him back to the truck. "Don't make no difference if you want 'em." Leonard climbs in, shuts the door. The window is open. "Paid five hundred for their mamma." The bed is loaded with odds and ends, pots and pans, personal stuff. "Somebody shot her." He steps back, looks hard at Leonard sitting, hands up on the wheel, looks at the gun rack which is empty. Leonard hardly seems to breathe. Nor has he spat in quite a while. Yet something's happening. Luther looks a little closer. He's making noise. Saying something. Luther comes up to the window, places his arm on top of the cab, bends down to hear:

"Shit," he says at first and often, "shit" and "goddamn shit" and "not worth shit" and "shit" on this and that with not much audible in between (it's hard to say to what extent communication is intended, whether Luther ought to back away and leave in any case, ignore the urge to listen in as to some point of personal relevance, something familiar overheard). A fragment here and there, a few words strung together, something now about the weather, how it gets too hot to sleep, too hot to something, "hotter'n shit," much "hotter'n shit," makes people crazy, don't eat something, don't eat right—they don't eat right; it gets so hot they don't eat right; they get too tired (by now, his arm and elbow resting in the window, Luther has his ear inside—it's like translating from a language just a bit removed from yours, a dialect just a little closer to the branching point, the trailer park from which, say fifty years ago at most, we all diverged). It's all discomfort and complaint. A low, continuous recitation like some literary form, a nearly vanished oral tradition, half-remembered—all events, all deeds, are driven by resentment, all resentments spring from fear: their aches and pains, their good-for-nothing friends and neighbors, every small dissatisfaction husbanded, reviewed (the trick is not to dwell on words or even expressions, but to get the rhythm first, the mood, the emotional point of view and then it comes), how that dang baby cried and wouldn't never sleep; things fall apart, won't hold together—not the car, the air conditioner, not the simplest little thing, it flies away; he hurts his back and gets laid off and she does too—or not her back, it's something else—but all the same they're quite reduced and still the baby—little girl his wife insists but he says baby—cries and cries, won't even let them sleep outside at night to get out of the heat, the goddamn trailer stinks as well, but they can't sleep outside the baby gets so scared it scares her mamma like there's something really out there every night. So it gets worse. He gets more angry at the small things than the big ones like when someone fails to wave back when their trucks pass on the road—that little thing you do when passing on a narrow country lane, that subtle lifting of the fingers with the palm still on the wheel as if to say, in some small way, well here we are both trying to get by, make the best we can of things in this poor undeveloped region—just that much of a rejection, unintended makes no difference, sets him off, just goes to show how bad it is, how not worth shit it's all become (and all this time he never moves, just keeps his hands up on the wheel, stares straight ahead, his knuckles white as if he'd lost his brakes on some treacherous stretch of road). "You ain't too tired to drink that beer," he makes her voice a faint and distant little whine, "don't hurt too bad to watch TV," it trails away in a weirdly sweet falsetto, "chew that damn tobacco." There's a trickle of it coming form the corner of his mouth. It's like he's bleeding. Like in the movies when that happens and you know whoever it is is going to die. It seems that fatal. Luther leans in a little closer. Then the TV goes out too and that really does it—just a dark and smelly trailer every night; she takes to standing in the screen door with the baby while he sits outside and has his beers, gets drunk enough to make her come outside and sit there with him but the baby won't shut up and she gets nervous, gets all scared, keeps having to go back in for something while he sits there facing away, listening to them, all the crying and all the crappy little sounds life makes inside a crappy trailer and the more he sits and listens and the more he gazes off into the dark, the more misfortune finds a presence, finds itself incorporated into the notion of what's out there, what the baby's wailing at.

One night they sleep outside regardless—it's so hot and so foul-smelling—leaving the child inside. Its cries are less hysterical if they do that, leave her single window open and a bottle of sugar water even though she's three years old. After a while the crying stops and then all night there's not a sound, a little breeze comes up, they fall asleep and that's that until morning when all the screaming wakes him up. He's getting really hard to hear at this point and Luther's somehow lost the knack or something, lost his sympathy—whatever it was that seemed at first to strike a chord now seems repellent all of a sudden as when certain familiar smells or flavors reach a degree of concentration that transforms them, makes them appalling, horrible, disgusting and all the more because they retain their familiarity. Luther jerks away—there's something unintelligible about the police, the little dog, and what they found up in the tree (some animation now from Leonard, a sort of clenching and unclenching of the wheel), a low and bitter-sounding whisper—almost spitting—about some woman, the religious woman, coming to visit, smiling at him, smiling and smiling. The tobacco juice has trickled all the way down his chin. Luther's standing away from the truck—can't hear him now, or maybe he's stopped. He can hear the crows off to the north; a distant pop from someone hunting the pipeline, probably, to the east. He backs away a little more, then starts to head back to the trailer.

"Hey," shouts Leonard. Luther turns. "Come here," he calls. "Come here," he calls again. He has something in his hand, something white, holding it out the window. Luther walks back to the truck. "Smell that," says Leonard. "Go on." He holds it up to Luther. Luther takes it—it's a garment, a blouse or something. Leonard's looking right at Luther. "Go on," he says. Luther brings it carefully toward his face. "Go on," says Leonard. It's perfumed. He brings it closer. It's familiar. It's the way she smelled that day at the barbershop but even more intensely floral, concentrated, overpoweringly sweet. He hands it back. "Ain't that heaven?" Leonard asks. "Don't that smell like heaven? Don't it?" Luther nods. For a second longer Leonard looks him in the eye, then stuffs the blouse behind the seat, starts the truck, and backs around, heads out to the road, just sits there idling for a moment as if deciding which way to go, then turns to the south and drives away, a thin white haze like all that misery trailing behind.

"This here; what's this?" says Sheriff Bobby. Evening light, just now beginning to break through the haze, sets everything out in that rosy shadowy sort of strangeness Luther hates. The object of Bobby's interrogation might as plausibly be the weedeater, the pile of boards next to the step—it all looks uniformly odd and arbitrary this time of day.

"Trap," says Luther. Bobby lifts the cobbled-together wooden door and lets it fall.

"Trap for what?"

Luther shrugs. Bobby looks at him, looks at the row of white-flecked tar-paper sheets stuck up with duct tape on the trailer—five sheets side by side, each one, from left to right, more liberally spattered than the previous: the first one patternless, apparently random; the last one clearly displaying the outline of a hand. "Monkey," says Luther.

"What?"

"Maybe a monkey."

Bobby's radio is making noise. He goes to attend it. After a minute he comes back. "Which way you say he headed out?"

"Went north," says Luther.

"Huh," says Bobby, removing his hat, fiddling with the band, "somebody seen him south of Gladewater." He looks at Luther, "Puppy getcha?" Yurang's growling behind the door. Luther looks down at his arm. "Ain't nothin' serious."

"I knowed this fella got his privates all ripped out by one of them chows." He keeps on fiddling with the band; it's got a little silver ornament, not quite centered at the front.

"New hat?" says Luther.

"Yes sir." Bobby puts it on, turns sideways, lets the setting sun shine on its whiteness.

"Damn," says Luther.

"Little more dignified than that straw one."

"No question about it."

"Yes sir"—he's looking around, surveying the place—"just a little more dignified." The shadows of trees are creeping across. His white hat glows. "No car."

"That's right."

"No phone." He looks at Luther. "TV?"

"Nope."

"Gets lonely here I expect."

"Not lately."

Bobby smiles and looks down at his boots—brand new as well, black shiny lizard—gives each one a little wipe on the back of his clean, pressed khaki pants and walks on over to look at the tar-paper demonstration. "So all he wanted was a puppy?"

"Yep."

"You see a gun?"

"Not in his rack."

Bobby shakes his head. "What is this shit?"

"You think he shot her?"

"Can't say I'd blame him. What the hell is all this shit?" He's studying each one, moving slowly left to right. The growling from inside gets louder, deepens, catches a subtle resonance with some cheap and rattly property of the trailer so the whole thing for a moment seems to vibrate very softly with all that cheapness and all that menace combining easily in the reddening evening light.

18

"You know she's the one had all them leaflets dropped all over."

"Which one?"

"The young one—one you saw. Paid for it anyway."

"Didn't know that."

"Hired that plane."

"No kiddin'."

"And I'll tell you somethin else she's got old Bobby tied in knots."

"He's got a wife."

"You seen him."

"Yeah."

"That stuff he's wearin'. Hell, he's puttin' on."

"Oh shit."

"Damned right he is. Well she's the one got Joe the sign."

"You seen it?"

"Seen it goin' up."

"So what's it for? He ain't open nights."

"God only knows. Dolores called me, said I oughta get on down and have a look, said it was spooky—'spoookee,' you know how she talks."

"No."

"Well she talks like that—says, 'Agnes, thees ees spoookee'; said she was closin' up, turned around and all of a sudden all these sparks and flashin' colors, people across the street start clappin', Joe out there dancin' all around and pretty soon they all get quiet and everybody starts ploppin' down there on the grass just watchin' the sign, not sayin' nothin', just baskin' in it like they was out there on the beach."

"Universal?"

"Yep."

"Universal what?"

"Hell I don't know. Universal Church and Juicy Burgers."

"Joe's Big Spooky."

"Ha."

"Look out."

"I see 'em."

"Hit your brights."

"Ain't got no brights."

"Goddamn."

"Hold on."

"Goddamn."

"Oh Lordy, just about got one."

"Just about did."

"I hate that—people dumpin' dogs. That's where you get that sorta thing, them packs of dogs. I betcha most a them things was dumped, people thinkin' it's a kindness. Oughta just kill it and be done. Just be done. I swear they get so nasty-lookin'. Seen a pack a them once looked worse'n anything I ever seen standin' out there in the highway over some old dead somethin' or other and wouldn't leave it, wouldn't move so I had to stop and this great big mangy sonofabitch stands there lookin' right into my headlights—ain't no hair left on him nowhere except a patch right here in front and down one leg. Looked like he used to be one a them real big curly-haired dogs, them big old friendly-lookin' dogs. I swear it don't take much. Just turn him loose, just open that door and shove him out, say 'there you go; go on get out, get back to nature,' and by God I guess he will but not the way they like to think. You wanna crack that window a tad?"

"Sorry."

"How's that arm?"

"Okay."

"Don't look okay. Looks like that bandage keeps gettin' bigger."

"It's okay."

"Oh my."

"What?"

"Lookee yonder. You think that's it?"

"What?"

"Lean over here, that side's all dirty."

"Yeah."

"My, my. You think that's it?"

"I guess. That flickerin'?"

"My oh my."

"Looks like it's movin'."

"Goodness me."

"It's got stuff movin'."

"What do you suppose?"

"It's got a cross on top there too. You see anybody?"

"No."

"Slow down. Let's see."

"No cars."

"Damn, look at it light up the courthouse."

"Just that squad car over yonder."

"Jeez."

"Don't see nobody here."

"Pull on around. Anybody out there on the grass?"

"Can't really tell. No, sure don't look like it. Lord almighty. Ha. If that ain't somethin'."

"Pull on around."

"If that ain't somethin' else again."

"Why don't you back it in up there."

"What?"

"Like a drive-in. Back it in so we can watch."

"Oh, Lord."

"Right here."

"Oh Lord, oh Lord."

"That's good."

"Oh Lord . . . don't mind me . . . Jesus . . . you figure now we're goin' steady?"

"Agnes."

"I'm okay . . . oh, Lord . . . just let me catch my breath."

"Shit, ain't that funny."

"Way too much fast livin'."

"Shit."

"Oh me."

"To hell with you."

"I'm sorry. Lord."

"Shit, look at that. You ever seen that many bugs?"

"Oh me."

"It sorta hurts your eyes. You think he plans to leave that thing on every night? Oh jeez, look there. Them little curly things. Just ever now and then them things go shootin' off like that. How 'bout that."

"Galaxies."

"Yeah?"

"Sure. Got your stars there, right? And don't you figure them funny-colored ones are planets?"

"How much you reckon that thing cost?"

"Five planets—that one there's a comet. Lord, no tellin'—even just to put it up; you oughta see the steel they got up there on top."

"What's that one there at the tip of that long red spiky part? Ain't that one too?"

"My, my, my, my."

"Six, then."

"My, my."

"No, wait . . . one, two, three, four. . . ."

"Shh."

"Eight. By God there's eight if you count that little bitty one down at the bottom."

"Listen."

"Whoosh. There they go again. What?"

"Listen."

"What?"

"Shh, quiet."

"Oh."

"It hisses, don't it."

"Yeah."

"My, my."

"It's all that current squeezin' through them little wires."

"You figure?"

"Yeah."

"Sounds like the beach."

"Look over yonder."

"What?"

"That squad car. Look in there—you see the hat?"

"Who is that? Willis?"

"I believe it is."

"Is he asleep?"

"I imagine so."

19

Agnes sets the rake down with its handle against a big white-painted rock, approaches the porch where Luther stands like he's been wounded, shot or something, holding his stomach, a straining, pale expanse of which shows through a gap in his blood-red shirt.

"So where's the button?"

"Hell I don't know."

"Well, where were you standin'?"

"Right here."

"Dang"—she looks around, walks out in the yard, looks around some more, looks back at Luther—"damn good thing I was out of the way."

"Aw, shit," says Luther, trying to hold his shirt together, walking over to take a seat at the edge of the porch, regarding the damage as if in fact it were an injury to his person. "Shit," he says again. "Aw, shit," and shakes his head and folds his arms across his belly, bending over as if recovering from a blow.

"You rip it?"

"Shit," he says and takes a peek. "Guess not," and folds his arms again and looks down at the ground. She comes around to stand next to him. He looks up. She's got the makeup on. It's really not the color of her skin at all. It's pinker. Maybe it's the color she used to be and she just uses it out of habit—you can see exactly where it stops, the places she missed. Or maybe that's not the point. Maybe it's just a sort of formality like the way she paints the rocks.

"I got a shoe box full of buttons."

He sits up and sucks his gut in, holds his shirt closed.

"Or I could take one off the cuff. You got a few more'n you really need."

He looks at his cuffs, each slightly frayed but adorned with four

David Searcy

white pearly buttons set in silver-colored bezels. He always liked the way that looked. "Let's see what you got."

They look around a little more. "You wanna check out by the road?"

"Shit," says Luther and follows Agnes into the house.

"Cigar box."

"What?"

"Cigar box. You said shoe box."

"Well whatever. Take your pick."

It's on the bed. The bed is made. He's never been in here before. The bedspread's tucked in under the pillows. It's an old white, nubbly bedspread edged with tassels. The windows are open behind the headboard. Evening light—gold sunlight just now breaking through—comes at a narrow, grazing angle across the nubbles casting little nubbly shadows and a fading patch of light against the wall next to the dresser. He can't bring himself to sit down on the bed, somehow; he stands there by the window with the box. She's standing over by the closet which is open. He can see a number of boxes neatly stacked up on the shelves. It's all just so. He pokes around among the buttons. Most are big ones, funny colors, funny shapes, the sort you find on women's clothing; but underneath, as if they'd had more time to settle, are a few that look all right—not anything fancy, just regular buttons like the ones that come on shirts he's had before. He picks one out and looks at Agnes, puts the box down on the bed—Garcia y Vega Elegantes; he tries to think the words to himself—closes it, places the button on top, and steps away.

"You need to take it off."

He looks at her a moment.

"Ain't no space between that tummy and the shirt."

He looks around, decides the kitchen might be better, walks past Agnes, trying to hold his stomach in as he untucks his shirt, undoes the pearly buttons, moves to yank it off and toss it, take a seat there at the table on the far side; but the sleeve sticks to his bandage, makes him yelp, sit down right there and gather the shirt that's hanging off his arm up to him, over his stomach, hold his arm against his chest with half the bandage pulled away.

"Now what in the world"—she's coming over, peering at it—"what'd you do? That ain't no dog bite."

"No."

"Goddamn." Bends closer.

"Told you."

"Dang." She sniffs it, lightly touches the red and swollen skin next to the cut which is seeping badly, the edges starting to evert the way a veined shrimp does when boiled. He jerks a little. "Hot," she says, "you got a fever in that arm."

"Put thinner on it."

"What?" She stands up.

"Thinner. Paint thinner."

"Lord." She turns and disappears into the bedroom, comes back muttering in fluttery, soft exasperation gathering items here and there. She helps him pull the shirt off, peels away the bandage, takes his arm, regards the wound a moment.

"What'd you do?"

"I cut it."

"Cut it how?" Just out the window the chickens are passing one by one back toward the cedars. "Cut it how?" The yard's in shadow, just the fence posts tipped with light.

"Can't say exactly."

She opens a little brown glass bottle with a thin glass applicator on the cap, a thin red liquid clinging to it. "Monkey blood," she says.

"What? Shit."

"Hold still. That's what my daddy always called it. That's what everybody called it far as I know. You never heard that? What do you mean can't say exactly?"

"Monkey blood."

"Yep."

"Why?"

"Beats me. Just one of them things you say to kids. Better'n Mercurochrome or Merthiolate or whatever." She's got it painted all around and in the cut; now blowing on it, pursing her lips and holding his arm and gently blowing across the wound. The light has left the tops of the fence posts. He can hear the chickens flapping, rising softly into the trees. "You better get that to the doctor."

"It's okay."

"It ain't okay."

It's all bright orange. It looks worse now than it did before. "We better go. You get that button on, we'll go."

"Go see Doc Kirby."

"It's all right."

"He ain't gonna hurt you."

"Get that button on and we'll go." He pushes the shirt across the table, takes the pad of gauze she's folded, takes the tape. "It's gettin' dark."

It seems, paradoxically, so much darker on the square with the neon sign. The little incidental lights—security lights, streetlights and such that pick out the edges of things, like pilot lights maintaining the possibility of everything coming to life again tomorrow—dim right out, as do the stars. It's such a glare. All light belongs to Joe's Big Juicy. All radiance gathers unto it while elsewhere all is dark. It isn't possible now to linger on the fringes. One is in the light and, therefore, passing in or one is not. There is no easy hanging around, no casual promlike coming and going; no transition, gentle, sum- mery, between one precinct and the other like the first time. People loom, rather than drift, into the light. They go right in as if they know to go right in, as if they know, as Joe must know, that, come to this, who cares to saunter about in the world, who gives a shit about the Wal-Mart.

Agnes pauses in the street. She's having a problem with her dress or seeming to have one, standing, fiddling with it, smoothing it. Luther takes her by the arm, guides her across into the softly hissing glow that makes her wince a little, he thinks, like stepping into chilly water. The door's braced open with Joe's big white limestone fossil. Luther sits her down right there, right by the door, just one seat in, and stands there by her on the door side for a moment just in case she tries to bolt. The others are standing and milling around—a few he knows; most are vaguely familiar faces. They're helping themselves to drinks from the Coke box, wandering back a few at a time to the little storeroom to pay their respects. Bobby's voice booms out occasionally. Sounds of amazement and approval. There's someone pushing past.

"Hey, Luther."

"Hey."

"Hey, Agnes."

Agnes brushes at her hair and stares at the picture on the wall behind the counter. It's a poster-size enlargement of the much-reiterated photo of the catfish. It's so big it falls apart; the image disintegrates completely into speckles of light and dark, uninterpretable, raw material for the common imagination which, apparently, is to be encouraged by the heavy gold-leaf frame of the very sort that might surround the standard misty upward-gazing face of Christ.

"Oh dear," says Agnes. Luther sits. Except for that—except for the picture and, of course, the electric murmur of the cosmos—it's the same.

"Fire up that griddle, Joe," says someone. People laugh. Joe's head appears in the service window, grinning, basking for a moment in the joke that dismisses all the mundane functions of the place, confirms the general sense of occasion and how easily and amiably the ordinary falls away. The chatter softens. People start to take their seats—there must be twenty or twenty-five. Joe comes around with folding chairs. Some people stand. The periodic, soft, reflected flicker of galaxies exploding and receding brightens the street, makes Luther glance out the open door into the dark as toward a lightning flash, a summer storm approaching. Little light-attracted insects flit about, hang in the darkness, drifting, weightless, here and there. His eyes lose focus, or rather conviction as to distance. The shiny specks themselves recede until they seem like a sort of starry residue.

Tap, tap. He turns. A pointer, the broken-off tip of a bamboo pole is tapping against the picture. "Who can see him?" A stirring of hands, a looking-around. Joe's got his up. She smiles and looks down at the register which she's made into a lectern, rearranging, now, the papers resting on it, sorting and smiling as from the rear a few more people drift back in.

"Y'all go ahead and unplug that light." Joe's leaning forward in his little school desk, motioning with his hand. "Just jerk it free; don't want that damn thing thawin' out." General laughter as if it were an established sort of joke, as if this were a matter for some anxiety. Joe's delighted. He looks ridiculous out of uniform, paper-hatless, hair slicked elaborately over his baldness, almost giddy to join the customers, surrender his concerns to a higher purpose. The little storage room goes dark. A settling in. A pair of children on the Coke box swinging their heels against the side very softly tappity-tap. "Who sees him? Who can see his face?" It's hard to see her face in a way—a vagueness to it, almost that look of features recovered, reconstructed from a burn so at a distance it's okay but sort of blank, erased a little. "Yes?" She smiles. It makes her smile come out of nowhere like a trick, like pulling flowers from a hat. It makes no sense. She smiles at Joe. He brings his hand down. Someone whispers to the children; tapping pauses for a moment, then resumes. Her eyes have closed; the smile withdraws. She's perfectly still, just standing now behind the counter like a manikin; there to occupy the dress, a dowdy dark-blue short-sleeved dress with little polka dots all over, nothing to it, the sort of dress you used to see in Hudgins' window and meant to appeal, one had to suppose, to older women who liked to shop there and to whom such drab white-polka-dotted dresses must have represented something—resignation, a state of grace. Her eyes still closed, she takes the pointer, turns around like playing pin the tail on the donkey, stands a moment, lifts her eyes— she must be looking—to the picture, applies the pointer carefully, deliberately, to the surface, various stations, reciting softly, almost a whisper, as if to herself not to instruct but to rehearse, to resubmit to the miraculous: "Here the thorns, the drops of blood. . . ." The sheriff, sitting on the far side, twists around; he cranes his neck and goes all squinty, holding his hat to keep it on. A woman sitting on the other side of Agnes grasps her husband by the wrist, emits a noise, a little cry, then seems embarrassed, brings her hand up to her mouth. Outside a car drives slowly by. ". . . the eyes uplifted . . ." She points to where one eye must be and then the other, back to the first and again the other. Now and then she points somewhere and simply pauses, saying nothing as if uncertain or in silent expectation of additional information, points of anguish; ". . . how he suffers. . . ." here the pointer makes a circle. Agnes stiffens. What could that be but a mouth—what she's suggesting? Open. Gaping. Luther looks away. Each lightninglike eruption of the sign makes the fluorescents dim a little, makes the buzzing worse, sets up a sort of oscillating strain inside the room which Luther senses as a periodic tightening in his stomach. Air moves faintly through the door, the distant whistle of a train. He takes a deep breath, brings his hand down over his stomach, feels the difference in the button sewn more heavily than the others—lots of thread wrapped round and round between the button and the shirt. ". . . His wounded side. . . ." A pair of eyes—her little boy's, he thinks—peers out from behind the far end of the counter, from between the rack of green and white and yellow packs of gum and, just below, the tray of peanut-butter crackers. That's the child she had to lift up on the freezer that first night to see the fish. His eyes are darting here and there. Again the flash, the dimming lights, the tappity-tapping somewhat louder as pairs of heels fall into phase; the pointer delicate, contrapuntal. ". . . oh my, yes . . ."

"Yes," says the woman next to Agnes.

"Yes," says someone in the back.

"Yes," mingled whispers. Luther looks around. Some fasten on the pointer, watch it closely. Others—most in fact—don't seem to want to look. They look away, look at the floor as if it's all too much right now, right off the bat. They need to hang back, keep their seats, gaze off at nothing like they're waiting for a burger, let it come to them like that, like something common, then—surprise—it's something else. A little breeze. A breath of air. His crew cut tingles, stomach tightens. He wonders where the woman is who Agnes said paid for the sign and all the leaflets, the very attractive one—you'd think she'd want to be here. Bobby's turned around, still baffled-looking, squinty, glancing occasionally and, sure enough, it seems with a certain disappointment, toward the street. His boots reflect the variable glare with rich reptilian corrugations; a brand-new buckle of commemorative proportions tilts away beneath his gut. What if he keeps on like that? Adding things like that? What would he look like in a month or two? A year? They've got the rhythm now on the Coke box, found a natural, indefinitely maintainable dirgelike frequency. Bright red-candy-colored liquid trickles down the chin of one onto his shirt.

"Is that my Jesus?" Such a breathless, anxious tone as if it might be someone else; or as if pretending some uncertainty just to heighten things the way you do with children—give them cause, before they pop out of the blanket, in the dark to doubt themselves. "Is that my Jesus?"

"Please," says someone. How is it possible, Luther wonders, just to slip right into this like this, go straight from all the ordinary stuff—from washing dishes, say, or anything like that—just drop it, head on down to Joe's and, bam, get worked up, get yourself right up against a thing like this. The catfish hooked them somehow. Bait and switch, he thinks. He thinks that's funny, leans to tell the joke to Agnes, feels his button start to give, and sits back up. The eyes are on him. From behind the candy rack, the little eyes. When Luther winks they look away.

"Oh." Now she gasps. She turns around and gasps again, "Oh," puts the pointer down and places both her hands across her chest, bends forward, shakes her head, and laughs and gasps once more, "Oh my," like someone much too old for such things exiting a funhouse. "Oh," she says more softly, smiling all around that strangely unsupported, pure, schematic smile. "It's right here isn't it? Yes?" Not false, it's not a false smile; merely uninvolved with any other aspect of the face and, so, exemplary in a way suggesting joy, exhilaration, can be senseless: here, it says each time, look here, behold, how joy erupts spontaneously out of nowhere; unencumbered takes you with it; purified to this extent reveals a subtle stomach-tightening commonality with terror. Luther folds both hands across the failing button, looks around again. A few have hands or tissues to their faces. Some still hold themselves obliquely toward it all. "Just here," she says, then, "Yes?" again, the smile expanding. Luther keeps his left hand pressed against his stomach, holds his forearm with his right—it's hot; he's feeling hot all over; he can't tell if it's a fever or the room or maybe both. She stands and smiles like that a moment, then she reaches under the counter, lifts a heavy, squat black object—a slide projector—takes it over to the service window, talking all the while in a sort of run-on, automatic, grade-school-teacher kind of voice: she's Sister Irene Mary Pincus for the newcomers; bids them welcome; wonders if they ever thought about the ways the world might end and how a thing like that—profound as that—might happen, really happen (she's got tangles in the cord; she has to loosen knots then draw the plug end through a couple of times), how subtle, roundabout, and odd such things historically tend to be—not the end of the world of course but like that, like the Ice Age, say; she walks around behind to plug it in, bends down, she's hard to hear now struggling with the plug or something, jerking at the cord to get more slack and going on and on about whatever it is; it's not the Ice Age now, it's changed to something else; she has a se-ries of examples. Here the tappity-tapping softens, loses precision as the children on the Coke box turn to watch the slide projector whir to life; she reappears describing fires—real ones apparently—that can burn deep underground for years and years in peat deposits, coal seams, spreading, unextinguishable, till before you know it, long be-fore you know what's even happening all the earth is compromised beyond recovery, burned away—not like your grass fires, forest fires, that sort of thing; that's like a first-degree burn, grows back pretty easily—but more deeply and never the same right under your feet and did you know (she stops to wrestle with the carousel which doesn't want to drop down into place) and did you know (she looks up) this whole region is shot right through with lignite, not just gas but lignite coal—you see the pits still from the twenties don't you? Mine shafts once filled in but slumping open now; just think about how perilous that is, how terribly precarious this whole area is in ways you can probably feel. You feel it don't you? Don't you really? Don't you think it makes us sensitive? Don't you wake up nights sometimes? And then she stops, surveys the room, regards the pro-jector for a moment, scoots it over to the left, adjusts the elevating screw, turns on the lamp, adjusts some more until it's centered more or less above the window at the front, the luminous field too large, distorted at that angle, spreading a little onto the ceiling.

"Joe?" she says.

"Huh?" Joe's slumped way down in his seat, mouth slightly open.

"Lights?"

"Oh," Joe gets up and reaches around behind the couple standing in the corner and hits the switch. Now just the trapezoidal glow above the window and, from outside, the complex periodic flicker.

"Joe?"

He's ready this time. "Yes'm."

"That little light?"

A silence.

"The one inside the freezer?"

"Yes'm."

"What is that, a forty?"

"Sixty."

"Still, that's not enough to thaw the fish out, is it?"

"No, I guess not."

"No." A pause. "What would it take do you think?"

"Ma'am?"

"What kind of light . . ."

"Ma'am?"

". . . would it take to penetrate the frosty distance, warm our hearts?"

"What kind?"

"Yes."

"Well . . ."

"The light of faith."

"Oh."

"It would take the light of faith." The first slide drops. The tapping slows. Luther leans over to his left as far as he can. He's got the worst seat in the house. It looks like a picture of a picture. Now it's focused. It's a picture of the picture on the wall, gold frame and all. It's getting really out of hand, it seems to him. It's like a rumor going around and around again. A few of the little gnatlike insects flit about in the projector beam. The outside lights—fluorescents like the ones inside—whose aging ballasts sometimes make them flash and flicker, start to do so now in sympathy with the sign. The buzzing acquires a lower pitch. It seems to mingle with and amplify somehow the soft collective sound of breathing in the dark. The next slide sticks, receives a tap. It's just a slightly closer view—the top half mostly; no gold frame. He looks at Agnes, thinking maybe she'll look back, confirm his puzzlement, shake her head or something. Light from outside flickers through her pale-gray frizzy hair, shows up the wrinkly gill-like gaps where the makeup missed. She's wearing perfume too, or something fragrant—floral, sweet, and childlike. Thunk—the next slide falls. She's timing it with the sign. She'll let it go a couple of cycles, then she'll change it at the flash. Kerplunk. It's nothing. Another shot a little closer. Luther looks around. There's no obliqueness now—it's all attention, pallid faces facing front. He leans way over, puts his arm up on the rail, and tries to lift himself a little. Flash—kerplunk. His arm hurts. Someone makes a noise. So what is that? The same thing blown up even bigger—centered on the same dark blotch a little darker than the other bits of decomposing photographic data. It's like something under a microscope, like germs or something scientific—pictures of a virus. "Oh," says someone. In the flash he can see the little eyes still darting back and forth behind the candy rack. The dark blotch fills the screen now. Someone whispers, "Oh my God," and "Oh my Jesus." Two or three start doing that. The bench is shaking. Someone's rocking—it's the woman next to Agnes. Luther lets himself back down into his seat. His stomach hurts. The button's giving way. The children on the Coke box have dropped off to find their parents. Agnes's hair looks quite electric in the stroboscopic light as she stands up, walks slowly out, and disappears across the street. His sleeve is sticking to the back rail of the bench. He has to twist around and use his other hand to pull it free so not to separate the bandage from the wound. This strains the shirt and pops the button. For a moment he just sits, bent over, looking at the insects in the beam of the projector. "Oh my blessed, blessed, blessed, blessed Jesus," someone's chanting. Then he's up and out the door.

She makes him drive. It's been so long he has to think about it, how to work the column-shift especially. It's so vague. He has to fiddle for a while to find reverse and Agnes paying no attention, no help at all, just sitting looking out the window.

Everything about the truck is sort of vague—slack in the steering which the huge thin plastic steering wheel makes worse (he gets it up to maybe fifty—the speedometer doesn't work—and swerves from one side of the highway to the other just to test it, see if Agnes throws a fit but she just sits there), something funny about the clutch that makes the cable feel like it's stretching, about to snap. It's all congenial. It seems to extend and accommodate his sense of personal dilapidation. He tugs and bangs on the window vent to make it open, get that steady stream of air across him, cooling his stomach herniating even further through his shirt (another button's about to go), his injured arm—blowing across it just like Agnes, carrying all the heat away. The act of hurtling down the highway in the dark, were he able somehow to maintain it, might be enough, just in itself, might be sufficient to sustain a sense of purpose. He could do this and do nothing else, he thinks, and be okay. Just bounce along in air-cooled vague coordination, imperfections in agreement. Here we go on down the road, the clear black asphalt. It's like a ship's wheel, he imagines—how you probably have to sense the slip and flow of things, anticipate a lot. He looks at Agnes—no anticipation there; she's leaning back, maybe asleep. Her head rocks side to side with the curves. He crests a hill. The headlights dip and fan out slowly. He hits the brights but they don't work. He squints. There's something in the road way up there—white, not moving yet. He looks for the weird reflective gleam of something's eyes. He slows a little as he passes—just a lump, a dead white something by the road, a dog or a cat. Probably a dog. About the size of a little dog.

20

It's not ineptitude exactly—just an overwhelming problem with the effort, countless little acts of will required to do the simplest thing in all this heat. He wants a single drop of paint to leave the soda straw and fall the seven feet from where he's sprawled atop the trailer to the foot-square tar-paper target on the ground. He wants to do it without leaning on his bandaged arm in such a way that little darts of pain shoot from the wound down through his wrist into his hand. He'd like his finger not to stick to the top of the straw when he lifts it to release a drop of paint thus causing the straw to shake and give a little flick which altogether screws up what he's trying to do which is be scientific as he can observing single drops of white paint thinned to varying degrees with mineral spirits in their plummet from this height (exaggerated to exaggerate the effects) upon release by various means. He'd like the puppies to shut up. In their excitement they're trying to climb the chicken wire and there's a chance—they've got so big—they'll tear it down. He tries a different way this time. He keeps his finger on the straw, maintains the seal, then with his left hand (bracing himself up on both elbows) squeezes down—a good idea except it's hard to do it smoothly; sweaty thumb and finger slip and grab and slip along the red-striped plastic straw. He runs his left hand through his hair and tries again. That helps. A blob of paint appears but won't release. He keeps the straw pinched just behind it, scoots himself out over the edge a little, blows in the other end while relaxing the squeeze. A drop of paint falls to the target, makes a splatter. For a moment he just lies there, folding his hands up under his chin, remembering spitting off a bridge when he was a child, remembering something on TV he watched with Agnes (from whom not a word in days) about some ancient Roman building with a dome so high they said a drop of water released from the ceiling would evaporate before it hit the floor. He leans out over, spits and misses, the taste of paint still in his mouth. How is that possible he wonders? How could it rain if that were possible? Or would that mean rain had to start in great big globs and dwindle down to little droplets? Maybe sometimes great big globs would reach the ground—he seems to recall big drops of rain. Sometimes it falls from a sunny sky, gets blown in sideways he supposes, and that's when, it seems to him (he sits up, throws his legs over the side and sticks the straw back in the paint), that's when it seems to him you get, for whatever reason, those great big raindrops. Out of the blue. Though even then they're not so big. He looks up. How he wishes it would rain, the haze condense, come down in torrents, bounce and sizzle off the trailer, lay the grass flat, soak the puppies. "Y'all get down." This just excites them even further. "Get!" he yells. They're really barking at him now. How is it down there on the ground they think he's fine but let him get up here on top—well that won't do. He gazes out across the field. Yurang's run off, though subtle partings in the grass appear to show where he has been. He stands up carefully—right at the edge to hold his weight, to keep from going through the roof. It's even clearer now. The pattern of what look like little trails. Just this much higher seems to help—the glare at noon is almost shadowless, almost as disinterested as the faint but clear and watery predawn light. He looks above the field, averts his gaze a little. There seems to be no sign at all of his own violent excursion the other night. Maybe it's habitual, an established circuit like the dog paths in backyards but more extensive, more complicated. One long furrow (he looks away and looks again; it comes and goes, picks up most clearly where it crosses natural dips and irregularities) arcs away off to the east and back around and seems to stop. He's on his tiptoes, slips and sits down quickly too far off the edge to keep his perch. He has to let go, push away, hope nothing breaks—the Pantheon, he thinks, amazed to know the name, a vision of it like one's life before one's eyes, detailed like that: the vast interior, ranks of stepped square niches, swirly marble, huge and empty space and at the top the dazzling hole. All this before he hits the ground and twists his ankle, has to fend off all the puppies pouring through where the wire's collapsed beneath their weight.

Yurang disdains the couch. He wants to go back out. He's at the door. He sighs. He lies down, gets back up, and stands there panting. Moonlight slants in Luther's window, lights his stomach which he regards, propped up in bed, with a kind of surprise, a kind of amazement bringing his hands around it carefully like a pregnancy or a crystal ball. It's monumental, brightly lit like that—a marvel. How in the world could this have happened? Why should bodies keep on growing, spreading out like old potatoes sprouting feelers? Going rotten too. He holds his arm up in the light. The gauze is dirty and discolored. He tries to make a fist. It's worse he thinks. He lets it down across his stomach, folds his other hand across it, shuts his eyes. "Hush." Yurang plops back down. In a moment he's up again and panting, pausing like he's listening—panting, pausing. Now he's quiet. Luther looks. He's on the couch, nose to the window, then he's back down, coming over to the bed to sit and pant by Luther's ear. The moonlight strikes across the muzzle and the eyes, the inexpressive convolutions of the face. Luther gets up, limps across to the little table, kneels on the seat, looks out the window, feels the shifting of the trailer. That's worse too; he needs to shim it up some more. He brings his face up to the screen—just moonlit grass, the smell of grass. A soft, metallic, gurgling sigh comes from the gas well to the west. He sits and turns to look at Yurang: pitlike eyes half shut, his black tongue lolling out and one tooth shining, almost glowing, in the moonlight in the dark.

He's got some soda straws, some paint, the broken-off corner of a sheet of pegboard, white glue, pliers, the hacksaw never returned to Agnes, drill and bits, a piece of paper (one of the leaflets whose obverse, below the photo, has a clear space good for doodling), scraps of wood from previous projects, rubber bands, a roll of black electrical tape—all spread out carefully on the table. In his hand a stub of pencil. In his thoughts the vaguest yearning toward design, mechanical drawing, schematization of a notion, vague itself but which, reduced to diagram, might achieve conviction. It should involve an array of droppers—like the thin glass dropper Agnes used to apply the antiseptic—precise like that, and antiseptic in its precision, but more active, forceful. Luther looks outside. Yurang's not happy on his chain. He keeps on jerking it, making an awful ratchety racket under the trailer where it's anchored. He's got the chain pulled nearly taut, just stands there like that, then he'll make a sudden lunge out toward the field as if it had to be a mistake, a misapprehension; a simple problem of technique—clatter, thunk. The trailer shivers. Morning light has begun to soften with the haze. Little glistening clouds of gnats hang here and there. They look like markers, buoys or something, how each floats above its spot. It seems a good idea at this point not to let the dogs run loose—to clear the field, to clear the mind as far as possible. Luther brings the pencil down. He makes a line—a little inch-long vertical line—and then another right next to it about a quarter inch away. That's the straw, a section of straw. He starts to make the smaller lines to close it off at top and bottom, then refrains, recalling something about conventions to represent an open tube. Kerthunk. "Goddammit." Another kerthunk. "Hey!" Yurang creeps back under the trailer. Luther takes the piece of pegboard, looks at the edge then holds the straw against it—same width—sticks the straw into a hole; it fits quite snugly. That's a break. He makes two sets of double horizontal lines on either side of the piece of straw to represent what right off the bat seems a fairly encouraging state of affairs—a one-inch section of soda straw stuck right in the hole. Tight as you please. Three-eighths above, three-eighths below—a little thing but vastly gratifying nonetheless. It speaks to rigor and precision. He extends the horizontal lines a bit, sharpens his pencil rubbing it sideways across the photograph above, then carefully terminates each end of the pegboard cross section with a little zigzag line to indicate the arbitrary truncation, that the pegboard should be understood to continue for who knows? He leans back, gazes out the window for a minute. Who knows how far; how large a structure is required? He looks at his drawing, then at the Xerox of the Xerox of the photo of the catfish now obscured entirely. What size was that plywood? Two-by-three? No, larger. Maybe three-by-five and still too small. He looks outside again, uncertain, once more vague about the notion, what the notion is exactly, why it seems to come and go—one minute sharp in its intention, clearly purposeful; and the next diffuse and clumsy, ill-considered. Even sunlight seems to hurt his arm. He scoots to the side a little, places his left arm in his lap, takes up the pencil, begins very carefully filling in the pegboard cross section with a shading of diagonal lines. He really likes the way that looks—he holds it up—like something technical, scientific. This much, then, is perfectly clear—just this little bit. The eraser is worn away to nothing. He takes the pliers, compresses the little brass-colored collar until the dirty once-pink rubber squeezes out, then, here and there, cleans up the smudges and the places where the diagonals overshot. He can imagine people designing rockets just like this—one piece at a time, making everything as clear as it can be, one little certainty next to another. How could it not work, they must think; how could this not be deeply meaningful.

He hates to walk out to the mailbox, hates to walk out to the road then have to turn and walk so far back to the south to where it stands, a great-big mailbox on a great-big cedar post so oddly removed as if to serve some larger house long since destroyed or never built. As if the mail (such as it is, junk for the most part) had somehow fallen to him by default—our plans have changed, go on, you take it, it's all right, you take the ads, the discount flyers, come on down and have a taste of how it feels to belong to the world in a proper sense. And so he does but not very often. Mr. Tuel takes care of the bills. It's mostly a matter of cleaning it out before the mailman starts to bring it to his door or decides he's dead. "Get back here." Yurang's trotting along, starting to drift out into the field. "Come on." The surface of the road is starting to crack, the old black oil-soaked dirt gone gray, dried out and crumbly at the edges. You can smell it though, still, faintly in the heat, the slightly volatile oily smell. His boots are going, too. His old gray ropers look just like the road; little cracks appearing at the instep fill with pale orange dust and look just like old nasty, crumbly road. "You get on back here." Yurang's sniffing, about to head out after something in the weeds on the other side. "Oh shit." The mailbox burns his hand. The little tab is bent out straight and hard to pull so he has to place one hand on top to get some leverage. It's his bad hand too, his bad arm, pain shoots back and forth along it between the elbow and the wrist. He stands and holds it tight against him for a minute, Yurang watching, sitting, panting in the middle of the road. It's like it's sunburned, like he'd driven across the country with it hanging out the window of Agnes's truck and now it's hot and red and sensitive to everything. He looks over at the dog, the eyes half-closed, on hold, just waiting; looks at the mailbox, gives it a whack with his other hand, gives it another right at the top where the flange of the door is bent and causes it to jam. The door falls open. A dirt dauber wasp crawls out and slowly climbs the arch of the opening, stops at the very top for a couple of seconds then departs. Luther looks inside, steps closer. Crows are making noise way off to the north some-where, just carrying on and on. There's not much mail, just some of those coupons—the kind with pictures of missing children. He brings his face right up to the opening, the coupons are curling; it's like an oven. There's some debris in there or something. He reaches in behind the coupons, burns his knuckle, withdraws a little bleached-white bone. It's sort of blade-shaped, like a collarbone, very small, warm in his hand; he turns it over a couple of times, peers again into the mailbox, reaches in, withdraws another, this one larger, more of a regular bone-shaped bone, clean as a whistle, ivory-white just like the first. It's like a bone that's been exposed for a while to the elements—he rubs his thumb along the shaft—not so dried out though. He takes another peek. There's quite a bit more. He looks around, walks across the road, and stands a moment. The crows are furious; crows are always fussing like that, making that racket; now there are more just to the east. Yurang's on idle still, ob-scure, just sitting, panting, gazing dimly toward the sound. How blunt and dim his face is, bred to be like that, all folded-in and placid-looking so the violence is surprising, he supposes, more effective, out of nowhere, no real sense of what he thinks. They hate the heat. But there he sits just panting, dripping on the road. It's hot as asphalt. Luther wipes away the sweat above his eyes, looks at the bones. The crows have stopped now. All of a sudden just the sound of Yurang panting. There's a sheen. He holds one up. A pattern of subtle, shiny streaks that looks like burnishing—even the complex knobby ends are polished free of all their fleshy associations. It's meticulous. The way museum bones must look, removed completely from the particular in order to represent the species, the hard essentials of something rare perhaps, exotic. Luther gazes at the mailbox, walks across, tosses the bones back in, and takes the coupons, walks back out in the road, holding the coupons, glancing at them, shuffling them, turning them to face the right way, right side up the way most cashiers like to do with dollar bills—the advertisements facing down; the missing children, faded-looking, depicted along with their abductors in that faded-looking shade of blue, all facing up. He stands there shuffling for a while, then goes to the mailbox, fans them out into a tray, and scoops the bones out onto this. It's all the same. It's all just perfect. Clean and white as it can be as if a chicken—which is what it is; a chicken—as if a chicken were something precious like that, endangered or extinct. The skull's here, too, although less perfect than the rest; there's a depression in the tiny cranial bulb, and a little crack. But other than that it's all complete, a perfect set, the whole thing somehow less surprising, less disturbing— how it got here, why someone would want to do it—than simply heartbreaking in a strange way. All the effort. Such a worthless pile of bones. He has to use both hands and still some pieces fall. He slings them out into the field, wads up the coupons, calls to the dog, and heads on back.

What wakes him this time in the middle of the night is a conviction— the literal sense of which departs now with the dream although the

David Searcy

effect, the emotional lurch, persists—that somehow he's come adrift, the trailer slipped its mooring, slowly, gently floating on the tide until it's so far out from shore that, should he look, there would be nothing. Only stars and grass—or water; he's not clear on that, not sure it makes a difference. It's a thought like: I'm not breathing. Like it's built up over time (when was the last time, for example, he heard a car come down the road). Like when your body forgets to breathe, the way you do sometimes for a minute and for a minute it's all right but at some point it wakes you up with a terrible start. As if the gentle slap of water against the dock were suddenly missed and realized to have been replaced some time ago by something else—the smooth, flat, uninflected surface of the deep and the deep uncertainty of what that may contain. He thinks there may have been a lurch, an actual lurch. Or else he dreamed it—a little bump the way a fish will bump the bait. He sits up, takes a breath, and puts his hands down firmly on the bed. He looks for Yurang, hears him now, his breath, not panting, just his breathing right beside him. There's no moon yet so it's dark as it can be. Now, there. No doubt—a little bump. The trailer shifts. He wants to think it's Yurang doing something, jumping off the bed or off the couch or something, acting strange but here he is. He starts to put his hand out, touch the dog, but reconsiders. There, again. He feels the bed shake just a little, just a quiver but all over like the structure of the trailer moved entirely all at once. A little bump but very broadly, very generally applied. He gets his legs up under him, backs into the corner. Yurang's breathing starts to catch a growly flutter. What if someone fell asleep in a little boat that drifted into a school of whales—there might be nothing he could do. He might just curl up in the bottom and wait it out. Each little bump might be just that—an incidental point of contact— huge and terrible events might slip right past and not develop, might not suddenly heave him up and over unimaginably like the world gone upside down.

The fluttery growl—the deepest, basest, most unstable state of threat—continues, it seems, for several minutes. It has a natural respiratory rhythm, joins the other normal functions. Loathing and terror just like breathing, just like falling off a log. A fairly bright star to the southwest is producing that illusion with the louvres of the window above the table, its reflected image rising as the star itself descends. Luther eases down and carefully gathers the pillow up behind him, watches the double star converging—one glass louvre, then the next until at last it sinks from view.

21

"**Y**ou wanna see one?"

"What?" she asks. They're in the Vingo Grocery parking lot. It's only nine or so but getting hot already. She's not feeling well. She'd like to put the sack of groceries in the car, direct the air-conditioning vents all toward her face and place the orange juice in the plastic Kleenex holder, drink the whole quart on the winding, hilly road back to the house.

"Come over here." He starts to walk back to the squad car, turns and motions with his head, his huge emphatic cowboy hat.

"I don't. . . ."

"Come on."

She can hear his radio making sputtery, urgent noises. He reaches in, withdraws the microphone and stands there with it, waiting, constituting, now, an official situation. It's Saturday, not too many people out. A package boy on break stands by the news rack smoking, combing a beautiful coif of auburn hair. He turns and nods. He's not a boy. His face looks old, bizarrely pinched beneath his pompadour as if some terrible trade-off were involved.

"Two-oh-one to one-fourteen"—the sheriff winks—"y'all hold off now, don't go messin' with that thing." A squawk returns. It might be laughter. The package boy keeps staring at her. He holds the cigarette and the comb in the same hand somehow, moving easily back and forth between the sublime and the grotesque, attending both sides of the bargain without embarrassment. "And get me a picture now, you hear?" The sheriff smiles and lowers the mike. "They're real good boys but they get sloppy." The grocery sack is getting heavy, awkward to hold. Her purse is slipping off her shoulder. He leaves the microphone dangling, comes and takes the sack, his huge thick hands replacing hers with too much contact; too much fragrance also—shockingly at odds with him, his bluntness and his bulk, such spicy, floral aftershave, cologne or whatever. It makes her dizzy almost—the fumes, the contradiction. "Bet you got one of them buttons on your keys."

"Oh, sorry; yes." She fumbles around in her purse a moment; there's a click, a flash of parking lights. He leans in, puts the groceries on the seat and pauses like that, feels the leather seat, the headrest, backs out, shuts the door, and stands there for a second looking thoughtful, turns, and smiles. His radio's squawking, blurting and hissing rather horribly—unintelligible exclamations, barks and static; occasional snatches of that dismissive official drawl designed to convey the most appalling information, she feels sure, with perfect ease. Such information, even now, might be encrypted, carried somewhere, thinned, compressed, within the noise as if the hiss itself were essential to certain kinds of really terrible information— the way those awful cockpit tapes of some poor aircrew's final moments always seem to require a transcript (the news reporter with her head cocked, looking grim) although the sound is quite sufficient by itself to give you chills.

"Well, you seen two—seen that first one fell apart I understand; and then that other"—he looks down and starts to hitch up his equipment—"makes you the expert I suppose." It seems to her he shouldn't try to look so neatly pressed and starched; he should be rumpled, let duty hang and sag about him. He should really let it go. "And anyway"—he takes his hat off, runs his hand across his hair too thin, it seems, to groom with fingers thick as clubs—"you wanna get back on that horse." He smiles. "You figure?"

"What?"

"You know."

"I think. . . ."

"Back on that horse that throwed you."

"I'm all right." He's coming over.

"This one's out there plain as day; ain't gonna sneak up on you or nothin'." Again the fragrance. She looks away. The coiffured package boy is gone. "Wood County. Not too far off. Not more'n fifteen miles." He calls it this one—just like that, just one in a series, un-

150   David Searcy

pleasant perhaps but one of those things. Just one of those things. "Them boys over there say this here one looks kinda silly."

"Don't say that."

"Beg pardon?"

"Nothing." Half the pine trees to the west look like they're dead. It's pine bore beetles—or pine borer beetles—someone told her.

"You know what she says?" He's come up right next to her.

"Who?"

"She says them things are blessed."

Where's her gum—she had it right here in her purse.

"That's what she says and know what else?"

"No." Here it is, a brand-new pack.

"Says course they're animal parts; that's the part gets left behind—you believe that?"

"No."

"Huh?"

"No. Not literally."

"Not literally?"

"Not exactly. No. Oh shit." The pack springs open, gum goes flying. "Jesus."

"Here."

"No please, just leave it." He gets up and simply stands there for a moment in the morning light resplendent, fragrant, vast.

"You got anything there gonna melt?" He nods at the car.

She thinks of her orange juice, shakes her head.

"You get your cattle?"

For a second she's a blank. "Oh no. Not yet. Soon though."

"Charolais?"

"Yes. Charolais."

"Good meat."

"Oh?"

"Yep. Real good." The hissing of the radio makes the fragrance seem to escape from him like gas. "We best get goin'." She looks around at all the Chiclets on the pavement, locks her car, and zips her purse.

. . .

The planted pines, the fully grown ones, are so odd. Especially where, as here, they constitute the forest—pine plantation on both sides of the narrow road; it looks almost like real woods until you catch the angle right and they line up like rows of corn. So odd to think of trees that way—provisional, warehoused in a sense; such fundamental and substantial things. Like finding where they store the hills and streams. It suggests the things you think should form a basic notion of the world are arbitrary, picked at random out of a bin; tends to make you regard even perfectly natural settings with suspicion and, by extension perhaps (she really shouldn't have come; she's feeling carsick, has to take deep breaths of air that smells like cigarettes and flowers and something else—the actual smell, the natural odor of the sheriff sneaking through; and the trees so close on either side she gets that apprehensive feeling, keeps her feet pressed to the floorboard as if to brake should something lurch into the road) . . . and by extension perhaps the world in general seems somewhat uncertain—at least this part of it which has always felt uneasy to her in any case, right at the vague, obscure convergence of three states just as they seem to lose distinctive statelike qualities; individual picture-postcard characteristics fall away toward something pleasant enough—the trees, the numerous artificial lakes—but slack somehow, without conviction. They even name it. Arklatex. Or The Arklatex. The local TV news reporters like to use the term a lot—the news from nowhere in particular live at five and there it is and sure enough it might be anywhere with pine trees, red dirt, artificial lakes. She thinks she might be going to throw up any second. "Whoa, look out." He almost overshoots the turn, brakes hard, and skids the car around then hits the siren as he bounces across the cattle guard which pretty much undoes her for a moment, makes her shut her eyes and clutch her shoulder strap. He makes a production of it, roaring across the clearing—lights and siren, kicking up dust— to the other vehicle, green with a silver pine-tree emblem, parked way out there by itself, its front doors open, two deputies it looks like, one inside the car, one standing watching the sheriff as he pulls up, climbs out, stretches, braces himself there lazily, elbows on the doorframe and the roof. She can't really see very well around him; out the window on her side it's empty field, some sort of stubble.

"Lord amighty look at you," the deputy says. The sun is well above the trees and making everything behind a hazy glare.

"By God, Cotton, when they let you carry a gun?"

The white-haired deputy removes his sunglasses "Boy, I sure do like them boots."

It's like dogs meeting in the street. She tries to see around the other car in front—the other deputy's eating something out of a sack, now leaning across—"Hey, next time sling a little more dirt"— a truly horrible-looking huge round yellow pastry in his hand.

"Well lookee there now." The sheriff hitches up his pants, walks over to him. "How'd you know I ain't had breakfast?"

"Hell you ain't."

"Don't be like that."

"Shit."

"Watch your language."

"What? Oh." Silence for a minute then more softly, "I'll give her some."

Oh God she whispers, now he'll come and tap the window and say this man of considerable importance in his county has offered her some of this revolting substance and to refuse would mean dishonor and disgrace. She shuts her eyes again. It's not here. It's not going to be simple. She's not to have a preliminary view, an easy approach across a field. They're going to drive somewhere to see it— through the trees and all of a sudden there it will be right in her face like something captured in the headlights in a graveyard on a date and meant to scare her half to death. By now her orange juice will be warm.

"So what'd y'all do just go ahead and haul it off?"

"It's over yonder." It's the white-haired one again. She looks around. They're standing together, facing away. The deputy's pointing.

"Why's it yonder?"

"'Cause that's where it is." He's got his sunglasses on again; he grins at the sheriff. "'Cause ole Bo ain't had his breakfast." Bo's still at it. Now and then he'll glance at her. She looks away, gets out of the car.

"Too silly for Bo?"

"It ain't the silly."

"What?"

"The smell. Bo felt quite strongly."

"'Bout two hundred yards. I guess he did."

"You can smell it now."

"Shit . . . Oh, beg pardon." She's come up to see where they're looking. She shades her eyes. A denser haze, almost a mist, above the stubble diffuses the glare. It makes a lovely golden glow. He's moved behind her, one huge hand now on her shoulder, turning her slightly, the other pointing (how can it point with any accuracy; it's much too blunt, too gross; it indicates whole acres at a time) but there; she sees it; something.

"Smell it?" says the deputy.

How could there be anything to smell so far away. It's not very big whatever it is and surely there's some sort of inverse square rule . . . "Oh," she says. "It moved."

"Yeah that's pretty silly too, the way it's hung up there real delicate like one a them things—you know."

"Piñata?" she says.

"Yeah." A pause. He looks uncertain.

"Mobile?"

"Yeah like one a them—my sister's baby had one hangin' over its crib; you just open the door and that thing goes to tiltin' back and forth and ever which way." He looks at her, white hair and dark glasses disconcertingly like the frightening mono-appellative German popular singer, Heino. An album cover in fact. Heino in curious local costume: Heino in The Arklatex; Deputy Heino. The sheriff's hand is still on her shoulder. She moves away. Bo has emerged. He's standing tucking in his shirt, a smiley crescent of yellow pastry in his mouth—he's coming over, still working to get it all tucked in, pastry stuck there idiotically; why doesn't he eat it; any second it will start to look congenial, colorful possibly, an exotic labial ornament. She feels a shudder, walks out in the field away from the squad cars toward the object a couple of yards. ". . . you shoulda seen that baby bat that thing around," the deputy's saying, "do it for hours, just go to hittin' at that thing, ringin' them bells . . ." At the edge of the field, right at the fence, on the other side of which is corn or something tall like that, a tree—a pecan perhaps—sends out a long and graceful branch. It hangs from that. There must be a cord too thin to see—the glare obscures it, the golden haze. The thing itself—it moves so slowly—must be flat or nearly so; sometimes it thins, elongates, almost disappears except for a bulgy part in the middle. Were she to stand here at this distance long enough she might deduce it in its phases, figure it out, not have to approach the thing at all, not have to take the personal risk. There is a faint, peculiar smell. ". . . like them kids you hear about got somethin' wrong, just sit around and bang their heads against the wall and stuff like that, well this here sorta got like that, got to where that's all she wanted to do; they'd try and take it down but, man. . . ." He pauses, after a while says, "Jesus," very softly. She can sense they're looking at her. It's stopped moving. She must wait now for it to tilt a different way—the air has changed, the cord has twisted, something's happened. She's about to let herself start seeing things, making things more than they are if she's not careful. She can feel it like a migraine, like those "cluster" headaches people claim to sense before they happen. Things acquire a sort of aura. Such a beautiful golden haze like in that lyric from the musical *Oklahoma!*—Gordon MacRae with his hat pushed back, arms out and singing in the corn. Now here it comes. Now tilting slightly. ". . . anyway." (They're moving now.) "She still don't talk a whole lot—tell you what though, she is just as sweet as she can be and purty too. I will say that. I will say that. I got a Polaroid. . . ." It appears to tilt this way because the sunlight plays across it for a second, just a flash, a glossy ripple. Is it wet? The smell again. It stops her. She's been walking toward it. This is fine. Right here. The smell and the delicacy of it, the shimmer and balance, are at odds. It's like the sheriff and his fragrance but the other way around—and worse, or deeper, the disagreement more profound. ". . . is that a angel, huh?" They're crunching across the field. "You oughta see the way they get her all dressed up. Is that a perfect little angel?" It's coming around now, about to show itself to advantage, the critical aspect, even though it's just a shadow, a silhouette against the corn or whatever it is. It's like that instant when, approaching something unusual in the road, you know it's going to be some sort of little tragedy before there's any particular feature to distinguish it from trash, a chunk of tire; as if the essential form of ruin, mortal damage, were described by a line as subtle and as strong and with as powerful an appeal to intuition as that which, made with one of those artful ocher crayons, say, to trace the reclining sweep of naked torso, hip, and thigh, evokes the sense of life, the whole thing just like that, the twist and surge of life in general. It has limbs, sticklike projections—now they're clearer—which are what, viewed sideways, looked like thinned extensions of the body. Sunlight catches the upper two; they're sort of flung out—being flung out, as it appears, by that illusion which, absent other visual clues, makes the rotation of distant objects so ambiguous, hard to determine in its direction, that the mind gives up in favor of the simpler, more spectacular explanation that the object is changing shape. It looks like that; the arms—the sticks, whatever they are—seem to thrust out slowly into a full and, in that way that even a stick figure can be so expressive, wildly celebratory gesture while the ones below, the legs (the anthropomorphic interpretation has taken hold as of course it will given half a chance; which is all it is; she's in control) . . . the legs, the sticks, cross very delicately at the ends like pointed toes—so oddly exultant and balletic for just a moment, holding the angle; something really very awkward with a bloated, lumpish body jumping nevertheless for joy, the painful-looking bend at top (as if whatever it is has buckled, possibly ruptured) joining the image (notwithstanding there's no head as such) as arcing back and neck, eyes lifted (one imagines eyes in any case), all weirdly buoyant as a cartoon dancing cow or sheep or something, straining upward— what if blessedness smelled like that? What if the real thing smelled just awful to the undeserving, unenlightened sticking up their noses at the stench of death transcended, *joie de mort*; it's easy enough for Gordon MacRae—he has a head; he has a hat; he's not been damaged, killed, run over as this thing, for all its Balinese-shadow-puppet-like exuberance, looks as if it may have been. The sheriff's hand is on her shoulder. "Hey." She flinches. "You okay?" She nods. "So whatcha think?" She thinks it's nothing all of a sudden. Now it's lost it, dead, not springing now but sagging, just dead weight, the strain reversed, the shape suggesting something hauled up, broken-jointed, by the extremities like a carcass or a handbag—now it looks just like a handbag. Now it changes once again; it turns again light as a kite. She feels a breeze. The deputies take an oblique approach across the field as if seeking a slight upwind advantage. She can hear them.

"Dang," says Cotton.

"Shit," says Bo.

The sheriff gives her a little pat and goes to join them. There's a mockingbird over that way, in that tree perhaps. A stream of little twitters, complex phrases, each one different. How can it do that automatically? Like a computer seeking primes, the value of pi; a "difference engine," tiny gears inside withdrawing, re-combining every time: no that's not it, no that's not it.

"Hey, look there now," says Cotton, "looks just like a tar baby, don't it?"

"What?" says Bo.

"A tar baby—you know?"

"What?"

"You know."

They're getting out of range. Just the mockingbird now. She wonders if, should it ever find it, it will stop. If all the mockingbirds will stop. "Oh goddamn, Jesus." She hears that. Bo stops. The others walk up to it. Now it looks like something else, from here at least, foreshortened—something like those ugly, spiky things you find on beaches. What do they call them—mermaid's purses—but in fact they're something's egg case. Hard black pillow-shaped little pouches with those nasty curly spike things at the corners. It's the egg case of a skate. That's what they are. Which tells her nothing— what's a skate?—except the adult form sounds unpleasant. Names of marine life—the obscurer kinds especially, the kinds that might not get a name except for fishermen or sailors who probably bother to name things only out of brutal necessity like cursing—tend to be unpleasant. "Skate." It makes her shiver—"mermaid's purse" sounds like that snickering sort of euphemism like "prairie oysters." "Beaver pie." Oh Lord don't poke it. Now the sheriff's got a stick. Of course that's right, that's what you do. Before you name it, hit it. Gaff it. Bo's withdrawn a few more yards. The sheriff reaches. Please don't let there be a sound. She can't imagine any sound that wouldn't make it even worse. He's got it swinging. Now just standing there and watching. Now he's looking at his stick. Is this police work? First you poke it. Surely that's inscribed in Latin somewhere— already sounds like Latin. Why is there a stick, a long straight stick there anyway, right to hand. It's probably evidence. It doesn't matter. It's still swinging. It's precessing, if that's the word. The arc it swings through rotates slowly. If a stylus hung down from it, as from a pendulum, into a smooth white bed of sand it would, after a while, trace out a pattern like a flower. The sheriff's waiting for it to come around to where its swing goes straight away and back so he can get a solid hit. He makes a feint as Cotton backs up just a little. Now he's set. The poke. A thump, a sort of snap, and then a whoosh as it collapses, folds up, spilling something out. She turns and walks back toward the car. "Oh shit." That's Bo. "Oh goddamn shit." There's really no compelling reason she should live down here; no reason not to stay in Dallas; teach, do something useful. This is silly. They can drop it all like that. Forget the cows. Go home. She stops and turns around. Bo's on his way, hand on his hat, equipment flapping, jingling change and labored breathing trotting past. The other two are where they were. Just standing, looking, someone repeating something—Cotton shakes his head; it must be him—it sounds like "darlin'" over and over.

When, as happened now and then when she was a child, she'd find herself at a scary movie in the company of braver friends she had a technique to filter out the scariest parts—though not altogether and not conspicuously—whereby, cupping her chin in her hands, she'd bring her index fingers up to close her ears (she convinced herself it looked quite natural) while her little fingers hovered very discreetly before her eyes like those fuzzy computer-generated shadows used to mask the faces of videotaped offenders and informants. She could allow herself to imagine something else was going on so, while she vaguely heard the screams, the horrible gnashings—just as now she hears the radio squawking away, Bo struggling to not just blurt things out, to take deep breaths and find the proper frame of mind, the proper cadence, squeeze it all, the horrible blurty parts and all, into that easy, thin transmissible tone of voice; just as she winces at the arrival of the sheriff and the deputy (standing near her; moving away—". . . don't need no records; bet you money. Poor little darlin'. Bet you any amount of money that thing's her. Poor little thing. Get me a Polaroid. Never seen one quite that little. Cotton? Yeah, I'll get a picture . . .")—so, though terror swirls about, impinges, it might be masked or filtered (not unlike a simple "la, la, I can't hear you" but internal, more creative) and the least offensive bits might recombine toward something comforting and bright: in this case Heino; not his lookalike but the real one—she leans back, she feels the breeze come through the car—the real one out there in the corn or whatever it is, if not as high as an elephant's eye, still high enough to make a back-drop for him, white-haired, dressed in white with two white German shepherd dogs like on a poster she saw once, all very Christ-like washed in a gorgeous golden misty morning light and singing a medley of favorite *Oklahoma!* songs in his native tongue. She thinks she's probably never wanted a drink as bad as she does now.

Heading back the trees look just the same except she can't quite catch the angle, find the rows. The hazy sunlight flickers through across her face with such suspicious regularity she assumes they're artificial. Planted pines. Perhaps they're staggered. Soon there will be no way to tell. They'll get so good, become so cunning with the artificial lakes and trees and whatnot. They'll adjust the way the sun comes through as well and all the rest and then who cares. Who'll know the difference. The floral aftershave has faded, overtaxed. He cracks the windows.

"Sorry. Guess I'm gonna need a change of clothes."

The pines thin out—perhaps they're real ones after all or maybe blighted; some look dead. They open up, give way to meadow. It's a very small dirt road.

"That didn't work out like I thought."

"No."

"That little girl . . ."

"I know."

". . . been missin' about a month."

He takes a turn. The road reduces even further to a grassy, rutted lane between wire fences, open fields. The left side falls away to terraced ponds and pasture.

"Where. . . ."

"Hold on."

They crest the rise. He stops and rolls the windows down the rest of the way, turns off the engine. Oh my God it is a date, she thinks; he's scared her really good and now she's ready. Just like high school. Oh my God. He sighs. "Look yonder."

"What?"

"Look yonder. Look over yonder."

She leans forward. He gets out. She sits a moment, opens the door, gets out, and walks over to the fence. "Oh."

"Ain't they purty."

"Yes."

"Old Harley's got probably two or three hundred."

"Charolais?"

"Yep, Charolais. Real nice ones too."

"They are."

"Yep."

"My." She folds her hands on top of the fence post. He goes back to reach in the car, returns with something. It's a bottle. He breaks the seal, unscrews the cap, and hands it to her. She looks at him a moment. He's stepped back. He looks quite rumpled now. He produces a tin of snuff, withdraws a pinch, inserts it, smiles. How touching, almost—a prophylactic. As if the smell weren't quite enough, it serves to limit his intentions; serves to purify the offering.

She looks at the flat pint bottle, rests it in both hands atop the post. When was the last time she had bourbon? Back in high school, she imagines, when to refuse it meant dishonor and disgrace. Mixed with Coke as she recalls. Or was that rum? Some sweetish, pungent sort of liquor. She leans above it, breathes it in. Oh that's it, yes. That wonderful sweetness like an apology; something medicinal like those cough drops, cherry-flavored—here, I'm sorry; you must take this with a little bit of sugar. It might hurt some going down but you'll feel better and you have been through a lot; and here's a vista—hard to come by in these parts—where all the bad thoughts can disperse; and cows. And cows, so pale, identical, gently scattered like a child's thoughts; like the room of a little child with cow-print wallpaper—cows to count and to believe in; in their passiveness and safety, their conduciveness to sleep.

22

"What you got?" asks Avery.

"Washers."

"Yeah? That all?"

"No. Got some cheese," says Luther.

"Cheese?"

"Yeah. Right here." Luther lifts the sack with the little packets of American cheese and gives it a shake—"cheese"—puts it down then lifts the other sack and shakes it—"washers"—puts it down on the bench.

Avery leans back, squints at the street and the courthouse, folds his hands across his stomach. "Cheese and washers." Sweat is starting to darken his collar. "Well, by God, I guess you're set." The square is more or less deserted. Over at Joe's across the way a tall young man with a scraggly beard is doing something to the sign. He's going up and down a ladder.

"Where's your puppy dog?"

"Home. Where's Royce?"

"He's feelin' puny."

"Yeah?"

"Just feelin' kinda puny." Avery yawns and shades his eyes, looks up and down the empty street. They've got the decorations up. It helps to have some sense beforehand where they are to get the overall effect. The somewhat ghostly wreathes and reindeer, stars and angels—fairly minimal tinseled outlines—tend to disappear among the supporting structures (light poles, traffic-light suspension cables), seem to hover about less like the things themselves than markers showing where they go or where they've been. The tall young man has gone inside. The sign is flickering, not quite catching, colors sputtering very faintly in the sunlight. Now he comes back out and stands there looking at it.

"What the hell you do to your arm?"

Luther puts it in his lap with his right hand over it. "Cut it."

"Yeah? On what?"

"On somethin'. I don't know. Ain't nothin'."

"Huh," says Avery, sitting up and taking a big white handkerchief from his pocket, folding it twice, wiping his forehead then his neck, holding it back there for a minute. The young man disappears again. The flickering stops.

"End of the world," says Avery.

"Yep," says Luther, taking a drink of root beer.

"How many shoppin' days you figure?"

"Shit."

"Huh?"

"Shit, who knows."

Joe's come outside to monitor the sign, yells something, steps into the street and yells again, stands there awhile then looks around and goes back in.

"You get some bread?" He's holding his handkerchief by the corners, leaning forward, waving it gently back and forth.

"Got some already."

"Good." He's flipping it up and over now until it's all rolled up, then back the other way; just doing that over and over first one way and then the other. "Know why?"

"No."

"So you can make yourself a cheese and washer sandwich."

Luther finishes off the root beer. Avery's folding up his handkerchief again; he dabs his eyes then sighs, emits a little chuckle, shakes his head. The framework Santa across the street on the courthouse lawn is starting to lean. The single board that props it up is bending in and slipping a little, making the tinsel all hang in away from the outline of the body as if a wind were blowing through him; making him lean back like he's looking at the sky. The grass is clear of leaves; it's just been mown it looks like. Dust and clippings yellow the walk, a faint dead-grassy smell in the air. The courthouse benches need to be put back on the lawn. You can see the dead spots in the grass where they usually go—two rows, four benches each; white-painted two-by-four and strap-steel benches facing each other across the approach to the courthouse steps. Someone's left them on the pavement. Luther puts his cheese and his washers into his backpack, zips it up. For a while they sit there without talking, Avery leaning forward, head down holding his handkerchief behind his neck. From over at Joe's a delicate tapping as of someone trying to loosen a rusted screw. Avery yawns again. He stands up after a minute, puts his handkerchief in his pocket, places his hands at the small of his back, bends backward, stretching. "Yessir, Royce showed up this mornin feelin' puny so I said just go on home." He brings his arms up, twists a little left and right. "Just go on home." He stops. The tall young man is back up on the ladder. Avery walks out to the curb, looks at the sky. "I told him might as well just go on. . . ." There's a sort of rumbling somewhere. ". . . don't know why we don't close up on Mondays anyway like them city. . . ." Now again. It sounds like thunder. Avery looks at Luther, squints up at the sky again. It's white. Not cloudy white. Just hazy, washed-out white without a hint of blue. Across the street an old man in overalls has appeared, regards the benches. He just stands there sort of hovering like a bird above a fallen nest. He can't sit down. There's something wrong. He looks at the sky. The rumbling rises to a level sympathetic with the window glass behind, which starts to buzz. Then it subsides. For a moment everything is quiet. The neon-sign man on his ladder pauses, looks in their direction or maybe past them to the south. The old man turns that way as well. A sort of haze, a thin white smoke, is drifting in from around the corner. From the street that runs from the south straight into the courthouse it emerges, spreads, diffuses across the square, the courthouse lawn. It has an oily, hot-machinery kind of smell. And now the rumbling, sounding nearer, starts again; this time in escalating surges—vroom, it goes; then louder, gradually gaining amplitude and volume like one of those toy cars—friction cars— you had to push against the floor a number of times to get them all revved up before you let them go. It's doing that. It's revving up— whoever it is is going to blow it. You can hear the cams or something start to clatter. Smoke is drifting into the square again. The sound booms off the buildings, off the courthouse—a terrible grinding rattly roar. He's got to be pushing way over the redline now. It sounds like something's really starting to go—like when you zoomed those little friction cars too fast they'd start to chatter, hit some oscillating frequency, shut right down and never work quite right again, although some kids just couldn't seem to grasp the principle; they'd keep shoving it harder and harder until the wheels came off or something. This is like that. This is taking it way beyond the point of recovery—no longer surging, just a wild ascending screech, a hair-raising complex of unlubricated harmonics mixing in at this point, steel on steel like when a drill hits granite. Avery's face is totally blank. The air is white. Now squealing tires. It must be a V-8—he burns rubber almost all the way to second. He hits third as he appears from between the buildings—a blue-green pickup with the bed piled up with stuff. It seems so odd to go to third right there a few feet from the curb as if he figured he might simply plow through everything, through the courthouse and keep on going. As he hits the curb the front end leaves the ground so then the rear hits and the whole thing's in the air and tilting forward; all the contents of the bed come flying out—the pots and pans, a set of box springs, open cartons full of dishes, clothes, and whatnot. Then he slams into the benches; the ones on the right get scattered, tumble across the lawn while the others stack up somehow right in front of the truck, precede it into the courthouse steps—a row of benches end-to-end that buckles violently like a train wreck throwing one so high it lands up on the parapet of the balcony above the entrance, teeters there as the truck flips over and slides tail-first up onto the porch with the three brick archways, going sideways, bending double with the impact as it lodges upside down in the central opening. There's a fairly gentle shower of loosened mortar, chunks of brick. The engine idles, burbles quietly for a second then cuts off. A sense of particles—smoke as well—but especially particles, tiny bits of stuff just floating all around; residual smoky swirls of turbulence in the air above the street. And for a moment not a sound except the soft, continuous cursing of the tall young man who's fallen off his ladder. Avery sits down next to Luther.

At some point before the fire truck and the ambulance and with people, even deputies and police, not certain quite yet how to approach the situation—the smell of gasoline, the steady bomblike ticking from the cracked and cooling metal—Leonard crawls out through the window, sort of half-rolls down the steps, then stands and looks around, steps back, looks at the wreck. He finds a bench that's landed upright, takes a seat, and spits a long dark stream then lies down like a vagrant and appears to go to sleep.

The courthouse lawn looks like a garage sale and, eventually, as the wreck cools and the gasoline gets hosed and the ambulance leaves with Leonard still asleep or comatose or dead and things seem more or less under control, the people start to wander around among the various scattered items, pausing now and then to look at this or that. Policemen tell them not to touch and so they don't but still they drift about well into the afternoon as shadows deepen. They look at every little thing as if they'd never seen such things or seen them like this, out in the open like this, things much like the things they have at home but not like theirs, just different enough that you can tell.

A wrecker tries to free the truck. His tires make great-big double ruts in the courthouse lawn. They try the winch but that begins to crack the limestone over the arch. They'll have to get a torch and cut it. Periodically, after the TV crews arrive, it glows, illuminated for the time it takes to interview someone or give a story posed in front.

The volunteer firemen hang around till almost everyone has left. They hose the steps a few more times and make a project of the Santa, getting him upright, adding a brace, and placing bricks along the base at front and back to keep him steady.

Luther has made room for Dolores. Now and then she shakes her head and whispers Goodness me or Dios or something in Spanish. She sits a while then goes back in, returns with sandwiches and drinks. It's getting dark. A couple of firemen roll up the hose while others lower the teetering bench down from the parapet. Others stand about. One turns to wave at Dolores.

"Whatever happened to that old man?" asks Luther.

"What old man?" asks Avery.

The neon sign casts intermittent flickery shadows. Dolores sighs and places a napkin on her knee.

23

There's nothing to stand on. Nothing to put on top of the trailer just to gain a little height, a little perspective. How strange to lack a simple thing like that. He hasn't a single piece of furniture as such. It's all built-in. He leans over the bed, looks out the window at the tree tops barely silhouetted now. It's nearly dawn. He folds up the little Formica table, tugs on the storage cabinet-seat. One side pulls free—it's only nailed—and the drawers collapse. The whole thing's falling apart. He tries to push it back into place, sits on it, bounces, feels the trailer start to tilt. Yurang is waiting. He still can't believe the door won't open to him, let him jump the step and shoot straight out into the field, into the grass. His ears are pricked. He lifts one paw and then the other. Luther stands, Yurang gets up, looks up at Luther. "Stay," says Luther. Yurang hops onto the couch and puts his nose up to the glass. Out there in the grass in the faint gray light his scent, his trails, are fading away. The door slaps shut. An extra push to make it latch as Luther looks down at the homemade wooden step. It's framed with two-by-fours and topped with half-inch plywood—hardly enough to make a difference. He kicks the lumber scraps beside it, looks at the trap, the one he made from Agnes's crate, walks over to it, leans on it, presses with his weight. It's maybe two-feet high on its side. He gets it balanced against his shoulder, both hands under, bends his knees, and heaves it up. It makes an awful-sounding crash and gets the puppies all excited. He hates to think about the mess if their box tips over. Now the hard part—one foot up on the propane tank, the other feeling for the narrow sheet-metal ridge at the end of the trailer, he has to jump to grab the ventilation pipe. He hauls himself onto the roof and skins his elbow trying not to use that hand. He scoots to the edge. His arm hurts all the way to the shoulder. He sits for a moment holding it up against his chest, which seems to help. He tends to hold it up a lot. Last night he tried to keep it up against the wall above his head, occasionally dozing off to repetitive dreams about his arm, himself and his arm somehow confused, his arm in the grass, his arm as bait and further confused, in that wildly irrational way dreams have when you have a fever, with the quarters of cheese sandwich placed at intervals out in the field away from the trailer. They seem to have calmed things, kept the trailer from rocking about in the middle of the night. It's still too dark. There's just the grayness of the grass. He scoots to the left, reaches for the trap and pulls it over, turns it crosswise to the trailer with one end at the very edge. It seems exactly what he needs, this sort of thing. At least it did last night in the dark with his arm propped up. One wants to elevate one's point of view. You want to see what's in the water. You want to stand up, keep your balance in the boat, be still, and look down past reflections, past the surface. He gets up, supports himself on the trap as he straddles it, gets one foot up and then the other, pauses like that on all fours on top of the trap on top of the trailer in the dark. Or not so dark. It's brightening. He can see the sticks—at least a couple he's pretty sure—that mark the locations of the sandwiches. Somewhere long ago he saw a trained pig walk a tightrope—parallel tightropes actually—just about like this, the pig's legs spreading so precariously farther and farther as it made its way along. He stands up carefully, moves toward the edge with little steps to keep from tipping left or right. Why should the simplest thing like this be so much trouble. Just to gain a little altitude. Just to get up out of bed sometimes, in fact. He's at the edge. He stands up straight and looks straight out across the field. It makes a difference. A foot and a half, two feet at most, and now he's in another realm. The waning moon is high in the south. He feels he's stepped right up here with it. He lifts his arms away from his side, imagines floating. Maybe vultures fly so high to get a better sense of the overall situation. Maybe you have to start with that; not try to look right at the thing you're looking for but rather seek the broader, deeper possibilities, the mortal tendencies at large. The grassy texture starts to emerge now here and there. He can see the sticks quite well—all four, spaced out in an arc, all to the south. It's just about right. The watery grayness. Even, colorless, indecisive morning light without opinion. You can see things for a moment with indifference, without having to think about them; thoughts of grass and trees are just as faint and clear as thoughts of air. You see into it. Where the grass has been disturbed, not quite sprung back, it makes a shadow—something's passage like a wake that closes slowly, smoothes out slowly. Almost as if whatever passed by were still passing. You can sense the general presence; probabilities like fishing, knowing sort of where to cast; where something's likely to have been and then a point where doubt collapses altogether, where it lies down, settles down into the grass there by the first stick (or the last stick) to the east and leaves a shadow of itself, a pressed-down place, just like a deer will do; and big as that, at least as big as that—he brings his arms up to his chest—and more expansive, not curled up but sprawling out snow-angel-like. Light strikes his face. Red morning sun flares through a gap low in the trees. He's dazzled, head and chest aglow. It's like he's burst up to the surface for a moment, treading water. Then he takes a deep breath, gets down off the crate, slips very carefully, still half-blinded, off the front end of the trailer to the ground.

Whack, goes the foot-square pegboard sheet with slots cut in it. Whack again. It slides across the other sheet without resistance almost. Washers act as bearings. One per straw. Sixty-six straws (or one-inch sections). Staggered rows (a straw in every other hole) to give an even distribution. Straws on bottom poking up into the slots—each made by cutting between adjoining holes—on top. A pair of rubber bands for tension. Whack. The top sheet slips across between the guides and strikes the stops; the straws compress. It gives him pleasure as if it had no other purpose. As if the effect, the gratification, might be a transferable sort of benefit, even marketable like those gadgets you see on TV late at night: for only nineteen ninety-five a thing, a device, which placed on a table, say, near a window—a narrow screened and louvred window through which all the world seems bleak as bleak can be, reduced to grassy apprehension, hopeless, vague, diffuse, and unrelieved by any point of reference where the mind can find attachment; from which window thoughts go out but don't return with any precision, come back scattered like the chaff or whatever they called it, bags of foil they used to toss behind a plane to fool the radar, like the gold flecks in the white Formica table (although sometimes, now and then, and especially now as setting sunlight finds the right reflective angle through the window above the couch, you pick out patterns, think you see things in the blips)—a device which, placed by such a window, then, or anywhere for that matter in the privacy of your home, engages anguish and uncertainty, gives them format, frames the question, lines up all those little doubts, those little apprehensive blips, into a regular linked array and turns them back upon themselves. It's not a camera. Whack. No mere receptive vessel can provide such peace of mind, can make this promise. Whack. And promise, to be sure, is quite enough; at least for now. The sunlight's fading. Flecks of gold in the Formica lose their glow. The puppies need to come inside. It's time for Yurang's evening walk. He gets the leash, stands by the door, flicks on the light for just a second. What a mess—the sawdust, inch-long pegboard cutouts scattered everywhere. It's all a mess. The model on the table looks absurd now. He's a crazy man. He turns the light off. When he gets back he'll make sandwiches. One cut straight across the way he always likes it, and another cut in quarters for the field.

24

He's outside the fence. Just standing and watching. It's been a week or more since he's seen her; long enough to feel he can't just walk right in. He puts his pack down, leans on the pickets. "So what are you doin'?" She's got a quart-size can of white paint on the ground next to her, bending with a brush in one hand, holding back her pleated skirt with the other, painting rocks.

"What's it look like?"

"Paintin' rocks."

"Well there you are."

"Huh."

"Goodness me." She groans and winces as she gets down on her knees to do the bottom, to get the line right, keep it even about an inch above the ground all the way around.

"How come you do that?" A bead of paint accumulates and here and there sends little dribbles into the sand.

"So you don't like it?"

"Sure, I guess."

"Well then I guess that's why I do it."

"Thanks," says Luther after a minute.

"You're quite welcome. Oh." She gets up with an effort, holds the brush away and looks down at the rock. It's glossy white. She hasn't thinned the paint at all. It tends to thicken and drag in places.

"Nice'n shiny."

"Yeah, they didn't have no flat."

"No?"

"Nope. All out." She steps back, looks around. She's finished. All the rocks are painted white regardless of size, even the ones too small for raked concentric ripples. She lays the brush across the paint can, looks at her hands. The sand is freshly raked, no marks except her footprints leading around from behind the house and among the boulders; here and there a round depression from the can. Her hands are spattered.

"Where's your chickens?"

She seems to think a moment, looks up, turns her hands out, "Ain't no chickens," as if to show him; as if to demonstrate there's nothing left but spatters. "Somethin' got 'em." Luther looks at her a minute. She bends down and gets some sand and starts to rub it between her palms. He shoulders his pack. The gate is locked with a little padlock. He climbs over, comes up to her.

"Somethin' got 'em?"

"Yep."

"All three?"

She gets more sand—"Yep"—stands there rubbing it, letting it sift from between her fingers. It seems to work or else it's just the reddish sand and white paint mixing to the color of her skin—a little too pink maybe sort of like her makeup. Too-pink hands; the pigment fills the wrinkles, makes them look like a child's hands except for the way the joints are swollen. Now she's looking at them too, just standing gazing at her swollen childish hands.

"When?"

"Other mornin'."

"Shit."

She shakes her head and takes a tissue from the pocket of her skirt, dabs at her hands. "I hate to use that water. Stinks so bad."

"Boy don't it."

"Yours too?"

"Yeah." He puts his pack down.

"Smells like somethin'—I don't know."

"So, what . . . ?"

"You know"—she looks away—"how sun can shine into a house and fill it up sometimes real early, fill it up just like the air is light and everything's so clear and bright and empty you just lie there for a minute like you don't know where you are exactly everything's so clear you're sorta lost?" She turns to face him. "Breaks my heart almost. You know?"

"Yeah."

"Breaks my heart and then to look outside and see them feathers scattered like they was. Not many. Just a few and some inside like leaves'll blow inside like in the fall—you know you just can't keep 'em out once they start fallin'. Sweep and sweep but in they come. You know they found that little girl." She turns and heads back to the house. He brings the paint can and the brush and sits beside her on the steps.

"Where?"

"Over in Wood. Not too much left but they could tell."

"What happened to her?"

"One of them things."

"What?"

"One of them things like what you saw I guess, like that one out there in the corn that time." She stands up. "I believe I like 'em better like that."

"What?"

"Them rocks. I believe I like 'em shiny. Dolores tells me you and Avery saw the crash."

"Boy we sure did. You see the truck?"

"No it was gone." She takes the paint into the yard as if to do a little touch-up, then just stands and looks at Luther. "How's your arm?"

"Okay."

"You sure?" She shakes her head, looks down at a rock, applies her brush. "Hell you don't know"—she moves to the next one, studies it, looks up, waves her brush—"hell you don't know she might be right. Could all just start to end right here, this little place, this little bitty part of the world might start to rot just like a dog bite—first it's sore and then a fever." Here she closes her eyes and shivers, puts the paint down, folds her arms, sort of hugs herself, and looks away.

"It ain't a dog bite."

"Yeah I know." She stands and looks across the road a moment longer, turns and looks at him again. "So where you been?"

"Home mostly. Fiddlin'. Really sorry about your chickens."

"Fiddlin' how?"

"I got them rejects—you can have 'em if you want." She comes back over to the steps. "Ain't no hurt feelin's there I'm sure." He smiles. She sits down.

"Fiddlin' how?"

"Or I could trade you for some lumber."

"Lumber?"

"Two-by-fours."

She leans against the post and kind of squints and makes a face.

"Well, you got some ain't you? Said you did. Said that was all you had, remember?"

She sits up, leans toward him, touches him on the cheek, just holds her hand there for a second then leans back. That stops him, makes him feel embarrassed all of a sudden, makes him stand up patting his pocket for a cigarette, one half-smoked down at the bottom of the pack. It takes a while to shake it out.

"You got a fever."

"No I ain't. I just been walkin' all this way. I had to jump your god-damn fence." He points to the fence. "Since when you go to puttin' a padlock on your gate?" He gets it lit, wads up the pack, walks out a ways into the yard and looks around, walks to the gate, looks at the padlock, looks at Agnes. "What you figure to keep out with that?" He gives it a rattle. She's sitting there watching him, leaning forward, both her hands up to her face. He gives the gate another rattle, feels the top hinge start to give, derives encouragement to shake the gate again so hard the whole fence whips a little, makes a snapping sound; a picket falls, the gate comes free and hangs there by the padlock. "Shit," says Luther. Agnes goes into the house.

"I could let you have a puppy."

She looks over at him, goes back to the sandwiches, the pre-assembled array of toasted bread and cheese, tomatoes, lettuce, pressed ham, all arranged just so. He likes to see it there like that on the white-tile counter, all the good things he can bring to mind al-most, just there as if it were a natural state of affairs, an inclination of the world to let good things emerge and fall into arrangements, presentations. "You want everything on this?"

"You bet." He's standing by the table, holding her hammer, rocking the rusty head on the handle, feeling its looseness. "They ain't mean, you know. In spite of what you think." She cuts each one diagonally, puts it on a plate. She brings his over with a glass of lemonade, keeps hers on the counter near the sink by the little window, stands with her sandwich gazing out. "Hell, chickens are mean." He sits; his arms stick to the oilcloth. He's still sweaty from his labors to repair the fence and gate. He puts his left arm in his lap. "They'll kill each other. Hell, they'll eat each other sometimes." It's exactly right—the toasted bread still warm, just crunchy enough. He takes a sip of lemonade. "I got this one, you oughta take him. He's a gray one. Gettin' big. They all got papers. He's the one old Leonard wanted." She just shakes her head and gazes out the window. "That's real good. Hey, Agnes."

"What?"

"Good sandwich."

"Good."

He shifts his chair around a little toward the window at his end and takes a bite, leans back. A swirl of dust kicks up out by the road, gets twisted way into the air and disappears. Now leaves and more dust as a whirlwind, a little dust devil, comes across the barbed-wire fence into the empty field next door. It makes a gentle steady rustling, lifting clouds of leaves and sand and stuff that looks like bits of feather as it sweeps into her yard across the back into the cedars. A puff of breeze comes through the window. Agnes puts her glass and plate into the sink. A clink of ice as Luther drains his lemonade. He takes an ice cube, holds it up against his forehead, rubs it back and forth and lets the drips run down. He hears her sigh.

"What in the world you gonna do with two-by-fours?"

And for a moment he can't say.

25

"**M**y daddy knows this stuff but I sure don't—now what do you call that?"

"Pegboard, four-by-four-foot sheets," says Luther.

"Pegboard." Shaking her head at the unlikeliness of it, having to deal with exotic items on her own, the pencil grasped in that funny desperate-looking grip with her thumb stuck out the way he's seen young people do. "So what's that for?" She checks the price. It takes forever. Agnes turns, walks back to the front, stands looking out the open door onto the square. It's getting dark.

"You hang things on it."

"Oh." She brightens. "That's real neat. And those are springs, I know what those are. One, two. . . ."

"Six. They're all the same."

"I can't believe they got him up there."

"Pardon me?"

She has to write the code or something, then how many, then the price. She has a silver ring on her thumb. It looks so childish with it stuck out there like that. "That little man. How many nails?"

"Four pounds."

"My daddy says that's where they kept some other guy one time—they called him 'Animal' somethin' or other. Right up there on top of the courthouse in that little-bitty jail. You hurt your arm?"

"Yeah."

"That's too bad. You think he can see out them little windows?"

"Four pounds."

"Oh yeah. Sorry."

"Seventy-five cents a pound."

"That makes. . . ."

"Three dollars."

"My," says Agnes from the front. They turn to look.

"Oh ain't that neat." She abandons Luther. "I just love that"—walks with Agnes out to the curb. The courthouse glows, a ghostly Christmas-lighted outline. Luther looks down at the sheets of pegboard, starts to count the holes, gives up, and turns to the aisle of hand tools. All the keyhole saws have blades about the size of the one he's got—too wide to start the cut at the outside of the hole; he has to come back with a file which takes too long and gives him blisters. It's impossible, he thinks. He really might be crazy. Maybe crazy really feels like this—he looks at his hands—just sort of abrasive. Maybe nothing more than that. "I can't believe he didn't kill hiself. My daddy says they do that—kill the ones they love then try to kill theirselves." It appears he's lost her. It's going to be too dark in any case. He could get an electric hand drill—Agnes might not go for that although here's one for under thirty—get a quarter-inch bit and rock it between the holes. It could tend to drift, though. He can see it becoming a struggle. "My friend Amy's mom and dad went to that meetin' over yonder." Such a childish, confidential little voice to carry like that. "Daddy says that big ole sign's in violation of some ordinance. They say all that stuff—what he done and all them things—is 'cause of some religious thing. Lord I sure hope not. God, you'd think if people think it's the end of the world they'd do somethin', not just hang around. You'd think that wouldn't you?" He takes a one-inch cold chisel down. "I know I would." It's much too blunt. He puts it back. "I might go somewhere. Get in the car and take a ride." Here, right here—a one-inch Stanley wood chisel with a steel cap on the handle. That's the ticket. He looks at the price then goes ahead and breaks the plastic away from the edge. He feels the edge. "I can see Jesus, though, in that picture. It's so easy. Can't say I like the way he looks too much but I could see him right off." It's what he needs, a simple sharp incisive gesture—whack, you hit it with a hammer, nothing vague or abrasive about it. He walks to the door unwrapping the chisel the rest of the way. He holds it up as Agnes turns. The teenage store clerk turns as well, beams. "That's a chisel. Oh my goodness, look at me run off and leave you all alone." She takes the empty package, trots back to the counter, writes it down. "What y'all makin'?"

David Searcy

Agnes stands there by the door. She looks at Luther, looks at the girl—"You have to promise not to tell"—smiles at the floor and shakes her head.

"Cross my heart." She makes the gesture.

Luther stands there with his chisel, with his thumb against the edge.

"It's a trap, right?" Agnes lifts her eyes toward Luther. "Right, I'm pretty sure of that. And I believe"—she looks around, looks out the door—"in light of everything, in light of what we know, what seems to be out there needin' further definition"—she turns around—"it is a trap for the Holy Spirit"—her eyes get wide—"or somethin' like that."

"Holy Spirit?" says the store clerk. Luther stays right where he is, says not a word.

"Yep, but it ain't like what you think." She lifts a finger. "No sir. Not any more'n the Rapture's what you think—ain't nothin' really like you think now is it, Luther?" Luther seems to have cut his thumb.

"I don't think nothin'," pleads the store clerk.

"I know, sweetheart. That's all right." She starts to laugh.

The teenage store clerk starts to laugh. "You're pullin' my leg."

"I guess we are. You want to help us get that pegboard in the truck."

"There's one."

"It ain't."

"Sure is. Slow down."

"Lord."

"Slow way down. No brights?"

"No brights. Good Lord."

"See, look. Pull over here."

"That ain't no catfish head. It's black."

"They turn black."

"Lord."

"No, look. Just stop now, turn it in and put your lights right on it. You seen ones like that. You got to."

"Yeah well guess I wasn't payin' attention. Why the hell they want to do that?"

"You don't like it?"

"Shit."

"Look yonder. Go ahead. Up there's a big one. Hoo, boy; somebody done some fishin'."

"Why the head and not the rest?"

"The rest gets ate. Besides the head'll keep. You salt it first. You cure it."

"Then you take it out by the road and nail it up. Sort of like way back there somebody misread the instructions."

"People do it. Go on."

"Jesus, all along here."

"Yep."

"There's two on that one there."

"Yep."

"All along here."

"Just a thing folks like to do."

26

He's got it down. He's got the technique. He's got his doorstep out in the yard to be a table, got a pegboard sheet on top. He pulls it along, whacks parallel cuts to join the holes, to make the slots, but leaves the cut-out pieces in place. Then when he's through he'll flip it over and punch them out from the other side. Whack, whack—it takes two whacks per cut. The only problem is his left hand keeping a grip. He tends to lose it. Now and then the hand just opens, the chisel slips. He gets some duct tape, wraps it around the hand and the chisel, twists it over the top three fingers and under the fourth to get the angle right, the chisel barely loose enough to twist to get the bevel facing in for each half-cut. That works okay. It goes much faster than he thought. Whack, whack, then twist and whack again. It's like a die-cutting operation. Like a factory (Yurang's jerking on his chain which adds an industrial-sounding counterpoint). Whack. Kerthunk. It's preordained to work, the whole thing, the whole idea seems sharp, coherent, perfectly clear as long as he keeps this up. Conviction in the act of manufacture inflects the enterprise itself, can bring the vaguest sort of notion into shape. Whack, whack, kerthunk. Another kerthunk and now a growl. He stops and gets up, turns around. It's Willis. Standing by his cruiser, behind the door a safe distance away as if he can't be sure if Yurang's chained or not. He's got a Big Gulp or a Slurpee or something, sipping it from a straw. He steps away from the car and stands there, makes a raspy, empty gurgle through the straw which really irritates the dog who snaps his chain so hard it jerks him off his feet. Now Yurang sits and pants at the very end of his chain as Willis walks up, stands above him, looks down at him for a moment, withdraws the straw from the plastic lid with a fingernail-on-blackboard sort of squeak and, holding the straw above the dog, lets fall a cherry-flavored drop. The trailer shivers and, for a second, half a second,

Yurang's got the cuff of his pants and Willis, caught on the cusp of events, seems to strain away from the realization as much as the fact; his buck teeth clenched without expression, not a sound from either party, just the pull of possibilities in that instant. Then the dog's just sitting, panting once again as Willis brushes at a bright-red slosh of Slurpee on his shirt, looks down at his pants, looks up at Luther with his chisel. Luther picks at the edge of the tape. "I knowed a feller got hisself ripped out real good—all ripped out here—like that." He gestures with the chisel, starts to peel the tape away. "Most dogs'll worry it, grab and hold and shake you know"—he looks at Willis—"like a rabbit by the neck." He wads the tape into a ball. "But chows are funny; they keep bitin'—chomp, chomp, chomp— just sorta work their way on up. You got some soda on your shirt." He turns and walks back toward the trailer.

"Hey," says Willis. He dumps his Slurpee, tosses the cup over toward the dog. "Leonard says you and him are real good buddies." Luther steps into the trailer, gets a screwdriver, comes back out as Willis approaches in an arc defined by the swing of Yurang's chain. "Real pals," says Willis. Luther goes over to the pegboard, flips it, lines it up so the first row hangs just over the edge of the step, waits for a moment, lets the pain in his arm subside, then with the screw-driver starts to punch the pieces out to make the slots. "Yes sir"— Willis walks up, stands behind him—"way he talks I guess it musta been one of them real meaningful-type relationships." The slots are a little fuzzy on the punched side but that shouldn't hurt, the straws will give. "That right?" Luther looks back over his shoulder.

"Where's your gun?"

"That right?" says Willis, nudging the pegboard with his boot.

"You didn't break it did you?" Luther straightens the pegboard. "You didn't go and break your gun?"

"What in the shit is that?" He kicks the pegboard again.

"I bet you did." He gets it straight again.

". . . the fuck"—again the boot and Luther's up with his left arm shoved in Willis's face and pushing him back into the trailer.

"You smell that?" It makes a funny boingy sound as his head slams back into the siding and his cowboy hat flies off. He feels Willis's teeth. "You smell that? Know what that is? I been goddamn bit by the Holy Spirit and you better back way off. Way off." He shoves himself away and stands there. Willis holds his hand to his mouth, looks at his hand. The dog's gone crazy. He's got the hat. He's tearing at it, dragging it back into his area, shaking it, biting it, getting his head up into the crown, one paw on the brim, and snapping through with a spray of straw, now getting it hung around his neck which really sends him into a frenzy, ripping pieces from the brim until he tears right through it, tossing the strung-out remnant, springing upon it, holding it down, and tearing some more.

They move away into the yard and stand together watching the dog. "You owe me a goddamn hat," says Willis after a while.

"I know." Yurang attacks each smaller and smaller piece in turn. He seems to intend a truly thorough, almost analytic, reduction.

"You gonna buy me a goddamn hat."

"I said all right." There comes a point where the dog will pause, just sit and gaze off into space and pant a moment then, apparently deciding some shred still offends, have at it again.

"So'd you stop by for anything in particular?"

"Think he's done?"

"You want it back?"

"Just wondered. Shit, there he goes again."

"So what'd you want?"

"Bobby'd like you to have a word with Leonard. Shit, look at that."

"Leonard?"

"Why'd you want a dog like that?"

"You want to tell me what you need?"

"Need you to have a word with Leonard. He won't talk to nobody else. Bobby figured maybe you could get him started." Here he turns. "Shit I was teasin'. What the fuck is wrong with you?" Turns back to the dog. "Why in the hell anybody want a dog like that?" Yurang's spinning around and biting his chain. He looks like a mad dog. "Holy Spirit my ass. You're gonna buy me a goddamn hat."

"I said I would."

• • •

It stinks in the squad car but it's cool.

"It's that sight thing."

"What is?" He's about to fall asleep.

"That goddamn laser sight don't point right." He keeps putting his hand to his mouth and doing something with his tongue. "I could arrested your ass you know that?"

If Luther leans back with his arms crossed just like this he feels all right, can't feel his left arm really at all except for a soreness in the armpit.

"Shit, look there."

Luther opens his eyes to note the tiny smear of red on Willis's finger.

"Shit," says Willis, "seven hundred dollars, thing don't point straight."

"Probably broke it playin' with it."

"Shit," says Willis.

"Where you goin'?" Luther opens his eyes again.

"Get me a ice cream." He turns in, pulls up to the speaker, rolls his window down and waits with his index finger doing something in his mouth. The heat drifts in. It's taking a while. Luther adjusts the a/c vent and closes his eyes as a pair of logging trucks come thrumming up the highway, winding out on the road to Longview. Other than that there's not much traffic. He can hear Willis shift around and wipe his finger on his pants, lean out the window.

"Hey," says Willis to the speaker, "all I want's a goddamn ice cream." He leans back. "I seen that picture they sent Bobby of that baby girl—the way she looked with all that stuff there on the ground." Luther crosses his arms the other way, looks over at Willis who's found a Dairy Queen paper napkin which he applies and then examines, re-applies and re-examines. "Wasn't much there you could really tell too much about." He unfolds the napkin, regards the Rorschach-like duplication of red blotches as if surprised, as if it were revelatory in some way. "Shit." He leans out again. "You people want some business? Shit." He looks back at the napkin, squinting. Sunlight shines straight in that side. He's sweating. There's a faded swirly ice cream cone of the kind he'd like to have on the plastic sign above the speaker. It's a hollow double sign designed to illuminate at night. The hazy sunlight shines into it, shows the cracks, a jagged hole, and what appears to be a bird's nest. Willis bleeps his siren, yells into the speaker once again. "I want a goddamn ice cream cone."

"Nobody home," says Luther.

Willis looks at Luther, pokes the napkin in his mouth, and pulls around to the service window. There's a yellow sign with leasing information. "Shit," says Willis, removing the napkin. "Shit." It's redder; he unfolds it, puts the car in park, and holds it up. He probably has bad gums as well. "You goddamn motherfucker, look at that."

"Looks like a angel."

"Huh," says Willis, looking at it. "What the hell's the matter with you."

The sheriff's preoccupied. "Henry, get them front doors open. Prop them back ones too. Let's get some air in here." He looks at Luther sort of blankly, glances at Willis, goes to supervise the maintenance supervisor in his opening of the doors—he wants them open all the way, both doors and all the way and both the back ones too. He wants to ventilate the courthouse, make a breezeway front to back. He steps outside, observes the workmen patching brick, replacing mortar; looks across the mostly empty square at nothing, stands a moment under the arch with his hat removed as if the better to receive some faint impression, make some subtle determination. He's gained weight. His belt twists nearly horizontal under his gut; his great-big silver rodeo buckle reflects the ground. And yet he's all tucked in, all pressed and scoured-looking, maybe even a little paler overall as if from too much laundering, bleaching of his khakis. Now he turns, comes back to Willis.

"Where's your hat?"

"Dog ate it."

"What dog?"

"His dog."

Luther smiles. The sheriff stares at Luther, shakes his head, and looks away, walks down the hall and stops and seems to sniff the air, comes back and shakes his head again, says, "Dang," and looks at Willis.

"What?" says Willis.

"Get yourself a regular gun, all right?"

"All right."

"And get yourself a hat."

"He's gonna buy me a goddamn hat."

"That's fine." He walks around behind them, hits the elevator button. "Go ahead and take him up." He wears cologne. It smells like flowers.

"Want me to book him on assault?" Willis grins.

"Not if you want your goddamn hat." He turns away; the elevator opens; they can hear him for a second as it rises, yelling, "Henry, find out what the hell that is; think somethin' died in here or somethin'."

"There you go," says Willis.

Luther doesn't move. "I seen him twice in my whole life."

"I guess it musta been real special. There you go." The steel door shuts. It's a little common room with steel and concrete tables and a window on the far side. It's quite warm. And now there is in fact a certain unpleasant smell. No sign of Leonard. No one at all. To Luther's left a little window shows the control room where a jailer sits and smokes. He's joined by Willis who stands and leans against the wall, applies a tissue to his mouth, looks up at Luther, jabs a finger toward the other end, says something to the jailer who's amused. Four cells on each side of the main room all are open. All the tiny-windowed red steel doors swung wide. There's a peculiar mechanical sort of noise. Other than that it's rather strangely quiet, hushed as if from all the extra steel and brick and whatnot jails require. It's like a test or something. Guess which cell he's in. From here he can see into the first two which are empty: toilet, sink, a little shelf, a sheet-metal shelflike mattress frame without a mattress. All the steel is primer-red. The walls of cinder block or cinder block and brick are the palest, vaguest shade of yellow. Everywhere are little doodles, random childish-looking drawings, names and numbers, scribbled figures on the concrete tops of tables, on the walls. It really is too hot, like being in an attic in the summer. He moves past the first big table, bolted, along with its benches, to the floor. The next two cells are also empty although in one, the one on this side, the decorative impulse has received a fuller expression. He looks inside. Most of the back wall is devoted to a very large heart with "Jesus" written above it on some kind of scroll or banner. Drops of blood like raindrops—drawn the way kids draw them all lined up in perfect rows—fall from the heart. It looks like scorch marks, like the whole thing's done with matches, made with sooty little streaks. The air-conditioning must be off. The front of his tee shirt's soaking through in spots. He pulls it away from his body, steps back out into the common room. The sound is almost regular but not quite—like someone stapling things together over and over, just the slightest variation in the interval. And another sound as well, though very faint, like someone singing or a radio playing somewhere. Two more cells, both empty. Now the sound like stapling suddenly stops. A shuffling movement. Leonard peers around the door of the very last cell on the other side. His pants are down around his ankles. He blinks at Luther. Seems to consider him a moment, reaches down to extract one leg, kicks off the pants from the other foot and leaves them there, goes back in his cell. "Won't give me shit for pain or nothin'." Now the sound starts up again. "Goddammit."

Luther walks around to the second steel-and-concrete table, stands there by it. Leonard's trying to flush the toilet. There's a button in the wall above the commode and he keeps pushing it, making that noise.

"Sometimes she'll catch," says Leonard, standing in his Jockey shorts and tee shirt looking down into the toilet with the utmost concentration. Push—therwhump. The sound of a bad valve shutting down. The smell is not so much latrine smell though; it's more like something dead and decomposing. Push—therwhump. What is that singing like a mosquito in his ear? "They showed me pictures."

"What?"

Therwhump. "They come up here and showed me pictures of my baby."

"What?" says Luther; then, "Oh, Christ."

"They think I done it but I didn't."

"Christ," says Luther again and turns to the window. It's barred with heavy vertical slats of steel. It faces the square. It's one of the little windows the girl at the hardware store had wondered about. He walks over to it. It's not very clean. The glare diffuses across the glass but he can see above the buildings of the square, the green of trees beyond, a couple of hills toward Gladewater and Big Sandy to the south. Whatever stinks must be substantial. Not that strong, yet with that rotting-cow-like quality of excess; disaster; more smell than you need to represent a single thing, it spreads beyond somehow, extends its implications. The singing seems to be coming from down there on the street. He squints.

"I tell you what." Therwhump. "I seen what did."

It's even hotter right here in the glare. He pulls at his shirt. It's hard to see. There's someone standing on the corner across the street but it's in shade and he can't tell. A woman's voice. It sounds like gospel. Something "Jesus." Very gentle but disturbing with the smell. "Sweet Jesus." Irritating like a mosquito; like someone whispering something terrible in the sweetest possible voice.

"I thunk about it." Whunk. He's really whacking it now. It sounds like Yurang jerking his chain. Therwhunk. "I reckon I'm pretty sure." He's using his fist. "That sonofabitch ought not to showed me them damn pictures." Whunk, therwhunk—a left and right. He's jammed the button. "See." He stands now with his hands down. "See. Ain't nothin' works worth shit." He's simply gazing into the toilet, standing like that, apparently disinclined to move. It must be ninety degrees at least. Luther looks around after a minute, walks to the front. The control room's empty. He taps on the glass. He taps again a little louder, tries to peek into the hall through the tiny window in the door. It looks like someone's held a cigarette or a match against it, scorched and partially melted the heavy plastic or whatever it is in several places making it hard to find a clear spot. There's some noise below, some yelling; maybe Bobby. Maybe they're heading off to lunch. He turns and leans against the door. He has a brand-new pack of cigarettes. He removes one, walks back up to the other end, stands by the table, lights it. Leonard hasn't budged.

"I wisht I had that shirt, you know; that one that smelt good."

"Yeah," says Luther.

Leonard touches the button gently, says, "Goddammit." Takes a breath. "I'm sittin' out there like I said and I can see into them woods, you know, a ways—them little sweet gums down that slope and then them pines, right where them sweet gums go to pines. . . ." A very faint and rather sweet melodic passage from the street—too faint for words but something, something "Oh my soul," and "Oh my Jesus," something, something. ". . . how the light gets kinda funny in towards evenin', gets all red and shines in sideways through them trees, I thought I seen a deer or somethin'—you know how it gets, the light, all striped and speckled-like and all up in them woods—and I'd look hard and shit if it weren't just like a deer and I'd yell Mama come on out here but she wouldn't, she'd just start to get all fussy with that baby and that dog starts goin yip, yip, not really barkin', more like scared or wantin' attention; that damn thing weren't good for nothin' sept the baby liked it; had them papers though I believe; I know it did. I know it had them papers." Whunk. He hits it really hard to no effect, looks at his hands, looks over at Luther. "Right there"—glancing at the toilet—"right there's where I'd like to put them goddamn papers; that damn thing didn't make one sound that night, not one little goddamn yip and not that mornin' neither—right there under the bed the whole damn time and all that hair all over, Mama screamin' and all." The singing has stopped. He shuffles over—little steps as if still hobbled—sits at the bench with his back to the table, facing the window. "She'll be startin' up again here in a minute."

"Who?" says Luther.

Leonard shakes his head. "That goddamn sonofabitch don't give a shit, don't even give a shit if I done it—big ole hat and big ole gun don't give a big ole goddamn shit." He's wearing that tee shirt with the parachute and the skull, the one he wore that day at the Mount Pisgah Feed and Grocery. Luther sits down facing the same way at the other end of the bench. Light falls between them; stripes of light across the bench, the top of the table picking out the hearts and flowers, names and numbers, *X*s and *O*s, all sorts of mindless little doodles like a glaze, a gentle dusting of empty thoughts. It looks like Leonard might be sick. He's leaning over. After a minute he sits back up, apparently only trying to spit. His mouth is dry but he wipes it anyway. Out the window it's just white. It's like they're way up in the clouds, up in the haze and heat, suspended. Not a sound now, just the odor of decay which is not so bad if he thinks of it spread out, part of the condition of things in general.

"Deer don't shake itself like a dog, though." Leonard wipes his mouth again. "And deer don't get up in the trees and go all fuzzy or somethin', get all big and dark. . . ." A thin pure note, quite high, descending—"Precious Savior, Precious Lord." ". . . and deer don't wait until you drank too much and go to sleep and make a little breeze and come and take away your baby." Now he leans way over again. "You know I was in the goddamn Marines." He's getting a little hard to hear. He's having trouble. "I was . . . shit." He sits back up. "You know I was in the goddamn Marines."

Troy has to come and let him out. The younger deputy's very nice, apologetic, just got in, can't take the time to run him back, though maybe later; thinks the sheriff very likely had to rush home to his wife who tends to make demands of late and even gets a little hysterical during the day sometimes, starts crying, calls him up; although—he stops to have a word with another deputy—he may have gone out on a call. Still he thinks Willis probably just went out to get an ice-cream cone and should be back here pretty quick if Luther wants to hang around although for sure it might be nicer on the lawn there where the workmen sit about beneath the trees enjoying lunch and, by all appearances, the performance. That's so strange, the way she stands there in her polka-dotted dress (it's not the same one, different color, though it looks about the same, the big white dots the size of quarters); how can someone simply stand there like that singing; if she had a bucket or something people could toss some money into that would be all right, still odd but not unlike some other things you see at Christmas; it would have a purpose then; you could toss a quarter in and then that's that, you've done your part, go on about your business, never mind about the singing, how the thin sweet voice drifts all about the square and seems to mingle with the smell which is detectable even out here on the lawn, here on this bench that wobbles now, its steel frame twisted so no matter how he sits it feels unstable. After a while he walks around and checks the parking lot—no sign of either Willis or the sheriff—then he wanders over to Joe's. Joe's got things all torn up; he's taken out the wall, leaving only the studs there at the back between the main room and the kitchen. He's standing, looking at it, thinking he can get more seating in here without that wall, or maybe a lectern at that end, a sort of pulpit; pull the counter out up front, put benches there, and that would do it. And if he left a sort of furdown he could hang that gold-framed picture right above where she would stand which Luther agrees would be quite nice. The griddle is covered with debris. Joe's white with sheetrock dust, his combover out of place and hinged way over to one side which makes him look like an open container, all the contents going bad. Luther steps outside and takes a seat at the edge of the walk, gazes up at the courthouse, traces the lines of Christmas lights along the structural intersections, just the outline of the building, which makes it look so insubstantial when they turn them on at night. As if a pickup truck might really drive right through it. "Take me up, oh take me up on wings of love, my Savior. . . ." Luther counts his money—two one-dollar bills, a couple of quarters, and some pennies—walks down to the Exxon, gets some peanut-butter crackers and a root beer, hangs around to see if Vernon needs a hand—his help didn't show this morning, hasn't shown in fact this week at all but there's no business really to speak of. Just as well. So Luther helps him stack some recap tires and sweep up here and there in hopes he'll get a ride at some point. Vernon gives him a five-dollar bill and says to come back—looks at his watch; it's three forty-five—in a couple of hours.

Now it's quiet on the square. The singing has stopped, the singer departed. It's like she's done all she can do. He checks the parking lot again. It's totally empty—looks like even Troy has gone. He walks on over to where it's shady on the south side of the square and smokes another brand-new cigarette, smokes it all the way to the end. He walks across the little alley, stops to peer in Hudgins's window. It says Hudgins still on top in big block letters above the awning but inside it's nearly empty—a couple of chairs, some sort of big gray plastic mat, a row of trophies in the window. It's a twirling studio now, a school for majorettes or something—there's a sign with crossed batons. He wonders how profitable that could be. He looks at the dates on all the trophies—faded glory for the most part. They've still got the old coin-operated scale outside by the walk like a public convenience. "How Much Do You Weigh?" it asks on the front. It must be anchored to the concrete; probably cost too much to remove. Just let the majorettes flow around it. "How Much Do You Weigh?" now barely legible through the rust-stained white enamel, a big floating question mark below—no fortune, nothing, just the basics—as if back then, back in the thirties or whenever it was installed, this might have posed a novel question, would have made people stop and think well, yes, if things have weight then people must have too—hey kids, hey Mama, get on over here, see what you weigh—like getting your blood typed or your I.Q., something weird and somehow critical that people never knew they had; that people lining up to step up on the scale might fear they had too little of or even lacked. He steps up on it, drops a penny in the slot and is surprised to hear the mechanism release. He bends down over it, shades his eyes. He weighs (it's hard to see, the cylinder's stained as well) just twenty-two pounds. That's it. That feels about right. He sighs, steps off the scale, walks down the walk—it looks like Avery's closed up early—takes a seat on the bench, leans back. He can see the scars on the curb where Leonard's truck took off. It sounds like Joe's removing studs. He sort of dozes on and off, allows himself to entertain a dreamy sense of the nearly weightlessness of things—like the Christmas decorations, like the tinsel-outlined Santa across the street. It all might blow away like fluff; the slightest breeze would be sufficient. The workmen leave; the shadows draw across. He wakes himself up suddenly with his snoring, sees the courthouse Christmas lights are on, and hurries to catch his ride.

27

"You listnin'?" Agnes asks.

"Yeah."

"No you ain't."

He's been up since the first gray light. He had an inspiration in the dark with his bad arm propped up, unable to sleep. He saw the trap as a more explicitly, mechanically active, and aggressive principle of knowledge—like the child's hand clapping down upon the cricket. That sort of sudden thoughtless compression of one's regard for a thing. That instant—not the capture, just that instant when the hand claps down and isolates the cricket from the world. A great descending, apprehensive definition of a thing (his arm hurts worse, especially up underneath the shoulder, in the armpit), whoosh, a sudden rush of air and for that fraction of a second there you've got it, what it is, but just for an instant—pick it up and it's too late; it blurs, becomes your friend, your meal, a little story about itself. He saw a complex parallelogram of links or hinging arms, the trap collapsing like a lawn chair; and it seemed he could imagine what it felt like, what it might feel like inside to something terrible, undefinable, yet which craves that big cheese sandwich—the biggest, best cheese sandwich possible—there in the dark just out of reach, and it can see the stars because the trap is open at the top; so that's all right, it comes right in; it's got the sandwich and the stars, it's all just fine and then—he winced; he actually shivered when he got to this part—then the sky is closed off with that whoosh, an awful clap (this way, too, you don't need springs to force the slotted Masonite across; it's all inertial, gravity mostly); whack, as if the stars were squeezed into those little squirts of paint, the paint like pins, like insect pins, and for that instant in its fear it is defined, it feels itself defined perhaps—how strange would that be? All its vaguely spiritual, deerlike—what did he call it, "fuzzy"—dark and wolfish, maggoty characteristics brought together and recorded.

"You ain't heard nothin I been sayin'."

"Yeah I have. Hold this." His hand's not working very well today. "Get down and put your weight right there and hold that steady." He kneels down as well and straddles the two-by-four and butts its end against the end of the one she's holding, drives two nails, offset a little, through the side of hers into the end of his. He gets a clear ascending ring each time he strikes—it's pretty good lumber. "Now this here."

She stands. "Goddammit. What do you think about that? That old man bein' up there dead like that?"

He's ready for her now at the other corner. She's not moving. He looks up. "He got throwed up there in the crash I guess." She stands there looking at him. He puts down the hammer, wipes his face. "Old man?"

"An 'elderly gentleman,' called him an 'elderly gentleman.'"

"There was one right there on the walk before the crash and then there wasn't. Knocked one a them benches up there, too, way up on top a that little porch thing. Got that down but guess they missed him. Wanna give me a hand here?" He picks up the hammer.

"You oughta tell 'em."

"Tell 'em what?" She's still not moving. "Tell 'em what?" He puts the hammer down again and stands. "Don't make no difference, Agnes. Sept to get ole Leonard charged with murder or somethin'."

"Ole Leonard?"

"Yeah ole Leonard. Good ole Leonard. We're best buddies, ain't you heard?" She cocks her head a little, studying him; takes a step. He backs away. "You keep your hands to yourself goddammit. All that shit don't make no difference. You gonna help me here or not?" He waits. She's looking at his arm, and at the lumber, all the parts laid out, the puppies in their pen and Yurang dozing in the sun. A soft, prolonged asthmatic wheeze comes from the gas well. She gets down to brace the corner of the frame. He butts it up and nails it, then the other two. "I need some hog wire. Need to stretch it across this here and lay some chicken wire on top." He stands with his bad arm held against him. "Need some ten-foot lumber too, so's I can make a outside frame kicked over forty-five degrees like this"—he shows her with his boot—"run cables down from here to here to keep it tight, from pullin' in; so when it gets inside no matter if it's heavy it don't touch the floor at all, don't smear the paint."

"The paint?"

"The picture."

"Picture of what?"

"You know."

"The hell I do."

"You said you did."

"I did?"

"Sure did. You scared that little girl pretty good, remember? The one at the hardware store?"

She gets up, wincing; holds her back and looks up. "Got another one missin', too, about that age I heard this mornin'—you know the MacNallys; one of them girls. That's what that fuss was all about, all that commotion, all them squad cars out here yesterday afternoon."

"I wasn't here."

"Oh dang." She makes a face, bends back as far as she can then straightens up and keeps her eyes closed for a minute. There's another wheezy gurgle from the west. It sounds a little bit like Willis with his Slurpee but much deeper and more final. "Oh my goodness." She opens her eyes and shakes her head. "Can you imagine what that smelled like bein' up there all that time. And all that heat?"

"I need some hog wire." He gets one of the four-foot uprights, has to kneel and sort of brace it against his shoulder, drive one nail then get it straight then drive the other. "Need some eighth-inch cable; some whatchamacallitis—tighteners. Turnbuckles. Need four turnbuckles; better get six." The gnats are bad; they get in his mouth. He spits, looks up. "So what do you think?" She's still just standing there.

"Where were you?"

"Town."

"You smell it?"

"Yeah. So what do you think?"

She looks around, walks over to the puppies—one's awake; he's got his paws up on the wire. "This him?"

"That's him."

"Hey there," she says. It growls. "Hey there," she says again.

"Is that their house?" asks Luther.

"Yep."

"Looks sorta burned."

"They had a fire a while back; never did fix it up."

It's hard to tell if all the more-or-less battered vehicles in the yard are permanent inventory or a supportive family gathering. Agnes slows. It's probably both. There seem to be people in the back. The puppy squirms in Luther's arms; he wants to jump right out the window and have a go at two rangy mutts up on the porch. Somebody's standing in the screen door looking out, an older woman; there are sounds like pots and pans and someone yelling, calling someone over and over. Dogs' heads turn to watch them pass. The older woman steps outside to watch as well. He glances back. Her eyes look wild. Her hair is crazy, implausibly black and very frizzy like it's singed. Does she expect each passing car to have her child? She looks as if she might combust from disappointment, loss, too hard a life, and now this final thing.

"Look here. Here's what you have to do." Her kitchen table is all laid out with plastic soda straws, a coffee can full of tiny sections of dowel, a tube of glue, that quart of paint she used to paint the rocks, some thinner, a pair of scissors, a little candle. He lights the candle. "Keep the flame right over here away from the paint." He cuts the straw. "One inch, that's all." He holds the one-inch piece of straw up to the candle. "This part here's the most important part—don't let it melt too much; just catch the end." He lets the flame approach the end then squeezes it flat. "If it hurts to do that, it's too hot; you let it melt too much; just barely let it bead. See here. Look here." He does it again. "It's got to seal but not so tight it can't bust open." He opens his fingers. "There." It's closed, the straw sealed flat. "You do it."

Agnes tries; the plastic catches fire; she tries again. "Ouch."

"There, you see?"

"Okay, okay." She does it this time. Seals it. Shows it to him.

"Perfect. Now, you got a dropper somewhere—like for eye drops?" After a minute she emerges from the bedroom with a dropper, stands a moment looking back into the room.

"So what's he doin'?"

"I can't tell. He's under the bed." She's leaning over trying to see.

"They like to chew on stuff. You got a worn-out shoe or somethin'?" Agnes disappears again. He hears her in the closet opening boxes. Hears her talking to the dog. "Come on," he calls. The puppy follows Agnes back into the kitchen with a tennis shoe in its mouth. He shows her how to thin the paint, to fill the sealed straw sections half full with the dropper, draw a bead of glue around the open end, and use the bits of dowel for plugs. "You hold it up like this, you get the air on top like when you get a shot, you know? Like how they do them hypodermics. Let the air seep through the seal; that way it don't break open when you put the plug in." Agnes leans back, folds her arms. "Right?" She says nothing. She's just looking at him. "Agnes?" Under the table the sound of softly ripping canvas. "It goes real quick once you get the hang." She looks outside, looks back at Luther, picks up the coffee can full of little wooden plugs and gives it a shake.

"Why don't you shoot it?" She gets a handful, lets them fall back into the can. "Why don't you just get a gun and shoot it?" She looks up. "Or one a them big ole traps with teeth? A big ole bear trap." Luther rises, hugs his arm, walks to the sink, looks out the window. Her back is to him. He can hear her messing around with the stuff on the table. It sounds like nothing—a bunch of stuff; a bunch of straws and glue and insignificant stuff.

"You know that woman was the mother."

"Yeah, I figured. Kinda old." He runs cold water—more like

lukewarm—on his hand and tries to make it into a fist. Her water smells as bad as his.

"How's this?"

He turns, walks over to her. She's completed one. She shows him, hands it to him. "Good." He hands it back.

"How many these things you need?"

"'Bout six hundred."

She sort of spins around in her chair which excites the puppy—now he wants the shoe she's wearing. "'Bout six hundred?"

"'Bout six hundred and eighty-four."

She's shaking her foot; the puppy joins the fight in earnest. "Jesus Christ."

"Once you get goin' you can do three in a minute pretty easy."

"Jesus Christ," says Agnes. Terrible sounds are coming from under the table. Luther goes to get the dog food out of the truck. He finds a bowl and fills it with water, puts some dog food in another bowl next to it. Agnes watches. The puppy seems to have settled down.

"Well guess I'm gone. We'll pick that hog wire up tomorrow. Right?" She sighs, looks at the table. Luther squats down, lifts the oilcloth—it's asleep. He gives it a pat. He calls from the porch, "Hey Agnes."

"What?"

"Might as well go ahead and lock that gate."

There's a big black long-cab pickup truck parked out in front of Luther's trailer. Luther angles across the field to get the henhouse in between him and the truck. It's Mr. Tuel. He can hear the muffled sound of Yurang having a fit inside. He drifts off-line a little to get a glimpse—Tuel's got the weedeater, trying to start it, muttering, cursing it sounds like, making little sputtery exclamations. Luther comes up to the henhouse, peeks around. He's found the gas can. He's going to go through the whole routine. He changes the gas and tries again to start it. "Shit," he says. "Shit, shit, shit, shit." He pours some gas on the ground and drops a match. He drops another match. He kicks the gas can, picks it up and dumps out all the gas then throws the gas can and the weedeater in his truck, stops for a moment to re-gard the four-by-six-by-six-foot two-by-four and chicken-wire con-traption. "Shit," he says, gets in his truck and drives away.

He jerks awake. It's not his arm; that's not so bad right now; it's hot—he can feel it's hot against his stomach—but the pain's not re-ally bad. It's something else. He looks for Yurang in the dark. He's on the couch with his nose right up against the window. There's no moon. Just stars and now and then—he blinks—a subtle flickering like distant lightning. He starts counting, stops at twenty. There's no thunder. He sits up. He forgot to put the sandwiches out; forgot to place cheese-sandwich quarters by the sticks out in the field. He just got tired. He just conked out. The dog is rigid. Luther gets up, feels unstable for a second, braces himself against the ceiling, feels the trailer shift a little as he moves to the other side (he has that sense of having come adrift, of bobbing like a lure, the trailer cast out like a lure upon the depths). He kneels on the couch next to the dog. The window's closed; it has no screen. He cranks it open. There's a sad, depleted sighing from the gas well. For a moment nothing else. Then Yurang stiffens as a flickering patch of pale-blue flame appears out in the yard, winks out, appears again and sends out little runners here and there across the ground, the central portion winking out again, the separate ripply glows then feeding back into the center which re-ignites and flashes up into a clear blue-edged with yellow swirl of flame that draws the smaller flames into it, flickers higher than the trailer for a second, then just disappears. The smell of gaso-line drifts in. A faint and distant peeping from the tree frogs in the woods. He gets his pillow, stands there with it for a while just look-ing out, then curls up sideways on the couch with the pillow behind him so he can sit like that as long as he needs to, keep his face right there by the open window, fully awake for a while, then dozing, vaguely drifting at the surface, in and out of not quite sleep.

28

She's unable to shake the oddness, the sense of artificiality, now at all. Where stands of obviously planted pines give way to something obviously nothing in particular, nothing elaborately intended—fields or thicket, whatever—still the feeling persists. There's no relief—ah, back to normal. No relaxation of the strain of disbelief. And even coming into town—you hit the outskirts and expect the terms to change; this stuff is artificial anyway; out-of-placeness is its nature: helter-skelter, false front, service station serving as a restaurant, piles of rubble (inexplicable, official-looking hills of broken sinks and toilets); cross the tracks and into town itself, the square still blighted here and there by that terrible moment of vague, uncertain architectural longing toward the up-to-date and hopeful which, sometime probably late in the sixties, draped the fronts of good old buildings with those shingled mansard roofs and brutal corrugated facings—even here, beyond the obvious insincerities, the little self-deceptive yearnings evident everywhere you look in every window almost, every decorative flourish (Lord, the Santa Claus—how desperate, tinseled, hollow a thing that is on the courthouse lawn; it's like the gesture of some cargo cult), beyond all this and definitely extrinsic to the effects of having had too much to drink last night (she drains the quart of orange juice) there is a thin provisionality as if one might at any moment out of the corner of one's eye glimpse suddenly here, right here, the same surprising lapse, the same unraveling that you do among the pines. She rolls the windows down. The hot air fills the car. It seems so empty. Hardly anyone out today. She waits at the light in front of Hudgins. Maybe others have gone missing. Maybe the rate is geometric—first just one and then you wait awhile and then another, then before you know it, whoosh, the big red-letter, bumper-sticker day is here at last. The light turns green. They've got the sign on. All the tubes are glowing nicely, though they're pale in the daylight; even the cross on top glows steadily now, faint neon white—about the color of the sky. She parks in front. The door's propped open with that big white-fossil rock, a stack of sheetrock just outside. She stands a moment by the car. It whispers now; they replaced the transformers or the circuit breakers or something. Now it whispers much more softly. Little whirligig spiral galaxies go spinning away with their own even softer whisper superimposed. That's that, they whisper. That's the end of everything, they say; and it is for a minute or so and then they do it again. "Hello," she calls at the door, peeks in. There's no one here. The counter is gone. There are little piles of swept debris, those wooden benches Joe's got turned around and pushed against the wall and not much else. A haze of dust. She steps inside. The kitchen's gone as well; it's all one big long space right back to the storage room. They've left the exhibit on in there it looks like. Pallid TV-colored light fans softly out into the dust. It alters slightly, dims a little, with each small increase in voltage, with each whispery open-ended universal loss of mass—or attenuation of mass, she thinks, to the point it amounts to the same thing, really. Hadn't she read that? Where's her check? She wouldn't have left it. She sits down at the end of a bench—he's got them facing to the rear like pews—and rummages through her purse. She finds the envelope with the check, a box of Chiclets, puts the purse down, puts the Chiclets and the check on the little desk and folds her hands. She read that somewhere didn't she? Mass and gravity—maybe only gravity, maybe both; it was probably both—depend, somehow, in their ef-fects, how we experience them, on all the mass in all the galaxies there are. And to the extent things tend to expand on a cosmic scale, thin out eventually, so do gravity, mass, and such. Until—she turns, looks out the window—after billions and billions of years you get these hot, depopulated afternoons; unpleasant dreams; a subtle weakening of some fundamental bond that tends to catch you by surprise like when in summer sometimes the pond will suddenly turn and all that bottom stuff comes floating to the surface. She gets up and goes to the window. They can't intend to be gone very long and leave it open. Sunlight angles in, projects the "Joe's Big Juicy" onto her dress—an actual dress-dress, simple shirtwaist, cotton, white, somewhat demure; not inappropriate, she decides, although one might wish for one of those pious little doilies to cover the head and maybe a pair of cotton gloves. That silly giant plaster hamburger's here on the window ledge along with the other odds and ends from the counter. What a thing. It has the mass-produced, exaggerated, semi-ecstatic qualities of a cheap religious statue. This is my body, she thinks and runs her hand across the nubbly sesame-seeded surface of the foot-diameter bun. This is my blood, along the shiny roll of catsup, the indecently plentiful, vaguely intestinal, drooping giant tomato slices. Lord, it's hot. She looks outside, squints at the glare, then looks away and looks again, walks to the door and stands a moment, waits for the whispery june bug sound of receding galaxies—it's possible actually to imagine, if she lets herself, a subtle sympathetic diminution of the natural light as well. A sort of tease—End of the World, just kidding; oops, no here it comes; just kidding; oops, no that's not it; no that's not it. She looks at the floor. She really wants another orange juice. She returns to her seat and takes a long deep breath and folds her hands again. A Catholic child she knew once told her how the wine was actually, truly transformed into blood and how he'd heard about a man who didn't believe it, charged the priest right in the middle of the ceremony, grabbed the chalice, took a drink, and dropped stone dead right there. How strange, she thought; he should have died before he had a chance to drink it. Maybe he had. Such stories tend to change. She places a Chiclet on her tongue and closes her eyes and waits a moment, then gets up, walks toward the back.

The floor is wet. The plywood sheet that covers the freezer is dripping a little. It's not a very good insulator—cool escapes, condenses, drips. The wood has darkened. The orange extension cord taped down along the floor creates a dam, a pool of water pretty much right where you have to stand to get a view. The cord looks worn. The fluctuation in the light is not encouraging. Presumably the faithful will be preserved from electrocution although she supposes the possibility should provide a little extra devotional kick. She steps to the freezer, places her hands on the cool wet plywood. Is there a tingling? Does it vary with the light? Shall love and hope all pass away? She chews her gum and bends to look. She brings her face down all the way into the layer of cool—an inch or so, it feels like, right above the plastic window—lets her nose touch. Nope. Still nothing, though it's larger. Like some ancient piece of wedding cake or something grown too frosty, too problematic, to identify or throw away—it must have great importance, otherwise it wouldn't be here. Better leave it. Let the children worry about it. Or the children's children. Let them now and then sneak down for a snack, a drink of milk, then open the freezer for a second, stand and gaze upon its hoary, vast, inclusive, humping whiteness no more catfishlike than anything else, than whalelike, mummylike, the way some look at least—she's seen them like that hasn't she, shrouded, flexed, and on their side, their limbs drawn back into the body in regression toward some limbless, ancestral bottom-dwelling form. The cool is nice. The sound of water gently dripping.

"Gobble you up," a little voice behind her says. She jerks around. It's Sister Mary Irene Pincus's little boy. She smiles. He smiles back. "Gobbled them girls." His name is Bud. He has a chocolate bar. It's smeared around his mouth and on his hands. She can't recall having heard him speak before at all—he doesn't quite pronounce his *R*s. He's looking down now at her feet. "Them sharks don't need no more'n that much water there." He indicates with the chocolate bar; a piece goes splash into the puddle. He looks up and smiles again. They're back. The lights come on in the main room; sounds of voices; looming backlit bulk approaching.

"Whoa there, no sir, no, no, no; ain't gonna gobble nobody up," the sheriff lifts the boy up high above the freezer, swoops him around (she ducks the feet), and brings him zooming right down smack, a little too firmly it seems to her, on top of the view plate— giggles, choking, smear of chocolate across the plastic which reminds her very unpleasantly of the smear of a swatted fly. Bud scampers off. The sheriff's breathing very heavily, looking at her. "Whoa," he says.

"I brought Joe's check," she says.

He nods, says "whoa" again, smiles. "See that belly?" His still heaves from the exertion. She's uncertain what he means. "You see that belly?" It seems about to become an uncomfortable sort of moment. "There." He taps the plastic window.

"Oh."

"That belly. See?" He points. "No eggs." It seems to be important.

"Yes." She looks.

"Huh?"

"Yes."

"That there's just what it is, the thing itself. You see it now?"

"I think so. Yes." She stands up. Now he's breathing easily, smiling, beaming at her, fragrance enhanced but compromised by the heat. He reaches over, takes her shoulder, pulls her sideways to him, holds her there next to him for a second as they gaze down at the exhibit like some couple hovering above a bassinet, gives her a pat, a reassuring little squeeze.

"I believe I need to take you fishin'."

29

I t's the last thing. Just a six-by-six-foot—actually slightly smaller—frame of one-by-twos with tar paper stretched across, the three sheets lapped and joined with duct tape underneath, wrapped over the frame and tacked on the back so all you have on top is an even dead-black surface. He would like to have fitted the bottom of the trap with slots or brackets or something so the frame could slide right under like a drawer or a film plate, an X-ray plate, everything cocked and ready to go, just slip it in real slick and easy with a disinterested, scientific, as he imagines ("place this under your tongue for a minute"), sort of gesture; but that's all right. There isn't time. He'll simply tilt the whole thing up and slide it under the trap that way. He's got it leaning against the trailer. It's brand-new tar paper, black as felt. Except that it's square, it looks a little—reminds him a little—of those portable peel-up holes you see in cartoons, the really crazy cartoons where the characters fall into these and come out in China or Hell or wherever. He lifts the bottom of his tee shirt, wipes his face, steps backward squinting at the tar paper, trips over a board and collapses heavily. For a while he sits there holding his arm—it's seeping again; he wonders if that's good or bad; it might be good; he supposes it's possible it might be good. Very likely—it seems very likely now, right now on the ground in the heat and the smell of spilled gasoline and his arm really hurting—there won't be anything to show for this. He squints again. He can make it look so black if he squints, make it look like unfathomable tar-paper depths and even imagine something rising, about to rise, like in those eight-ball fortune things. He starts to get up, feels quite dizzy, sits back down. What very likely there will be, at the very best, is an awful mess. He's built a machine to make a mess, to make a mess of things. A machine to make no difference. He feels dizzy even sitting down. He lies back, sort of falls back, shuts his eyes against the glare. He can hear the puppies acting excited, piling up on this side of the pen and putting a strain on the doubled wire, the rein-forcements. They're going to be too old to place before too long. What will he do with all these dogs? He never even put a sign up. What was he thinking? There's a faint, exhausted-sounding little whoosh from the gas well, followed by an even softer sigh as the tank receives the distillate, almost seems to gasp. It's starting to sound pretty lean, he thinks. When did he last check on the cows? He's probably fired. His boots are coming apart—the right one; he can feel it; he can feel the old gray leather coming apart.

When Agnes gets a certain way sometimes he senses habits, behav-iors, coming through that don't refer to him exactly. Or not origi-nally. It makes him feel somewhat displaced, a little bit ghostly. She keeps sighing deep accusatory sighs and shakes her head, says "Lord, Lord, Lord," or "Goodness me," declines to look at him directly, getting ice and pouring water, which is almost drinkable if it's cold, plugging in the little oscillating fan which for some reason fails to screech, just whirs and blows across his face. She tosses a bright red-wrapped and ribboned Christmas present onto the bed next to him, stands in the doorway just gazing out.

"What's that?"

She turns and looks at him for a second, goes to the counter by the sink and starts to fiddle around with the radio.

"Hey," says Luther.

"You got to wait until tomorrow if you're alive." She's trying to turn the radio on.

"That button on top."

"I'm gonna get you into town to see Doc Kirby."

"Not on Sunday; not on Christmas Eve you ain't."

"Dang."

"You gotta turn the whole thing a little one way or the other." Fluttery static, hiss and squawk; the edge of a signal. "I don't use it much." It's Christmas music, "Silent Night" or something.

"There." She stands, the signal fades. She backs away; it strengthens sightly. "There." She turns, steps out the door.

"You got 'em?" Luther calls.

"I got 'em."

Luther pours the last of the ice water into his palm and splashes his face, the back of his neck. It's Perry Como. He leans back. He's feeling better. "You gonna help me plug 'em in?" he yells.

She slams the door of the pickup. "Come on now. Come on." She's got the puppy with her. "That's right. Come on." It looks fatter, fluffier or something. It's been bathed. It's on a leash with a big red ribbon tied in a bow around its neck. Yurang is up, at the end of his chain. She has a grocery sack; she holds it up and shakes it.

"Jesus Christ, don't shake it, Agnes."

"I'll do worse'n that unless you make me a promise."

"Shit." The puppy's trying to jerk away toward Yurang; she's about to drop the sack. "All right, just bring it here. Don't drop it."

Perry Como night apparently. Christmas Eve with Perry Como. Agnes sits on the floor with the last of the Masonite panels—double panels; three-by-three-foot; slotted top sheets screwed down tight with safety screws to be removed as each of the four is locked into place on top of the trap. One end in her lap, the other resting on the couch, it looks like needlepoint or something perfectly natural like that, peaceful. She inserts each little paint-filled section of straw with the same firm, competent nod of her head as if she were taught how as a child. As if her mother had done it just that way. "O, Little Town of Bethlehem" comes softly through the gentle hush of static. Evening sunlight slants across. The slots and straws make complex, delicate shadowy patterns.

"Get that fancy kind of cheese?" The flecks of gold foil in the top of the little table catch the light. A redbird is singing.

"Got that smelly kind of cheese. I had to get it at the bait shop."

"Bread?"

"Got kaiser rolls."

He nods, leans back, and takes another bite of his own cheese sandwich, looks outside and finds himself, for a moment, suddenly buoyant, almost overcome with a sense of momentousness—

quite serenely overcome. He looks at Agnes. How deliberate, calm, resigned. Perhaps momentousness is serene. Even the sound of sirens, somewhere way beyond the lake it sounds like, seems to contribute, carries only a sad, reflective little note like that of the redbird. Almost finished. Almost done. "The hopes and fears of all the years. . . ." What was it like, he wonders, just before the first atomic bomb, say—out in the desert, wherever it was. Was there a moment like this—someone sweeping up, a radio somewhere playing something—Perry Como maybe, he was around then wasn't he—deep red evening sunlight streaming into the Quonset hut or something like a Quonset hut, all corrugated, temporary, just enough to house the thing, the moment.

"Bait shop?"

"Yeah, they use that stuff for catfish bait."

"Huh."

"Yep; they mix it with some other stuff but that's the place to get it."

"Huh."

"Yep, that's where you can get it."

They can hardly budge the trap. It weighs too much. They have to tow it behind the truck with Luther riding, standing astride the projecting members of the eight-and-a-half by eight-and-a-half-foot outer frame whose prowlike angle helps to part the grass. The low red sunlight shows their wake and exaggerates the ripply surface of the grass, the clouds of gnats and other tiny glittery insects, floating bits of grass and dust, a golden-rosy glow of dust that lifts around them and seems to concentrate and hold the light, hold everything in a dreamy, slowly fading, reverential sort of light as Agnes trails the rope around and draws it up to turn the trap the way he wants, helps lift one side to slip the tar-paper panel in, presents the sandwich—triple-layered and double-cheesed and kaiser-rolled and such a fragrance, such a rich conflicting density of smell, so good and bad at once, especially out in the open, so far out in the field so late in the day away from any context or politeness.

. . .

"See where I put them springs in there?"

"Yeah." Agnes sits on the wooden step which now is back where it belongs, works on the knot in her puppy's ribbon which has had its little bow yanked into streamers.

"That worked out real good I thought." He sits in the door. It's nearly dark but he can see it, just the top part raised like wings way out there just above the grass. "The way them levers come together in that slot and made it easy just to put a spring in there to work both sides like that. I thought that worked real good."

"Looked good to me." She's got it loose now, pulls it free. The puppy plops down with its head across her foot.

"I think you got yourself a dog."

She turns and holds a finger up into the light—it's got a beige Band-Aid around it.

"Shit," says Luther. Perry Como's fading fast. The stations tend to lose their power in the evenings, tend to settle below the horizon— which is what it feels like anyway, part of the general sense of falling out of phase.

"I think I fucked up, though."

"Yeah?"

"Yeah. What's gonna keep a coon or somethin' else from settin' that thing off?"

"Well. . . ."

"Dammit."

Agnes stands.

"Goddammit, I coulda figured somethin' out."

She bends and clips the leash onto the puppy's collar.

"Shit."

"I tell you what," she says—the puppy's not inclined to move; it seems to have turned in for the night; she tugs it gently—"I am truly of the opinion that no self-respectin' regular sort of critter's gonna go anywhere near that thing. Come on." She tugs again more firmly, finally reaches down and picks it up. She holds it like a baby, turns and looks across the field. It's getting too dark now to see anything at all.

"Thanks for the present."

"Don't you open it till the mornin'. Lord, I'm beat." She heads for the truck. She turns it around and backs up, leans out. "Merry Christmas."

"Same to you."

She takes the bridge too fast as usual—rattling tailgate, clash of gears, a little intermittent backfire, poppety-pop, as she winds it out, as she recedes, until that's all he hears, just every now and then a little pop way in the distance.

He has Christmas Eve type dreams, the kind a child will have where it all goes wrong and it's all subverted, ruined, all your best and clearest wishes just a mess; and then you wake up, shake it off, go back to sleep but it's the same, a gloppy, smeary mess, raccoon and possum tracks across it, great big splurts of white like pigeon droppings, nothing subtle, fine or forceful, nothing terrible, nothing much. He kicks awake. His sweaty sheet he half-imagines soaked with paint. He kicks it off. He's got the radio on, turned down to static mostly, just a hint of music possibly now and again, but it's the noise he wants to wash out any tendency to listen for the trap, to lie awake and wait and listen for the sound of something—reindeer on the roof, whatever. Still it's not very restful. The whispery noise is like a blanket, seems to overlay his thoughts and redirect them right back down into those dreams. He thinks of Willis, Deputy Dawg, and how he looked there in his squad car that time, sound asleep, completely lost in the static. Maybe that's what puppies hear when they get all piled up together for the night—the sound of all their little heartbeats, circulation, respiration, indiscriminate, all for one and one for all and all the same. "Hush now," it says, "it doesn't matter; makes no difference." He turns it down a little more. Is that what Perry Como says? It probably is. He turns it off. He plumps his pillow, adjusts the fan, and tries to get his arm braced up into the corner, tries to make it stay like that, gives up and holds it across his chest. There's no momentousness. There's nothing. Where's his present? Where did he put it? He rolls over and feels around on the floor, feels down by the foot of the bed and finds it there. He places it next to him, leans it against the window screen but that tends to make a little noise whenever he moves so he tries a couple of different arrangements, finally puts it under his pillow.

David Searcy

30

L uther sighs. He sits up, tries to fix the ribbon, tries to pluck it up a little, runs his thumbnail back and forth along the creases. Yurang's quiet on the floor, head on his paws, awake, although it's hard to tell sometimes with chows—you have to look for that little twitch above the eyes which are hard to see. He turns off the fan. The redbird's out there again; he looks—that must be him out by the road there on the wire. The sunrise flickers through the thin parts of the pines, flares through the tops, across the grass in rosy streaks, across his bed. He scoots back, shoves his pillow behind him, crosses his legs, and holds the present in his lap. He slides the ribbon over the corners, slips it off, the ribbon and bow in a single piece; she actually tied it, made the bow herself. He places it on the bed. He turns the package over, pops the tape and lifts the perfectly folded triangular flaps, unfolds them, spreads the paper open, lifts the shiny white enamel-finish cardboard box and turns it right side up, lifts off the top, lays back the tissue. It's a cowboy shirt. Bright red with pearly buttons. He looks at the tab inside the collar. Extra large. He leans back, looks down at his stomach, folds his arms across it, takes a deep breath, slowly lets it out.

The milk is bad; he puts it back. He stands at the counter and munches Kix right out of the box. They last forever, taste like nothing in particular. They make eating more like breathing.

He changes the bandage without actually looking at his arm. He sort of sloshes some of that red stuff Agnes gave him over the wound—the countertop is pretty well stained by now. He holds his breath and turns away until he gets a layer of gauze around it. Then it's a little easier finishing up with a folded pad, more gauze and tape.

How bright it is this time of day inside the trailer, morning light still clear and pink bouncing in off dusty ground, the yellowing grass. It practically glows.

"Hey." Yurang's eyebrows wiggle a little. "Hey," says Luther. Hardly a twitch this time. The tail moves very slightly. Luther sits on the edge of the bed, looks at the cowboy shirt in its box, looks at the dog. The puppies are stirring. Luther lies back down and shuts his eyes. He concludes there should be nothing. Nothing much. That would be good. That would be just what the doctor ordered. Nothing makes a lot more sense. He waits for the shooting pains to stop. He keeps his eyes closed for a while. Then he gets up, puts on the shirt—he lines the pins up on the table, counts them, five—rolls up the left sleeve to the elbow, steps outside.

It's already starting to get hazy. Already hot. The redbird's gone. He walks a little way into the yard and stops, comes back up onto the step, back up in the doorway for a moment, squinting, raising himself on his tiptoes, dropping down, regarding himself in his undershorts; the shirt's that fancy kind though, long tails hanging down in front and back. He trots around to the end of the trailer, climbs onto the propane tank and scrambles onto the roof—it's not so hard without his boots which tend to slip—steps carefully sideways along the edge to where the chicken crate can give him some support. He squats beside it, gazes out across the field. A sort of brightness, fairly subtle but from here he can see it clearly—all around the trap there's a delicate sort of brightness like a halo. He stands up and starts to climb onto the crate but changes his mind. It feels unstable, probably warped up here in the heat. He kind of half stands for a minute with his left hand on the crate, considers jumping, reconsiders, looks around, looks everywhere, behind and all around at the pine trees and the field, the grass, the whole scene, wants to take it in, establish what that looks like, just the basics, just be sure what nothing looks like. There's no question—he stands up—the trap is closed, the top is down, it's dark, the Masonite is dark—and there's a halo around it. That's enough, he thinks. Just that right there—it's even beautiful in a way—just that right there would be enough. He slips and nearly falls off the end, skins up his knee but protects the shirt, trots in a limping sort of trot into the grass which feels, against his bare white legs, like freezing water— not the cold part but the shock of jumping in, of giving up. He can't quite see it. There's the trap but there's no brightness, not from here. He slows. What if it's something optical, sort of imaginary like a rainbow? He keeps waving away the gnats. It's like he's swimming. Something's coming. He stops. A big truck—it's an asphalt truck or a gravel truck or something; it comes roaring around the curve. The driver waves and Luther waves back. In his underwear and cowboy shirt he waves. It's automatic. He stands and watches until it's gone, until the dust has drifted away. His knee is bleeding. There are a number of little scratches on his legs. He turns. He sees it now he thinks. It's in the grass. As he gets nearer it's more obvious. He breaks a stalk of grass, examines it, breaks another closer in. It's paint; it rubs off like a powder. Like a dusting of ash or something. It's quite clear. He circles the trap but keeps his distance. The clapping shut, the whole thing must have been more violent than intended. Probably the springs were a little too much. The ground, the grass, around the trap looks bleached as if from some bright light—a tiny nuclear event. Here and there he can actually see the shadow of the structure on the grass. He steps in closer. It's like a light still shines inside. Although it's dark. He peers in under the top. The chicken wire is white. He feels the inside of the upright—the paint is dry, perfectly dry. The hog wire's white in places, mostly around the edge. He can't really see much more than that. The sandwich is gone. He stands and backs away, retreats a little farther, stands a moment simply looking, turns, and runs back to the house.

It's more of a problem than he thought, just raising it up. "Now here we go." He talks to himself. He's got his jeans on and his boots. He's on his knees. He's got his good hand under the trap. He's brought two sticks to prop it up if he can get it onto his shoulder. "Here we go." The gnats are getting in his mouth. He sets it down and tries again, gets one stick under at an angle, shifts around to find some leverage, brings it up a little more. "That's got it." Now the other stick.

• • •

The tar-paper panel is much too cumbersome to carry. He has to drag it through the grass. It's covered with insects. Little bugs all over it—gnats and tiny grasshopper things and lots of those little bug-shaped bugs that hop all over the place; their hoppings fall in and out of phase, sometimes a whole bunch will just vanish all at once and reappear somewhere or not. There must be something in the paint. They must like something.

Puppies wander about, some drifting in and out of the tall grass, others hanging around, getting underfoot. "Yurang." He turns around and calls; he whistles once, turns back. It's leaning against the trailer. It's important not to think he needs to see it right away. You don't read X rays just like that, not really. You might think you do but it takes training, surely. Time to learn to see it. It's so compli-cated, seemingly complicated, subtle, lots of little parts. A subtle suggestion, at least, of parts, extensions or something sort of pecu-liar. Not a coon, though. Not a possum. Not by any means. Not any-thing like that.

It's really a matter of concentration. If, for example, in the darkness he illuminates certain sections with a flashlight, it gives a sense of breaking the problem up and making it more approachable. He's re-moved his mattress, placed it on the floor, tossed out the puppies' box. They're loose. The door is open so they come and go at will—they mostly come; one's in his lap. He's got the panel leaning up against the bed. It fills that whole end of the trailer. He's on the mat-tress leaning back against the wall. What seems to have happened is the capsules sort of exploded. The paint was atomized. It must have formed a cloud—so what you've got is not a shadow, not exactly. It has depth in a way. There must have been a violent sort of swirling of the mist up under things and how it swirled and settled must re-flect the shape, at least in places—that's the impression. He uses the flashlight like a pointer. Here, for example—he likes to think of himself as saying that: "for example"; as if the puppies were an audience; as if he had summoned this great detachment—here, for example, away from the great big somehow unpleasant-looking truly shadowy part in the very center you start to get a sense of form, and there's a fairly definite outline here where the tip of something, one of those extensions, must have hung down through the hog-wire/chicken-wire floor and actually touched the tar-paper surface. He waves the flashlight back and forth across the panel very quickly to get an overall view again. You'd never get that in a photograph, that sense of something touching, reaching the surface, coming nearer. It is, however, he supposes, like a photograph insofar as it's a negative, black on white, so in his mind he tries to correct for that, reversing it, reversing also its actual physical orientation: something white and rising toward him. There's a little breeze. The night air smells of gasoline. "Hey," Luther calls the puppies. "Y'all get in here." Here they come. One, two, three, four, five. . . . He's got them all. "Y'all don't crap in here too much." He puts a bedsheet over the panel, goes outside to call for Yurang, stands and listens for a while.

31

"What's that?"
        "It's bourbon."
"Bourbon?"
"Yep."
"Oh dear."
"Don't say that please. Don't say oh dear or anything. Just don't."
"Want some of this?"
"No. What is it? No."
"It's good."
"You put in too much hot—too much hot pepper."
"It's *arrabbiata*."
"I don't care. I mean I'm sorry. I'm not hungry. Thanks for the robe, it's very nice."
"Looks nice. You sure?"
"Yes. Tell me. . . ."
"What?"
"Have you ever caught a fish? Gone fishing? Done that kind of thing?"
"That kind of thing?"
"Like fishing."
"Well, when I was a lad. . . ."
"No really."
"No. Here, this is good; it's not too hot."
"Not ever?"
"Have a seat. I think I caught a carp once."
"Carp."
"Some pasta, very lovely *penne* pasta; little sauce."
"Don't do that."
"What?"

"That fake Italian accent thing."

"But you're okay with the general tone—the simultaneously fawning, patronizing. . . ."

"What's a carp?"

"A carp, my dear. . . ."

"Oh stop. Just never mind."

She takes her drink out on the deck, leans on the rail. A swarm of something teeny tiny—gaggle, flock—departs the cypress tree and flitters into the dark. The frogs are going. She can see the Milky Way, at first quite faintly, overhead. It looks like a cirrus cloud, then as her eyes adjust she sees it better, all the stars. Orion hangs above the dam. And in the water. All the stars there on the glassy, optical surface. If she were standing on her head she couldn't tell. She swirls her ice. The frogs are making that plunky noise that sounds like "testing." One will start then others follow here and there along the margins of the pond. They all say "testing" with exactly the right inflection over and over, all night long. She takes a drink, regards a bright star in the water near the shore. It splits, dissolves into a ripply smear of light as something twists and thrusts away beneath the surface. She looks up without even thinking as if to see the event reflected.

Why should there have to be such clatter simply cleaning up and putting things away? And such a pause to let her know he's pausing, waiting for her to come back in before he turns the light off. Such forgiveness in that gesture. She'll just wait. She'll nurse this drink, a pretty stiff one, watch the stars rise over the pond and sink into it—if she lays her head down sideways on the table she receives a reasonable impression, seems more reasonable in its left-hand/right-hand symmetry she decides, of the expanding universe, especially, she's pleased to note, if one allows the black reflected line of trees along the shore to represent the primordial obscurity, the darkness at the center of one's knowledge. She's not tired. She'll stay out here with the doubting frogs and finish this drink and wait until he goes to bed. He never reads. He's asleep in seconds. There's a faint glow barely peeking above the tree line, right in the middle of her cosmology—she still has her head down sideways on the table; it's quite comfortable. It interfers—the glow. There shouldn't be one. How to explain—she takes a drink and puts her head back down—a subtle leak of information across the boundary of our ignorance like that? It compromises linearity as well as other things, she's certain. She goes ahead and drains the rest. At last: the rattly, clinky hum of the dishwasher. That's the final thing. It's always the very last thing. The light goes out behind her. She sits up. She waits a bit then slips inside, makes another bourbon in the dark. She comes back out and stands by the rail. It must be Gilmer, that little glow. She almost imagines now and then she can see the faintest fluctuation. She sits down and swirls the ice. She tries to think—she has a blouse and jeans in the dryer but her purse and keys are probably in the bedroom. She should wait awhile. There's half a bottle left. More frogs are joining in the chorus. She imagines drifting out across the pond in the old canoe into the obscurity, into the blackness toward the shore.

It's probably not a good idea for her to drive, but it's okay if she takes the back roads; she prefers them really anyway, prefers to avoid any sort of traffic, having to deal with two-lane highways, someone's lights—they always want to go so fast, come up behind too close and make you go to the shoulder; but it gets a little confusing, especially at night. You really have to pay attention. She messed up somewhere. It's hard to tell. She may have actually backtracked, might have been down this particular stretch before. She hits her brights. That little house with the dirt front yard and the purple car seat on the porch looks sort of familiar—the display of catfish heads as well, three on one post. Or maybe not. Three on one fence post—that's the first time she's seen that. She shivers, dims her lights. It's like they climbed it, crawled up out of the ground one after the other like those cicada things, those empty cicada shells you see on trees and the sides of houses in the summer with their backs split down the middle where the newer form emerged. She breaks a rule and gets the little pint of brandy from the glove box—Armagnac and quite expensive to discourage this very thing, but brandy nonetheless for emergencies, for the chill.

She slips into town, thinks of herself as slipping into town, somehow as if she weren't supposed to, shouldn't be doing this, sneaking a peek, turning onto the square now, slowly, quietly. And in fact—it nearly takes her breath away—it is like something embarrassing, some appalling secret, not so much the huge and maybe a little embarrassing neon sign itself, but just that it keeps on running all night long with everything else closed down, completely dark, as if it had some surreptitious job to do at . . . what, she looks at the dash . . . at three o'clock in the morning. "Oh," she says aloud as she pulls to a stop in the middle of the street, gets out and stands looking over the top of the car for a moment. "Oh," the galaxies sputter away so sadly, so emphatically in the dark; she seems to follow them in her mind, her currently augmented state of mind, into the night beyond the sign, imagines cinders falling out somewhere, way out beyond the city in some field, a rustling pitter-pat of cinders falling into a grassy field. It's awful. How the world should end—and here it is for all to see; she looks around—and all night long in case you forget; in case you wake up in the night and think: Now what did I forget? Was it the dishes? No. The cat? No. Was it . . . oh. Yes. That was it. And you can come down for a look if you really want. There's no one here. She backs the car into a space across the street, rolls down the windows, turns the engine off, and looks around again. No sign of life at the courthouse. Still—she pops the cork on the little bottle—there's an open-container law and she can't bear to pour it out.

What was that Kafka story? Something about a prisoner somewhere strapped into a machine that over the course of hours or days—she can't recall—inscribed his crime, the name of his crime, into his back with a sort of stylus over and over, deeper and deeper, until he got it, understood. The periodic stuttery recession of the cosmos flickers softly through her eyelids. Warm night air moves very faintly through the car; the sound of trucks, just every now and then a big one, hauling logs as she imagines, removing the props, the better furnishings, getting out while the getting's good.

32

She's being touched. Just here and there—her wrist, her neck—
very lightly touched by something heavy like being lightly
brushed by livestock. She's not home. She opens her eyes. She seems
to have fallen across the passenger's seat. It's dark. Up through the
windshield she can see the neon cross with its pale-blue radiating elements, once in a while a flickering from below that lights the inside
of the car. A hovering presence. There's a complex, contradictory
sort of fragrance. It withdraws.

She's being lifted. Not ungently but very briskly as if habitually, a
very usual bit of business not unlike, in her dim, reflexive surrender
to it, being gathered out of the car at night when she was a little girl.
The fragrance, at least the floral component, now is almost overpowering, overlaying everything else as, for a moment, she's against
him, gets her hair caught in his badge which requires her face to be
pressed hard against his shirt as he untangles it, pressed right past
the loud cologne into the scent of whatever nastiness he's been at.
She jerks her head. "Oh God," she says. "Oh Jesus."

"What?" he whispers, carefully lets her down into the front seat
of the squad car. There are other voices nearby. They recede. She's
being given a tall white Styrofoam cup of coffee with his hands
around her hands around the cup until it burns—her hands kept
tight against the cup like that. It's like a police technique, as if she
were meant to confess to something.

"Please," she says. He lets go, sits back, shuts his door. Whenever
he moves the whole car sways a little. She supports the cup from the
bottom, takes a sip.

"I'll get them boys to bring your car," he says in a voice not used to modulating down toward kindness, softness. He gives her some-thing else—it's awkward, on a napkin, rather large. He tries to place it on her lap. She has to take it. It's a huge round yellow pastry. She assumes it must be yellow.

"This is my body."

"What?" he whispers; why does he whisper?

"What?"

"Thanks."

"You bet," very softly he says, "you bet," turns and sighs a wheezy sigh, looks out the window. "Been a night."

She smells it—past the sugary pastry, floral aftershave and every-thing she can smell the kind of night it's been. He shakes his head. He doesn't have to tell her. "You don't need to. . . ."

"Them things. . . ."

"Really. . . ."

"Them things sure get in your clothes."

She's feeling ill.

"Had two this time, 'bout, oh, five miles apart and one. . . ."

"No, please. . . ."

". . . little bitty ole thing but the smell. . . ."

"I'd rather not. . . ."

"Hoo, boy."

"Please."

"Lordy."

"Yes."

He's looking at her now.

"You gonna be okay?"

She nods. The neon galaxies disperse. The pastry is yellow. It re-ally is. It's soaking through the paper napkin.

"I can cut that up in pieces for you. Here." He leans to get his knife; the car sways.

"Oh no, really."

"Sure?"

"Oh yes."

"Hey lookee here; this here's real cute"—he takes an object from his pocket; it's his keys—"look here what happens when you push this here." His key chain has a clasp shaped like a fish. He holds it up into the glow, the fish mouth opens to release the ring which has a little fish hook on the end. "Got that for my birthday—ain't that cute?"

"It is."

"Just push that little fin on top and snap it back."

"It's cute."

"Boys at the courthouse give me that."

For a while they watch the sign. "What kind of fish is that?"

"What?"

"On your key chain."

"It's a shark. They said they couldn't find no key chain with a cat-fish."

"Oh."

"A shark's about as close as they could come."

"I think I'm probably able to drive."

"You wanna take a little test?"

"A shark's not really very close."

He shifts around. She shuts her eyes. "You ever seen one on a line. . . ."

"No."

". . . comin' off that muddy bottom on a trotline, you can't see him till he's tired—a really biggun. . . ."

"No."

". . . he'll wait until you're right on top and take that line and run this way and that, near turn you over. . . ."

She can feel his breath and smell him, feel his hand against her leg.

". . . you shine your light down there at night into that water it'll look just like them big ole sharks way out there in the ocean, how they look—you seen them movies, ain't you?"

"Yes."

"You seen 'em."

"Yes."

"You start to haulin' on that line at first ain't nothin', just the water and the mud but then look out, hoo boy." He's quiet for a moment. She can feel him turn away, remove his hand. He starts the car.

"My purse."

"We got it." He pulls out. The pastry eases very slowly from her knee onto the floor.

"I got the record."

"Oh?"

"Still do. I caught him out here where we're goin'. Ain't nobody knows this spot. And this right now's the best time, right now."

There's a suggestion of gray—false dawn, whatever that is—the faintest possible premonition of the morning.

"Usually keep a trotline out here all the time."

"Was there another . . . ?"

"Gonna pass a spot up here you might remember—sorry?"

"Wasn't there another?" He turns onto a smaller road. They lose that straight off in the distance glimpse of faintly graying sky. The trees close in.

"Another what?"

"Another catfish. That first big one someone caught as big as yours."

He shakes his head.

"I heard. . . ."

"There weren't no other big one."

"No?"

"Nope. Just somebody talkin' or somebody heard somebody talkin' 'bout a dream or somethin'. I don't know." He's slowing.

"Just a dream."

"Look here. Just fishin' talk. You know how people talk. Look where we are."

The trees have opened up again on either side—a sort of corridor that sweeps away up over gentle rises left and right, a hint of color. Rods or cones—whichever—struggle in the half-light but there's color. Yellow. Gold. He starts to speed up.

"Wait."

He pulls off to the side.

"Wait," she says softly, feels around to find the button, lowers the window, holds her face to the air a moment, opens the door, steps out, and leans against the car. She's still unsteady. She breathes in a long deep breath. It's still that smell like VapoRub or not that; something like that. Something. All those sticky yellow flowers, such a concentration of them. Such a gash straight through the trees and then the flowers like an ointment on the wound. He's getting out. He comes around. She walks to the fence; he follows.

"'Course ain't nothin' here."

She looks for a gap in the barbed wire.

"Here go." He lifts one strand, puts his boot down on the other, strains to make it easy for her. She slips through.

"We hauled it off, you know." The wire snaps off his hand and hits his shoulder, snags his belt as he rolls under into the flowers. "Dang." Retrieves his hat. "Can't leave them things just sittin' out." He walks up to her. "Can't just leave 'em out."

It wasn't VapoRub but like that; stronger, yellow, greasy, aromatic stuff beneath the hot towels on her chest; she felt quite certain—the way a child, without real certainty, without the concept, can imagine she finds it anyway, anywhere, lurking in the most discouraging places—she was certain it was medicine for her heart which had become infected, damaged in some way. He shifts his weight a little now and then from one foot to the other, jams his hands into his belt behind his back.

"Why can't you leave them out?"

He looks at her. A gust of wind sends waves across the flowers, makes him hold his hat. "What?"

"Like those catfish heads. Just leave them out." The breeze is chilly, whips her hair across her face. She rubs her arms. Thin wisps of pink are fanning out across the sky. She takes another long deep breath. Sometimes she'd wake up in the morning having breathed that stuff all night and for a moment entertain the brightest hope, entirely permeated, cleansed. She shakes her head.

"What?"

"What's a carp?"

"It's just a fish. Ain't good for much."

"Not like a catfish."

"Nope."

The wind is kicking up, the flowers toss this way and that. "And that? What's that?" She nods. He looks across the flowers up the rise.

"What?"

She can see it, flowers parting; it's a dog or something.

"What?" He walks on out into the flowers.

"Can you take me home?" She has to yell. He turns.

"What?"

It's just like those movies. He can't see it yet but it's right there—a sort of darkness in the flowers at his feet. She turns away, sits down in the flowers, shuts her eyes, and puts her fingers in her ears.

33

He sees it now. He sort of saw it first thing, soon as there was light. A breeze came up, he felt the trailer rock a little, just enough to wake him—puppy on his stomach, a red one (why don't they have names?), the little red one; others piled up on the bed-sheet which they'd pulled down off the panel. It surprised him. In the nearly dark he didn't know at first quite what it was—like when you wake up in a strange room, it can take a minute, maybe even longer. He kept thinking he was looking through it, looking through a window at a dark shape, not remembering what was there. It looked like something outside, hovering, backlit. Even, after a while as the light improved, as he became aware—a part of him became aware—of what it was, he held that notion, kept that sense of being in a strange room where it had an abrupt and thoughtless, almost photographic presence, that sort of imminence—just the smallest detail, the slightest revelation at any point and everything would fol-low, would resolve. And, in a way, it did. He glimpsed a hand imbedded in the overspray—what he thinks of as the overspray: that secondary, atmospheric, halolike effect that, here and there in the dim light, fell away, allowed a sense of outline and his practiced eye to find a hand, a little hand like a child's, its fingers spread like a child's will do when being traced with a piece of chalk, and from the hand a little arm; and along the arm his will to imagine all the rest led into the dark unpleasant center from which all the spidery parts, extensions, runners, consequences of the thing—he had to look away at last—from which details began to emerge, began to suggest themselves like a whisper which, though not exactly intelligible, lets you know by the tone or something it's indecent.

He's still lying on the couch. The puppy doesn't want to move; she likes the warmth. The breeze is cool and Luther probably has a fever. He looks out. The morning sky is aglow with color. Wind is whipping out of the north across the grass. He feels a chill. He sits up, draws his legs up to him under the covers, lets the puppy slip to the floor. He watches the grass, the sweeps and swirls of wind. It's like a clean slate; Agnes raking her yard. Whatever leaves a trail now leaves it unmistakably. There's a siren somewhere. "Hey." One of the puppies starts to sniff around in that preparatory way. "Hey." Luther gets up, opens the door. They tumble past him into the yard. He gets his jeans on, rounds them up into the pen, checks on the chickens, stands for a while in just his boots and jeans, no shirt, and lets the change in the weather hit him, pale and thin-skinned, start him shaking like the grass. He must have fever—he must have it like a quality by now, a characteristic, like his stomach hanging out; he feels the cool against it, looks down at it shaking, shivering; big old stomach shivering. He can feel his injury standing out here shivering, feel how it runs right through him, constitutes an apprehension, a sort of knowledge; indisputable. You can't argue with it. Look at this. He's shaking now like crazy. What a sky. He's never seen a sky like that. He heads back in as sirens, more of them and nearer, seem to come from different directions, seem to keep on getting louder. By the time the first car pulls in way too fast and sort of bounces sideways, skidding into the soft dirt, raising huge amounts of dust, he's cut the tar paper halfway off the wooden frame. It's curling down out of the way so he can see them out the window, flashing lights and sirens and all—two more nearly collide head-on, each trying to beat the other to the turn-in. Then they fan out, park their cars at funny angles like they've seen it on TV. "Where's that damn dog?" one yells. "Look there"—that sounds like Willis—"look there underneath that trailer." Luther's almost got it now. He has to cut through duct-tape seams along the bottom then just goes ahead and rips it the rest of the way. He rolls it up and stands there with it for a moment to see if maybe he'll stop shivering. Bam. The door shakes. He can hear the puppies putting up a racket. Bam. "Hey Luther, where's your dog?" It's not a voice he knows. "Hey." Luther rolls the tar paper tight as he can and jams it up behind the sink in the little bathroom, tries to close the plastic door but it's still sprung where Yurang bent it out that time. He throws the mattress back on the bed. "Hey, Luther Hazlitt." Luther grabs his new red cowboy shirt and slings it on and stands there by the door and sneaks a look. Bam. "Luther, where's that goddamn chow?" He presses his boot against the bottom of the door then turns the knob and lets the door pop open suddenly so it bangs the side of the trailer. It's a tall, lean, sort of stern-faced deputy Luther's seen maybe only a couple of times. He takes a backward step or two but doesn't throw a fit or anything like Willis.

"He run off," says Luther. Troy walks around from the side; he's peeking into all the windows.

"Run off when?" The stern-faced deputy's lips are all that move, just barely, the only part; it makes him look like one of those characters in that really cheap cartoon show years ago where real live mouths were superimposed on otherwise motionless cartoon faces.

"What the hell's the matter with you? You sick or somethin'?"

"Shit," says Luther. He can't get his shirt to button. Wind comes whipping around the trailer, slaps the door into his shoulder. Sawdust swirls around the other deputy way out in the yard—another one he doesn't know; he's got his eyes scrunched up; he holds his hat on, kicks around in the lumber scraps and stuff. Willis Beagle hangs back by his car, just stands there.

"What?" He's having a problem with his left hand, trying to button his shirt. "Oh"—he looks down and tries a different button—"run off . . . let's see . . . yesterday. 'Bout this time. Just took off." Maybe it's not so much his voice that's shaking as his shaking makes him hear it like that. "What'd he do . . ." it won't stop. He looks away across the field. He tries in a whisper, "What'd he do, go rob a bank?"

"What?"

Luther shakes his head.

"Hey."

"Nothin'."

"Look at me."

He looks at Troy who's finished peeking in the windows, now he's standing by the puppies, trying to let them sniff his hand and driving them crazy. It's an awful noise right now, a useless, irritating noise, the wind and everything and that just makes it worse. "Shut up," he yells. They just get louder. Troy steps slightly away from the pen and looks at Luther. All four deputies look at Luther. None of that easy, sly, professional look you usually get though, none of that; it's all right on the surface: they could be plumbers, pure and simple; duty imposed or superimposed upon the face so clearly, sternly, lips can barely move to request he sign this form that lets them search his trailer, do whatever they want. It takes a while. They go all through it like debris from some disaster, make remarks about each thing, dismiss it, make a face and throw it down and ask him lots of questions; all but Willis who's outside, at one point pissing on the trailer in that same spot like a dog. They jerk the tar-paper panel out from behind the sink and tear it, flop it halfway open, shake their heads, and toss it away, don't give it a thought. They look at his hands and ask what happened to his arm. He has to show them. Jesus Christ, they say and back on out, good Lord what in the world's the matter with him and then they're gone except for Willis. He just stands around in the yard for a couple of minutes, looks at Luther still with his shirt unbuttoned, stomach hanging out, still shaking. "Bobby's dead," he says across a swirl of sawdust. "Shit." And turns and leaves.

34

The pink clouds spread, go red then violet, thicken slowly into gray, low, heavy overcast. The wind, by midday, comes straight out of the north, and even colder. Puppies huddle up in their pen. The chickens stay in the lee of the coop, all puffy and quiet. Luther's got his Army jacket on, zipped up. He sits on the stump with a sandwich, facing the trailer, watching the open door swing back and forth. It slaps the side then swings back, almost closes but not quite, swings open again. It's like how you think of a house abandoned; there'll be wind, a swinging door or gate or something. He can imagine someone coming upon a trailer like that, glancing inside and passing right on by. No one but kids with secret beers and cigarettes would even bother with it. What do they do these days—still beers and cigarettes and things like that he wonders? Maybe worse. A little dope. A couple of girls. Much tittering—look at this old thing whatever it is, this old pathetic this or that, this incriminating, sad, old thing and toss it away and giggle. Stains all over the mattress. Scorch marks. After a while he goes inside and clears the bed, sweeps all the stuff that got tossed over there onto the floor, lays out the tar-paper panel facedown without looking at it, trying not to see the front at all, repairs the tear with duct tape, rolls it up again, face-in, as tightly as he can, puts tape around it at the ends and in the middle, thinks a moment. Wind comes whistling through the windows; bits of paper fly around and out the door into the yard, receipts for things, to be turned in to Mr. Tuel; some of those leaflets he collected with the picture of whatever—catfish, Christ, whatever. There they go. He finds a little space between the bed and the outside wall just big enough to stuff the rolled-up tar paper in.

By late afternoon there's a dusting of snow. It doesn't stick so maybe not an actual dusting but it's there, the tiny crystals on the dark-green canvas sleeve of his Army jacket, each one present for a moment, for a while the overall number pretty steady, each one winking out, replaced.

Sounds seem to carry so much farther in the cold. He hears her miles away, the little pop, pop, pop. She needs to tune it; needs to not downshift like that, just use the brakes. She rises, breaches; spray-can white on mottled white looks like the skin of some old fish, a whale or something as the truck ascends to grade, appears to rise up through the grass. She pulls in, parks sort of far away as if she weren't quite sure—the way it looks with all his stuff tossed out and scattered in the yard, a little like the courthouse lawn that day last week, whenever it was. She cuts the motor, lets the puppy out. It makes a couple of wild, ecstatic circles around the truck, spots Luther sitting on the stump and dashes over for a tummy rub, a scratch between the ears, then to the pen with loud reception. Agnes climbs out rather stiffly, she's so bundled up, her arms sprung out away from her sides a little like a child's. She's wearing mittens and a big plaid cap with earflaps, pulled way down, her gray hair flying out from under. She walks over, stands, and looks around awhile at all the gutted-out odds and ends, the tacky crap it's so surprising life requires.

"See anything you need?" he says.

She looks down at him. He's quite glad for the mittens, other-wise she'd probably try to feel his forehead. She just stands there. "Hear 'bout Sheriff?"

"Ain't heard much."

"He's dead."

"I heard that much." The wind sorts his belongings as to weight or maybe value. Pots and pans and things like that stay put of course right where he tossed them. Somewhat less substantial articles such as socks and more or less empty plastic containers tend to concen-trate in a crescent away from the center where they seem to mark the sweep of gusts that swirl around the trailer. He can't decide if what appears to be a fainter segregation of those sorts of things you can't quite throw away, those small regretful things that gather at the bottoms of kitchen drawers, is real or not. In any case the final stage is mostly paper, what just blows away.

"Real bad is what I heard."

"Huh."

"All messed up, all tore up—right out here somewhere this mornin'. Hear them sireens?"

"Yeah."

"He had that woman with him."

"Huh."

"That's what I heard."

"Huh."

"Lord." She looks around again. "What are you doin'?"

"Cleanin' house."

"Lord"—she looks all around and pulls her earflaps down and snaps them under, holds herself and sort of shivers—"Lord, Lord, Lord."

"Need you to help me."

"Heard they think she musta seen whatever done it."

"Need to haul that trap back here."

"Goddang, you know I hope it was her husband. Don't that make more sense . . ." She's looking out across the field; she sees the trap. "Goddang," she says more softly, looks at him. "You get it?"

"I got somethin'."

"Somethin'?"

"Yeah, I guess."

"You guess?"

"I guess."

"Well did you?"

He's inclined to think there is a clearly separate phase of matter fanning subtly out, revealed between the not quite insubstantial things like rags and socks and beer cans, and the abstract, spiritual (catfish, Christ, whatever) stuff that simply blows away. Although it's hard to say exactly what it is.

• • •

"Don't jerk; you'll snap the joint," he yells. The trap is hard to budge and she keeps trying to yank it—revs the motor, pops the clutch. "Whoa." He hops off and lifts the frame a little. "Easy."

"What?"

"Don't rev it up like that—just take it easy."

"What?" The wind is loud and she's still got her earflaps down. She leans out. "Gotta gun it; it'll conk out in the cold."

"Okay, just go."

"What?"

"Go." The rope snaps through the joint, the turnbuckled cable, already under considerable strain, lets go, whips back into his knee. The motor slowly chugs to a stop, she gets out, comes around, and stands there as he uncontorts himself, gets up, and limps around, a bit to test it, leans against the trap. It's getting dark. A brush of snow against his face. He looks at her. There's no expression; she's on hold as if she'd hit a dog, some poor old feral dog, and waits to see if it will rise. He rubs his knee and takes the rope and ties it to the next joint over. "Twist it out," he yells, then walks back over to her. "You can pull it from the side, just go on straight and it'll twist right out." She nods but stands there looking at him like that for a moment. Snowflakes settle on her cap. He hears the puppies yapping faintly above the wind in wild, inadequate response to other distant wilder yappings, squealings, howlings to the east.

He rides the trap back with his eyes closed, almost stinging, blowing snow right in his face, the rush of grass like waves as darkness falls and all this distant crying and yelping now, all around, from creatures so reduced, so interbred, so unspecific that their cries seem all the purer and more ghastly—sounds of any terrible creatures you can imagine rising, breaching here and there around a little ship in some uncharted region.

"What the hell am I gonna do with all this stuff?"

"Just keep it, sell it. I don't know." He tries to pile the heavier items, kitchen things, on top of lighter things like clothing, tucking it all at the front of the bed behind the cab, trying to make it look like something ordered and reasonable is going on; it's hard to see, though, in the dark and he winds up just sort of tossing everything in. He looks around. "How 'bout the puppies?" Snow-flecked light fans out the open door of the trailer across the yard to where she stands by the trap. She lifts one panel slightly, lets it down; bends over, peers into it, through it, as if to check for any faint residual presence. He walks over. "Best way, I figure, is you go ahead and get in first and get all situated behind the wheel, then I can put 'em through the window." Agnes stands.

"Doc Kirby's open tomorrow."

"Fine. You got any more of them two-by-fours?"

She turns and walks to the truck.

"Got any plywood?" he calls; she slams the door and waits as he conveys the puppies, all six, one by one, each petted, spoken to, and carefully introduced into the cab.

The house, the trailer, is now abandoned. He's still here but like a transient, fully dressed with one old blanket and a pillow huddled up into the corner on the mattress—nothing worse and nothing sadder, more abandoned, than an old bare mattress. Even the door and windows left wide open to prove the point: there's nothing worthwhile, nothing substantial here at all; don't even give it a second glance. So might this be what spiritual is? Completely adrift? That's it? Completely disconnected. Final thing you get a two-by-four and whack at the power line right there at the power head up there on top of the trailer. Sparks will fly but do not fear, just whack away; once you begin you mustn't stop, the sparks shoot out and there's that terrible spit and hum of severed current (you may never, surely never, use that much, but there it is, it's always there; it holds you to it like you're always told don't ever try to pull someone away who's grabbed a live one, get a two-by-four or something).

There are benefits to cold. What little food is left will keep. And he imagines, by that token, so will he, his arm at least, a little longer.

Wind is good. It rocks the trailer now and then, keeps him awake or at the verge of being awake; of being alert, now that he's thinking along those lines, to things of the spirit. It's a spiritual sound, he decides—the periodic, wildly disconnected screaming, hooting, yelping in the distance of the coyotes, feral dogs, whatever they are. Whatever happened to the wheezing of the earth, the gas-well noise? It's been a while. What if it's really wheezed its last and now at last it's getting cold.

He'll have these dreams, just little short ones—Yurang's back, he reaches out; that's it, there's nothing. Not much to it: Yurang's back but no he's not. No he's not.

Yet something enters at some point and wakes him if he is awake— he hesitates to move, to make a determination. Just a flickering—red like the numbers on his now discarded clock—and right at the cor-ner of his eye; it darts around; he can't quite catch it, then it's gone, he starts to drift off after a minute (which suggests but doesn't prove he was awake), and now it's back. It's Tinkerbell. He sees it now— a little dancing spot of light; pure spirit; the opposite of Yurang. Tinkerbell—except she's red not gold the way he seems to remember. Still, it moves around like that. It holds a moment, streaks away, and comes right back. The wind makes gentle whistley noises around the trailer, in the background rushes softly over the grass and now and then blows in a little puff of snow, a couple of flakes against his face. How pure, how simple. And now he sees it. All you do is simplify, then sure enough, of course, it's there, the Holy Spirit. Tinkerbell. It comes right in and dances around in the cold, the empty insides of things. The trailer creaks and tilts a little, suddenly lurches. It's too dark outside. The doorway's dark. He jerks up. There's a dazzling flash of red and an explosion. It's as if some-one had clapped his ears, just whacked him; he can't hear or see a thing and it occurs to him within this deafened, blinded half a sec-ond it would be like this of course, would feel like this—he's seen those TV preachers do it, take someone and whack him, clap his ears, and then the eyes roll up and then they fall, saved, healed, for a minute and maybe a minute is all you need, enough for practice for the real thing which, presumably, this must be. Or possibly not.

"Oh fuck, oh Jesus fuck."

He hears that, sees a white light rolling around on the floor, a flashlight, and a large unstable figure leaning, snatching at it, trying to pick it up while cursing, "fuck" and "Jesus fuck" and "Goddamn fuck oh fuck oh fuck, you hit?" now shining it right in his face and almost blinding him again. It's Willis Beagle, dog-face wild above the flashlight, looking at him, poking at him, smelling of beer and something stronger, standing back and trying to shake his flickery flashlight back to life, gigantic pistol in his right hand counterbalancing these efforts, waving all around, its laser sight still on, his finger probably on the trigger. Darkness now and little fairy streaks of laser light again. He turns it off. Thump goes the flashlight onto the floor—it's either the flashlight or the gun; must be the flashlight. Gust of wind. A tingly aerosol of snow blows through the screen and Willis stands there as if stunned back into shadow, empty, unspecific.

"You all right?" he says at last.

"Not bad, how 'bout yourself?"

"Shit." There's a stagger as the trailer shakes a little; flashlight kicked into the wall, a short-lived glimmer. "Fuckin' thing. Thought you was the dog. Where is he?"

"Run off like I said."

"Fuckin' thing." Another stagger. "Saw your door was hangin' open. You all right? Oh shit." He comes and leans on the bed. Some kind of sweet liqueur, it smells like. "God. Look there." He's got one hand on Luther's shoulder, got a knee up on the mattress and his head right next to Luther's. Tap, tap, tap against the wall beside the window. "Shit, look there." It's hard to twist around with Willis hanging on him.

"What?"

"You gotta get your head down here."

He tries. "So move your hand. Oh yeah." A little hole with gray light and a tiny stream of cold air coming though it. "Drilled it good."

"Sure did."

"You think them little buzz saw thingys worked?"

"Oh shit." He falls back onto the mattress. Luther pulls his feet up. "Scared me, door wide open and all, you risin' up like that. Thought you was the dog or somethin' else." The sound of wild ones yipping and howling far away above the wind. "I hate them things." His breathing catches in his throat, sounds all congested like a cold. And for a while that's all there is, just Willis's nasty-sounding breathing. Luther wonders if he may have actually passed out, where his pistol might be pointing, what the odds might be of taking it away without objection. Willis makes a drawn-out gurgling noise and coughs and whispers, "Hate them things," and coughs some more and sighs. "I quit 'em."

"Huh," says Luther.

"Fuckin' Emmitt Dobbs, oh yes sir, he's the one—the logical successor. Ain't that shit. He is the logical successor." He exaggerates the phrase and strains his throat or something, goes into another coughing fit, hacks something up but doesn't spit. He's got the hiccups now which makes him have to pause every now and then in mid-complaint. "You seen . . . you seen him right out here this mornin', how he was, that skinny . . . shit . . . that skinny sonofabitch ain't been here near as long as me; ain't never been chief deputy or . . . shit." He holds his breath a minute. "Shit." He takes a deep breath, tries again. The trailer rocks, the door slaps hard against the side. He lets it out. "What in the fuck . . . it's freezin'; what you got the windows open for? You got no sense to close the door?" But he just lies there . . . "Shit" . . . and hiccups, moans some more about unfairness, county politics, and how it's not official but he'll quit. He'll quit tomorrow. But right now he's inexplicably here, laid out across the foot of Luther's bed, and, notwithstanding little periodic spasms, fast asleep.

. . .

The wind has stopped; the door hangs open to the strangely pallid darkness; Willis stirs, tugs on the blanket. "Shit," he whispers, tugs again and rearranges himself a little, belches, sighs a couple of times. "You shoulda seen him. Shit. All cut up everywhere all over. Smelled bad too. You know? Like he'd been dead a good long while but shit he ain't. And I ain't never seen nobody act as crazy as that woman— kept her eyes tight shut the whole time, wouldn't say a goddamn thing but sorta sang a little song like to herself the whole damn time real soft you know like to herself so it was hard to make it out." He sits up slightly, gives a good long belch, and lies back down. "Troy said he knew it though—he listened to her, said he was pretty sure it was from some musical somethin' or other about Oklahoma or somethin' like that." He sits back up and gives another belch and sighs again, lies down. "Goddamn it's cold." A little later Luther hears his pistol thump onto the floor.

35

The chickens are gone. Just gone. Eight Reds, three Leggerns just like that, no feathers, nothing. Feathers, of course, would all have blown away. He walks around inside the pen; there's just a little snow on the ground, enough to make him think to look for chicken tracks and think how odd to think of chicken tracks in the snow, and odd to think they might mean something if he found them but there's nothing. Not a thing to suggest what happened or that anything actually did. What if they all just blew away, being mostly feathers, like balloons. He recalls that weirdly empty feeling the other day, the sense of weightlessness. He looks across at Willis, who's emerged bewildered-looking, amazed, as from a spaceship. Stock still, arms limp at his side. One careless move and he goes flying, bounding up like some poor astronaut, limbs flailing, lost above a whitened, weightless, dying world. He coughs and spits and sort of stumbles off the step and walks around behind the trailer, pauses briefly at that corner he seems to like, then goes on out into the field to relieve himself.

It's hard to use the little hand-cranked drill. It's not just the usual problems with his left hand—he adjusts for that somewhat by getting the handle braced in tight against his chest. The bit's too dull. It skitters across the metal siding, refuses to bite; he leans into it but the siding bends away. It's strange. The trailer, all its materials seem so fragile, cheap, and temporary, vulnerable, but when it comes down to it somehow you can't touch it; like those peanut-butter cracker things in cellophane—it's nothing, cheapest thing you can imagine but just try to tear it open. It's a struggle, big and strong as you might be, it drives you nuts how cheap and crappy stuff resists you and you wind up crushing half the crackers just to get a couple. He

David Searcy

sits down—right on the ground. He wouldn't mind a pack of peanut-butter crackers and a root beer. He leans back against the trailer. Already-fallen snow gets lifted, swirled around, blown off the roof, as dry as dust. It settles like that, very slowly just like dust, drifts here and there across the yard. He wonders how long Willis plans to hang around. He's been out there in his car all morning, sacking out apparently, windows all rolled up against the noise of Luther bashing the trap apart. It's not the squad car. It's his own, his personal vehicle. That seems so peculiar somehow, even alarming, just a step away from meeting his mother or something. Nor is it helpful that it looks like it belongs—as if it had been out there awhile, a couple of years, sort of off to the side, its nose in the tall grass, one of those boxy early-eighties station wagons, fake wood panels on the side, the wood grain worn away to white in several places. Luther gets up, takes the blocks of wood he's cut and drilled, and holds them against the trailer just to make sure where he wants them, either side of the door and a little below the level of the window. It doesn't have to be exact, just more or less. He licks his finger, makes three smudges where he wants the holes to be then finds his pencil, marks them again as dark as he can and walks on out to Willis's car.

He stands a moment. He'd just as soon not interfere. A snowy powder sifts across the fogged-up windows—not so fogged that he can't see him though, sprawled out across the back seat, mouth wide open. From inside there comes a gentle steady hiss. It's like some sort of incubation is taking place. He opens the driver's door—no whoosh of decompression; quite a smell though—turns the radio off. A jerk of the head, a gagging sound from Willis.

"Hey," says Luther. Gagging complicates to wheezing, coughing, farting. He recalls it takes a while. He backs out. "Hey." He gives the top of the car a whack. "Need you and your gun out here a minute." Then he walks back to the trailer.

"You're a weird-ass, goddamn, motherfuckin' idiot."

"What's the matter, can't you hit it?"

"Shit yeah, I can shoot your trailer. Hate to waste a goddamn bullet."

"Wasted one last night."

"Shit."

"Gotta hit them marks though, see?" He taps the penciled marks. "See, that's the thing." He taps them one, two, three. "Don't have to be dead-on, but close."

"Shit, it'll go clean out the other side."

"That's fine. Don't make no difference, sept you gotta hit them marks."

"Shit."

"Straight through."

"Shit." He draws the slide back, seems to get it jammed or something. Now he's got it, chunk, a bullet in the chamber. He walks up to fire point-blank then reconsiders, backs away a couple of steps, then gets himself into that crouch.

"Straight through."

He stands up, turns his laser on, assumes the crouch again, stands up again and says, "He fixed it so it's locked on thirty feet," and looks at Luther. Luther shrugs. Now Willis steps off thirty feet away from the trailer, gets all set. The little laser dot is dancing all around within a circle maybe the size of a dinner plate.

"Sure hate to wound it."

"Fuck," says Willis, switches his laser off. "Fuck"—turns and walks away back toward his car—"fuck"—comes right back, walks up to within ten feet or so, and shoots the trailer. Bam, just shoots it. None of that combat crouch or anything. He just walks up, points, and shoots the way someone might suddenly lose control and shoot another person. Doves fly up behind the trailer, whir away off to the west. It's hard to tell if he hit it at all. They walk up to it. There's no hole that Luther can see. "Shit," says Willis. "Sheeut." Looks at Luther with a look almost like pleading so bizarrely is it rendered, canine features struggling through the lower emotions toward the higher, toward some pure and perfect uncontingent joy. He's got his finger in the hole—he's shot the mark out. Luther allows his jaw to drop and backs away. Bam, bam, like that he shoots the other two as if afraid to lose his moment of grace and, sure enough, he gets them—not right on the mark, not like the first, but close enough and more than adequate to the purpose. Willis walks to the stump and sits there with his pistol gently cradled in his lap. He watches Luther attach the blocks and then the four-foot pivoting two-by-four shimmed out with a piece of plywood so it clears the door-frame stripping. Luther tests it: opens the door and leans the two-by-four against it at the hinge, then slings the door closed with a bang. The board falls right across the door into the L-shaped wooden cleat on the other side. He tries it ten times. Twice it strikes the top of the block and fails to drop. He saws an angle off the inside of the block; he saws it badly but it works—ten times and then ten times again the door slaps to, the board falls, whack, into the slot, and bars it shut. Now Luther grabs the doorknob, yanks it. There's about an inch of play. He yanks it hard as he can then stands away and looks at Willis, waiting to let him take the opportunity now to say how Luther's even more of an idiot than he thought and what kind of bullshit deal is that, to bar his door shut on the outside, maybe unless he really plans to catch a woman. And with that—to make that joke, to think to make it—there would be such dumb, mean-spirited gratification it could grin and sneer away to some extent what seems to Luther, suddenly now, an awfully strained and ominous sense of things reduced to true essentials, all come down to what—if you only understood it, dogs and chickens, all distractions notwithstanding—life is really all about. Snow lifts and swirls around in the yard, collects like sawdust here and there; there's not enough to cover the grass except in places. Willis isn't going to do it, come insult him. Luther sees that. Willis finds himself invested. He just sits there with his pistol having done the very best that he can do—that he can ever do perhaps—and it's not in him now to question what proceeds from that, however strange it looks.

A little later Agnes shows up with some plywood, makes a big deal of it, backing her truck around like it's a load of reinforcing steel or something, dropping the tailgate, kicking it out with too much effort onto the ground, and roaring off without a word or even a glance at Luther and Willis on top of the trailer undertaking to poke some holes in the roof with a very large Phillips-head screwdriver Willis happened to have in his car.

"You wanna look here what you're doin'."

"Ain't that Agnes? That is ain't it." Willis lets the screwdriver drift and watches her go. "I seen that truck in town sometimes." As if he felt it were important to identify, consolidate these little scattered certainties. "She needs to get it tuned."

Luther puts the hammer down and watches the truck dip into the trees. They hear it clatter over the bridge. "You go to town we need some stuff."

"Ain't goin' to town."

"I thought you was."

"Nope."

"Said you was."

"Yeah well"—he turns and dangles his legs—"I got to thinkin' and I think I quit already."

"Yeah?"

"I figure I probably did."

"You had some words."

"You got that right." He looks at Luther with a great big buck-toothed grin. "You got that right." Then looks away across the field and says it again more softly, then a little later once again more softly still. The wind whips snow up out of the grass and now and then imparts a twist, a whirling motion making little snowy whirlwinds. Willis scoots back just a bit so he's not sitting on the seam. He brings his hand up to his pistol to protect it when he moves. "So what you figure?"

"Figure 'bout what?"

" 'Bout this right here; 'bout all this here."

"In what respect?"

"Shit, I don't know." He's got a bullet out. He turns it, shines the tip against his shirt. " 'Bout what it's for."

"We're gonna catch ourself a woman." Luther sits back, leans on his hands to take the weight off his damaged knee. "Don't that sound right?"

He turns and grins but only shakes his head and turns back to the field.

"So ain't that right?" says Luther.

Willis puts his bullet back in his belt. "How come you called it what you did?" He's had his hair cut. You can see where it's actually rubbed a little thin right in the back where his hat came down.

"How come you still ain't got a hat?"

"Shit."

"Huh?"

"By God, you still gonna buy me a goddamn hat. How come you called it that?"

"What?"

"You know. Holy Spirit."

"That's what Agnes calls it."

"Shit." Wind shakes the trailer. "You gonna buy me a goddamn hat."

"Hell, it's a deer stand!" Willis, sitting on the stump, yells with delight that's muffled somewhat by a bite of Sonic chili dog; he rises, spills a portion of his super-giant limeade, points at the wobbly four-legged structure Luther's struggling to erect on top of the trailer. "It's a deer stand; shit, I know all about them things," as if herewith the mists withdraw and he's released from all uncertainty and doubt.

"You wanna give me a hand?"

"You bet."

"Right now?" It's not very stable. Kick one eight-and-a-half-foot leg into place against a block, another shifts, the whole thing sags one way or another; just a bad idea to try to pre-assemble all the parts. "Goddammit, Willis, put that down, I'm 'bout to lose it." He's not thinking very well; he shouldn't force things; he can't even force his injured arm to work. "Goddamn don't step there, you'll go through. Here." Willis takes it. "Hold it like that." Luther gets one leg nailed down to the piece of two-by-four they bolted to the roof. "Now that one there. Watch out that other's startin' to slip. Just watch your feet." He nails one more and then the final two are easy. Luther follows Willis down the makeshift ladder they contrived of hog wire stretched between two boards. It works all right except for being a little springy. Luther's boot slips out. He clatters down the last three feet or so like running a stick along a fence. He staggers back and almost falls. His legs feel weak. He sits on the ground and looks at the way the structure leans, the way it's all loose-jointed, not quite right—the six-by-six-foot frame at top not holding things to center as he'd thought, or sort of thought or just expected. He's not really thinking now. He's tired. His pants are getting wet. He's found a little drift of snow to sit in. Willis walks up.

"Know what?" Munch of chili dog, slurp of limeade.

"What is that, a limeade?"

"Yep. You want some?"

"Shit, it's freezing."

"Know what?"

"What?"

"You need them whatchacallit braces things." He holds his arms in an X across each other, spills a little limeade.

"How the shit you drink a limeade when it's . . . Jesus." Now he's starting to shake again. He needs to get up off the ground. He stands and brushes off his jeans.

"You know?"

"What?"

"Braces."

"Fine. You do it."

"Huh?"

"You do it." Luther makes it to the trailer, to the mattress; after a while awakes to noises—soft, uncertain; then more violent, uncoordinated noises on the roof.

. . .

At some point all the racket stops, winds down, replaced, in Luther's vague not-quite-unconsciousness, by subtle fluctuations in the light. There'll be a shuffling, then a shadow, through closed eyes a gentle lowering of the brightness like the drawing of a shade, then light returns, and after a minute the same again. This seems to go on for a while; it's hard to say how long as Luther tends to drift away and back to his awareness of it, lying on his side, face toward the door; at last his eyes come barely open: there's the open door, gray light now going darker gray toward evening; now the shuffle, elbow, shoulder, and the rest of Willis Beagle silhouetted, leaning, peering, grinning possibly. "You awake?" He steps inside. It's either a grin or a sort of grimace. "Come on out here now, okay? You come on out."

It's pretty horrible. Boards of different lengths and widths are nailed together—lapped and nailed in whatever order, it appears, he picked them up to make the piece sufficiently long to span the distance. It's a distance, furthermore, that quickly diminishes with materials. So in front—he obviously started on the south side here in front—you've got a great big X-brace spanning top to bottom; as he worked his way around, though, like a child who starts his sign with letters too large for the paper, things get smaller, sort of desperate, till at last here on the west side—Luther walks around with Willis, silent, following—it's a small and frail and tragic little X-brace rendered frailer, even sadder, by attempts to compensate with scraps of really trashy lumber forming hopeless little supplemental buttresses and struts. He looks at Willis. Willis looks down, seems to discover something caught between his teeth. More snow is falling, just a few big fluffy flakes that you can see even in the distance very clearly against the trees. "Okay now," Luther says to Willis rather softly, "that's okay. You need to go on into town, though; get them things we talked about and get on back here pretty quick." He's turned away a little now, still with his finger in his mouth. "They ain't gonna arrest you or nothin' are they?" Willis shakes his head. "All right then; I gotta knock some wood off the henhouse, get us a rail up there." He finishes with his teeth and stands there looking at his work. "All right?" says Luther.

"Shit," whispers Willis, walks away, turns back with that grimace to look it over one more time, then heads to the car.

The snow is perfect. It's the way you imagine snow, the way someone who seldom sees it thinks about it. How a child might draw it, perfectly uniform with big slow flakes, each one intended, each deliberate as spitting off a bridge. It's an illusion probably caused by the surrounding tree line, that it seems to fall just here within the field, as if directed, come straight down with great precision, great big flakes like radar blips about to happen, any moment bouncing back to light the screen but not quite yet—where is it? Here? No. Is it here? No. Not quite yet.

36

"Oh shit," says Willis, "ain't this somethin'."

"Huh," says Luther.

"Ain't it?"

"Huh."

"What?"

"You oughta see the way you look."

"This here's the way it's supposed to look—it's like them mountain climbers use; keeps all the heat in."

Willis looks sort of like a giant purple grubworm, but with teeth, big doglike teeth.

"This here one—you got one just like it—this here one is rated down to ten degrees, except it's orange, the one I got you. Ten degrees. Can you believe that? That okay?"

"What?"

"If it's orange."

"Oh yeah, I guess."

"That's cold, you know it?"

He keeps wriggling around inside the purple sleeping bag, exploring all its comforts with an undulatory enthusiasm Luther finds unpleasant. Luther stands. The plywood floor, not very accurately fitted together, has more bounce than he would like, the sections laid right over the chicken-wire/hog-wire grid from the earlier trap. Now Willis's hands poke out and pull the drawstring tight so just his nose and open mouth are visible. Luther turns away. It makes him think of Agnes's story about the "wolves," the terrible maggots she imagined made that howling sound at night when she was a child. It's getting dark. The grass is quiet, and from here, from way up here—it feels much higher than the fifteen feet or so he figures it is; his eyes seem level with the tree line—he can see into the stalks down to the thatch and the ground in places where the last brief fall of snow left patches of white. His yard is white. The chicken yard is mostly white, the henhouse roof—not really white now; lighter gray—the double-rutted path to the road. It doesn't take much to remove yourself from things, to get that sense of life's exposure— "Oh," you think, "well look at that." Just fifteen feet or thereabouts. He takes a grip on the corner post which extends a foot above the rail, with the tar-paper curtain tacked along it all around. He spreads his feet and gives it a shake. He grabs the rail and tries again and puts his weight into it; somewhere there's a snap. He does it once again but gently in that delicate, sort of formal way you tighten a screw you think you may have stripped.

"Got this here too."

Another little presentation. Luther's struggling with the zipper on his bag. "What?" It's like Willis is at camp or something, showing off his stuff, his focusable flashlight, giant fighting knife.

"Here."

"What?" It's dark. A sloshing sound. He takes it, takes a drink. "Oh Christ, what is that?"

"Southern Comfort."

"Shit." He takes another, leaves the zipper, leans back. "You go all the way to Gladewater?"

"No, I had it."

"Shit." It tastes like cough syrup, burns a little, spreads, and just like that involves him altogether like a hot bath, lets his breath escape, his limbs go slack. His arm slips off the much too frail and flexible one-by-two and pops the tar paper loose right there but it's okay; it's tacked on top. They pass it back and forth awhile.

"So," Luther asks—he's got himself propped in a corner, feels himself to have gained his sea legs as it were—"you had some words, huh?"

"Yep." Whenever he drinks it makes a little popping sound the way a child will do with a bottle of soda. "Yessiree." He hands it back and Luther wipes it. "Told him he was just a stupid skinny sonofabitch that didn't know a goddamn fuckin' thing bout bein' a sheriff or nothin' at all and all he was was somebody's stupid skinny fuckin' brother-in-law. That's what I told him." Luther feels the tap on his arm; surrenders the bottle.

"Yeah, I guess you probably quit."

That little popping sound. "You figure?"

"Yeah, I figure you probably did." He starts to laugh; then Willis—choking, snorting laughter dwindling gradually into hiccups. Pretty soon the bottle's empty, just a hiccup now and then. It's strange, the flimsy dead-black tar-paper-curtained darkness totally open at the top like this like hiding behind a bush, like something childish like that, hopeless. If he stares at the paler darkness of the sky and lets the rest just go to shadow, he can make out certain features in the overcast, detect its motion—north to south he thinks, although right now he's not too sure which way he's facing. Willis hiccups, shifts around, and make the floor creak. Every now and then he does that—hiccups, shifts a little, clears his throat.

"So what'd you catch them other times?"

The clouds are racing past it seems. "What?"

"You know. All them other traps you made."

He's let himself slip down and sideways till he's almost on his back, his head supported by the middle rail, the one-by-two; it bends; he didn't nail it very well; he hopes it holds. The clouds are shooting past as if terrific winds were blowing right above them, just above the stillness. Luther lifts himself back up into the corner, gets his arm up where it doesn't hurt so bad. "I tell you what."

A hiccup.

"Tell you what I didn't catch."

"All right."

"Okay?"

"All right."

"Didn't catch a rabbit."

"All right."

"Coon."

"No." Hiccup.

"Possum."

"No."

"No possum."

"No."

"Nor snake."

"God I hate snakes."

"Nor skunk." (He's conscious of the "nor," its chant, its biblical conviction.) "Bobcat."

"Shit."

"Nor weasel, monkey . . ."

"Monkey?" Hiccup.

". . . no particular thing."

"Shit."

"No particular thing . . ."

"A monkey . . . shit."

". . . that you could pick it up and say that's it, that's all it is, right here, ain't nothin else but this right here no matter what you thought, how bad you thought, how sad and empty, not worth shit and all you thought and all that other too, that other shit that's goin' on; and it would just come down to that so you could say well lookee here that's all it is don't that beat all."

A muffled hiccup. Creaking floor.

"I didn't catch me nothin' like that." He listens. Not a sound from Willis. "Know why?"

Nothing.

"'Cause it ain't like that." A whispery sort of noise he thought might be inside his head is just the random sound that gathers like the whisper in a seashell. Just the sound of tar paper tacked around a frame, left open, way up here on stilts like an antenna, like some radar dish or something. "'Cause it ain't a simple thing." More creaking. Willis sort of lurching to his knees, dark, unclear top half of him swaying above the tar paper for a second, turning possibly, sticking his head up, looking around like someone awakened by a noise, then slumping down and scooting back into his corner. There's a hollow little pop, a belch.

"I figure it got Bobby."

"Mm," says Luther.

"Don't you? Don't you know them assholes gonna look so god-damn stupid. Ain't they. Shit. It cut you too. Holy Spirit my ass." Another belch. A sudden movement shakes the floor. A quavery sad receding whistle as the bottle sails away.

37

For a long time Luther took for granted one of those marvelous declarations too bizarre to not be true—that from the bottom of a well the daytime sky looks black as night and you can even see the stars. It was a notion simply received and carried around, no more to be questioned than some assertion about strange properties of the pyramids or the orbits of the planets, altogether beyond him, outside his ability to doubt or even think about it much until one day as he was peering through a length of half-inch pipe he saw how silly it was, how easily disproved and how peculiar that he'd allowed it. He supposed it was the "well" part as if wells, deep holes in the earth, were somehow special, exotic places where you might expect weird stuff to happen, like that huge, domed Roman building, between whose ceiling and floor a falling drop of water would evaporate. How easy it is to think whatever you want, to make stuff up without even thinking. Dig a hole and there are the stars. He hates the sound of Willis breathing in his sleep. It won't get light. It must be a property of this particular exotic enclosure that the morning is repelled like beads of water off the tar paper; whispery, oily tar-paper darkness trapped inside; that, lying awake for who knows how long with the sense of imminent daybreak, nothing happens—Willis snoring in the corner, scudding overcast. Or maybe it's the end of the world already and this is only how it goes; it just stays dark, that's how you know, like in those countries close to the Arctic where in winter there's no sun for weeks and weeks or maybe that's just one of those stories, one of those marvelous things to say. One day no sunrise; guess it's winter. Guess it must be the end of the world and Deputy Dawg's going to snore right through it. Luther gives him a little kick to no effect. It's too much trouble. Luther sighs and shuts his eyes and counts to twenty, looks. No difference.

David Searcy

Counts to fifty very slowly. How remarkable if this were really it—it just stayed dark and people never quite recovered, never quite got back in the swing, got up and brushed their teeth and so forth; never really quite recovered. Counts to one hundred with his hand across his heart to time the count, to keep it slow, then does it again. There might be something. Now he shuts his eyes not counting, waiting as long as he possibly can. There. He can tell it's getting light because his sleeping bag is orange. Willis wasn't kidding—it's that color they use for life rafts, warning signs. It pops right out: help me, I'm sleeping; or look out, stand back, I'm sleeping. Willis's purple one is slower to emerge. He hears the redbird, traffic somewhere far away. The clouds look like they're starting to thin, break up perhaps. He tugs at the zipper, gives up, squirms his way half out and into the corner, sits up, holding his head for a moment to let the dizziness and the pain at the base of his skull subside a little. There are perfect, separate snowflakes on his sleeping bag. Looking closely he can see them, only a few, a delicate sprinkle; not enough to have felt apparently. Luther forces himself to sit there in his tee shirt in the cold a little longer, takes a few deep breaths, kicks out of the sleeping bag, puts on his Army jacket, crawls to the rail, and looks. He's turned around. He's on the north side—he can see the notch in the trees where the road dips through; he can smell a sour sort of smell and, now, recall the peculiar sounds he'd semiconsciously in the night preferred to think were somehow something other than Willis standing and staggering at the rail, relieving himself. He moves away to the other side. The air's dead still. It's at that point, almost, of release, things shifting over night to day, when the field is clearest. As when, sometimes for a moment when you wake up, there's a residue of dreams, a sense of all of them, just flashes, very clear and very brief and then they're gone. There should be no doubt whatsoever if there's anything to see; from way up here, the field erased by wind; the snow might even help—a careful dusting like the way they check for fingerprints; it ought to pop right out. A simple trail, a simple incursion is what to look for—now he stands—what he imagines he should see. He should receive a sense of tentative approach; that's all he wants, just confirmation. No big deal. He has a plan, regardless. Still, there should be something. Grass is all there is though, scattered patches of snow; he stood too quickly, has to hold on to the post. His head is spinning. Willis's breathing sounds like someone about to die. He thinks he heard somewhere more people die at dawn or just before than at any other time. That's what they say. The breath goes in, the breath goes out like through a pipe stuffed full of leaves. Right now the grass—the snow and dirt and grass; it's all so clear; too much detail almost—the grass makes patterns at the edge of his field of vision. What was that word—the way she used it in that leaflet (leaflets; Lord, how many were there? He collected quite a stack)—that word he didn't like somehow, or understand: "expressed" disturbed him, how she used it. "That He is expressed within the commonplace. . . ." He'd read it like you read a cereal box; he'd have a sandwich, take a leaflet, look it over, sort of give it another shot. He'd turn it; try to find the Savior like the monkeys in those comic book puzzle-pictures drawn in that complicated squiggly sort of way to make it hard to find them hidden among the ordinary things, the trees and shrubbery, clouds, whatever. "He is expressed. . . ." It sounds so soft and matter-of-fact like breathing or something. It seems colder. Just a few frayed trailing clouds now as the overcast moves off. In a minute sun will gleam through the pines beyond the road. He takes a glance that way—not yet, not quite—turns back and there's no question all of a sudden. Small suspicions, apprehensions, run together, send out feelers here and there, extend themselves across the field along the subtlest (by themselves you'd think just accidental) partings in the grass until it's clear as it can be. "Hey." He gives Willis another kick. It's not a simple, limited thing. It's not like what he would have guessed. It makes his heart sink somehow, makes him think it's gone too far already in some way he's not quite sure he understands; it's like that word; it's like that rotten piece of board that's lain up underneath the trailer much too long; you pick it up like you can use it but it feels so light and then you see those wormy little channels, little trails. "Goddammit, Willis," Luther jerks him up one-handed, overdoes it, almost loses him over the rail, gets him to kneel and pull his arms out, makes him hold on, eyes and mouth wide open, yanked straight up from death without preliminaries, gaping.

"What?" He drools a little. "What?" he whispers.

"Look there. See them trails? See that?" He points and moves his finger slowly all around in sweeps and arcs that curl and cross each other back and forth. "Goddammit, Willis, not my finger. Look. It's been out there all night just movin' around see, look there all around behind and everywhere; see all them trails, the way they hook up? It's been movin'. Look here"—Luther points down, physically redirects the other's gaze—"look there, right there where it come right up to the yard almost. Goddamn. It must have set for a while—you see that spot?" He looks at Willis. "Huh?" It's hard to tell—he just looks stunned. A rosy glow spreads gradually, delicately over his face. It's like embarrassment or enlightenment or a blessing or something, his eyes half closing. "Willis?" It's the sunlight. Luther looks across the road and squints and zips his jacket up the rest of the way.

38

"I think he likes it up there." Agnes stands away a little, both hands shading her eyes to catch an intermittent glimpse of just the top of Willis's head. "Lord." She walks out a little farther into the yard and turns and shades her eyes again. "What is he doin'?" Now and then the structure seems to sort of shiver.

"Somethin' or other with his gun."

She shakes her head and looks at Luther. Luther looks down at the grocery sack she brought; she saves them, folds them up and saves them—he can tell by the way the creases look, the paper crisp, unwrinkled; closed at top like a schoolchild's lunch sack, folded over, creased, and folded over again. He picks it up to keep the bottom from getting wet.

"I hear he better not be totin' that thing," she says. "I hear they laid him off or somethin'."

"Says he quit." It feels like sandwiches and chips or cookies maybe; something warm he hopes is coffee. Agnes walks back over to him. She looks odd so bundled up in brilliant sunlight, clear blue sky. The snow's burned off somewhat, evaporated; much too cold to melt, it draws away, recedes to little drifts and patches.

"Buried Bobby."

"Yeah?"

"This mornin'. Over in Longview." Willis is peering over the rail. They both look up. He disappears.

"You go?"

"No. Saw it on TV. That's where he's from."

"Yeah?"

"Showed his wife. You ever seen her?"

"Guess I ain't."

"Boy, she ain't much."

"Huh."

"Like she's hardly there at all."

"Huh."

"Actin' crazy kinda. Lotsa people actin' kinda crazy." She just stares at Luther. Luther shifts the sack more to his good arm, looks away. "So when you want all this?" she asks.

He shrugs. " 'For dark. Just any time 'for dark I guess."

The tower shakes; the sound of something heavy dropping to the floor and Willis cursing.

"It's a quick-draw thing," says Luther. "Sept he does it lyin' down."

"Ah." Agnes gazes up.

"He ain't quite got it yet."

Willis sits on the stump with his hands in his jacket. Luther stands at the edge of the yard and watches Agnes going in and out, retrieving things from her truck. She stops by the door of the trailer, turns. She's holding little plastic bags of produce—lettuce, tomatoes, something else.

"Want onions?"

"What? Oh." Luther looks at Willis, looks beyond him to the trees, the reddening sun, looks back at Agnes. "No," he yells.

"What?"

"No."

She steps into the trailer. He can see her getting things laid out—the shadowy, practiced movements. He can hear a plastic package—it's a new one—tearing open. Fresh pressed ham in little rounded-cornered slices. She'll remove them all and fan them out on a plate as if to say behold, look here how many, look how much we have. She seems to be cutting something now. He thinks how nice to be there watching—it's that time of day the sunlight comes straight in and lights the flecks of gold in the tabletop (tomatoes; it's that slip and thump of the knife when she cuts tomatoes)—of anticipating, being right there, holding out the hope, immediate hope. A glance from Willis now and then—he must receive some sense that they are not admitted, have to hang back as if Agnes were a bomb expert or a midwife. Something like that; something technical, maybe even sacrificial (he regrets the stains on the counter) going on. There's running water—Agnes washing up; she brought a towel, she even brought a towel. She turns and dries her hands (how odd the sound of water running—way out here, to hear it; running, splattering into the sink from way out here, the very last thing he'd expect, a gentle, comforting sound like that); she's through; she cleans up, carries all her stuff in a grocery sack to the truck, and then she's gone.

For a while they stand around not doing much of anything. At some point Willis moves his car a little farther away out toward the road and locks it up. He walks around it, checks the doors, the tailgate, stands there by it looking back toward Luther—toward the trees, the brilliant orange-red western sky—all squinty dog-eyed, mouth half-open as if he had never seen a thing like this, the sun, as bright as day, go red and sink, the shadows come across and catch him, nothing he can do but stand and watch.

It's hard to get the spring to hook into the hole at the top of the door—it takes two hands so he has Willis do it, lets him set the release as well while Luther holds the door back under tension, makes sure Willis ties the cord right with a little bit of slack. Then they just stand for a moment, outside looking in, the last red glow withdrawing visibly and, it seems, almost heartbreakingly from what she's done, from what she's left—good plates, it looks like, china, flowers—something, flowers probably—delicate little flowers around the edges and the very edges gold, it looks like gold; it looks like something real, not made-up, but remembered, reconstructed: toasted bread triangles (cold, now, maybe frozen—and, therefore, he wants to imagine, does imagine, with the sense of being toasted in her kitchen frozen in; that smell, that moment) stacked around a jar of something, mustard probably, in the center, all just so; and next to that tomato slices overlapping all around a stack of cheese whose

David Searcy

staggered squares create a spiral with a thing on top—an olive, pickle, flourish of some sort as if she couldn't bear to stop without a gesture saying more, there's always more; and ham of course, and lettuce torn that careful way and mounded up; a glass of milk. A glass of milk. And all the good things, all the kindness, all the comfort, consolation, in the world, it seems to Luther, set out finally, placed at risk.

39

W hen you go jigging, what you do is hold the line, the line itself, no pole or rod, and let the hook sink down to the bottom; then you bring it up a little, not too much, and keep it there—a
dock can make a pretty good place; the fish like shelter from the sun,
but even at night; the biggest crappie Luther ever caught was off a
dock at night—you lie there, hold the line and jig it, every now and
then just give it a little flip, a couple of flips. Some people jig it all
the time, just keep it going and that's fine. They catch some fish. But
Luther always felt the big ones had disdain for that; or something
like disdain—what in a fish might correspond; and you can't help
but think, just lying there and gazing down beyond reflected stars to
where the fish live, that you have a sense of them and what they
think or almost think or feel, whatever. That you imagine them
somehow and find their thoughts will overlap with yours at certain
points. So what he'd do is wait, imagine he could see down there,
and wait, ignore the incidental bump and tug, replace the bait, and
wait. Sometimes, if it were still enough, if he could be that still, the
water calm enough, the stars upon its surface might reveal the slight
disturbance, something there to be considered, make the wrist tense
and the shoulder muscles stiffen at the prospect of that dark thin
sympathetic line of thought connecting, jerking back with something. Luther shifts a little, squirms a little farther to one side to
keep the bag from getting pinched between the sections of plywood
flooring, pulls his folded Army jacket under his head, and feels
around to find the cord again. He lifts it just to take the slack up,
keep the feel of what's attached to what and what should happen.
When it happens there should be an actual presence; weight; a shifting of the structure maybe. Who knows what; but something.
Luther twists up on one elbow, gets the jacket how he wants it, lies
back down, and takes a deep breath.

● ● ●

If he tilts his head back he can see a smudgy sort of star among the bright precise ones. One that won't quite focus—it's a galaxy or something; he knows that somehow, was told by someone, had it pointed out. And almost straight up there's that little cluster of five called something or other; and Orion—where is that with those three bright ones in a row? Too low still. All the rest is random; scattered stars— you have to wonder how they managed to find the constellations, all those complicated shapes, and give them names and make up stories. "Willis," Luther whispers and gives him a little nudge. His breathing starts to get too loud sometimes; it helps to give him a nudge. But not too hard and not to wake him—that's the trick; he's got his bag unzipped, his pistol right beside him—just enough to keep the noise down to a labored whispery sigh; the breath goes in, the breath goes out, like in the movies when there's someone in a space suit floating away against the stars, adrift and running out of air. No, there's another one—five stars, but more spread out, that make a *W* or an *M*. It has a name but he forgets. He keeps one finger under the cord. He'll curl it, lift it now and then to feel the braided nylon pull across the two-by-four, to hear the little sound it makes against the edge of the tar paper. What's the name? He used to know. It has a name.

"Shit." He keeps shivering. It won't stop. He brings his arm in; "Shit," it's hard to know what's cold, what's fever; "Shit," he whispers softly; he can see his breath; it makes the stars look hazy. Ten degrees. Yes sir, you bet. They must have marked him. Must have seen old Willis coming.

One by one the three bright stars of Orion's belt come into view. They slip along the top of the tar paper, skim the edge, and slowly lift above it, one, two, three; he leans to see them clearly; and that red one, that big red one higher up there by itself; that's probably part, its arm or head or something; eye; could be an eye.

· · ·

So he imagines how it went. Here's Willis coming into the store but he's not wearing his badge or gun. He doesn't even have a hat. It's just old Willis and by now they will have heard (it makes him mad that they would do that, having no idea, no notion what it's for, how much there is at stake, how cold and how exposed the situation— what's required, in fact, is sleeping bags like space suits, space-age sleeping bags) but here's old Willis; right away he spots these brightly colored ones and oh yes sir, you picked yourself a couple of good ones there, those there'll keep you warm as toast right down to ten degrees, and shows him how they're filled with special scientific stuff and so on till he has to have them, knows that nothing less will do, no question. Warm as toast. No question. What's he doing? Sort of kicking in his sleep. Just like a dog. He's chasing rabbits. Luther thinks about that; Willis chasing rabbits.

He needs to not let go of the cord. It's like a string around his finger to remind him. Otherwise (his arm pulled in to get it warm) the fever tends to sort of take him where it will, he tends to drift off task a little, things get dreamy, eyes half-closed he lets himself get vague, his thoughts get vague, uncertain.

There's a difference, watching the water, holding the line, between those incidental ripples from some source entirely removed from the business at hand and those that demonstrate the imminence of something, show the actual presence. There might be a beaver out there, way out in the lake and you won't know it, but you'll see this long slow gentle undulation come across, the stars slip in and out along it, and you think, well that's a beaver, you can tell. It has that look of beaver passing through the water, beaver wake. And you'll get other quicker, sharper little ripples—those are frogs or some-times snakes and all that's easy enough. It's when the surface goes a little funny all of a sudden, sort of loses definition, stars get smeary, that you tense up, even get a little queasy having set your gaze for so long on that spot and gotten used to things reflected as they are, as they should be; to have it all become uncertain just like that—and never mind it's what you're waiting for, or what you think you're waiting for. And, too, you have to watch out not to lose your focus, get yourself involved, with all that waiting, in too broad a possibility, let it spread and get so big that you can't find it like this old boy he once knew who went to bag himself a buck, knew it was going to be his year to get a big one; so he got up in this oak tree near a firebreak where he knew deer liked to cross and settled down in a wide smooth crotch with his twelve-gauge pump and waited and waited until right out into that firebreak came, as clear and plain as day, the biggest buck he'd ever seen alive—a twelve- or fourteen-pointer—whereupon he begins to pump and fire his shotgun, pump and fire again and again until he's out of shells without ever bringing his gun to bear or lowering it even, pretty much blowing the top right out of that tree as his brother told it.

It disturbs him that his breathing tends to fall in phase with Willis's, makes him feel like here they are at last the same. A pretty sad and sorry pair just lying here and breathing in and out together. Not a penny's difference finally. Luther holds his bad arm tight against his chest; he tries to force the muscles, twist and bend the wrist to get the damage all bunched up until it hurts to keep it there like that, to try to keep the sharp distinction of it.

It's so odd, the Milky Way. The way you start to see things in it; not much there, just barely something in the sky that you can see, not points like stars, not really things so much as just a place where vague indefinite thoughts can go. Sometimes you get a light rain or a drizzle on the lake and you'll see shapes appear on the surface of the water, usually out where the water's deep and there appears to be no reason for it—how the rain will give a different shine, a different feeling to one part and you think maybe it's the temperature or something but it's really hard to say why there should be a place on the water. Water's water, you think, like sky.

He comes awake. He's shoved his hand right through the tar paper. He was reaching out for something—Yurang; something. Now he pulls it back. He's torn it loose a little there at the bottom. Air moves softly under, lifts the tar paper slightly, makes a little fluttery sound; the cold, dry, empty grassy smell slips through. He holds his hand very lightly against the tar paper just to feel the cold, the thinness of it, feel the breeze against it. Tappity, tap; his hand shakes so much. He can't help it. Tappity, tap. It makes that noise.

The fever makes him even colder. Just like how they say cold water comes more quickly to a boil. It's just like that but in reverse. It's like a running start or something. He can feel it. How the heat comes to the surface, too much heat, and overflows, shoots through his arm and out the line into the water, grass, whatever. Grass. Whatever.

Here and there at some point—pretty late; it's hard to tell how late; the Milky Way sweeps almost straight up overhead—the Holy Spirit seems to move among the cows. They start that mooing like they do sometimes at night but not so many usually, not so far apart and not this cold, not all spread out and near and far. It's hard to know what moves a cow but you imagine something pretty fundamental. Not like wild dogs; not like crows, which just go off for any reason; anything at all almost and off they go.

"Hey," Luther whispers. Willis's breathing starts to get so faint, so shallow it's as if he might be fading out. "Hey." Luther holds his bad arm tight against him, tries to feel it in the cold.

· · ·

It's sad, somehow, how it subsides, the mooing, gradually, one by one it seems until just two or three quite far away, more deeply touched, are left to cry and bellow out to one another for a while across the fields. There follows such a sense of quiet. Such a sense of pause, remission, in between, like in the trough behind a swell. The air stirs faintly. Tar paper moves a little one way or the other, bellies softly in or out like laundry, makes that sound like laundry on a line. The little creakings, all the tiny little noises in the structure have reduced to just a faint and intermittent sort of sighing at the smallest scale where things lose their affinities in the cold, release the last of that conviction whacked into them, sag away until there's nothing but geometry holding it up. He finds it hard to get his breath. As if the air's too cold, too thin, or else the shivering interferes. He can't hear Willis now at all. And now the nightbirds. Gently twittering all of a sudden all around, just for a little while, then nothing. It's as if that's that—that silent, sad as that. As if it worked its way down through the orders of things, down through the greatest, most compliant and benign, on down through flittery, less particular sorts of creatures; down to what? He makes himself take in a long deep breath and slowly let it out. It seems to him the hush, the subtle background whisper that you get, must be the grass. The sound of breeze across the grass, of movement in it—every tiny little insect moving in it, every accidental touching and untouching of the grass against itself. And not, he thinks, just here, but everywhere; beyond the field, to other people's fields, along the roads. All over. All the grass. It is, he's sure, if that is what it is, the very lowest order of things. Where you begin to listen closely, pay attention. It develops—what to listen for develops—out of that. And if you're careful, use your judgment, don't go casting all about, be still and listen, it should separate a little from the noise—the noise will sort of part around it. There will be a point toward which consideration is extended, concentrates (like anything extended, drawn out in the cold, contracts), refines the apprehension to a sharpness, narrows, thins it to a ringing (if he blinks he thinks he'll lose it), periodic, now and then, the ring of truth as he supposes, out there somewhere in the grass and coming closer, softly jingling like some change in someone's pocket. Snap, goes something. Right below, inside, a little snap of something and it's clear, somehow, immediately—there's another snap, a clatter as the pieces fall away—the milk has frozen, burst the glass.

"Hey Willis." Nothing. "Willis." Nothing. "Willis." Nothing now at all. It's like snow-blindness. Not a whisper, not a sound. It's like a vacuum. Outer space. The Milky Way drifts down and spreads out to the southeast, shows the tar paper, where it stops; the corner post, its shadow, sticking up another foot or so. A fairly bright star hangs above it as if indicated by it. Luther fastens on this. How the star is poised above the shadow of the post, just there, at zero as it were, all things adjusted back to that. A point of reference. Any deviation instantly detectable—as now the post deflects a little, moves away from the star a little then moves back. He's still. It isn't him. He holds his breath. It's like the pointer on a scale—it starts to move again—an astronomical scale for things too large to sense directly. He can't feel it. He can't sense the tilt at all. But there it goes. It's leaning toward a different star a little higher to the south. The one at Vernon's Exxon goes up to a hundred pounds and Vernon likes to do it, likes to weigh your catch himself and tease you with it, take his hand off very slowly then he'll pause and let you think that must be it but, whoa look out, shit, look at that, he'll let it down the rest of the way and no one breathes to see the pointer swing around that little bit— that little bit, but you project it way on out there like that, billions of miles, he's sure; he's heard that. Billions. He can't see it too well now; it's off the edge of the Milky Way. It makes him gasp, he thinks, or something—makes him make a startled noise as if the jigging line had jerked through flesh to bone, his joy preceding terror barely, merging with it, bleeding into it. Willis heaves up, coughing, spitting, flings the bag aside, and rises in one motion. Luther pulls. He throws his weight into it, shoulder joint endangered as the body turns before the arm can follow, big old belly slung that way pulls all the rest of him along into a roll that takes him into Willis's feet. He hears the steel retainer clip tear through the tar paper, feels it strike him in the back as Willis fires, and feels the legs of Willis stiffen, jerk with every shot the way a child will do as if to sling the bullets out. There may or may not be a scream or yell or something; or, again, it could be him. He tries to get away from Willis, kick the sleeping bag away and get himself into the corner but the bag gets all bunched up around his feet and he's just kicking, thrashing around and Willis's shooting, little flashes here and there against the stars, the structure jerking, starting to sway and snap as Willis seems to leap with every shot (it really is just like a cap gun, on and on, how many bullets can it hold, why would they make a gun like that, that just keeps shooting, boom, you have a gun like that it must be all you think about, how many bullets it can shoot, boom, it must take all your attention and concern to have it, boom, kaboom, no thought for anything, thoughts fly away like little pinwheel whizzy bullets. Boom. A spray of something—splinters). Luther goes for Willis's knees, gets both his arms around and twists and throws him sideways with a terrible, complicated-sounding crash, a trampoline-like bounce that compromises something pretty seriously, floorboards flying; he can feel the wire mesh give, sag like a hammock. Creaks and pops from somewhere lower in the structure then it's quiet. Perfectly still. He's still got hold of Willis's legs. No movement. Nothing but the laser dot that shines against the tar paper to his right and makes a gentle oscillation up and down. At least he's breathing. Luther rolls off, lies a moment trying to listen, pulls one leg free, reaches down and frees the other, feels around for Willis's stuff—behind his head (he's still not moving), gets the flashlight, lies back down, just lies back down across the jumbled plywood flooring. There's a freer sort of movement to the air with all the wire exposed. He's cut his hand, he thinks; his good hand; sliced it on the chicken wire; his fingers feel all sticky on the flashlight. Where's the button? He jumps up, attempts to spring up to his knees and shine the flashlight out there, shine it all around but nothing happens, it won't work, he only makes a lot of noise and drops back down. Where is the button? He fucked up. He should have waited. Willis fucked up. Where's the button? It's so cold. What if the sleeping bags are fine; it's just that cold. The air moves gently, kind of circulates up through, around him, brings a tiny jingling from the field. You push it down first—that's the deal. He eases up into a crouch and grabs the rail. His stocking feet slip on the wire. He gets his elbows up on top to keep from slipping, listens. There. He points the flashlight, presses down and pushes up. He has to shut his eyes a moment. It's so bright. It's such an awful light, pure white and tightly focused krypton, halogen, whatever kind of light it is. It lights the air. It penetrates the cold, removes all doubt. There's Yurang, sitting steaming in his breath way out there panting in the grass the way he does when he's been after something, pausing to reflect, his eyes upon it—rabbit, coon, no matter; he knows where it is.

"I shot my foot," says Willis softly.

"Shh," says Luther, plays the light across the grass between the trailer and the dog. There's something.

"God," says Willis.

"Shh," says Luther. Something like a person sitting, resting, leaning over in the grass.

"I shot my foot." He's going to cry.

"Hold on." He shines it back to Yurang but he's gone, a sort of haze perhaps—or not—hangs in the grass. The light's so brilliant he can't stand it really, looking right into it, right along the beam; his own breath drifts into it. He can't seem to find the other right away, just grass, but there it is, now standing, all spread out somehow like someone in a coat, a big black coat held open all the way the way you see them do sometimes to show the stolen watches or whatever; no not watches.

"Jesus God." Almost a sense of resignation now from Willis, crying softly as for things beyond repair or consolation.

Or the way a child will do that with a sheet or something, make it be a cape or wings or something, then go running all around like that, as if to be a bird, an angel, pale and chubby face uplifted, scrunched up just like that against the light. And here it comes. "Hey."

"Christ, oh Jesus . . ."

"Willis."

"Jesus."

"Hold on."

"Shit."

"Hold on to something."

There's an odd delay between the sound of impact (sort of muffled, almost gradual) and the railing kicking back into his chest which makes him grab it, lose the flashlight as he flails about and hooks his arm around; both feet slip right across the wire and through the tar paper so he's hanging for a moment as the whole thing now swings back the other way in total unadapted darkness which allows that sort of dreamlike sense of falling that continues on and on—the whole thing; tower, trailer, everything—past vertical, he imagines, center of gravity shifting now out over the grass; that's why it's quiet, there's no strain, it's weightless, falling; everything is coming down and he's just hanging there and waiting till it's too much, takes too long, his arm gets tired, he lets his legs down, finds the floor and gets back on it.

He can see a few stars now and, if he turns his head, looks down through the wire, the whiteness of the trailer. He's not shivering. But he stinks or something stinks. He banged his bad arm pretty badly; now it's wet. It might be that or who knows. Who can say what stinks. Why isn't he shivering? He's not cold. What's Willis doing? He can hear him in the corner doing something with his gun and saying something. It's not crying but it's like that. Sad like that. "I seen all kindsa shit," he's saying, making little fiddly noises with his gun. Like trying to load it. Having trouble. "Seen all kindsa shit," the "seen" and "shit" get emphasized at points of special effort—little bullets that won't fit or something, won't go in the clip. It's sad to come down to such things. The little things. He stops the fiddling. Now he's quiet for a moment, breathing hard. "I can't believe I went and done that." Very deep and raspy breathing. "Guess you got a pretty good look." It isn't clear if he wants a response. "Huh?"

"Yeah." Luther's voice comes out in a whisper.

"Huh?"

"Yeah."

"Ain't old Leonard is it?" Sort of laughs.

"No."

"Know what I wish? God, what's that smell?" More raspy breathing; now a sigh. "Know what I wish?"

"No."

"Wisht I had me a goddamn ice cream."

This time the impact has a deeper and more penetrating quality. Nothing sways, has time to sway. The force expends within the structure, whips up through it in a rippling, snapping, popping-loose of bracing; stiffness goes, it all just slumps, the floor tilts, sags away a little to one side where all the bending strain gets taken with a sudden cracking jerk into the joints where the legs bolt on; a sound of splitting, all along some length of two-by-four that slow, reluctant sound of good wood splitting, sort of tearing, flooring sagging even more in little increments it feels like as the staples start to go, pull loose in sequence as it cracks along that side, the far side (don't you call them staples; aren't they called that—U-shaped double-pointed nails he tacked the hog wire with and took such care to drive in at an angle to the grain so not to split it? Such a little thing. A careful little thing, and there it goes). A pause as things find equilibrium for a moment and below, inside the trailer, very quiet very gentle sounds of china touching china, soft and delicate little sounds while here above (a strange and perfect opposition) what must be the narrow, canted heel of Willis's pointy cowboy boot attempting to find purchase as the wire begins to sag beyond some point at which the forward-slanty heel becomes a problem. Luther grabs the corner post. What must be Willis's right hand tears the rest of the tar paper, the whole panel, clean away; he feels him swinging past his head a second time just grabbing air, thin air; a ringing in the air, continuous now, a tiny ringing growing louder—it's just dog tags but it carries all that sense of termination: tiny bell, polite, insistent, put your pencils down and fold your hands and sit back in your seat, that's it, that's that. The two-by-four cracks through, a brief cascade of springy little pops, a staple zings past Luther's ear as all the flooring sections slide away and Willis, with a deep breath, simply follows.

Luther hardly has a chance to pay attention. He's concerned to twist himself around and get at least a toe into the wire before his hand slips off the post. He's looking down and so can't help but notice how the top of the trailer seems to open, how the seam splits almost silently as Willis drops into it, plywood clattering off the roof into the yard. It's all he can do to hang on, try, as everything now falls away, to get his fingers, toes, through chicken wire, which cuts and tends to break, into the heavier, stronger hog wire but it springs away it seems, released from tension, sort of curls up out of reach to leave him hanging there on nothing, almost nothing, swaying slightly, gazing out through gaps in what remains of the bracing toward the pines beyond the road, their silhouette a little darker than the sky. He hangs there briefly as if weightless, something drifted down and caught there for a moment on the wire, remains of something, then he falls.

It takes a long time to discover he can breathe and move a little; can identify the basic facts around him—stubbly grass, a patch of snow; once in a while a jingly panting sort of warmth above his ear—he's on his side—that comes and goes. The sounds of earnest mechanical activity—intermittent flickers of light, occasional muttering—makes him think how sleeping late on riverbanks, on camping trips, you wake up sometimes, get to lie there, simply listening to the coffee being made, the little camp stove giving trouble; someone's been up first and caught one, caught a good one, got all generous, grand about it and determined he'll have everything all ready for the others just to show what can be done. Such grace in that. Forgiveness. Now the warmth again. It smells like death. It licks his cheek. He eases up as slowly, carefully as he can, and waits to see if that's all right, then puts his arm around the dog. Some things get tossed on the ground next to him. Willis limps past. Luther puts the jacket on and then the boots. He hears the car start. Headlights shoot out through the tall grass by the road; it backs out, comes around, and parks with the engine running, headlights shining on the trailer. Luther squints at the lights a moment, gets up slowly, finds his balance, takes a step and stops, bends over with his hands on his knees to wait for things to stabilize. Exhaust drifts into the headlights.

Willis stands at the front of the car. Yurang trots over, sits next to him. After a second Luther follows. It's just there in the light. Half hanging out the door; the broken-in door—the lower part below where the board was, cracked and bent back in somehow. He tilts his head to see it better; see the face. They walk up to it after a minute. Yurang stays, eyes sort of half closed, panting. Willis takes a piece of bracing, lifts the coat or whatever, turns it back to show the things stitched to the inside, bits of stuff, all kinds of stuff; some cloth and paper, little bones, some dried-up things that could be anything; a little pocketknife hangs from a string. The face is damaged on one side; also the throat of course is very badly bitten, torn. The blood looks almost black. The plumpish upside-down face, hairless, perfectly smooth except for the damage sort of shines up through the smell; its eyes and mouth are tightly closed. The car is laboring. Willis walks back to it, guns it a couple of times then turns it around and backs it up. His muffler makes a little burbly, rattly sound. The air smokes up, glows red in the lights. They drop the tailgate. Willis grabs it by the collar underneath, gets both hands on it, jerks and tugs; things catch so Luther has to help as best he can and try to lift it up a little, get his good arm under, ease it onto the ground. They stand for a minute, get their breath, then haul the top part up on the tailgate, lean it back, and then the feet. Then Willis stops. "Hold on," he says; he lets the feet back down, has Luther help him carefully lay the rest back on the ground. He walks around to the passenger side, comes back with his pistol, nudges Luther out of the way, and empties the clip. The sound, projected off the trailer, seems to take a while to fade; it seems to roll away like thunder, here and there reverberating, interacting with the various natural features in that complicated resonant sort of way. They get it back up on the tailgate, shove it forward onto the old shag carpet, close the gate, roll all the windows down as Yurang hops in, takes a seat up front in the middle.

There are lights in the Rhonesboro Store. They pull in. Willis bangs on the glass till someone comes and lets him in. He comes back out in a couple of minutes with a cheap-looking cowboy hat and two Eskimo Pies, hands one to Luther, takes his boot off, pours some stuff all over his foot, some more on his pants where a cut bleeds through, replaces the boot, adjusts his hat, unwraps his ice cream as he drives.

They back the car into a space across from Joe's as Luther and Agnes did that time to watch the sign. It's going full blast. End of Days is here; so many in attendance some are standing on the side-walk, children kneeling on the little window ledge and looking in at what appears to be a pause, a moment, deep reflection, silence. Heads are bowed. The stars and galaxies fly away as Willis leans back, cuts the engine. Luther holds the Eskimo Pie stick so the dog can lick it. Willis has some left. He likes to eat the chocolate first, then sort of turn the stick around and around until the ice cream's gone. Then just the stick from side to side and in and out. He gets out, lowers the tailgate. Luther helps him pull it out on the tailgate on the carpet, rearrange it so it's lying on its back and facing up. They find some wads of paper napkins in the back seat. Luther spits and wipes his hands, the front of his jacket, dabs at Yurang around his mouth and on his neck. The parking spots across at Joe's are full so Willis takes it down the street and comes back up and stops as close as he can behind the cars, in front of the sign. It hisses softly. People glance around, turn back. For a moment Willis sits there qui-etly then he gets out, Luther takes the dog by the collar, kind of stumbles—one leg seems about to go—over to a pickup truck with a big wide tread-plate bumper he can sit on. Willis climbs onto the fender of his car and looks around, climbs onto the roof and stands there flickering in the neon, courthouse Christmas lights behind him. "Precious Jesus," issues faintly through the hiss—a sort of whisper, not a song ". . . oh precious Jesus." Luther lets himself lean back against the tailgate, slump a little to one side to keep his hand on Yurang's collar. He feels numb, somehow, all over. Willis bounces very lightly on the roof. It makes a funny little boingy sort of sound. "Oh precious Savior, precious Lord." It's like a whisper right behind him, in his ear, so soft that he can barely hear it. Boingy popping of the metal in and out as Willis bounces, seems to find some purpose in it, starts to put his weight into it, gets the whole roof bending, popping with that deeper thundery noise sheetmetal makes. He gives a whoop. He's got it going now. The car rocks side to side. He's got the rhythm, whooping now with every bounce, his arms flung up and down to get more force into it. Luther slumps a little more. "Shit," Willis yells. "Y'all don't know shit," he yells and bounces toward the rear where the body lies, white-speckled coat laid open, odds and ends revealed to intermittent stuttery flashing neon light, the white face flickering, further blemished by a bullet hole or two it looks like, rocking with the bouncing rather gently like a big fish caught and laid upon a gently rocking deck. "Y'all don't know shit." They must be coming out. He's screaming, "Holy Spirit my god-damn ass." There's not much bounce left in the roof. It's all caved in. He twists and drops and grabs his foot, bangs with his fist to keep it going. "Shit. This here's what done that shit. This here"—he waves down at it, strikes the roof—"this here, come on look here." A few emerge from between the cars; they start to come out one by one into the street like at a carnival, people drifting out from one thing to another. Some just stand and look at Willis; others seem to gaze away. "Shit, what the shit you think that is? We killed it." Luther feels he might be about to tumble off the bumper. "What the shit you think that is? You think that there's the Holy Spirit? Shit." He's spitting, jerking around on top of the car and acting crazy, waving his cowboy hat down at it. "Shit," he screams. "Shit. What the shit you think that is? Shit." Luther finds he's gradually slipping off the bumper to the ground. Receding galaxies cast such sad uncertain shadows into the street. "Shit," Willis keeps on yelling over and over again.